Praise for Sean Slater

'A satisfyingly authentic debut from a man who really does know about the bleak side of the human psyche . . . v[illegible]ten with an unexpected gentle irony, and featuring a [illegible] character that the author clearly likes, it's a neat, stylish thriller from a writer to watch'
Daily Mail

'The USP of this energetic debut thriller is that it's w[illegible]itten about a Vancouver cop by a Vancouver cop . . . In [illegible]act Sean Slater writes the sort of pacy superior pulp you'd expect from an author who'd never eaten a doughnut on a dull stakeout'
Daily Telegraph

'[illegible]ast-paced, gripping and impossible to put down, Sean [illegible]later's novel is an explosive, action-injected tale told by a great new talent. A fantastic read'
Chris Carter, author of *The Death Sculptor*

'Gritty, dark and graphic. A terrific read'
D[illegible]niel Kalla, bestselling Canadian author of *Pandemic*, *Blood Lies* and *Of Flesh And Blood*

'Slater has a knack for grabbing the reader's attention and making them want to keep turning the pages'
beasbooknook.blogspot.com

Sean Slater is the pseudonym for Vancouver Police Officer Sean Sommerville. As a police officer, Sommerville works in Canada's poorest slum, the Downtown East Side – an area rife with poverty, mental illness, drug use, prostitution, and gang warfare. He has investigated everything from frauds and extortions to homicides. Sommerville has written numerous columns for editorials for the city newspaper. His work has been nominated for the Rupert Hughes Prose Award, and he was the grand-prize winner of the Sunday Serial Thriller contest. His debut novel, *The Survivor*, was shortlisted for the Arthur Ellis Award.

Also by Sean Slater

The Survivor
Snakes & Ladders

SEAN SLATER

The Guilty

SIMON & SCHUSTER

London · New York · Sydney · Toronto · New Delhi

A CBS COMPANY

First published in Great Britain by Simon & Schuster UK Ltd, 2013
A CBS Company

This paperback edition first published, 2013

3 5 7 9 10 8 6 4 2

Simon & Schuster UK Ltd
1st Floor
222 Gray's Inn Road
London WC1X 8HB

www.simonandschuster.co.uk

Simon & Schuster Australia, Sydney
Simon & Schuster India, New Delhi

A CIP catalogue record for this book is available from the British Library

B Format ISBN: 978-1-47110-137-3
Ebook ISBN: 978-1-47110-138-0

Typeset by Hewer Text UK Ltd, Edinburgh
Printed and bound in Great Britain by CPI Group (UK) Ltd, Croydon CR0 4YYY

This book is dedicated to two people who shared my childhood and helped make it such a magical time.

To *Billy*,
who I gave an airplane ride into a tree.
I am sorry for that (not really).

And to *Cindy*,
whose Barbie dolls I drowned in the bathtub too many times to count.
I'm sorry for that, too (again, not really).

The Guilty

Part 1:
Fuse

Wednesday

One

The bomb may have been set to go off in three hours, but the fuse had been lit nine years ago. They had been long years. Hard years. And the notion of it all brooded in the bomber's mind like a nuclear winter haze.

He knelt on the concrete floor of the steel barn and stared at the woman who was strapped to the chair in front of him. She was attractive. Middle-aged. Dark-skinned. And she was crying softly – had been for damn near an hour now. Mascara-thick tears stained her ebony cheeks.

Her sorrow meant nothing.

He turned his eyes away from the woman. Ignored her sobbing and waffling and suffering. Instead, he focused on the burlap sack, for it was what mattered now. As he opened the bag, the orange light of the barn lamp tinted his face, making his damaged skin look like a dried-up peel. It was a sight to behold, and the gobsmacked woman tied to the chair could not help but stare.

He focused on the strange motley of items he was removing from the bag.

Yellow sponge . . . *check.*

Micro-tape recorder . . . *check.*

Red file folder . . . *check.*

And of course, the toy – a hand-crafted wooden duck, dressed in a policeman's uniform. That was the essential piece . . . *BIG check.*

The bomber stared at the toy. The wooden duck was roughly the size of an iron, and had been personified with arms and legs, so that it somewhat resembled a Daffy or a Donald Duck, and not a real one. Painted on its chest was a bright red number *6*. The sight of it made the bomber smile sadly. He stuck his finger through the steel O-ring, gave it a pull, and listened to the bird's voice-box come to life:

'These criminals are making me quackers!'

The recording ended, and he looked at the duck for a long moment. His smile slipped away, but he did not frown. He did not show any emotion. He just knelt there looking at the wooden duck and feeling overwhelmed by memories – ones which were slanted and out of order.

Like a row of freight train cars that had gone off the tracks.

When his thoughts derailed, he stared at the woman. A strange mix of emotions distorted her face. Confusion. Fear.

Pain.

She choked back her tears. 'Pl-please. I've told you *everything*. You don't . . . you don't have to do this.'

In an instant, his expression changed. Turned dark. And his blue eyes looked like ice under the jagged rim of black hair. When he angled his head to see her, his face looked maniacal in the strange orange hue of the barn lamp.

'*I'm* not doing anything,' he said. 'You're the reason for all of this. And you bloody well know it.'

The woman broke down.

He barely heard her sobs. Already he was looking at his watch, going over timelines, analysing strategy. So far, the operation was going well.

Battle One of this long war had started.

Were it not for the fact that he really didn't *want* to do this – hell, he didn't want to hurt anyone – the bomber would have smiled. Because everything was going perfectly well. Spot on without a glitch.

And then the teenage girl stumbled through the first-floor doorway.

And everything went to hell.

Two

Homicide Detective Jacob Striker sat in the driver's side of the undercover Ford Fusion and sipped from a cup of Tim Horton's coffee, black. The brew was hot – too hot for the summer heat wave which had moved in late June and was still residing like a bad tenant, halfway through July.

He drank the coffee anyway. Caffeine was needed. It was only five in the morning, and – judging by the heaping mounds of workflow back at the office – the shift was going to be a tedious one.

In the passenger seat, Felicia sat with her visor down, staring at herself in the mirror. Her own cup of coffee, thick with cream and sugar, sat untouched in the pullout tray between them, and that was unusual.

Striker gave her a few more seconds of looking into the mirror, then spoke:

'Having a staring contest?'

Felicia let out a long sigh and flipped up the visor. She said nothing at first, but Striker knew the problem: Felicia's birthday was today, and she didn't like it.

'Do I look thirty-three?' she finally asked.

'No,' he said. 'Not any more.'

She cast him a look of daggers, and Striker grinned. After a moment, her expression lightened and she let out a small laugh.

'Yes, I'm being vain,' she admitted. 'But it's my birthday, so I'm allowed to be. And for the record, any more comments like that one and you'll be sleeping alone on the couch tonight.'

Striker sipped his coffee and stared back at her. Having a working partnership and a secret relationship was exciting no doubt, but it was also a lot of work. Sometimes it was difficult to tell where the two lines met.

'Thirty-three,' he finally said. 'Hell, I should be so lucky. I crossed that bridge a long time ago.' He gave her a smile and winked. 'Don't fret it, Birthday Girl. You'll be happy when the day's done.'

She cocked an eyebrow at him. 'What's that supposed to mean?'

'Little surprise I've been working on.'

Felicia gave him a wry look, like she was calling his bluff, but Striker just kept on smiling. He *did* have something planned – a romantic getaway for two in a quaint little bed and breakfast at Whistler Mountain Ski Resort. The reservation was set for Thursday. Just the thought of getting away brought Striker a sense of peace, and for the first time in as long as he could remember, he felt good.

Really, really good.

Then the call came in.

Sue Rhaemer, the Central Dispatcher for E-Comm, came across the air, her voice smooth yet rough, like sand in honey: 'Got a 911 coming in,' she broadcasted. 'Cell call. Girl's screaming. Not making a whole lot of sense. Says she's in the industrial area, somewhere down by the river . . . Keeps talking about two giant chimneys.'

Striker thought it over. 'The cement plant.'

'She's talking about the smokestacks,' Felicia agreed.

Striker dropped his cup in the tray holder, spilling some of the brew onto the carpet. He rammed the gearshift into Drive and pulled out onto Granville Street. Within seconds, he had the Fusion up to eighty K and was flying through 29th Avenue.

Sue Rhaemer came across the air again: 'Okay, we've lost her now – how close is the nearest unit?'

A patrol unit replied: 'Alpha 21 – we're the only car available right now, and we're coming from Dunbar and 2nd.'

Striker swore. 'That's over in Point Grey – they'll take twenty minutes.'

Felicia grabbed the radio and pressed the mike. 'This is Detectives Santos and Striker. We're three minutes out. We're heading down.'

Striker hammered the gas so hard, Felicia fell back against the seat and almost dropped the mike. As she plunged it back into the cradle, Striker swerved into the fast lane. They raced south down Granville Street, now at over one hundred K per hour, with speeds increasing.

Striker had a bad feeling about the call.

'Why the hell would a young girl be down by the river – in the industrial area – at this time of the morning?' he asked.

'No good reason,' Felicia replied.

Striker agreed.

He hit the gas and brought the car up to one-twenty.

Three

Factory smoke roamed the black waterways of the Fraser River like lost souls. Where the winds were strong enough, that same smoke spilled back through the pulp mill and concrete plant, blurring out a series of industrial lights so that they looked like distant dim halos.

Striker turned to Felicia. 'Roll down your window so we can hear – the girl's got to be close now.'

The words had barely left his lips when a small, awkward figure stumbled out into the centre of the gravel road. Striker hammered on the brakes to avoid hitting her, and the cruiser slid to a stop with the sound of crunching gravel.

He jumped out into the clouds of swirling dust and drew his SIG Sauer. Only when the hard rubber grip of the pistol melded with the firm flesh of his palm did a sense of reassurance filter through him.

They'd found her.

'Check her out,' he told Felicia. 'I'll cover us.'

The girl was crumpled on the road now, in front of their car. The bright halogen glare of the headlights made her face appear ghostly white and highlighted her long dishevelled hair. She was missing one high-heeled pump, and her short miniskirt and halter top were both torn.

The left side of her face was covered in blood.

'Jesus,' Felicia gasped.

She dropped to one knee in front of the girl.

Striker moved in front of them, shielding both with his body as he scanned the smoky haze of the concrete plant and, beyond that, the rumbling waves of the Fraser River. Everything out there was dark. Quiet. Unmoving.

'Are you okay?' Felicia asked.

'He's after me! He's *after* me!'

'Who's after you?'

The girl started to cry. She looked back over her shoulder. At the other end of the lot was a small steel barn with an orange exterior lamp. The light looked unnatural in the smoky darkness.

'He's got her in there! In the steel barn!'

Striker's eyes narrowed at the comment, and a coldness spilt through him. He turned around and met the girl's stare.

'Got *who* in there?'

'Some woman. A black woman – she's tied to a chair.' The girl let out a sob. '*He's going to kill her.*'

Four

The girl's words ended any hope of waiting for backup.

'I'm checking it out,' Striker said. 'Stay here with the girl.'

Felicia frowned. 'Forget that – I'm coming with you.'

'You *can't*.' He gestured to the bloodied girl. 'You need to protect her until Patrol arrives. She can't be left alone and she can't come with me.'

'Then wait, Jacob. You need cover.'

'No manpower, no time.'

Before Felicia could fight him on the issue, Striker wheeled about.

As he crossed the lot, the air grew thicker. Loose cement powder and gravel dust floated in the air and stuck to his face. Everywhere he looked, there was only darkness, blurred by the desperate light of industrial lamps.

He rounded a row of cement trucks and the steel barn came back into view. Now at this closer distance, Striker could see that the building was on a separate lot, nestled in between the concrete plant and the Fraser River. Thick blackberry bushes covered the perimeter, and surrounding the lot was a tall chain-link fence.

An odd spot.

Wasting no time, Striker climbed the fence, landed on the other side, and kept moving. When he reached the entrance to the barn, he stopped hard.

The door was half open.

He reached out. Pushed it open. And the hinges squeaked loudly. He looked inside.

The place looked *old*, long since deserted. All the windows were lined with rusted iron bars and covered with a fine layer of dust. From somewhere up high, a strange white light flickered.

Striker took out his flashlight. Readied his pistol.

'Vancouver Police!' he called.

No reply.

'Is anyone in there?'

When no one answered a second time, Striker made entry. The moment he was inside the barn and out of the doorway, the soft rolling hush of the river faded and was replaced by a heavy silence. There was the strong smell of fuel and oil in the air.

Diesel.

Striker kept moving. He worked his way past several stacks of old tyres and some piles of broken cement bags until he reached a narrow wooden staircase leading to a second level.

He aimed his forty-cal at the top of the stairs and moved slowly up them. The old wood groaned with every step, screaming out a warning to anyone above that he was coming.

Once at the top, the narrow beam of Striker's flashlight revealed a small square loft with four windows – one on each side. A quick sweep of the flashlight showed that all four corners were empty of threats.

No one was there.

Sitting dead centre in the loft was one empty chair. Striker moved towards it and a bucket of water came into view. There was also a yellow sponge. And an old forklift battery, sitting three feet behind the chair.

As Striker stared at the battery, the wind blew in through the open windows; the wires extending from the terminals touched.

The current arced and a quick spark of light flashed through the room.

In the brief illumination, Striker noticed that the wood under the chair was discoloured. At first he thought it was blood, but a closer look suggested it was probably water. Lying in the centre of the stain was a crescent-shaped piece of rubber with one long wire extending from the flatter end.

Oh Jesus.

A darkness washed over Striker as he connected all the items in the room: the steel chair, the water-soaked floorboards, and the battery terminals hinted at much. But the rubber pad with the wires – *that* was the clincher. It told Striker everything he needed to know.

He was standing in the middle of a torture chamber.

Five

Striker whipped out his cell phone. He was about to call Felicia when a flicker of something caught his eye.

Movement.

He swivelled left and looked out the south-facing window. There, down by the river shore, were the vague outlines of two figures. They were marching eastward through the thin wisps of factory smoke, one ahead of the other.

Striker moved flush with the window for a better look. He aimed his flashlight and pistol at the silhouettes, and called out.

'Vancouver Police! Don't move!'

For one brief moment, the two figures stopped. Then the second one turned around. Though faceless in the darkness and fog, this one was taller than the first, and thicker in build.

Definitely a man.

For a moment, the man seemed to be complying. Then he raised his arm and the sharp hard *crack* of gunfire ripped through the night.

The window shattered.

Instinctively, Striker dove backwards, landing hard on the wooden floor. Shards of glass rained down around him. Bullets punched through the old boards and ricocheted off the iron support beams.

He kept low on his belly. He covered his head, rolled for the stairs, and crawled down to the first level. By the time he hit the concrete, the angry sounds of gunfire had stopped and were replaced by a distant, undulating wail.

Police sirens.

Striker scrambled to his feet and raced outside. By the time he'd made it across the small lot, everything north of Kent Avenue was aglow. Police lights tinted the skyline red and blue.

Striker headed down the trail that led to the river. Along the way, he used his cell to call Felicia. She answered on the first ring.

'He's running the river,' Striker warned.

'Jesus Christ, Jacob, what the hell was that – gunfire?'

'Just get containment going. Start up a dog. Call in the chopper.'

He hung up and plunged ahead, keeping his body low with the bramble, making himself as small a target as possible. After one hundred metres, he emerged between two blackberry bushes and stepped down onto river silt.

He looked east, then west. But both ways were empty.

Barren.

'What the hell?'

The sight made him frown. He'd made it to the shoreline in less than two minutes. No matter which way the two figures had gone, they should still have been visible.

Striker turned his eyes to the river. A summer fog hung overtop the waterway, one thin enough to see through. Visibility was good for a hundred metres at least. If the suspects had fled that way, even in a vessel, he should have been able to spot them.

But the waters were empty.

It made no sense.

He shone his flashlight all around the riverbanks. In one patch of silt, right at the end of the trail, were a set of footprints. They faced east and disappeared after only three steps, where the ground became firmer.

A few metres beyond was a small dock.

Striker approached it. Keeping his gun at the low-ready, he stepped onto the pier and the old planks groaned beneath his one hundred kilos of weight. The entire platform felt unstable. At the end of the dock, on one of the posts, hung a thin rope. Striker moved up to it, then aimed his gun and flashlight into the river below.

Nothing but black water.

The two figures had just . . . *vanished.*

Frustrated, he was about to head back towards the barn when the beam of his flashlight caught something near his feet.

A *gleam.*

He knelt down on the dock. Gloved up with latex. And plucked the object from a wooden plank. Turning it over in his hand, he saw that it was a long thin bracelet, made of silver and gold designs. Celtic. Or Gaelic. He wasn't sure. On the links was a red-brown splatter. He took out his flashlight, and shone it on the links.

Not blood. River muck.

The sight should have filled him with relief, but it did not. No blood meant less evidence for the lab. Less of a trail. Hopefully the barn would provide some decent DNA samples. The forensic techs would have to start processing ASAP.

Striker bagged the jewellery and his cell went off.

He answered. 'Striker.'

Felicia's tone was one of relief and anger: 'Where the hell are you now, Jacob?'

'Down by the river. They've escaped.'

'Well just watch your back. A dog's coming down from the south. Chopper's almost here, too.'

Striker could already hear its distant approach. The rotating blades were like soft thunder cutting the air. One minute, the bird was nowhere to be seen; the next, it rose up over Mitchell Island to the south, and the entire shoreline was flooded in the blinding white glare of a 30-million-candlepower spotlight.

Striker felt his jaw tighten at the sight. The chopper had arrived. So had the dog. With any luck, one of them would find something to go on, because so far the immediate crime scene was offering him zero.

The thought of this hit Striker like a physical force. Left him winded. He had been too slow in reaching the woman. He had failed her. And that failure might have cost the woman her life. It was a fact he had to face.

Sometimes reality could be cold.

Six

A quarter-mile downriver, at the westernmost precipice of Mitchell Island, the bomber pulled himself and the woman in between the logs and flotsam that were jammed up against the shoreline. The woman was waterlogged – an anchor pulling him down. Had it not been for the scuba gear, they would never have made it.

Two hundred metres across the river, to the north, the entire area from Granville to Main was spotted with red and blue police lights. Completely knackered, it was all he could do to focus on them.

He tore the breathing apparatus from his lips and pulled himself and the woman up the steep bank of mud, deep into the island bush, until they were under the thick overhang of a pair of weeping willows.

There, he dropped to the ground and rolled the lifeless woman over so that she was facing upwards. He cupped a hand under the back of her neck. Angled her chin. Parted her lips. Blew air into her lungs.

Nothing.

He interlocked his fingers over her chest and began compressions. Finished. Breathed again. And repeated the process several times.

'Breathe, for fuck's sake. *Breathe.*'

Finally, when hope was almost gone, the woman made a gagging sound. She jerked and hacked and spewed, then rolled away from him. She formed a protective ball and lay shaking in the sand.

A numb relief spilled through the man.

He lay flat on his back and tried to control his breathing. He was thirty-six now, and though he did not feel old, he definitely felt worn. Damaged from the years of abuse and trauma.

He killed the thought and focused on the immediacies.

The nylon sheath of the prosthetic was soaked and it was losing suction against the stumpy end of his disfigured leg. He reached down, pulled the sheath tight, and felt the surgical screws inflaming his bones.

He tried to gather his breath.

Found it difficult.

High above, the eastern sky was lightening, turning from blood-pudding purple to a lesser bruised blue. All along the shoreline, the blinding glare of the police chopper spotlight was turning the riverbank white. The bird was far away right now, way down by the Arthur Lange Bridge. But that meant nothing. It could reach Mitchell Island in seconds. Even now, as it floated westward, the steady *whump-whump-whump* of the helicopter blades shook the air with a physical force, and they shifted his mind back to harsher times. More violent times.

The bomb going off, blowing him to pieces.

And the tragedy that had followed.

The recollection was vicious, malignant. And yet oddly enough, it slowed his frantic heart. Helped him breathe. Allowed him to regain his sanity again. It actually *relaxed* him.

And still the woman coughed and spluttered beside him.

After a short moment, the police helicopter floated all the way to Heather Street – too close; dangerously close. So he got moving. He dumped the flippers, oxygen tank and breathing apparatus in the river, then grabbed hold of the retching woman's underarms and began dragging her through the grove. They headed for Twig Place Road.

Where the backup vehicle was parked.

Once under cover of thicker tree tops, a place where the chopper could no longer illuminate them with its omnipotent eye, the bomber took a moment to reassess the situation. The woman was awake now, fully conscious of what had happened – of what was *still* happening – and she gaped at him with large wide eyes. A disbelieving stare.

'You . . . you *saved* me,' she finally whispered.

He merely nodded.

'Of course I did. You're not supposed to die this way.'

Seven

Striker bypassed the steel barn with the orange lamp.

He hiked up the river embankment and cut through the loading zone of the cement plant. It was barely quarter to six now, and despite the police emergency lights, the early skyline was still cloaked by a charcoal fog.

Quarter to six, Striker thought disbelievingly.

The chase had felt so much longer.

He detected movement and looked left. Walking towards him, coming from the opposite end of the yard, was a familiar face: Sergeant Mike Rothschild – one of Striker's oldest and dearest friends. In one hand was a roll of yellow police tape. In the other was a paper cup with a plastic lid. Coffee, no doubt.

'Mike,' Striker said.

As always, Rothschild had a warped smile on his face, one that made his moustache slope unevenly across his upper lip. His face held a look of concern.

'You okay there, Shipwreck?'

'Guy's a friggin' magician.' Striker pointed towards the river. 'I lost them down there somewhere. By the pier. It makes no sense.'

'The dog'll find something.'

Striker hoped to God so.

He looked at Rothschild. In the murky light of the factory's glow, every line on the man's grizzled face was apparent. He was pushing fifty now, and the years of policing and shift work had left their mark on him. Like it did every cop. But today Rothschild looked especially aged.

Striker knew why. Rothschild had a lot on his plate right now. Like Striker, he too had lost his first wife. And raising two grief-stricken little ones made the situation all the more difficult.

Striker asked him, 'You almost done your shift?'

Rothschild laughed bemusedly. 'Just beginning, man.'

'*Beginning?*'

'Yeah, I know, I look like shit – thanks for the vote of confidence.'

'You just need some sleep.'

'Tell me 'bout it. The twins haven't been sleeping well. They've been giving me grief about this whole move thing; they don't wanna leave the old house. Too many memories of their mother, I guess.'

Striker made a point of looking the man in the face. 'I'm sorry I wasn't there . . . to help with the move.'

'Duty calls.'

Striker shook his head. 'I'm the kids' godfather. I should've been there. This damn job – it eats up your life.'

'Yup. Faster than a fat kid devours a Mars bar. Get used to it, man, it ain't gonna change.'

Before either one of them could say more, Air 1 – the Vancouver Police Department's helicopter – roared overhead, the heavy percussive blasts of its blades beating down on them, stirring up the dirt and gravel of the parkway. As the chopper floated south, Felicia and their young witness were lit up on the side road.

Striker focused on them. 'Something's not right with that girl.'

Rothschild just nodded. 'I'll tape off the scene for you.'

Striker nodded his thanks. As Rothschild hiked down to the river, Striker beelined across the lot towards their witness.

The girl was still crumpled at the front of the police car. The unforgiving glare of the halogens made her tight face look like white rubber. She sat on the gravel of the road, her arms wrapped tightly around her torso as she rocked nervously back and forth. Her miniskirt rode up her thighs, exposing the curves of her ass, and her long blonde hair spilled over her knees as her head snapped from side to side in response to any sudden movement.

With more time now, Striker took a really good look at her. She was maybe seventeen. His daughter's age. And the thought of Courtney being out in an area like this, at this time of the night, bothered him. The blood that had covered her forehead had now been wiped away.

He looked at Felicia. 'The blood?'

Felicia stood up from her crouched position. 'It was her own. From a small cut on her forehead. She banged it on something when she was scrambling to get away. Looked a helluva lot worse than it was.'

Striker knelt down in front of the girl and touched her arm. Despite the warm summer air, her skin was clammy, sweaty. And she flinched from the contact.

'Look at me,' Striker said softly.

No response.

'*Look* at me.'

The girl lifted her head slowly, and Striker shone his flashlight in her eyes. The pupils were large – too large, even for this darkness – and they remained so, despite the glare of his flashlight and the car's headlights. She licked her lips several times and rolled her tongue in her mouth as if it were too large to fit.

'What are you on?' he demanded. 'Special E? Jib? What have you been taking?'

'Uh, nothing. No. Nothing.'

Striker wrapped his fingers around the girl's chin and made her look at him. 'This is no time to screw around, kid. I'm not looking for charges, I'm trying to save a woman's life. Now what the hell are you on?'

The girl stared back through glassy eyes. 'Beans, I took some beans.'

Striker nodded. Beans. MDMA.

Ecstasy.

Judging by the size of her pupils, she'd taken an awful lot. And who knew what else she'd mixed in with it? There was more than just ecstasy in her. She was zoning out bad for that.

'Why were you even down here in the industrial area?' he asked. 'There a rave somewhere?'

She nodded again, licked her lips. 'Yeah, yeah. Big party.'

'Where?'

The girl looked up for a moment, her eyes twitching left and right. Her teeth chattering. 'Over there . . . somewhere. I dunno.'

'Why did you leave the party?'

'Had a fight. With Billy . . . we had a fight.'

'Billy who? He your boyfriend?'

'. . . so cold.'

'Where did he go? Did he come after you?'

'It's so *cold.*'

Striker resisted the urge to swear and looked at Felicia. 'Ambulance en route?'

'A mile out.'

Striker turned silent. He watched the girl sniff and tremble as he thought things through. When she let out a strange hyena-like laugh, he frowned. She was high, confused, and her story was all over the place. But she had definitely stumbled onto *something.*

He looked back at the river's edge. When thoughts of the bracelet entered his mind, he looked back at the girl. 'Were you down by the docks?'

'Huh?'

'By the pier. By the river.'

'No no no.'

'This man you saw in the barn – did he take anything from you? A necklace or anything like that?'

'Uh . . . no?'

Striker gloved up with fresh latex, then pulled the evidence bag from his pocket. When he opened it up and removed the bracelet, the girl looked at it with obvious confusion.

'Do you recognize this?' he asked.

She shook her head.

He put it away and tried coming at this from a different angle. 'What do you remember about the woman in the barn?'

The words seemed to bring the girl a moment's clarity. She blinked, sat up straighter. 'Her cheeks . . . the bones were, like, really high.'

'High?'

'You know, like, *prominent.*'

'And the man?'

The girl's face tightened. 'He's a worker. From the plant.'

'How do you know this?'

'Had . . . had on overalls. A uniform or something.'

Striker took a moment to write this down in his notebook, then continued with his inquiry. But the more he questioned the girl, the more she contradicted herself. In the end it was all gibberish. And when paramedics finally arrived, Striker's frustration level had reached new limits. He stood up, curled his fingers into fists, and looked at Felicia, whose eyes were filled with concern.

'Can you take care of this?'

'Of course.'

'Thank friggin' God.'

Feeling precious time slipping away, he turned around and headed for the one place he hoped would shed some clues on this whole mess.

The torture chamber in the steel barn.

Eight

Ten minutes later, Striker stood alone in the loft of the steel barn, directly in front of the chair where the woman had been bound. No restraints had been left behind. No ropes. No straps. No belts. No wires.

Using his flashlight to illuminate the area, he focused on the chair. It was an old thing, sturdy, made from steel legs and a solid steel backing. It was dusty, grimy, dirty as hell.

Not the greatest material for fingerprinting.

As he crouched down and examined the surface more closely, looking for any traces of hair or other DNA-testable substance, he noticed that there was no blood. The torture appeared to have been entirely electrical.

It was odd – something he had never seen.

Behind him, a plank groaned. Striker swivelled around and spotted a wizened old face at the top of the stairs. Barely reaching Striker's shoulders, and weighing in at a measly sixty-five kilos, was Inspector Tekuya Osaka.

At fifty-five years of age, Inspector Osaka was nearing his 80-factor – that magical total derived from age plus years served. It allowed for superannuation, and for Osaka, retirement was fast closing in. The look on his face suggested he wished he'd taken an early leave. Striker couldn't blame him.

'You don't look happy,' Striker said.

Inspector Osaka just frowned. 'This is downright creepy.'

'Tell me about it. Guy used electrical torture.'

'A stun gun?'

'More like a wand of some kind.'

Inspector Osaka moved nearer. 'A rather unusual instrument, don't you think?'

'The guy who did this is a pro.'

Osaka came to within a foot of Striker, his face better illuminated in the flashlight glow. With his thick white hair brushed back over his head and a matching goatee, he looked just like an Asian Colonel Sanders. 'Haven't heard of an electrical wand being used in years – not since that renegade biker got taken out back East.'

Striker made no reply. He was too intent on the scene before him.

Beneath the chair, the floorboards were no longer discoloured. The water stains had all but evaporated in the humid, growing heat. But the bucket was still there, half full of water. On the ground beside it was the old yellow sponge.

Everything would have to be swabbed for DNA.

Striker turned to look at the inspector. 'I want this scene processed like no other, sir. Top priority. Private labs, if needed. If a woman really is missing, every minute counts.'

Inspector Osaka nodded. 'Authorized.'

The word brought Striker a modicum of relief.

He stood up, feeling the haunts of two previous knee injuries, and took a final glance around. To the south, broken glass littered the windowsill and floor, and recollections of gunfire flooded him. He could still hear the shrill sounds of the glass breaking and the heavy, damn-near palpable blasts of the gunfire. It had been distinctive.

A forty-cal, for sure.

Striker moved up to the window. Analysed a few of the entrance holes in the frame. They were uniform, roughly ten to twelve millimetres in diameter, and the exit holes weren't much wider. No mushrooming. In some areas, the wood from the beams had exploded outwards in uneven chunks.

Full Metal Jacket.

He looked at the holes for a long moment, at the broken and splintered wood, then let out a long breath. The rounds hadn't missed him by all that much. Inches.

Inspector Osaka saw this too. 'That was damn close, Striker.'

Striker said nothing; he just stared out the window. In the southeast, the sun was slowly creeping out from its earthly blanket, turning the skyline from a light bruised colour to a deep crimson. The natural light illuminated the waters below. Down there, the helicopter had already scoured the shoreline, but a much more thorough search still needed to be done.

He headed for the river.

Nine

Striker watched Inspector Osaka return to his police cruiser. His responsibility was to report the incident up the chain of command. With the unexpected health scare DC Hughes had suffered this past month, Superintendent Laroche was acting as the fill-in Deputy Chief.

That was bad news for Osaka, because Laroche was notorious for poking his nose into ongoing investigations and for being unfairly demanding. Striker had dealt with Laroche too many times to count, so he felt for Osaka.

By the time Striker had hiked down to the river, the sun had risen just enough to flood the entire waterway with a reddish glow. Being careful where he stepped, Striker crossed the sandy expanse and stepped onto the pier. At the far end, tied to the last post, was the rope he had found earlier, still dangling in the wind.

He walked down the pier and studied the rope. Unlike the thick nylon normally used to harness vessels, this rope was thin – a twine that could be bought at any hardware store. Definitely not easily traceable. Also of note, the knot fastening the rope to the post was of the ordinary overhand kind. Nothing unusual like a bowline, hitch or cat's paw. Just a regular old knot.

The suspect had left them little to go on.

Striker took out his notebook and wrote all this down. By the time he had finished, Jim Banner had arrived on scene.

Banner – Noodles to all his friends – was making his way down from the roadside. Striker knew the man well. Hell, Striker was the one who had given Banner the nickname, after Banner had almost choked to death on a creamy linguine at the Noodle Shack. In return, Banner had nicknamed Striker Shipwreck – which Striker thought only fair, since it had been Banner's boat Striker had destroyed in a not-to-be-discussed water-skiing incident.

Striker waved the man down. 'Over here, Noodles.'

'Yeah, yeah, yeah. Hold your friggin' horses.'

Short, stubby, with white bushy eyebrows that made him look more Muppet than human, the ident technician waddled as he walked. He cut through the concrete plant loading zone and approached the dock. When he reached the river's edge, Striker nodded.

''Bout time you got here – should I send you a special request next time?'

'Sure. Address it to your mother's bedroom.'

For the first time since this nightmare had started, Striker managed a bit of a smile. He explained to the technician all that had happened, then got Noodles to swab the bracelet for DNA and examine the cut rope. Once done, he guided him a few metres back towards the trail.

There, he stopped.

In the softer region of sand and silt were the footprints he had seen a half-hour earlier, during the chase. Three separate indentations. In the morning light, it was obvious that they were poor at best. Little ridge detail, blurred by the twisting motion in the sand. But one thing was for certain – the prints pointed in the direction of the dock.

'Any chance of casting these?' Striker asked.

Noodles placed his toolbox down on an unblemished section

of land and crouched down low. Breathing hard from the exertion, his big belly protruding out, he pulled the flashlight from his tool belt and aimed the beam down into the first set of prints, then the second, and lastly the third.

He made some unhappy sounds.

'Not good?' Striker asked.

'Poor. But we'll do what we can . . . Any others?'

Striker shook his head. 'Not that I've seen – but we haven't done a full sweep of the beach yet. Got a canvass team being called out as we speak.'

Noodles just nodded.

Striker studied the footprints alongside the tech, assessing each one individually, then viewing them as an ongoing chain. After a moment, he pointed at two of the three shoe prints – the right ones.

'The heel kicks out every time,' he noted.

Noodles nodded. 'Could have a fucked-up gait.'

'Or a previous injury of some kind.'

'Could be. But the ground here slopes down towards the river. So his foot would naturally slip a little, especially if he was trying to turn as he ran. Size is probably an eleven.'

'An eleven?'

'Or a ten.'

'Great. We've just narrowed it down to eighty per cent of the adult male population.'

A few feet ahead, they found another print, this one much smaller. Possibly the victim. Noodles studied it. 'There's some basic ridge detail on this one,' he said. 'Enough maybe for a sample comparison . . . maybe . . . but the odds of discerning a brand and model are poor at best.'

'Poor as in your chances of being voted Cop of the Year?'

'Worse. Poor like *your* chances.'

Striker smiled weakly, then swore under his breath. He breathed in deeply, and the reedy stink of the river hit him.

Torture rooms. Rave girls. And vanishing suspects – this call was turning out to be the case from hell.

He was about to leave the river's edge when something else caught his attention – something he noticed in only the first of the three footprints. He knelt down, took a pen from his pocket, and used it to point into the instep of the first footprint. There, in the dirt, was a small patch of a whitish-grey powder. In the mottled tones of sand and silt, it was almost indiscernible.

'What is this?' he asked.

Noodles took a long look. 'Cement. Guy probably tracked it in from the plant yards – the stuff is everywhere.'

Striker said nothing for a moment, then nodded.

'Analyse it anyway,' he said.

'If you want.'

'I want,' Striker said. 'At this point we're looking for miracles.'

Ten

Striker met Felicia back at the cement plant in the foreman's office. The manager – a man who had run the concrete plant for twenty years without a glitch – had been called in from his Vancouver home and was now being questioned by Sergeant Rothschild in the back room.

Striker looked through the glass partition. The manager was wearing a pair of jeans and a New England Patriots jersey. He looked like he'd thrown on the first thing available upon getting the phone call. His befuddled expression also held notes of worry and shock.

He was clearly out of his comfort zone.

Felicia bumped Striker as she moved past him to the nearest work desk. She dropped a laptop down – one of the department Toughbooks – and punched in her password. Then the system known as PRIME – the Police Records Information Management Environment – initiated.

PRIME was essentially one giant police database, listing the majority of police contacts, with the obvious exception of privatized files, invisible entries, and anything attached to a sealing order set forth by the courts.

Felicia looked over at Striker. 'You were right. Our witness was high as a kite. Paramedics were worried she could overdose right there on scene, so they rushed her off to the Children's Hospital.'

'Children's?'

'Yeah. She's only *fourteen*.'

'Jesus Christ, are you serious? I thought she was older than that.' Striker took a moment to think of such a young girl being alone and high in a dark secluded industrial area. Thoughts of the scanty way in which she'd been dressed made him frown as his fathering instincts kicked in.

A situation like that could only lead to bad things.

And it had.

'Anyway,' Felicia continued. 'The girl says she saw something on the woman's shoulder. A tattoo of some kind.'

'What kind of tattoo?'

'A bird. An eagle, she thinks. Something *red*.' Felicia turned back towards the laptop and resumed typing. 'I'm running anything that's even remotely close. But this machine is old and slow. The search keeps crashing . . . We'll have to do a full scan at HQ.'

Striker was not surprised about the crashes. The portable laptops were notorious for failing during data searches. From what computer techs had told him, the problem was not so much a hardware issue as a software one.

Too many firewalled security checks.

Laptop issues aside, the notion of the girl spotting a tattoo on the victim's body was troubling. A tattoo was a great lead, no doubt, but Striker wondered just how valid it was, given the girl's mental state. He looked at Felicia. 'What *exactly* did she say the victim was wearing for clothing?'

'She didn't.'

'Why not?'

'She's high, Jacob. The details were poor. Hazy at best.'

'Yet she was clear on this tattoo?'

'Does it matter? It's all we got to go on. If you think you can do better—'

Striker held up his hands. 'Hey, I'm not criticizing here, Feleesh. Just thinking out loud. For this girl to see a tattoo on the woman's shoulder, then the victim must have been wearing something like a tank top. Or she was undressed.'

'So you're thinking this might be a sexual assault as well?'

A sick expression took over Striker's face. 'God, I hope not. I'm just talking this thing out.' He thought of a woman being strapped to a chair in the loft of the barn. '*Plus*, it was dark in there. *Plus*, the woman was black.'

Felicia cocked an eyebrow at him. 'So?'

'So how well does red ink show up on black skin, especially in a dark environment?'

'Probably not all that well,' Felicia admitted.

Striker looked back through the window at the plant manager, who was still being questioned by Rothschild. The man's New England Patriots jersey made Striker think. 'Some sports teams have winged logos. Like the Detroit Red Wings. Heck, their logo is even red.'

Felicia typed in the data, then sent off another search.

As they waited for a return of information, Striker moved to the exit and looked outside. Across the lot, yellow police tape cordoned off all the crime scenes: the incoming road; the entrance to the cement plant; the barn with the orange exterior lamp; and the dock area below. Yellow lines were pretty much everywhere he looked, marking off a half-dozen secondary crime scenes.

It was disheartening.

'So much forensics . . . this is going to take time we don't have.'

He took a step outside to get some fresh air. High overhead, Air 1 still hovered. The bird had been combing the riverbanks for over an hour now, and air time was expensive. Once she landed to refuel, financial costs would come into play. Budgetary considerations.

The air search would be called off.

Striker could feel the seconds ticking by. He turned to look at the inspector. Seeing Osaka as the Road Boss still felt wrong for some reason. For anyone with ten seconds of operational experience, it was easy to see how hard the job was on the man. Terry Osaka was damn near a wizard in Investigations, and a legal genius when it came to Planning and Research.

But for all his skills off the road, he had an equal lack of ability on the road. During operations, he often was the epitome of a second-guesser, and his lack of confidence led to long bouts of dangerous hesitancy. Striker could see the stress in his eyes at every call.

'How low is the bird on fuel?' Striker asked.

'You got twenty minutes, nothing more.'

'I'll take every one of them I got.'

Osaka looked ready to say more, but his cell went off. He raised the BlackBerry to his ear, then met Striker's gaze and frowned. '*Laroche*,' he whispered, then walked back towards the Road Boss car – a white unmarked sedan.

As Osaka climbed the hill, Mike Rothschild came down. The sergeant smirked and jabbed a thumb at the inspector. 'Did you ask the Colonel about the eleven herbs and spices for our barbecue tonight?'

Striker smiled at the joke, then frowned at the remembrance.

The barbecue with Mike and the kids . . .

'I wouldn't hold your breath on that one,' he said. 'I got a feeling this call is going to be a long one.'

Rothschild frowned. He pulled out a pack of Old Port winetips and lit one up. 'Fuckin' hope not, man. Kids are really looking forward to seeing you. Plus, I picked us up some thick-ass T-bones. Gonna try this Jack Daniel's BBQ recipe I found on the net. Supposed to be great.' He took a long drag on the cigarillo and blew out a stream of wine-scented smoke. '*Real* great.'

Striker barely heard him. His mind was preoccupied with the list of tasks that still needed to be done. Without responding to Rothschild's remarks, he pulled out his cell phone and called E-Comm. Sue Rhaemer answered with more of her usual 80s slang.

'Word up, Shipwreck.'

Striker tasked her with notifying all the hospitals. 'Tell them to be on the lookout for anyone coming in with injuries indicative of electrical torture.'

'I'm on it,' Rhaemer said, then hung up.

As Striker lowered his cell, his eyes caught sight of the land mass in the centre of the strait. Mitchell Island was a small section of land, connected by only the single-lane off-ramp of the Knight Street Bridge. The area was home to industrial plants, warehouses and shipping docks. Only factory workers ever ventured there. It was a good kilometre upriver and another kilometre across the waterway.

Striker looked at Rothschild. 'You think this guy could have swum there?'

Rothschild let out a laugh filled with smoke. 'Mitchell fucking Island? I guess that depends.'

'On what?'

'On whether our suspect is Aquaman.'

'I know it's a long ways off . . . but it's not impossible.'

Rothschild shrugged. 'Not impossible. But that's *far*, man. And the currents are really bad. This guy would have to be one hell of a swimmer. Strong, and in great friggin' shape.'

Striker said nothing back, he just stared silently across the way. When Inspector Osaka returned from his phone call, Striker got the man's attention and pointed at the island. 'Order the bird there, sir. And send in a search team with a dog.'

The inspector gave him an odd look. 'You honestly think he could have swum all that way? Especially while holding a woman hostage?'

Striker offered no further explanations.

'Just send the bird.'

Eleven

Garbed in a black tracksuit, the bomber drove down West 52nd Avenue and stopped at Cartier Street under the shadowy overhang of a cherry blossom tree. On the seat next to him were two piles of *The Province* newspapers, today's issue and thirty in all – props to explain why he was out so early in case the police pulled him over.

Just delivering papers, Officer.

Sometimes the most simple explanations were the best.

In the back compartment of the van was the woman. She was bound and gagged with duct tape.

She would be no problem.

For what seemed like a long time, the bomber waited, listening to the van idle and savouring the minty taste of the chewing tobacco he had stuffed under his bottom lip. It was Skoal – always Skoal. Wintergreen pouches.

He'd been craving some baccy for the last two hours now. It was because of the job, he knew. The stress always did that to him. Heightened the addiction. Made time slow down on him. It fucked up a lot of things. He preferred chew over fags for one reason – cigarette butts were easily found and made perfect DNA cultures for forensic techs.

Which was unacceptable.

He cracked his fingers, one by one. Edgy, he was getting edgy.

He needed to blow something up. Send it sky fucking high. In an effort to maintain control, he closed his eyes and muttered his favourite old rhyme:

> *Tommy Atkins went to war*
> *and he came back a man no more.*
> *Went to Baghdad and Sar-e.*
> *He died, that man who looked like me.*

He finished the rhyme. It was one he recited often. Like always, it stirred up old feelings, ones he could not define or place. *That* – the lack of recollection – bothered him more than anything.

He spat the baccy out the window. Grabbed another pouch. Inserted it.

Finally, the radio came to life – one soft click of a mike, followed by Molly's tinny but decisive tone: 'West 52nd is clear from Cartier Street to Adera Street. Proceed.'

He pressed his own mike: 'Copy. West 52nd is clear from Cartier Street to Adera Street. Proceeding.'

When the bomber reached the entrance to the command centre – an area wide open for the general public to see, yet a place everyone drove by every day and never so much as looked at – he slowed down.

He pulled onto a side road, just off the thoroughfare, and killed the engine. He had barely stepped out of the van when Molly, ever the silent ghost, was suddenly right there in front of him. Her drab brown hair was pulled back over her head into a short ponytail. Her pudgy face was tense and her fingers clutched the silver pendant around her neck so tightly that the chain dug into her skin.

'Where's your uniform?' she asked.

'I discarded it.'

'*Discarded it?* Where—'

'Don't throw a wobbly, all right? I did it safely. *Safely.*'

He stared into her eyes. Molly was tense. So tense. He could see that, hear that, *feel* that. It was her way. In past times, he had tried hard to change that part of her. To project a sense of calmness into her being. But it never did any good and he had long since stopped trying.

Nowadays, he just let her be.

He opened the side door of the van. There, lying on her side, hands and legs bound behind her back, blindfolded and gagged, was the woman. Molly made a choking sound at the sight of her. Her face paled noticeably, and she shuddered.

'This . . . this isn't a game, love. These are *real* people.'

'I understand that.'

'Do you?'

He said nothing.

'Did you get the information we needed?' she asked. 'Did she talk?'

He nodded slowly. 'They all talk.'

'But did you get *confirmation*?'

'We were right all along.'

Molly closed her eyes and let out a long breath. She looked ready to cry. 'Well thank God, because nothing else is going according to plan. Absolutely nothing.'

He touched her arm. 'We'll assess. Adjust. Adapt. Like we always do.'

Molly said nothing. Her face looked hard and her thin lips were pressed together tightly.

For a long moment, the bomber studied her gentle face. The tenderness in her eyes. And the memories flooded him – moments that were good and bad and somewhere in between, but all of them jumbled in time. Without uniformity or order. Like marbles rolling around uncontrollably in a porcelain basin.

For a moment, he tried to sort through them. Like he always did. When he failed miserably, yet again, he broke from his thoughts and focused back on Molly. Her small hands trembled, and he found that strange. Over the years, she had been on more missions than him. She had faced death *numerous* times.

So why so edgy now?

And then, slowly, it dawned on him. He reached up and gently took her hands. Pulled her close. Kissed the top of her head. 'I'm fine.'

She looked up at him intently. 'I don't want the darkness coming back on you.'

'Sunny days are here again.'

'I'm serious.'

'I love you, Molly.'

'I know,' she replied. 'I know.'

Twelve

Striker watched Felicia exit the cement plant. The morning light glinted in her brown-black eyes and made her long straight hair appear thick and flaxen. She looked beautiful, and Striker couldn't help but stare at her for a moment. When she climbed into the passenger seat, he started the car.

'Well?' he asked. 'Anything on the tattoo?'

'Nothing I can directly connect to a black female.' She spoke the words almost begrudgingly. She struggled to secure the laptop back into the mount; the brackets were notoriously fickle. 'This friggin' laptop keeps crashing. How the hell are we supposed to do our job when the department can't even fix their own software?'

Striker felt her tension like a hot breeze.

As the engine warmed up, he filled Felicia in on everything that had happened in her absence: his alerting the border and the hospitals; Noodles now processing the crime scenes; and how the police chopper was sweeping the shores of Mitchell Island. So far, nothing positive had come back – not from Noodles and not from the helicopter.

It was all one big zero.

'So what *do* we have?' Felicia asked.

'A bracelet and one hell of a strange torture weapon.'

Felicia nodded as she thought back to the scene. 'What a

weird torture device . . . and yet I think I've seen something like that before . . .'

Striker grinned. 'You're thinking of a curling iron.'

She gave him a hard look.

'Or maybe a hair straightener,' he added.

'Don't patronize me, Jacob. Not today.'

When his smile only widened, and she realized he was playing with her, Felicia laughed softly. She shook her head and ordered him to go south. 'Starbucks on Granville – if I'm going to be able to put up with you all day, I'm gonna need some caffeine and carbs in me. *Fast.*'

Striker nodded; he felt like some java himself.

Five minutes later, they'd exited the drive-thru with a pair of coffees – a standard black for Striker, and a vanilla latte for Felicia. The brew smelled wonderful, enticing. Yet when Striker raised the paper cup to his lips, his hand trembled. Thoughts of the bullets tearing through the window, back in the steel barn, hit him hard again, and he took in a slow deep breath in an effort to stabilize himself.

Adrenalin, he justified. *The jitters.*

Hoping Felicia hadn't noticed, he gulped down some coffee, then dropped the cup into the holder. He handed Felicia the raspberry-lemon scone she had requested and smiled.

'Happy birthday,' he said.

She took it. 'No candles?'

'I'd need a whole cake for that.'

Felicia gave him a deadpan stare. 'Are you trying to incur my wrath?' When Striker didn't answer, she tore off a chunk, and stuffed it in her mouth. After a few chews, she let his comments go and returned to going over the file.

Striker did the same. He wondered: had they prevented what was to be a gangland execution here? The fact that the victim was a woman made it seem less likely – unless, of course, their witness had been mistaken. Given the girl's drug-fed mental state, her anxiety, and the dimness of the barn loft, the victim could even have been a man with long hair. To tell now was impossible; they didn't have enough information, and Striker wasn't into making assumptions.

'We need to talk to a weapons expert. And the sooner, the better.'

Felicia agreed.

Only one person came to mind – fellow cop, Jay Kolt. He was the only expert the Vancouver Police Department had on these matters. Kolt spent the bulk of his time teaching Use of Force tactics to cops on training days, and also to recruits at the Justice Institute. And with a name like Kolt, he was damn well born for the part.

Striker telephoned the man on speed-dial. When the call went straight to voicemail, he left a message, asking for a return call ASAP. Then he turned back to Felicia. 'Weapons expert will have to wait for now.'

Felicia remained undeterred. 'The bracelet then.'

Striker reached into his inner jacket pocket and pulled out the brown paper evidence bag. He handed it over to Felicia. She removed the bracelet and studied it for less than a second before her left eyebrow raised in admiration of the piece.

'This is a Campetti,' she said.

'A what?'

'A Campetti. He's a well-known designer here in Vancouver.'

'How do you know that?'

Felicia grinned. 'Anyone who loves jewellery and lives in Vancouver knows of Campetti. The man's an *artist*. He has a shop in the gold building – for those who can afford to go there.'

'The gold building . . . you mean the Granville high-rise?'

'That's the one.' Felicia used her iPhone app to look up the phone number. She found it, called, then hung up. 'They don't open till eight-thirty.'

Striker looked at his watch. It was eight-fifteen now. He put the car into gear and drove north through the rush-hour grind. They headed for District 1, the downtown core.

Destination: Campetti Jewellers.

Thirteen

What would normally have taken fifteen minutes for Striker and Felicia turned into a half-hour commute. The rush-hour jam was thicker than usual and every traffic light was red. When they reached yet another backlog on the Granville Street Bridge, Striker grew frustrated. He pulled out his cell phone and called his voicemail. It was the third time he had done so in two miles.

Felicia gave him a sideways glance. 'Doesn't your phone alert you when you get a message?' When Striker pretended not to hear her and pressed the cell tighter to his ear, she smirked. 'Oh, I get it.'

'Get what?' he asked.

'You're worried about Courtney.'

Striker said nothing at first. Courtney, his sixteen-year-old daughter, had left for Ireland with her boyfriend, Tate, over fourteen hours ago now. Striker had driven them to the airport himself, and he couldn't help thinking of her.

'She's fine, *Daddy,*' Felicia added. 'God, you're such a worrywart.'

Striker had no messages, so he put the phone away. 'She was supposed to call the moment the plane landed. She *promised.*'

'And she will. God, give her a break, Jacob. It's not like she's gone to some Third World country. It's *Ireland*. And she's with Tate.'

He grunted. '*Tate.* That's what bothers me.'

'Oh, come on. It's not just the two of them – his whole family went. Besides, you should be happy she has Tate. He's a good kid. And he treats her well. After all Courtney's gone through the last year – getting shot and all – she's lucky to have someone who supports her and cares for her.'

'She's got me.'

Felicia laughed softly. 'Oh joy.'

'She hasn't even finished her therapy yet.'

'So what? What the girl really needs is some time away. Besides, this has nothing to do with therapy, or Tate, or her trip to Ireland, and you know it . . . Courtney's growing up, is all. And you don't like it.'

'She's only sixteen, Feleesh.'

'So what? I had two kids by the time I was sixteen.'

Striker turned to look at her. '*What?*'

'Gotcha.'

She laughed out loud and Striker said nothing. He just let out a long breath, steered into the fast lane, and drove across the Granville Street Bridge.

They couldn't get there quick enough for his liking.

The Gold Building – a 27-storey high-rise, located in the very centre of the downtown core – was not the actual building name, but a nickname cops had given it due to the high amount of gold vendors it housed.

Striker had been by the place a thousand times in his career – mainly because the Granville strip was a magnet for problems – but had never once set foot inside the building. Now, as they rode the elevator up to the top floor, he took the bracelet from the bag, turned it over in his hands, and looked for a signature or a serial number. When he found none, he looked back at Felicia.

'How'd you know this was a Campetti?'

She smiled. 'Any time you need information, baby, you just come to momma.'

He shook his head. 'You can be so annoying.'

'*I* can be so annoying? Wow, talk about the pot and the kettle.'

Striker let the conversation go. When the doors opened, he wasted no time in walking down the hall.

Campetti Jewellers was the last door at the end of the corridor. All that gave away its location was a simple black sign with copper writing. Striker pressed the buzzer and watched the exterior camera pan down on them.

He held up his badge. 'Vancouver Police.'

Seconds later, the electronic door clicked open.

Inside, the office was small but immaculate. Everything was cherry wood, black felt casings, and glimmering glass. Behind the front desk, the entire north wall was one continuous floor-to-ceiling window. The morning sun blazed through it, making the jewellery in the cherry wood display cases gleam.

From a side room came a man so big that, despite Striker's 186-centimetre height, he felt small. This man behind the desk was easily 200 centimetres and 140 kilos, with hands so big they looked like hockey gloves. His square face held a look of forty years, and his olive skin colouring was deepened by the contrast of his greying short hair.

Striker knew him at a glance. 'You gotta be kidding me – are you Monster C?'

The man behind the counter smiled. 'Now there's a name I don't hear much any more.'

Striker shook his hand. 'Detectives Striker and Santos. VPD.'

Felicia looked genuinely surprised. She turned to Striker. 'How did you know his nickname?'

Striker smiled. 'Any time you need information, baby, you

just come to poppa.' When she gave him one of her irritated looks, he explained. 'Monster C here used to be a tight end for the Seattle Seahawks.'

The big man nodded. '*Was.* Until Tyson Williams blew my knee out.' He spoke the words with obvious disdain.

Striker asked him, 'So what are you doing here? Security?'

'No, I design jewellery.'

'You mean, *you're* Campetti?'

The big jeweller laughed softly. 'I get that a lot. People expect some old Italian dude with tiny hands and thick glasses. Not these meat hooks.'

Striker grinned at that; it was true.

The three of them talked openly for a few minutes, then Striker got down to business. 'I need you to look at something and tell me if you recognize it.' He pulled the bracelet from his jacket pocket.

Campetti sat down on a stool and examined the piece for less than five seconds before speaking. 'Of course I recognize this. It's one of a kind. I made it.'

'You remember for who?'

'It was a *gift.* For Sharise Owens – the trauma surgeon who worked on my boy after he got jumped by a gang of pricks at the fireworks two years ago.' His face darkened. 'Cops had to carry him into St Paul's Hospital. He was barely hanging on.'

'Is he okay?' Felicia asked.

'He is . . . now.' Campetti stared at the bracelet and his eyes took on a faraway look. 'It's made from gold and sterling silver. A Celtic Knot. The *Triquetra.* It symbolizes life, death, and rebirth – which is exactly what Dr Owens did for my boy.'

'Dr Sharise Owens.' Striker wrote the name in his notebook 'This might sound funny, but is she black? African-American?'

'Well, yes . . .' Campetti's face suddenly took on a concerned expression and he stared at the bracelet. 'How did you get this? Is everything all right?'

Felicia interjected. 'We're not sure what's going on yet. This bracelet might not even be related. It's just something we're checking into right now.'

The words didn't appear to offer Campetti any comfort.

Striker took the bracelet back and placed it in the evidence bag. He then gave Felicia the nod to leave.

'You've been a great help,' he said to Campetti. 'We'll be in touch.'

A nervous expression still covered the jeweller's face. He stood up as they opened the door. 'If you need anything, just call.'

Striker said he would, then closed the door behind them. Once in the hall, Felicia cocked an eyebrow at him.

'St Paul's Hospital?' she asked.

Striker nodded. 'Time for a doctor's appointment.'

Fourteen

'Run her,' was the first thing Striker said when they got back to the car.

Know who you're dealing with: it was a standard rule he always went by – one learned from his first sergeant, once mentor, and now best friend Mike Rothschild.

Information was the key; it opened new doors.

Felicia ran the name Sharise Owens through the database. A few seconds later, the laptop beeped and the feed came back. On the screen was a list of names. There were three entities for Sharise Owens. Two of them lived in the City of Vancouver, and one resided in Squamish.

Felicia clicked on the first entity, saw a date of birth that equalled eighty-six years of age, and ruled the woman out. She then clicked on the second name – age forty-two – and the entity popped up on the screen. Felicia pointed at the information in the Particulars section. 'Look what it says right there. Trauma Surgeon. St Paul's Hospital.'

'Check if there are any tattoos listed.'

Felicia did. Frowned.

'None,' she said.

Striker wrote down all the listed telephone numbers. While Felicia read through the rest of the documented history, Striker began calling.

The first number, listed as *Cell,* was no longer in use. The second number, listed as *Home,* rang three times and went straight to voicemail. Striker left a long message. The third number, labelled *Work,* was the number for St Paul's Hospital. Striker called it, and was soon transferred to the nurses' station.

'It's Detective Striker,' he explained, 'with the Vancouver Police Department's Homicide Unit. I need to speak to Dr Sharise Owens. She's a trauma surgeon there.'

The nurse's tone gave away her weariness. 'One second, Detective.'

For a moment, the line clicked and Striker was stuck listening to pop music. John Secada or Marc Antony – he wasn't sure. Then the line clicked again and the nurse returned. 'I'm sorry. But Dr Owens isn't in just yet.'

'When does she get in?'

'Her shift starts at eleven.'

Striker looked at his watch. *An hour and a half.* 'Do you have another number I can reach her at?' When the nurse made an uncomfortable sound, Striker read off the numbers he already had. 'Are there any others?'

'No, those are the same ones we have here.'

'Does she hang out with any of the other doctors or nurses?'

The woman made a doubtful sound. 'Dr Owens doesn't really socialize with anyone – she's a very private person . . . but I'll ask around for you.'

'I'll wait.'

'Just give me a minute, Detective.' After another long moment, the nurse came back on the line. 'I'm sorry, but no one has seen her. And the only emergency contact we have is her cell phone number.'

Striker found that odd. 'No family or friends?'

'None.'

He let out a long breath, debated in his mind. 'I need her to call me the moment she arrives. *The moment.* Understand?'

'Yes, yes of course.'

He gave the nurse his cell number, hung up, and then turned to Felicia.

'I'm shooting zeroes here. Anything on your end?'

She looked up from the laptop. 'No. Same here, I'm afraid. The woman has no known associates. Not even one family member. From what I can tell, she's the only daughter of deceased parents . . . I say we flag her.'

Striker agreed. Flagging was the equivalent of an All Points Bulletin. If any emergency response worker came into contact with Dr Sharise Owens, Striker and Felicia would be notified immediately.

He called up CPIC, the Canadian Police Information Centre, and got Dr Sharise Owens flagged on the system as a Missing Person and a Person in Danger. While he did this, Felicia called Sue Rhaemer at Dispatch and got her to notify the hospitals, ferries, airports and borders once more.

After a long moment, she hung up.

'Done,' she said.

Striker said nothing. He just put the car into Drive and got going.

Sharise Owens' home address was just two miles away.

Fifteen

Striker and Felicia headed just around the bend for Beach Avenue, where Sharise Owens lived in an apartment overlooking the sandy stretch of English Bay.

They made it there in five minutes and took the elevator up to the twenty-second floor. The doors opened into the hallway, directly across from the suite, and Striker wasted no time. He took up his position at the side of the apartment door, waited for Felicia to parallel him, and then knocked three times. When no one answered, he looked down the hallway at the neighbouring suite.

'Maybe there's an onsite manager,' he said.

Felicia shook her head. 'I already checked. These are privately owned suites, and the concierge is offsite. We'll have to call him.'

Striker frowned at that. They had reason to believe the woman was in danger. She wasn't at work. She wasn't answering her cell. She wasn't answering her home phone.

'I'm kicking it in.'

'We should at least *try* to get the concierge.'

'Just be ready.'

'Jacob—'

Striker leaned forward and gave the door a solid kick. The entire structure bowed inwards, but held. A good lock, a better frame. Seeing that, he turned around and gave the door three solid donkey kicks, landing the heel of his shoe between the door handle and frame. On his third attempt, the entire structure burst inwards and the shrill cry of an alarm filled the air.

'Security system works fine,' he said, and drew his pistol.

Felicia swore in frustration but did the same.

They made entry and began clearing the suite. As they worked from room to room, two things became immediately obvious. One, Sharise Owens was a wealthy woman. Everything was top end, from the imported Kuppersbusch appliances to the genuine Persian carpets and teak floors.

The second obvious detail was that, if Sharise had been kidnapped, no struggle had taken place here. The woman clearly took pride in her home, keeping everything in its place, from the fanned-out *Oprah* magazines on the coffee table to the folded laundry in her closets.

Everything was immaculate.

By the time they finished clearing the residence, the alarm had stopped blasting. Felicia holstered her piece. 'This is a dead end.'

'So far it is,' Striker responded, his ears still ringing. 'Let's do a detailed search – see if we can find anything relevant.'

'Fine. I'll start with the kitchen.'

Striker nodded. That left him with the bedroom and the office area. He got right to work, searching through drawers and scavenging through the closets. But in the end, the bedroom yielded nothing. He grabbed the phone and hit the callback feature to see what number had last called the Owens residence. It was him. He hit redial to see the last number dialled. It was St Paul's Hospital.

The time of the call was late last night.

No leads there.

Felicia called out from the other room. 'No evidence in the kitchen or living room. I'll search through the den.'

Striker yelled back okay and went into the office. On the shelf, in two long rows, were a series of micro-tapes and compact discs. Striker examined them. Each tape and disc said 'copy' on the cover, and was followed by a description:

Arlington, Jonas – fractured pelvis, Motor Vehicle Accident.

Booth, Amy – punctured lung, Workplace Accident.

Chavez, Ricardo – appendix removal, Cause Unknown.

The list went on.

There were many tapes and discs, all appearing to be audio files of past surgeries Dr Owens had performed. Eleven years' worth. Striker was impressed. Most doctors kept reports, but it appeared that Dr Owens went a step further.

The woman was meticulous.

He put back the tapes and finished his search. When he approached the computer, he saw that the screen was black. He moved the mouse and a password request appeared. Having little personal knowledge of the woman, he didn't even hazard a guess. Instead, he sat down, opened the drawers, and started rifling through the files.

Most of it was ordinary bills with some tax information slips and the odd photocopy of a medical certificate or diploma. An old address book was relatively unused. It had the numbers of two other doctors listed in it, but nothing else. Striker called them both, but neither of them had seen or heard from Dr Owens in weeks.

After a long moment of searching, the alarm went off again. Striker gave up and returned to the living room. Already two of the neighbours – both middle-aged women, both cupping their hands over their ears – had come to investigate the alarm. Normally, they would have appeared nervous, even timid, but standing with them was a patrol cop – a tall Slavic-looking guy Striker had never seen.

Striker took out his badge and showed the cop and the neighbours. 'Detectives Striker and Santos.' He asked the women if they'd seen Dr Owens lately. Both ladies began chirping like a pair of overexcited hens, but in the end the result was the same. Neither woman had seen Sharise Owens since yesterday morning.

It was no good.

Felicia exited the den and joined them. She looked at the two women, then at the patrol cop, and then at Striker. She shook her head and spoke above the high-pitched alarm. 'You find anything?'

'Yeah. Another zero. You?'

'Zero plus zero equals zilch.'

Striker frowned. The lack of progress and the alarm was getting to him. He moved into the hall, away from the drone, and pulled out his phone. He tried calling Dr Owens' cell one more time, and was yet again directed to voicemail. He hung up.

Before leaving, he explained to the patrol cop what was going on with Dr Owens, then asked him to guard the suite until members of the City Maintenance Crew arrived to fix the door, or until Owens returned. The constable agreed, and Striker and Felicia left the scene under his care.

Back in the car, Striker scoured his notebook, hoping to see something they had missed. But the more he went over things, the more he ended up back where they had started.

'We need to know how Owens' bracelet got down by the docks,' he said. 'Even if she turns up okay, it's too coincidental.'

Felicia shrugged. 'For all we know someone stole it.'

Striker hadn't thought of that. 'Any history of thefts or robberies in PRIME?'

Felicia did a search. 'No . . . but this is interesting – she was arrested once.'

Striker closed his notebook and looked at her, surprised. 'Really? For what?'

'For refusing to leave an anti-abortion rally.' Felicia read through the report. 'Interesting. She was fighting with the protesters.'

'I guess that makes her pro-choice.'

Felicia nodded. 'Look here. She was also arrested a few more times. At different rallies. Who knows? Maybe this entire call could be a pro-choice thing.'

Striker let out a groan. 'Abortion activists? That's the *last* thing we need. It would be a political nightmare.'

He leaned closer to Felicia to read the screen and smelled her musky perfume and perspiration. She smelled good and, like always, her scent calmed him a little. He focused on the computer, on the entity known as Dr Sharise Owens, then spoke.

'We need to learn more about this doctor,' he said. 'So we got two options here – we can either wait at St Paul's until she shows up for work, or we can hightail it back to HQ and start searching the databases.'

The choice for Felicia was simple. 'I've had enough of hospitals to last me a lifetime.'

'Good. Because there's no guarantee she'll show up there at all.'

The moment Striker spoke the words, he regretted them. It was as if they were taboo. The fact that Sharise Owens might already be dead was a sobering thought. But there it was – the cold hard reality of it all.

Welcome to Homicide.

Sixteen

The clock read 09:45 when Striker logged onto his work computer at Homicide headquarters and waited for the Versadex program to initiate. It was a standard Wednesday, midweek hustle, and the office was half-filled with weary investigators. As always, the building echoed with a mechanical thunder from the prehistoric air conditioner that rattled sometimes, clanked others, but almost always blew out warm air – especially on hot summer days.

While Striker waited for the program to load, he walked to the kitchen area and poured himself a cup of the sludge the office brass called coffee. Normally he drank it black, but this brew required chemical creamer and sugar to smooth out the burned taste.

For the next five minutes, he sipped his coffee, checked his voicemail for messages from Courtney, and found that there were still none. He tried calling her twice himself, but to no avail. In the end, he called up the airlines and was told that the plane had landed without problem.

The information soothed and angered him all at once.

'Damn kid,' he said.

He scanned the office. All around him, rows and rows of makeshift cubicles were set up, each one a carbon copy of his own work station – a desk, a chair, a pin-up board, and an archaic crappy computer that was one generation away from being a Commodore 64. Hell, the monitors weren't even widescreen.

On Striker's pin-up board were two pictures. One of his daughter Courtney standing with her friend, Raine; and the other of his parents, who had died two decades ago in a motor vehicle accident, leaving him as the sole provider for his three younger siblings. He stared at the photos for a long time. When the program finally started, it was an emotional relief.

Immediately, he sat down and typed:

Surname: Owens. Given 1: Sharise. Given 2: Chandelle.

Then he entered her date of birth.

Before hitting send, he added in a request for information from LEIP – the Law Enforcement Information Portal – and also from PIRS – the Police Information Retrieval System. Both were older databases, used by municipalities that had not yet transferred over to PRIME.

The results came back almost instantly.

'Desktop system's fast today,' he said. 'Look at this.'

Felicia was seated in her own cubicle behind him, trying to get a hold of weapons expert Jay Kolt. Having no luck, she hung up, swivelled about and looked over his shoulder at the screen. 'What you got?'

'Same pro-choice arrest you had for Sharise Owens. But look at this – there was also a death threat made against Sharise. And it's a Vancouver file.'

'Vancouver? That's strange . . . I never saw it in PRIME.'

Striker nodded. 'Of course you didn't. This file is eight years old. PRIME didn't exist back then. We're not reading the actual report – this is an electronic summary.'

Felicia cursed, and Striker echoed it. Retrieving information could be extremely frustrating in the world of policing. Older cases often existed only on paper. Some were reintroduced to the system as electronic summaries, but they were few, and they almost always lacked vital information.

Striker let out a heavy breath. 'We're lucky this call even had an electronic summary; otherwise we wouldn't have known it existed at all. The original report should be filed away somewhere.'

'In Archives?'

'It's a Vancouver file. So, yeah, hopefully.'

Striker read the summary. It was about as bare bones as it gets – critically lacking for something as serious as a death threat. The suspect in the file was a male named Chad Koda. In the remarks column was one word:

Unfounded.

Felicia pointed at the entity. 'Chad Koda . . . is he a pro-lifer?'

'Apparently.' Striker looked at the last line of the summary. 'Says Koda had a "relationship" with Owens, but it doesn't specify what kind of relationship. Looks more and more like this was a domestic someone didn't feel like writing up properly, so they changed it to an Unfounded Threat call.'

Striker ran the name Koda, but nothing else came up. He looked at the name for a long moment, knowing he had heard it somewhere before. Then he made the connection. 'Wait a second . . . Chad Koda . . . isn't he that high-end realtor you see on all the billboard ads? The self-proclaimed multimillionaire?'

'Oh yeah. That's right. The guy who colours his beard.'

Striker raised an eyebrow. 'Colours his beard? If you say so.'

'It's obvious, Jacob – to a woman.'

'Remind me of that when I go grey.'

'So, tomorrow then?'

Striker just shot her a wry look.

He picked up the desk phone and called Archives. The woman who answered had a smoker-rough voice and Striker was familiar with her. He gave her the file number and year, then waited when she put him on hold. When she finally picked up again, almost ten minutes later, her one-word answer bothered him.

'Purged.'

'*Purged?*' It was all Striker could do not to swear. 'But this was a violent call.'

The clerk made a weary sound – like she'd given this explanation one too many times and was growing tired of it. 'I wish I could say it was unusual, Detective, but the department purged a lot of stuff back then. Especially the year the basement flooded and all the records had to be moved.'

Striker felt his blood pressure rising. 'Try one more for me. See what you got on a guy named Chad Koda.'

'Hold on.' After a few seconds, she came back to the phone and her response was the same. 'You're batting zero today, Detective. I wouldn't bother buying any lottery tickets if I were you.'

Striker sighed. 'I'll cancel my prostate exam too.'

The woman gave a soft chuckle before Striker finished the conversation and hung up.

'Well?' Felicia said.

'Purged. All of it.'

'But that call was a *death* threat.'

Striker shook his head. 'Why does this feel like *Groundhog Day*?'

He scratched his chin as he thought. With no known victim, their weapons expert still unreachable, and Noodles needing another four hours to process the crime scenes, they were quickly running out of leads.

Felicia said, 'We're at a standstill.'

Striker agreed. He stood up. Put on his coat. Adjusted his holster. And made sure that the magazine was seated securely. 'Come on.'

Felicia stood up as well. 'Chad Koda's place?'

'You got it.' Striker grinned. 'Time to see how a multimillionaire lives.'

Seventeen

Striker stared at the inlet and faraway border of Stanley Park as they drove across the Burrard Street Bridge, his mind not able to enjoy the glorious view and instead focused on the details of the case.

Where they were headed – the 1300 block of Pacific Avenue – was the lateral edge of the downtown core, an area nestled in between the sprawling urban jungle of city life and the tranquil walkways of the sandy-beached Burrard Inlet.

The seawall below Pacific Avenue ran all the way to Stanley Park. Felicia looked at the bay, at the sun shimmering off the waters, at the people windsurfing, and sighed. 'I wish I could own a place down here. But I'd have to sell my soul to afford one.'

'That wouldn't get you the down-payment.'

She let out a bemused laugh. 'You're probably right. I've probably lowered its value over the years – I've been known to be a bad girl from time to time.'

Striker grinned. 'Not often enough.'

They exited the bridge.

On the southwest side of Pacific Avenue, apartment complexes rose up twenty storeys high. They blocked the view of the bay that the northeast houses had once boasted so many decades ago. Not that people living there could complain. The view may have been blocked, but those houses were still within throwing distance of Sunset Beach.

Striker drove past the row of homes, each one in its own Victorian style, and took note of the surroundings. The house Chad Koda owned was a single detached residence, three levels high, with a steep wooden stairway. The exterior wood sported a brand new burgundy paint job with clean white trim. Out front was a wall of recently trimmed hedges and a red brick patio with garden.

Everything looked professionally maintained.

Felicia whistled. 'Something tells me he's not operating on a policeman's salary.'

'A cop couldn't afford the gardener. You do a history check on this place yet?'

'Yeah, but there's nothing relevant. Only call ever made here was a noise complaint, and that was six years ago.'

The information was disappointing; Striker had hoped for something more.

They parked away from the traffic flow, on Thurlow, and walked down the sidewalk with the hot sun pressing down on them. By the time they reached the front walkway, Striker felt stuffy in his suit. It was only ten-thirty in the morning, but already the day was beginning to swelter. And being next to a row of cars spewing out exhaust fumes didn't help.

At the front door, Striker went to knock, then hesitated. There was no known history of dangers connected to this address, but he never took chances. He leaned over the railing and tried to peer through the window, but it was too dark to see.

'The window's got some kind of tint on it,' he said.

'Wards off the sun.'

'Sure. And it stops people from seeing inside.'

Striker approached the door and rapped hard, three solid

knocks. Less than thirty seconds later, footsteps could be heard inside. A latch rattled. The front door creaked open. And Striker got his first real-life look at the man from the billboard ads.

Chad Koda.

Realtor extraordinaire.

Striker was somewhat surprised. The man was not what he had expected. Chad Koda was a bit shorter than average height, a bit stockier than his billboard photo suggested, and he looked every bit his fifty years of age. His silvering hair was almost gone on top, and kept short on the sides. His goatee was darker than the hair on his head – Felicia mouthed the word *dyed* once more – and it stuck out against his deeply bronzed skin. He wore a wine-coloured kimono that hung half open and matching slippers.

Koda gave them both an impatient look. 'Well, what is it?'

Striker badged the man. 'Detectives Striker and Santos. We'd like a few minutes of your time, if you don't mind.'

The man rubbed his eyes. 'This really isn't the best time.'

'It won't take long.'

'I've heard that one before.'

Striker made no move to leave. 'You are Chad Koda, correct?'

'Yes.'

'And you once used to date Dr Sharise Owens?'

Koda's face tightened at the mention of the name, and he let out a long weary breath. 'Now what has she done?'

Striker took out his notebook. 'Dr Owens hasn't done anything, as far as I know. But there's a lot of convoluted things going on right now, and I'm trying to find the woman. I was wondering if, perhaps, you had seen her.'

'Only in my nightmares.'

'Not a fan, I take it.'

'I like my women *warm*-blooded.'

Striker just nodded. 'Have you been home all night, Mr Koda?'

'Yes, I have been – look, is there a reason you're asking me all this?'

'It's coming.'

'Well, make it come quicker – or I'm closing the door and going back inside.'

Striker gave Felicia a sideways glance to see if she wanted to give it a try. She caught it and spoke. 'Is there anyone who can corroborate your being home last night, Mr Koda?'

'Yeah, the Kardashian sisters. Kim's in there cleaning up right now.'

Her eyes hardened on the man. 'Look, Mr Koda—'

'No, *you* look, Detective. Sharise was my common-law wife – no doubt you got records on that. And you know what? It was a goddam nightmare. Every fucking minute of it.'

'We understand there were problems.'

'Problems?' The tanned flesh of Koda's face reddened. '*Problems?* Is that what you call it – a fucking problem? That bitch aborted my son! That was more than a *problem* to me, okay?'

'I didn't know that.'

'Then you need to become a better investigator.'

Felicia's face coloured at the comment, but she continued questioning the man.

Striker, meanwhile, said nothing. He just wrote this information down in his notebook, not only to record the detail, but as a way of giving Koda a second to either calm down or say more – hopefully, something that might incriminate himself. After another long bout of hostile responses to Felicia's questions, Striker put the notebook away.

'Mr Koda,' he began, 'my partner here has asked you some

pretty serious questions about Sharise Owens. And yet, there's something here I find off – you haven't even asked if she's okay.'

The man's face darkened even more. 'That's because I don't give a rat's ass. The moment that bitch aborted my son, she ceased to exist. I planned on keeping it that way for the rest of my life – until you two clowns showed up. As far as I'm concerned, it's ancient fucking history.'

Striker studied the man. Saw him red-faced and sweating. 'Your emotions would suggest otherwise.'

Koda's jaw tightened. 'Are you legally detaining me, Detective?'

'No.'

'Then fuck off – you want to speak to me again, you go through my lawyer. He's at KDM. I'm sure you've heard of it. All cops have.'

Koda stepped back. Slammed the door. And Striker and Felicia were left standing there in silence.

'Well, that was pleasant,' Felicia said.

Striker said nothing. He was preoccupied with analysing Koda's reaction. Deep in thought, he walked back down the steps and headed for the car. When they reached the cruiser, they climbed inside and shut the doors.

Felicia asked, 'What the hell is the KDM firm? I've heard that name somewhere before.'

'You should have. KDM sues cops under the Police Act.'

'Great.'

Striker was about to say more on the matter when his cell went off. He looked at the screen, saw the name Rothschild, and stuck the phone to his ear. 'Gimme some good news, Mike.'

'Okay – you're looking more and more like me every day.'

'I said *good* news.'

'Then how's this for you? The dogman just found a pair of

flippers and some scuba gear on the northwest shore of Mitchell Island. Can you fucking believe it? You were right. Our gunman actually *swam* across the divide.'

Striker closed his eyes as he took in the information. Some of the oddities fell into place for him. 'The cut twine – it wasn't there for tethering a boat, it was used to hold the scuba gear.'

'Looks like it.'

'I want that gear processed. Swabbed, traced, everything.'

'Noodles is already on it. I'll make some phone calls to the rental companies. See if any of them dealt with some strange customers lately. Who knows, maybe one of them even has some gear missing.'

'I won't hold my breath.'

Striker thanked Rothschild and said goodbye. He then told Felicia what had happened. As she listened, her expression became one of disbelief. 'Electrical torture devices, breathing apparatus, and a guy who can swim to Mitchell Island . . . This file is getting weirder by the second.'

Striker couldn't have agreed more. Any single one of those oddities would have been unusual on its own; but collectively, it was downright peculiar. Unnerving, even. More than ever, it made him wonder what they were up against.

Just what kind of people were they dealing with here?

Eighteen

The bomber stood cloaked in the shadows of the bridge overpass on the Granville Island docks and waited for the toymaker to arrive. She would be there soon. Keisha Williams was always on time. Like clockwork.

Today it would be her undoing.

The thought of it made the bomber shiver with anticipation. Despite the growing heat of the day, a coldness filled him – one that came from somewhere deep within. He understood why he felt this way, even if he could not put it into words. The past had made it this way. Made *him* this way. Killed any warmth left inside of him and scrambled his mind like a grey-matter omelette.

Like always, he tried not to think of it. He closed his eyes. Felt the humid wind sweep in off the False Creek waterways. Smelled the reek sourness of the salt water and seaweed and—

The radio crackled at his side:

'The target's en route. Five minutes until arrival.'

He opened his eyes, squinting against the pale white sun. He pressed his radio mike. 'Copy. Five minutes until arrival.'

Five minutes. It seemed an eternity.

Dressed in a workman's suit, he slid the radio into the inner pouch of his orange utility vest. He then lifted the binoculars from his chest and used them to examine the toy shop.

Inside the store, all the toys had been removed from the far shelf and replaced by one wooden duck. It stood there now, a twelve-inch bird, dressed in a blue policeman's suit with a big red number 5 painted on its chest. In behind it was the bomb; just a small cardboard box containing miscellaneous cell phone parts, a steel pipe, aluminium wiring, explosives, and a power source consisting of nothing more than D-Cell batteries.

It was armed and ready for detonation.

The bomber checked his watch.

Three minutes to go.

The wooden boards of the dock bobbed beneath his boots, making him shift his weight to maintain balance. The action caused the screws in his leg bones to burn – burn like the tension inside of him. There was an anxiety there, an inner swelling difficult to control. More than anything, he wanted some Skoal. Wintergreen. Spearmint. Hell, even Regular would do.

But this was not possible. People noticed a man chewing tobacco.

It would have to wait until after the mission.

He focused in on the Toy Hut. It was a quaint little place. Just a small Swiss-style cottage that sat beside a duck pond and an adjoining playground, one which would be filled with children by noon.

Next door, in the same building but separated by a wall, was a coffee shop. The Ol' Bean, its wooden sign read. There were people inside. Three of them. And a woman in a patio chair outside with her dog tied up nearby.

Collateral damage.

He watched with a sense of numb acceptance as the toymaker finally came walking down Anderson. She was a big woman, rotund, and black as night. She was dressed in a fuchsia shawl with purple tights – easy to spot.

Target Number 5.

In the bomber's pocket was the remote detonator. The first button armed the fusing system, and it had already been pressed. The second button triggered the igniter. He kept his finger alongside the trigger as the toymaker approached from the south. She walked past the Ol' Bean coffee shop, singing a song only she knew.

The moment the target went inside, the bomber left the docks and walked quickly up to Anderson Street. Staring through the toy shop window from across the street, he saw the woman milling about. Preparing for the day like it was just another ordinary Wednesday in July. When she spotted the toy duck in the policeman's uniform, she paused, and a bewildered look crossed her face. She moved towards it.

And he knew the time had come.

He stepped forward, moving into the middle of the road, and stopped in front of the Toy Hut. Immediately, the radio crackled at his side and Molly's digitized voice came across the air: 'What are you doing? You're too close. You need more distance.'

He ignored the command.

'*Get back.*'

He pressed the mike. 'I need this.'

'No! You're too close! *Too close—*'

The bomber reached down and turned off his radio. Detonator in hand, he took one step closer to the toy shop, swept both his arms out to the sides, tilted back his head, and closed his eyes.

Then he pressed the button.

Click – spark – *combustion.*

And the entire south side of the toy store exploded in a ball of light and flame and smoke, engulfing him in the process.

Nineteen

Dr Sharise Owens did not show up for work and was still not answering her cell phone. Aside from flagging the woman as a Missing Person, there was little else Striker and Felicia could do on the matter. So they headed for Cambie Street Headquarters to locate the department's weapons expert Jay Kolt.

Striker was driving over the Granville Street Bridge, passing over the market, when a horrific thrashing sound filled the air and the entire bridge shook. Automatically, he hammered on the brakes and gripped the wheel so tightly his knuckles blanched.

Beside him, Felicia jolted in the passenger seat. 'What the hell was that?'

'Sounded like something exploded right below us.'

Striker hit the gas and cut down the off-ramp that circled onto the Granville Island Market. By the time he made the sharp turn onto Anderson Street, the screams had already started.

And what he saw shocked him.

On the south side of the street, the front section of one of the buildings had been completely destroyed. Thick white smoke poured from a large gaping hole, and flames climbed all along the building walls. In the street out front, shattered glass, splintered two-by-fours, and metal fragments littered the pavement. And covering everything was a thick layer of grey-white dust; it floated through the air like a poisonous pollen, dissipating slowly into the harbour beyond.

'Looks like a gas main went off,' Felicia said.

Striker was unsure. He cranked the wheel, turned the car sideways, and blocked access to the area. 'Call it in. We need ambulance, fire, and every patrol unit that's not already on a Priority 1. Notify the gas and electric companies too. And get Rothschild down here – we're gonna need a good sergeant to set up containment.'

Felicia got to work.

While she called Dispatch, Striker climbed out to look for casualties. Immediately, his ears were hit with the harsh roar of the fire and the strident cries of numerous car alarms.

On the opposite side of the road, a group of paramedics – perhaps already on scene when the explosion had occurred – were tending to a small group of people who had obviously been injured by the blast. Most of them looked stunned and bloodied, but conscious and aware.

Striker pointed at them. 'They okay?'

One of the paramedics nodded. 'Nothing critical. But who knows who else needs help.'

Striker turned his eyes away from the medic and scanned the perimeter. Here and there in the road, cars had been abandoned. Citizens wandered through the smoke like brain-dead zombies, gaping at the fire. Under an awning on the next block, a group of shop owners and customers was gathering, with many of them snapping shots with their cameras or taking video with their cell phones.

YouTube was just a click away.

Striker approached the front of the burning building. Splintered wood, torn-apart aluminium, broken concrete pieces with embedded rebar, and other rubble covered everything from the sidewalk to the docks. Also within the mess were numerous toys – wooden cars, dolls and other such stuff, most of which was half blown apart. The sight of the toys made him realize that kids could be victims here, and his guts tightened as bad thoughts flooded his mind.

He killed the thoughts and got moving. He searched through the area for more casualties, but found none.

Just smoke and fire and destruction.

At the south end of Anderson Street, a patrol car emerged. Striker waved them to a stop, then crossed the road to meet them. The car doors opened, and two young constables jumped out. Both of them looked newbie fresh from the academy and out of their element.

Striker grabbed the first man, a tall, thin East Indian guy. 'You, block off the road and start stringing up tape.'

Then he turned to the other cop, a smaller but stockier Chinese kid. 'And you, go around back and assess the damage. Look for survivors – but *do not* go inside. We don't know what we're dealing with here.'

When the two constables raced off in different directions, Striker ran back to the front of the building and began searching through the rubble. Smoke made the air thick, and the hot ash burned his throat. He had just finished lifting up a large piece of blown-apart drywall when Felicia joined him in the haze.

'Everyone's en route,' she said. 'Medics, fire, patrol – you name it.' She looked around. 'Any casualties?'

He threw the drywall to the side. 'Still looking.'

Felicia stared at the building. The flames had grown larger and were rising up over what remained of the roof. The fire was out of control. A hungry beast devouring everything in its path.

'Someone might still be in there,' she said.

She started for the building; Striker grabbed her by the arm.

'No,' he said.

She pulled away from him, but he held her tight. 'Someone could be trapped in there, Jacob.'

'There's no one alive in there now.'

'You don't know—'

'No one inside could survive that explosion, Feleesh . . . *No one.*' He looked at the flames devouring everything in their path, and at the poisonous smoke flowing out of the building. To attempt entry was beyond foolhardy – it was suicidal.

There was a reason why firefighters called cops *blue canaries.*

'We're not going in there,' he said.

Felicia pulled her arm away. 'But what if—'

She'd barely spoken the words when a second explosion rocked the street. A giant spire of flame burst upwards and was followed by a dirty gust of wind that sent the dust and plaster particles hurtling into their eyes. Striker raised a hand to shield his face. He turned away, closed his eyes, grabbed Felicia.

'Get back,' he said. '*Back.*'

Together, they retreated.

They moved out of harm's way to the far side of the road, then began scouring the area to make sure no one else had been injured in the second blast. The building was now completely engulfed by the fire and shrouded in a thick unfurling smoke that was quickly blocking out the blue sky.

Felicia looked back at the flames with a sick expression on her face. 'I hope to God no one's in there,' she said again.

Striker offered no reply. It was going on noon, he realized. And a Wednesday. That made the odds pretty good – almost a guarantee – that *someone* had been working today. He expected fatalities.

The only question was how many.

Twenty

When the first fire truck took a wide turn onto Anderson Street, only to be blocked by the undercover police cruiser, Felicia called out for the keys. Striker threw them to her, underhand, and she ran back up the road to move their car.

As she went, Striker covered his mouth with his hand and tried to dampen out the burned smell. He began analysing their surroundings to make sure he hadn't overlooked anything.

The small crowd that had gathered across the street moments after the initial blast was now thickening as more and more onlookers came to watch the fire burn. Several times, he'd warned them about the toxicity of the smoke and the randomness of the explosion, but it made no difference.

They were sheep.

Reporters were already on scene too. A guy with a CBC news shirt. Another from Global. A woman from News 1130. And all of them screaming out questions:

What caused the explosion?

Was it a gas tank?

A bomb?

Do you have any leads?

Striker ignored their questions, but soon the entire crowd was muttering about 'the bomb' that had destroyed the toy shop.

Having had enough, Striker grabbed a couple more patrol

cops, and the three of them guided the crowd down Anderson Street to a safer gathering point. Then he pointed out an access line. 'Cordon off the entire street starting *there*. No one in but emergency personnel. And don't speak to any of the reporters about what's going on. Leave that to Media Liaison.'

The two cops nodded, then got to work.

With the scene now preserved as good as they were going to get it, and with fire crews now preparing to tackle the ongoing blaze, Striker began the slow, monotonous process of a grid search. No doubt, search and canvass crews would be called out – Inspector Osaka was a stickler for following procedure – but an extra pair of eyes never hurt anyone.

Striker started at the farthest end of the sidewalk, just up from the dock, and got to work. Searching was always a painstaking task, and a job that could never be rushed. In ten minutes, he'd gone less than six metres.

But he found something – two dark squares on the boardwalk.

He crouched down for a closer look and saw that they were actually glass fragments. Their cuboidal shape suggested safety glass, likely blown from one of the nearby car windows, or perhaps that of the toy shop.

Striker gloved up with fresh latex, picked up the two pieces, and turned them over. As he did this, Felicia came up behind him. 'Take this,' she said. 'We might need it with all the chaos going on.'

Striker looked back at her, saw that she had brought two portable radios from the car, and nodded. 'Good thinking.' He clipped the portable to his belt, then held up the glass for her to see. 'Look at this.'

She did. 'Safety glass. Probably blown from one of the toy shop windows.'

'Look at the *colour* of the glass. It's tinted.'

Felicia took a closer look. 'That's not tint, it's *residue* from the smoke.'

Striker nodded. 'Exactly. The glass surface is oily and dark – which could suggest there was a fire in there *before* the first explosion occurred. Otherwise, the surface would have been clean.'

He looked back at the shop, then at the road and walkways before continuing.

'Look at those large flats of drywall that were sent flying onto the road. And this smoke residue on the glass . . . This explosion might have been the result of faulty gas lines.' He moved back to the front of the building that had once been the Toy Hut. He gestured to one of the large squares of drywall that was still lying flat on the road, then to the area where the gas lines ran. 'There's definitely a natural gas source there. And the way the walls were blown out, it could be indicative of a pooling effect.' He pointed to another large chunk of wall in the street. 'See?'

Felicia shook her head. 'No, I don't see. It all looks like rubble to me.'

Striker tried to explain it better. 'This could be another case of copper thieves. They turn off the valves, steal the lines, then recycle them for cash. Problem is, they don't always shut off the valve when they're done. Then you get a pooling effect of the gas. One spark is all it takes.' He looked at the gas lines one more time and then shook his head. 'Either way, gas or bomb, we need to call the City.'

'Already done. An engineer's en route.' Felicia gloved up and took one of the cubes from Striker. She studied it for a moment, then spoke again. 'You're assuming, of course, that this glass was a result of the first explosion and not the second.'

'It had to be. There was no window left when the second explosion occurred.'

'No window maybe, but there could have been fragments stuck in the frame. Bits that were blown out when the second explosion went off.'

Striker thought this over; she was right about that, and it frustrated him.

'We're gonna need a tech here,' he said.

Felicia handed Striker back the glass, and he dropped it into a brown paper evidence bag. He marked the front with black felt and was in the process of stuffing it into his pocket when something caught his eye – a gleam of sun on something metal.

It was coming from across the harbour.

Striker turned westward for a better look. There, on the small section of grass that fronted the Granville Island condos, was a man. He was standing under the foliage of a cluster of maple trees, a foot or two back from the seawall. His attire – dark orange vest; tool belt; a baseball cap with sunglasses on the rim – suggested he was a utility worker. But something about him didn't fit.

'He's watching us through binoculars,' Striker said.

Felicia saw him too. 'Maybe he's with the gas company.'

'Then why doesn't he come down and help?' He turned to Felicia. 'You got your monocular on you?'

'Always.'

'Give it.'

She took it from her inner jacket pocket and handed it over.

Striker peered through the mini-telescope. As he focused in on the man across the way, two things became apparent. One, the man was Caucasian. Two, he was bleeding from the left side of his cheek.

From exploding glass?

Striker tried to zoom in for a better look, but the man suddenly let the binoculars fall to his chest. Slipped the sunglasses down over his eyes. Spun away and began walking.

Striker lowered the monocular.

'Something's wrong with that guy,' he said. 'I want him checked. *Now.*'

Twenty-One

Harry Eckhart heard the check request come over the radio as he drove his unmarked patrol car across the Granville Street Bridge. Part of him wanted to ignore the call. Ignore everything about this whole rotten day, and just go back home, get into bed, and pull the comforters over his head. Maybe drink some rum. Some vodka. Do whatever it took to get him through another 21 July.

It was always a hard date. Today was the twelfth anniversary of Joshua's death, and he missed the boy as much now as he ever did. Maybe more.

The hurt never went away.

Normally, on every 21 July, Harry wouldn't even manage to drag himself from bed. But today Ethan had roused him.

Little Ethan. The boy born six years after Joshua's death.

Little Ethan. The boy who had brought Harry back to the world of the living.

Little Ethan. The only thing that mattered any more.

The boy was a six-year-old little saviour with foppish blond hair and chocolate-brown eyes. And the boy had not only roused him, but somehow managed to *lighten* him. To bring him back from that dark and hollow place, just as he had so many times before. Even now, the thought of the little boy brought a weak smile to Harry's face.

The child was innocence and joy.

Over the radio came several responses to the check request. Bravo 11 said they could do it, but they were coming from the downtown core. And Fox 13 said they could also take the call, but they were just as far. Even Car 10 – the current Road Boss, Inspector Osaka – offered to perform the check, but he was currently out on foot.

Too far from the scene to be of any use.

Harry cursed under his breath. He was the closest unit, and his conscience wouldn't let him ignore the plea from another officer. He reached the turn-off onto West 2nd Avenue, glanced west, and spotted the exact man Homicide Detective Striker had been describing on the radio:

A utility worker.

Orange vest with tool belt.

A baseball cap and sunglasses.

And binocs.

The man was limping a little as he hustled along, his right leg kicking back on him but moving well enough. He was heading south towards West 4th Avenue, cutting into the laneway behind the Starbucks.

Escaping.

Harry grabbed the mike and pressed the plunger.

'I'll take that check,' he said.

He turned down the off-ramp, ready to perform another one of the millions of checks he'd done in his 25-year career. But within ten feet, the traffic came to an abrupt stop. Swearing, Harry tried to steer around the gridlock, but there was nowhere to go. And far below the man in the utility vest was running now – fleeing in long, awkward strides.

Harry pressed the plunger on the mike one more time.

'We got us a runner.'

Twenty-Two

Striker was already racing around the seawall when he heard Harry come over the radio. The suspect was running. Goddammit, he was running! And with most of Patrol already dealing with the explosion scene, and only him and Harry in pursuit, the odds were against them.

Striker grabbed his radio and hit the plunger: 'I'm coming north from the harbour. Can you take him from the south, Harry? Trap him in?'

'Negative. I'm boxed in on the bridge.'

'Okay then, just hold your position.'

Striker raced on.

Outlining the harbour, the swerving red-brick path of Island Marina Trail slowly angled southward around a man-made lagoon. It was the centrepiece for the Granville Island condo development. Striker raced around the path into the complex. He knew the area well from previous Patrol calls. Up ahead, Marina Trail bifurcated, with one path leading west along the inlet to Kitsilano Beach, and the other cutting south through the condo complex.

When Striker reached the mouth of the divide, he stopped. Glanced west. Saw nothing but dock workers. Glanced south. Saw a winding brick pathway leading between two Japanese plum trees.

In front of them, an elderly woman was walking two Yorkie terriers.

'Did you see a man run through there?' Striker asked her.

She glanced back the way she had come. 'You mean that construction worker? Yes, he went that way.'

Striker bolted on.

The trail cut deeper into the condo development, then ended on West 2nd Avenue. To the west sat an empty stretch of road with no one on it. To the east was a Starbucks coffee shop. And three storeys above it, on the off-ramp, was Detective Harry Eckhart, yelling and pointing.

'Through the lane! The *lane*!'

Striker raced in behind the Starbucks. Within a half-block, all visual contact with Harry was cut off by the Honda dealership. Littering the lane were bald tyres, rusted oil drums, and bags of recyclable oil containers. Trash.

But no sign of their man.

Parked in the lane was a white van, and behind it was a small woman with sandy-brown hair. She had wide sturdy hips, and beneath her blue bandana was a pale and pudgy face. Other than the bandana, she was dressed in a pair of blue jeans with a beige work shirt. She was carrying a cardboard box.

'You see a guy run this way?' Striker asked her.

She put down the box and took a moment to wipe her brow. 'You mean that tourist?'

'What tourist?'

'Guy with the binoculars round his neck.'

'That's him.'

She nodded and pointed. 'He ran that way. Up the alley. He was really motoring though – what he do, steal somethin'?'

'Stay here,' Striker said, and raced on.

When he reached the end of the lane, he found himself

standing at the mouth of West 4th Avenue. All his hopes faltered. Cars were backed up all along the drive, running from east to west, and the backlog extended all the way up the off-ramp onto the bridge where Harry was stuck.

The explosion had turned the area into a congested nightmare.

Striker looked left, looked right, looked straight ahead. There was no sign of the man. And when he approached many of the drivers who were stuck in the backlog, none of them recalled a man in a utility uniform.

He was gone.

'*Goddammit.*'

Striker grabbed the radio from his belt and broadcast the man's full description and last known direction of travel. Then he headed back. Halfway down the lane, he looked for the woman he'd seen loading the van, but she was already gone. And there was no surveillance video he could see. Not a single camera adorned the lane.

Frustrated, cursing this entire day, Striker headed back down the walkway. The explosion scene was waiting for him.

Twenty-Three

As Striker made his way back towards the scene of the explosion, his iPhone went off. He looked down at the display and saw the word 'JaKo'. Short for Jay Kolt. He picked up. 'Jay – thank God. Where the hell you been?'

'Testifying.' The man let out a weary sound. 'I'm down at Georgia right now. Been here all damn day.'

'You almost done? I need to talk to you about a case we got going on here. A real weird one. Involves electrical torture. A wand of some kind.'

'Hmm. Not exactly a layman's tool.'

'It's not a layman's file,' Striker replied. He took a short cut between the condominiums and started walking back around the seawall. 'Torture session down by the river.'

'Sounds nasty all right.' Kolt broke from the phone to talk to someone, then returned. 'Listen, Striker, I'm back on the stand any second. It's gonna be a full day here, but I'll call you once I'm done.'

'I'll be waiting.'

Striker stuffed the cell back into his jacket pocket and continued walking around the inlet's bend. When he reached Anderson Street he stepped off the kerb, and almost slipped on the fragmented remains of one of the toy shop's wooden toys. Cursing, Striker started to walk past it, then stopped.

Something about it intrigued him.

A second, closer look told him why. The toy appeared to be a doll of some kind, though it was difficult to tell for sure, because the head and feet had been blown right off in the explosion. The remaining torso – the back half of which was also missing – was covered in grime and garbed in a blue uniform of some type.

A *policeman's* uniform.

Striker gloved up and picked up the toy. He brushed away some of the grime with his thumb. With the dirt and plastery powder removed, the uniform was much more distinct – as was the strange number painted amateurishly onto the front chest of the doll.

A large, red number 5.

Striker stared at the number for a long moment, wondering if there was some significance. When nothing came to him, he looked around the road at the array of broken-up toys and figured it was just another part of the debris. He bagged the broken remains for evidence and headed back to the primary crime scene.

There was still much to do.

It was going on three by the time the primary explosion scene was under control. There was less chaos now, but sprawling examples of the destruction everywhere Striker looked. The whitish smoke had now all but dissipated into the harbour, and the only hints of the pre-existing fire were the clusters of HAZMAT members still hosing down the rubble.

Striker leaned under a slash of yellow police tape at the south end of the block and looked at the gallons of water going down the drain. With it went so much evidence. Screens should have been set up.

Someone had really dropped the ball.

The thought angered him, and it took some determination to tear his eyes away from the drains. He found Felicia. Even though she was busy talking to Inspector Osaka – and a tall Native woman Striker did not recognize – she gave him a nod to let him know she'd seen him. After a few more seconds, she broke from the group and met him halfway.

'EDT's in full effect,' she said wryly.

Striker grinned at the comment: EDT was cop slang for the Evidence-Destroying Team – a nickname police often used for the fire crews.

'We should have screened the drains before they got here,' he said.

'We don't have any screens. Osaka's already called for some, but they haven't arrived yet.' Felicia reached up and brushed some cherry blossoms and ash out of his hair. 'I'm just glad you're okay. Last thing we need is you getting hurt in some useless chase.'

'It was far from useless—'

'That came out wrong.' Felicia pointed up the road. 'I ran south on Anderson in case he doubled back. But he was long gone by the time I got there. And then you came over the radio and killed the search.'

Striker listened to her words and came to the realization that the man must have escaped south or west. 'He ran for a reason, Feleesh. They always do. The question is *why*? Was he involved in this explosion? Or was it something else?'

'It could have been something simple. For all we know, he had a warrant – they always run when they have a warrant.'

'Maybe so, but I don't like the coincidence.'

Striker let the issue die, and Felicia filled him in on the scene details. 'Fire crews have all but gotten the flames out now. Everything's just smouldering. I called up the gas company and had the line shut down. Also, the City's sending down an engineer right now to condemn the place.'

Striker nodded. 'We're going to need some help on this one.'

'We already got it.' Felicia jabbed a thumb over her shoulder. 'Corporal Summer's on scene.'

Striker paused. '*Corporal?*'

'You heard right.'

Striker immediately didn't like it. The Vancouver Police Department didn't utilize the rank of corporal; instead, they employed different classes of constables, ranging from 5th all the way up to 1st. After that, the rank jumped straight to sergeant. So if this *Summer* person was a corporal, that meant only one thing:

The brass had brought in the Feds.

Striker looked at Felicia. 'Why'd Osaka bring in the RCMP? What's wrong with our guy – Christiansen?'

'He's back east at a funeral.'

'What about Truc Tai then?'

'She's on annual leave.'

'Then call her in.'

'Hey, it's not like they haven't tried. She's not answering her cell.' Felicia glanced back at the tall Native woman who was walking around the crime scene with Inspector Osaka by her side. 'Like it or not, the RCMP is all we got – and she's it.'

Striker rubbed his hands over his face. It was frustrating. Not that the members of the Royal Canadian Mounted Police weren't of the highest calibre; they were. But they brought with them a lot of red tape. And a lot of different rules and regulations, most of which led to infighting between the integrated units. Whenever possible, Striker always tried to keep Vancouver files in-house.

It prevented a lot of unnecessary headaches.

As if on cue, Corporal Summer began barking orders to her searchers: 'Gear up, people – masks and gloves, everyone. We need evidence of *components*. Anything you can find related to a fusing system: batteries, speaker wire, steel brackets. Nothing is trivial. And someone get some screens over those drains – we're losing trace evidence!'

Screens on the drains?

It was music to Striker's ears.

He watched the woman work for a moment, and he had to admit that something about her commanded presence. She was tall – a head taller than Felicia – and lean yet muscular. Athletic. She was also quite pretty. She looked no more than thirty-four – which would be ridiculously young for a federal bomb investigator, so he assumed she was older.

Her thick straight hair fell to her shoulders and was dyed a soft honey-blonde that contrasted with her darker skin tone. All in all, her looks were entirely civilian, yet her middle-of-the-road business suit screamed cop.

Striker turned to Felicia. 'Well, I'll say this – she takes command well.'

Felicia rolled her eyes. 'She'd better be able to take command. She's a *corporal,* after all – she's told me that three times.'

Striker smiled. 'Corporal. The dreaded C-word.'

As if sensing that their conversation was about her, Corporal Summer stopped walking around the crime scene and glanced in their direction. Upon seeing Striker, she beelined towards him. When she was near enough, she extended her hand and offered him a wide smile.

'Are you Detective *Striker*?' she asked.

He took her hand, a bit wary. 'Yes . . .'

'The same Detective Striker who dealt with the St James massacre?'

He raised an eyebrow. 'Oh, yeah, well, that was a while ago.'

Her already wide smile got even wider. 'Oh my God, it's such an *honour* to meet you, Detective. Really. I've read all about you and the active shooters you took down at St Patrick's High School. That was such a . . . such an *extraordinary* case.'

The memories of that time were bad, and Striker tried to make light of it. He forced a laugh. 'Well, I'm an extraordinary detective.'

Corporal Summer laughed wholeheartedly.

Felicia, meanwhile, just crossed her arms. 'I seem to recall being beside you during the St James attack.'

Before Striker could respond, Corporal Summer brushed her long blonde hair over her shoulder and continued speaking to him. 'You know, I would *love* to buy you a drink sometime and hear all about it – strictly in a professional manner, of course.'

'Of course,' Striker replied. 'Corporal . . .'

'Summer,' she offered. 'But you can call me Kami. We might as well be on friendly terms since we'll be working together for a while.'

'Tammy?'

She laughed. '*Kami* – with a K.'

'Oh. Well, I'm Striker – with an S.'

Felicia rolled her eyes. 'And I'm confused – with a C. Shouldn't we be investigating *this* case?'

Striker gave her a surprised look, then nodded. 'Of course, of course.' He looked at Corporal Summer and changed the direction of the conversation. 'So what exactly is your designation here?'

'I'm a Certified Fire and Explosion Investigator. I'm also a member of the IABTI.'

'Which is?' Felicia asked against her better judgement.

'The International Association of Bomb Technicians and

Investigators. I trained down in Huntsville, Alabama, at the Hazardous Devices School. It was quite the course, really. You should try it sometime.'

Striker gestured to the front of the shop. 'So, with your training and experience, what would you say this is – a bomb, or an accidental explosion?'

Corporal Summer adjusted the badge clipped to her belt and studied the scene. 'Well, any determination at this point of the investigation would be merely *preliminary*, of course. But I will say this – I have mixed feelings. Could have been a natural gas explosion, the way the front wall was blown forward like that.'

Striker agreed. 'And I couldn't make out a definable epicentre.'

A look of surprise covered Corporal Summer's face. 'Well, well – someone's been doing their homework.'

'I like to dabble.'

Felicia gave him an annoyed look, one that Striker pretended not to see. He was about to suggest deploying a bomb dog when one of the firemen hosing down the smouldering rubble let out a startled cry. The man raised his hand in the air, alerting everyone of a casualty find, and the moment made Striker's heart drop.

'What have you got?' he called out.

The fireman said nothing for a short moment, then his voice took on a nervous tone.

'Looks like a woman,' he finally said. 'I just can't tell for sure.'

Twenty-Four

The bomber gripped the walkie-talkie tightly as he struggled to navigate through the tunnels. It wasn't easy; everything kept moving around on him and distorting – like the images in a funhouse mirror. The percussive blast had hit him good. Bits of plaster debris. Glass too.

Molly was right – he had been too close.

All in all, it had shaken his foundations, but that was okay because it had jarred his mind right again. To a place where everything almost lined up. Following the blast, he'd felt like he was floating on clouds. Or filled with a fever and lifting above it all. The memories . . . the memories slammed into place:

He was off to war again.

Father was spinning him round in the air, giving him an airplane ride.

Then his men were dying all around him – chunks of flesh being punched from their bodies by AK-47 fire.

And Mother was crying, not wanting him to go.

Then Father was leaving. Standing at the car. And he was sobbing, peeking out between the drapes, saying, 'Don't go, Daddy, don't go.'

And the helicopter was dropping down – the loud whup-whup-whup of the blades sounding like angry thunder . . .

The timeline was wrong, he knew. Still in shambles. Out of place.

But it was better than before.

Despite the external chaos of the world around him, an inner calmness found him. A serenity. Because the jigsaw of his years was slowly unscrambling. And he hadn't felt this good since . . . since . . .

Well, *sometime.*

He placed one hand against the cold wet concrete of the tunnel wall and took a moment to ward off the dizziness that was slowly submerging him. At his side, the radio crackled:

'All clear. Proceed.'

'. . . copy, all . . . all clear . . . Proceeding.'

When he reached the end of the tunnel, he used the ladder to climb out. It took all his strength. Once at street level, he slid into the back of the utility van, and Molly took care of the rest. He heard her climb into the driver's seat, start the engine, and the vehicle got moving.

For a long time there was only silence. After many kilometres, Molly spoke.'You were too close.' She turned around to look at him and let out a gasp. 'God in Heaven – your face. You're going to need stitches.'

He said nothing.

'Did you hear me? You were too close. *Again.*'

He closed his eyes, tried to bumper back his pinballing thoughts. 'It . . . it helps,' he finally said.

'It does *not* help. You're scrambling your brains even worse.'

'Molly—'

'And enough with the ducks. This isn't a game – it's a higher calling.'

The bomber looked away. Grinned bemusedly.

A higher calling . . .

The notion sat in his head like a benign tumour. The whole idea of God was a foreign concept to him, a subject he could not understand. *Codswallop*. At times, Molly's theological and emotional conflicts ate away at him. They were good people doing bad things. He got that.

But it changed nothing.

'Everything went according to plan,' Molly said softly. '*This* time.'

He offered no reaction, he only spoke. 'With Target 5 dead, we can go back to dealing with Target 6 – the way we intended. Get back on track.'

'The sooner the better.' Molly let out a sound of concern. 'My God, if she escaped—'

'She's going nowhere – not unless she can uncuff herself and navigate her way out of that maze.'

For a long moment, only silence filled the cab of the van. When Molly spoke again, her voice was low and soft.

'I just want this to be done.'

'It will be,' he said. 'Already, one target is down and one is our prisoner. That leaves only four more to go.'

Molly made an uncomfortable sound. 'We need to use less explosive from now on.'

Her words stirred something within him. 'Less?'

'Yes, less. Or we'll end up killing someone innocent.'

He closed his eyes. 'Innocent.'

'Less than a half-kilogram,' she pressed. 'It's enough – these are high-grade explosives, after all . . . Are we in agreement? *Are we?*

He opened his eyes. 'Will it make you feel better, Molly?'

'Yes.'

'Okay then,' he said. 'Okay.'

Twenty-Five

Normal procedure at any fatality is for the coroner to pronounce death before the body is removed. In most situations, this is gospel. In this case, however, that procedure was overruled by Inspector Osaka.

For obvious reasons.

As Striker waited for the Body Removal Team to arrive, he gave the victim a cursory look. The blast had all but destroyed the head and neck regions. As for the body, it had suffered extreme trauma from the percussive force. And the flesh had been exposed to high levels of heat and flame, which had burned away the fat and turned the muscle tissue black. As a result, the remaining limbs had contracted into something of a foetal position.

But one arm was missing.

Striker examined this. From the yellow line, news media – digging for a front-page storyline – kept taking pictures from every accessible angle. Their usual lack of sensitivity made Striker angry, and that anger disrupted his thought process. He wanted the body moved to protect the family.

And he got his way.

When the Body Removal Team arrived, they found the victim hidden beneath a blue police tarp. The three orderlies, all dressed in civilian clothing, donned latex gloves and loaded the body into a generic white van. Body in possession, they drove through the frenetic cluster of reporters and headed for the basement of Vancouver General Hospital.

That was where the morgue was located.

Striker watched them go. When the patrol cops sealed off the road with more yellow police tape, Striker and Felicia assisted in a secondary sweep of the area. This time, they weren't looking only for bomb components, but for body parts too.

It didn't take long.

'Over here,' Striker called.

He pulled back a square-shaped chunk of support beam and pointed. Wedged between chunks of wood and concrete was a twisted fleshy mass. Perhaps the remaining limb. It was hard to tell.

Striker got forensics to bag and tag the tissue for the Chief Medical Examiner.

'Good work,' Felicia said.

Striker didn't respond. A deep concern filled his belly. There were too many unanswered questions here. About the case and about the person in the rubble. Not much was known about the victim so far: the body was that of a female, and – from the few lower-limb parts that weren't completely burned – the female appeared to be of non-Caucasian ethnicity.

African-American was a possibility.

Felicia touched his arm. 'Hey, you okay?'

He turned to face her. 'A black woman is kidnapped and tortured this morning down by the river. Now there's a black woman killed in the explosion here . . . I hope to God they're not related.'

Felicia nodded. 'I've been talking to some of the people in the area. The owner of the Toy Hut is a woman by the name of Keisha Williams. She's black.'

Striker listened, but the information somehow didn't connect.

He was tired. The day felt long, yet it was only four-fifteen. He looked at the different pods of forensic and search crews, and tried to keep track of everything. There were so many divisions. Multiple departments. It was an inter-agency nightmare.

'Come on,' he finally said. 'We need to round everyone up and make sure we're all on the same page here.'

Felicia agreed.

Striker gathered together all their counterparts. Once everyone was listening, he began listing the tasks of all the associated units. He ended the speech by discussing the role of Victim Services. They would be escorted by Patrol to the Williams residence for two reasons: One, to verify that Keisha Williams was not, in fact, safe at home and alive. And two, to prepare the family for the worst case scenario. The thought of telling the family left Striker ill – it always did – but he fought to suppress his emotions.

There was work to do.

With the primary and secondary scenes now contained, Striker gave Felicia the nod to get going, and they headed back for the car. He wanted to attend the morgue, not only to inspect the body, but to ensure that extra tests were conducted – complete swabs of all body tissues for explosives residue, and full-body X-rays to determine what kinds of shrapnel were lodged inside those same tissues. Grim though it seemed, it was an absolute necessity.

Striker looked at Felicia and spoke the words they had both been thinking but wanting to avoid. 'We may just have a bomber on our hands.'

Twenty-Six

Ten minutes later, Striker and Felicia reached Vancouver General Hospital. They took the freight elevator down to the sub-levels, feeling the booth chug and jerk with every foot descended. Felicia made a nervous sound when the booth stopped for a moment, her claustrophobia kicking in. She switched the portable laptop from her left hand to her right, and looked at Striker. 'Hopefully, the ME will find something to connect the explosion to the torture scene at the concrete plant.'

Striker nodded. 'Maybe there'll be some explosives residue on the body. Otherwise, we'll be waiting on word from Kami.'

Felicia cast him a cool glance. '*Kami*, is it?'

'What?'

'Forget it, just you and your ego again.'

'My *what*?'

'Oh please, Jacob. Like you don't know, with all the cheesy lines you threw out there.'

'What lines?'

'"*I'm Striker – with an S.*" "*I like to dabble*."' She shook her head. 'You're an obsessive-compulsive flirt.'

'I wasn't flirting—'

She held up a hand. 'Spare me.'

Before Striker could say more, the booth jolted, descended to the next level, and the doors opened. In silence, they walked on with the only sound being the clicking of their heels against the floor. They reached Examination Room 3. Before Striker could so much as knock, the large grey door opened, revealing Kirstin Dunsmuir, the Chief Medical Examiner.

Kirstin Dunsmuir looked as artificial as she always did. An overabundance of injected collagen caused her chiselled lips to perpetually purse, and the muscles between her eyes had been Botoxed so many times that her face showed little emotion, even on those rare occasions when she actually expressed any.

Striker forced a weak smile. 'Hello, Kirstin. Still the life *and* the death of the party?'

Dunsmuir said nothing. She just stared back through icy-blue contacts – ones that matched the blue shade of her smock and surgical cap. 'Come inside, Detectives.' She wheeled about and walked deeper into the room, expecting them to follow.

Once inside, Felicia placed the laptop on the nearest counter and brought up all the information they had on the toy shop address. As she read, Striker approached the examination table, where the body of their victim lay.

Against the dull metallic glimmer of steel, the blackened tissues stood out and appeared terribly fragile. The face and head regions had been completely obliterated by the blast, and the rest of the remains looked somewhat inhuman.

'God in heaven,' he said.

'God has no part in this.' Dunsmuir smiled bleakly. 'This is *my* domain.'

Striker offered no response. The more he looked at the body, the more disconcerting it became – had these remains really been a living, breathing person just a few hours ago? It didn't seem possible.

He worried about the woman's family.

'I want this one done right away, Kirstin.'

The medical examiner's lips parted enough to suggest a weak grin. 'You obviously haven't heard about the shootings this morning.'

'What shootings?'

'Just the latest round of gang warfare.' Dunsmuir spoke the words without emotion. 'I have two dead from the Sharma gang in Rooms 5 and 6, and one unknown in Room 1. And with both my assistants away at the body farm, we've got no one extra for coverage.'

'Meaning?'

She met his stare. 'If I get to your body at all today, consider it divine intervention.'

'Fuck the gangster. This woman comes first.'

'That's not how it works down here, Detective, and you know it. We're looking at tomorrow morning – at best.'

Striker cursed under his breath. He was about to further debate the issue when the door to the examination room opened and Detective Harry Eckhart walked through.

'Harry,' Striker said, somewhat surprised to see the man. 'What are you doing here?'

The detective shrugged. 'Was picking up some medical release forms at the pick counter when I saw you two come down. After this afternoon's chase I thought I'd pop in and see what was what.'

Striker said nothing. With the exception of the chase this morning, he hadn't seen Harry in a long time – not since Harry had transferred to the General Investigation Unit at Cambie Street Headquarters, away from Main Street's Major Crimes Section.

Despite the time that had passed, not much had changed in the man. Harry was in his late forties, maybe early fifties, and the silvering lines on his light-brown hair were a testament to his years on the job. The red rash of broken blood vessels that coloured his cheeks made his blue eyes look cold and were framed by a jowly chin and padded cheekbones. He always looked worn thin, and today he looked especially beaten down.

Harry looked at the examination table. Moved forward. Stared down at the body.

'Jesus mercy,' he said.

Striker nodded. 'You got some information on her?'

Harry said nothing for a moment, then blinked. He looked away from the body on the table. Splayed his hands in frustration. 'I lost sight of the suspect behind the Starbucks building. With all the traffic jammed up on the bridge, I just couldn't get around, Shipwreck. I'm sorry.'

Striker nodded. 'It was chaos.'

'Yeah, chaos . . .' Harry let out a long breath. 'Listen, I'll send you my notes through the internal mail. Need a police statement?'

Striker nodded. 'Mandatory.'

'Okay.'

The room went quiet; Harry said nothing else. His face took on a deep, despondent look as he stared at the body on the table. 'Jesus mercy,' he said one last time. Then he gave Striker a nod and left the room without so much as another word. The door closed behind him with a soft click.

Felicia finally looked up from her laptop.

'That was weird,' she said.

'*Harry* is weird,' Striker replied. 'But a good man – he's been through an awful lot. How's it coming over there?'

Felicia just shrugged and looked back at the laptop. 'Things are slowly coming together. We got some history on the toy shop.'

'Do tell.'

'Six months ago, Patrol was called to deal with a stubborn panhandler who kept harassing all the customers. The complainant's name was Keisha Williams, and at the time, she was the store owner. So that matches what the other business owners were telling me. She's the one.'

'You run her name through the other databases?'

Felicia nodded. 'Yeah. She comes up as a black woman, one hundred and eighty centimetres tall and a hundred kilos. Big woman.'

'Any tattoos?'

'None listed.' Felicia kept reading down the page. After a moment, her face tightened. 'Oh boy. She's a single mother of *five.*'

Striker felt like he'd been sucker-punched.

'And look at this,' Felicia continued. 'Guess who's listed under her Associates tab? Dr Sharise Owens. They're *cousins.*'

Striker beelined to her side and stared at the screen.

'This is too much to be a coincidence.' He looked back at the medical examiner, who was now in the process of detailing a body chart. 'This changes everything, Kirstin. I want the works done on this one. Full swabs, tox tests, X-rays – you name it.'

Dunsmuir gave him a cool look, as if warning him not to tell her how to do her job. But, eventually, she nodded silently.

'Is there any way you can move this examination up?' Striker pleaded. 'I'm desperate here.'

The medical examiner said nothing in reply. She just completed the chart she was holding, then snapped closed the metal binder. When she looked up and met Striker's stare, her eyes remained uncommunicative and cold.

'No promises,' she finally said. 'But I'll see what I can do.'

Twenty-Seven

Once in the parking lot outside the morgue, where they could finally get a cell signal, Striker got on his phone and once again tried Dr Sharise Owens' cell number. Like before, it rang several times, then went straight to voicemail. He left yet another message, then called her apartment and did the same. Last of all, he tried her workplace.

The nurse who answered the call this time was not the original one he had spoken to before. This girl sounded very young and very tired. After Striker explained the situation, her reply caught him off guard. 'Dr Owens? Oh yes, she's in.'

'She's *in*? Why the hell did no one call me?'

'I'm sorry?'

'I told that last nurse that this was a police emergency and to get Dr Owens to call me the moment she walked in – she's flagged on CPIC, for Christ's sake.'

The girl flustered. 'I-I . . . don't know who you dealt with, Detective. But Dr Owens probably didn't call you back right away because of the sick baby that got rushed through.'

Striker closed his eyes, pinched the bridge of his nose. 'Are you telling me Dr Owens is there now?'

'Yes. She's in the trauma room. With the baby.'

That was all Striker needed to hear. 'Don't let her go anywhere. I'm heading up.'

* * *

Not ten minutes later they arrived on scene.

The moment Striker walked into the admitting ward of St Paul's Hospital, he found himself swallowed up in the crowd. A bad smell filled the stuffy air, one of sweat and cleaners and sickness. Murmurs and sniffs and sneezes played louder than the Muzak filling the waiting room, and in the corner, a drunk was crying openly.

Striker swept his eyes around the room. A lot of memories of this place bombarded him – all of them bad. This was where he had come so many times before. With his wife, Amanda, during her depressions. With Courtney after the school shootings. And most recently, with Mike Rothschild, following the death of his wife, Rosalyn.

He hated this place.

Surprisingly, Rosalyn's memory hit him the hardest. Maybe it was because she'd been so good to him over the years, ever since Amanda's death, or maybe it was because Striker was the godparent to her children. Probably, it was because the memory of Rosalyn was the freshest – she'd passed away just four months ago.

Not a long time for the grieving process.

'You okay?' Felicia asked.

Striker blinked and looked at her. He realized he'd stopped walking and was standing there, looking down at a family that was seated in the waiting area. A little boy around six, a little girl near eight, and their father. It reminded him of Mike Rothschild and his children, Cody and Shana.

'I should have been there this week,' he said softly.

Felicia shook her head. 'Where?'

'Helping Mike and the kids move into their new home. I *promised*. But this goddam job – it just kills every plan you ever make . . .'

'Mike understands that, Jacob. He's a cop.'

'Maybe he does. But Cody and Shana don't.' He shook his head in disgust. 'They're six years old, Feleesh, and all they know is that I'm the godparent who never shows up for anything. Not for the move. Not when he took them sleigh riding at Whistler last Christmas—'

'You were a little busy saving people from The Adder, Jacob.'

'—and not tonight for the barbecue. Hell, I'm lucky I even made their mother's funeral, for Christ's sake.'

'Don't talk like that.'

Striker broke away and approached the triage nurse. She was pretty. Long brown hair and big doe eyes. She looked dead tired – a fact that didn't surprise Striker in the least. Nurses had just as bad shift schedules as cops. Given the fact it was now going on five-thirty p.m., the nurse was probably nearing the end of a twelve-hour shift. Who knew, maybe she was already working overtime.

She looked at Striker as if she had been warned he was coming, and offered him a wary smile.

'Hello, Detective,' she said.

Striker tried to be cordial. 'I need to speak to Dr Sharise Owens.'

'Sharise?' The triage nurse narrowed her eyes, then looked back at the large whiteboard behind her. 'Just . . . one moment, please.' She disappeared into the back, and when she returned five minutes later, an uncomfortable expression marred her pretty features. 'I'm sorry, Detective. But there's been a bit of a mistake here . . . Dr Owens isn't in – and she hasn't been all day.'

Striker let out an exasperated sound. 'I just called down here.'

Felicia sensed his mood. She placed her hand on his forearm and took over the conversation. 'We were told she was in surgery when we called—'

The nurse frowned. 'Oh, that was probably the new girl you spoke to. She's just learning the system and probably got confused by the whiteboard. You see, we have *two* Dr Owens at this hospital – one's a trauma surgeon, the other's a paediatrician.'

Felicia nodded. 'So what you're telling us is Dr Sharise Owens is *not* in today?'

'No, I'm afraid not. She was supposed to be . . . but she's missed her shift.'

Felicia asked, 'Has anyone tried to make contact with her?'

The nurse nodded earnestly. 'Oh yes, I have myself. Several times. But she's not answering her cell phone.'

'Is that unusual for her?'

'Yes. But to be fair, Dr Owens worked an extended shift yesterday – almost twenty hours – so we figured she'd just gone home and crashed straight through. It does happen with the doctors from time to time, and it's been a crazy day.'

Striker moved closer to the glass partition. 'How long have you worked here?'

'Uh, ten years, I guess. Maybe eleven.'

'And has Dr Owens worked here all that time?'

'She's been here for about seven of them, I believe.'

He nodded. 'So in all those years, how many times has she no-showed for work?'

The girl's cheeks reddened as she thought it over. 'Well, not once, really. At least not that I'm aware of.'

'Can you describe Dr Owens for us?'

The girl gave him an odd look. 'Describe?'

'Does she have high, prominent cheekbones?'

The girl nodded emphatically. 'Oh yes. And Dr Owens is *very* fit. She used to do those Ms Fitness pageants every year. And she's also done the Ironman race in Kelowna three times. Finished in the top twenty.'

Striker thought it over. 'Do you have a photograph of her in the computer? Or in her personnel file? Something we could see?'

The girl nodded. She typed the woman's name into the computer and an image came up on the screen – a black woman with long, straight hair that tucked around her ears and had been dyed a lighter shade of brown. The bones of her face were well defined and her teeth looked near perfect. Capped, maybe. She was attractive and appeared confident. Strong.

'I'll need a copy of this,' Striker said.

The girl looked uneasy. 'Is . . . is everything all right?'

Striker barely heard the words. He was too busy staring at something else, and when he saw it, his stomach knotted up.

Behind the front counter, a woman was busy sorting through some medications. She was Asian, with thick red lipstick and a round pudgy face. But neither the woman, nor her medications, were what concerned Striker.

It was her *uniform*.

He pointed her out to the nurse. 'Is she a doctor?'

The girl looked over. 'Yes.'

'Tell her to come here.'

The girl gave him a nervous look, but did as instructed. When the Asian doctor approached the front desk, the wired look in her eyes made Striker think she must've been on her thirteenth cup of coffee this shift. 'You requested to see me, Officer?'

Striker only nodded. 'Yes. Turn sideways.'

'I'm sorry?'

'Turn sideways. Please.'

The woman gave him a queer look, but turned.

There, on her shoulder, stitched into the side of her uniform, red on white, was the image of two snakes wrapped around a long staff, with wings extending from each side. The symbol was a caduceus – the ubiquitous emblem of the medical community. And the sight of it told Striker everything he needed to know.

He pointed the emblem out to Felicia and spoke gravely.

'I think this may be it,' he said. 'What your witness saw on the woman in the barn – the winged tattoo.'

Twenty-Eight

Dr Sharise Owens did not have a private practice. So before leaving the hospital, Striker and Felicia demanded to see her office. The room was located at the other end of the facility, several floors up. When they finally reached it, Striker found himself disappointed.

The office was small and sparse. The only books that lined the shelves were medical texts. And all of the patient folders and tapes were stored in archives. A cursory search revealed nothing but standard stationery in the desk drawers – Workers Compensation Board charts, the Insurance Corporation of British Columbia templates, and numerous other forms from Medical Service Plan. Nothing significant.

Nothing that could lead them anywhere.

Striker turned on the computer and was happy to see there was no password protection lock. On the screen were three folders:

Patient Reports.

Research.

And Miscellaneous.

He went through all the folders and saw no surprises. In the folder marked Patient Reports, there were over a hundred names. Striker scanned through them, saw nothing that stood out, and emailed himself the list. In the folder labelled Research, there was a string of articles on new surgical techniques. And in the Miscellaneous folder, there were a few links to pro-choice websites, but nothing more.

Striker wrote them all down. Once done, he opened the woman's email and scanned through it. He saw nothing of note.

Disappointed, Striker called up one of the computer techs he knew well, a man everyone called Ich. After filling Ich in on all that had happened, Striker ordered him to attend the office, seize the hard drives, and start processing the data immediately.

'Call me if you find *anything* unusual,' Striker stressed.

'Even porn?'

Striker grinned. 'Just call me, Ich.'

He hung up the phone, gave Felicia a nod, and they left the hospital.

Once inside the police cruiser, with the doors closed, Striker checked to be sure that Sharise Owens was still flagged on CPIC as a Missing Person and a Person in Danger. He had already requested the addition, but mistakes were often made.

Double-checks were good practice.

Once done, he got on the phone with Dispatch and, for the third time that day, had Sue Rhaemer notify all the neighbouring police, ambulance, and fire departments of the updated events. She followed up by once again alerting the hospitals, ferries, buses, and the US border. He even had her call the cab companies.

Nothing could be overlooked.

Last of all, Striker sent out his own personal computer message to all the mobile Patrol units: If anyone comes across Dr Sharise Chandelle Owens, detain her and contact Detectives Striker and Santos immediately. 24/7. He then added both their cell numbers to the message.

He let out a sigh and almost felt relieved. 'Done.'

He turned to Felicia to discuss their next course of action, and saw that she was on the phone. Her face was tight. 'We'll come down right away,' she said.

Striker gave her a wary look as she hung up. 'What's going on?'

'That was Victim Services. The kids are home at the Williams residence and it's not going well.'

Striker felt his jaw tighten. He blipped the siren three times to clear the traffic congestion, then hit the gas and U-turned on the busy strip of Burrard. They drove over the bridge into the False Creek area and headed for Creekside Drive.

It was the last place Striker wanted to go, but as always . . .

Duty calls.

Twenty-Nine

They reached Creekside Drive.

Striker got out of the car and looked at the building before them. It was eight storeys high and *old* – looked like one of the first subsidized family dwelling units in the area. Behind them was the harbour, and less than a quarter-mile east of their position was what remained of the toy shop. Police cars and fire engines still blocked the streets down there, and crowds of onlookers still gathered like prairie dogs, popping their heads up to see the smouldering wreckage.

The proximity of where they were was not lost on Striker. 'I chased our suspect right up that trail,' he said, and pointed.

'One more tiny coincidence?'

'There are no coincidences.' Striker was about to say more when the high-pitched wail of a young girl's voice filled the night:

'Momma . . . *oh, MOMMA!*'

The cry came from the building in front of them, high above on the fifth floor. One of the Williams children, no doubt. And it broke Striker's heart to hear it. Head down, feet feeling heavy, he walked up the sidewalk, entered the apartment building, and took the elevator to the fifth floor.

Once they entered the suite, the sound of crying grew louder.

In one of the bedrooms, a civilian support worker from the Victim Services Unit was huddled in a small circle with the children. They ranged from nine years of age and up. The youngest – a small boy – was hard-faced and looked to be in shock; the rest were all sobbing uncontrollably.

The moment made Striker feel like he'd slipped back in time. Memories of Rothschild's children sobbing for their mother returned to him, as did the recollections of his own daughter, Courtney, after she'd learned of Amanda's death. As always, the memories manifested physically.

His stomach felt like it had stones in it.

He studied the children before him. The oldest of the kids, a teenage girl of maybe eighteen, stood in the far corner of the room, separate from the rest. Her eyes stared at nothing, her face was as hard as rock. She looked up as Striker and Felicia entered the room, saw them, and then walked out.

Striker gave Felicia a nod. 'She shouldn't be alone.'

'I'll talk to her.'

'Keep her away from the windows.'

'I know the routine, Jacob.'

'And the knives.'

'I *know.*'

When Felicia was gone, Striker paused for a moment and closed his eyes. He wished he could close off his ears too, because the sound of the children's weeping was gut-wrenching. Instead, he steeled himself and got to work. He scanned the rest of the apartment and had a hard time believing that six people actually lived there. The place was small – tiny. Certainly not much to look at. Just a narrow strip of kitchen, where a half-eaten sandwich remained on the counter; another two bedrooms at the end of the hall; and a small living room that consisted of nothing but an outdated TV set, a threadbare chesterfield, and some old beanbag chairs thrown in the corner.

The TV was on. The local news.

Striker crossed the room and turned it off for fear of what footage might be displayed. As he did this, the sound of weeping caught his ears. It was coming from the opposite side of the apartment.

One of the bedrooms.

Striker walked down the hall. When he opened the first door and saw nothing but a pair of empty bunk beds and one single bed, he moved on to the next bedroom. When he opened that door, he expected to see one of the children crying, but instead there was a small black man sitting on the bed.

He was older, mid-forties, and balding in a horseshoe pattern of curly hair that was greying at the sides. He was holding a family picture, weeping openly, and looked up at Striker with lifeless eyes. 'Why?' he asked between sobs. 'Keisha was good, she was so good. Always *so good*.'

Striker stepped into the room and left the door open behind him. 'I'm sorry for your loss,' he offered. 'I'm Detective Striker with the Vancouver Police Department. And you are?'

'Gerome,' the man said between sobs. 'Her brother.' His face took on a desperate, wild look. 'Are they sure it's her? I mean, do they really know for certain? One hundred per cent?'

Striker said nothing at first. His mind flashed through the facts of the case: Keisha Williams was the shop owner. She was black like the victim. She had left for work fifteen minutes before the explosion had gone off. She hadn't returned home. And wasn't answering her cell phone.

'DNA tests will need to be done,' he finally said. 'But with the information we have at this point, I believe it's her. I'm sorry.'

The man on the bed looked like he'd been stabbed in the heart. For a moment, he looked ready to cry again, but then he gathered himself. Stiffened. Set his jaw. When he stood up from the bed, Striker saw that he was short – barely 165 centimetres

– and he looked even more weak and fragile in his broken-down state. He gently placed the picture of Keisha and the children back on the dresser, then angled it to face the room.

Striker spent fifteen minutes discussing with the man everything from the woman's job, her relationship with her cousin, and her past personal relationships. The answers were all straightforward. As far as her brother knew, Keisha Williams had loved her job as a toymaker, and she had gone into work seven days a week. Yes, Sharise Owens was her cousin. And yes, the two women were close.

Always had been.

As for more intimate relationships, Keisha Williams' deceased husband, Chester, had been the only man for her. The two had met at a toymakers' convention in Seattle two decades ago, and had been married happily ever since – until a drunk driver had ended their hopes and dreams.

'Any other men since then?' Striker asked. 'Any at all?'

A dark look distorted the man's features. 'There was one.' He spat the words with venom. '*Solomon* . . . But she got away from him.'

Striker took notice of the wording.

'What do you mean, *got away*?'

The man wiped away a tear. 'He beat her. In front of the children. I don't know all the details – Keisha wouldn't talk about it. And every time I tried to get her to open up, well, it just created a distance between us. So I stopped.'

Striker nodded. Looked around the room. 'Was this her bedroom?'

'It is.'

'I have to search it.'

Gerome looked like he resented it, but made no objection. He just nodded in a resigned sort of way, as if he understood that this had to be done. 'I'll check on the children,' he said, and left the room.

The moment he was gone, Striker got to work. He approached the dresser and looked at the picture of the once-happy family. In it, five children – all of them younger – smiled wide. They were half giggling, as if sharing some kind of joke. Three girls and two boys. A big family. In behind the children stood a tall bald man with a full beard and a great, wide, captivating smile.

Chester, Striker figured.

The father.

Wrapped in Chester's left arm stood Keisha Williams. Big golden hoops hung from her earlobes and a red floral shawl draped across her shoulders. She looked wonderfully alive. Happy. The sight of them was difficult to see. A once-perfect family destroyed by a drunk driver in the past and now by a highly suspicious explosion today.

Life could be cruel.

Striker put down the picture and started going through the drawers, one by one. They were sparse, filled with few clothes. And the apparel that was there was clearly old, but clean and folded neatly. Keisha Williams may not have had a lot of money to spend on herself, but she clearly respected what she had.

Striker finished searching the drawers. He found nothing but clothes, a few cheap necklaces, and some pill bottles with *Zestorol* on the label. He used his iPhone to Google the medication name, and learned it was a blood pressure drug.

He moved on.

In the closet, he found much of the same. Old shoes that had been recently polished, faded jeans ironed and draped over hangers, and two women's suits, one of which still had a Value Village tag on it. On the top of the shelf was an organizer. Striker pulled it down.

As he fanned it open, several of the tabs caught his eye: Gas Bill, Phone Bill, and Rent Receipts made up the first partition. Taxes, Child Credits, and Family Allowance Receipts made up the last half. At the very back of the organizer was a letter-size envelope.

Striker took it out and looked at it.

On the front was the name 'Solomon' in thick black felt, and right beside it someone had written 'VPD 105419 – CHRO'. Striker immediately made the connection: Vancouver Police Department. File number 105419.

A *Criminal Harassment Restraining Order.*

He removed the paperwork and read it through. Within two pages he saw an image that gave him a bad feeling. The photograph was a booking shot of a short-haired Caucasian male with narrow eyes, a square prominent jaw, and a wide thick forehead. He looked very Eastern Bloc.

Solomon Bay.

Striker was surprised to see the man was white; he'd assumed he'd be black.

As he studied the photo, Felicia entered the room. 'These poor kids,' she said softly. Her voice struggled for emotional neutrality.

Striker offered no response. He just stared at the photograph in the file. At the man's hard face. At his distant stare. At his dark eyes – glazed and lifeless and hollow.

Felicia saw the file. Then the photo. 'Who is that?'

'Solomon Bay,' Striker said. 'Our next lead.'

Thirty

'Run him,' Striker said the moment they climbed back into the undercover cruiser. 'Solomon Bay. Put him at age forty.'

Felicia nodded and typed the name into the system, then hit Enter. After a short moment, the computer beeped and the feed came back. She read it out loud: 'Solomon Elijah Bay . . . Oh man, this guy has a *ton* of history in PRIME.'

'What kind of history?'

She clucked her tongue a few times as she scanned the page. 'Most of the files are disturbance calls and assaults. Some consensual fights too. Looks like he spent a few nights in the drunk tank . . . Likes to drink and fight, this guy.'

Striker thought of the man beating Keisha Williams in front of her children and his fingers curled into fists. 'Let's hope he feels like fighting when I find him.'

Felicia patted his arm. 'Calm down there, Iron Mike.'

She compared the Criminal Harassment papers they'd found in Keisha Williams' bedroom with the files on the laptop. 'Says here, Williams met Solomon at the Ministry of Child and Family Services. Who knows what the hell he was doing there. Soon afterwards, the two of them started dating . . . He's thirty-six years old now, and by the look of things, a real prick. Goes by the nickname Sunny.'

Striker stared at her, deadpan. 'You gotta be kidding me. *Sunny Bay?* Sounds like a goddam timeshare.'

Felicia raised an eyebrow like she couldn't believe it either, then she returned to reading the information. 'Look here. Keisha Williams has Sharise Owens listed as her cousin in this report too . . . And here she is again in this one – hell, Owens is the one who called 911 for police assistance.'

'Thus the restraining order,' Striker said.

Felicia nodded. 'Both women have a connection to this man.'

'They also have a connection to Chad Koda,' Striker reminded. 'We can't forget our realtor friend either. There's something *off* about that guy . . . Any connection between Chad Koda and Solomon Bay?'

Felicia shook her head. 'None I can find.'

Striker thought back to the scene at the steel barn by the cement plant. He turned to face Felicia. 'This Solomon guy . . . does he have any ties to organized crime? Or anything like that?'

Felicia scanned the numerous pieces of information they had acquired. 'Not that I can see. He looks like your stereotypical abusive prick. Oh wait – he did work for BC Gas for a while. As a gas fitter. So he has some training in related matters.' She looked up at Striker. 'A guy with that kind of training could easily rig an explosion.'

'How many times did Sharise Owens report Solomon?' he asked.

'Three. But there are a lot of other calls with him listed as the Subject of Complaint and the Suspect Chargeable. Odd though, they just suddenly stop after a while.'

Striker looked at the screen. It showed three domestic assault charges and six harassment files in a span of six weeks, and then nothing. 'Maybe he's in jail.'

'I'll see if they locked him up,' Felicia said.

As she called Corrections, Striker read through the restraining order. Moments later, Felicia got off the phone. 'Nope,' she said. 'Solomon's not in any of the pens – federal or provincial.'

'Well, *something* happened to the guy. Pricks like him don't just stop.'

'I know. I'll keep searching.'

Striker pointed to the man's last known address. 'Portside Court. That's out east. By the Burnaby border.' He turned the wheel and hit the gas. 'I hate wife-beaters. This prick's gonna regret it when he gets out of line.'

Felicia's voice dropped a level. '*When* he gets out of line?'

Striker cracked the knuckles of his left hand and nodded.

'We can only hope.'

Thirty-One

Harry sat in the undercover police cruiser and gazed vacantly down the long stretch of Pacific Avenue. Out there, beautiful girls in Lululemon tights walked back from yoga classes while others rollerbladed in mini-shorts and bikini tops down the seawall.

Harry saw none of it. His mind was busy, preoccupied with bad thoughts from bad times.

Pieces of a past better left forgotten.

The explosion at the Granville Island Market had rattled him. Shook him so hard that it flung out all his feelings of grief and depression. In their place now were some new feelings. Concern. Trepidation.

Disbelief.

Could it all be connected?

Keisha Williams. The toymaker. Dead. It scared him.

When Harry had seen her remains on that cold steel slab at the morgue, he'd gone lightheaded. Felt his blood pressure spike. And he had damn near keeled over right there in the room. Even now, sitting in the cruiser, that numb jittery feeling spilled all through his legs.

He looked down at the two photographs he was holding and felt haunted and desperate all at once. The first photo was of his deceased son Joshua, and had been taken just two weeks before the boy's death. The second one was of Ethan, taken just one year ago.

Harry prayed to God that nothing bad was in store for this son. He couldn't take losing another child. Losing Joshua had broken his heart in every way possible. Calcified the tissue and scarred the membranes. It was a wonder the organ even beat any more.

But it did. And that was solely because of Ethan.

Ethan was what mattered now. The boy was *everything.* And nothing would ever come between them, Harry knew, because he would not allow it. He believed in that. He had faith in that.

So why would this numb uncertainty not leave him?

He closed his eyes. 'Oh Christ. Please oh fucking please.'

He rubbed his hands over his face as if this would erase the emotional turbulence he was experiencing, but it did nothing. The past was like a bad dream that recurred every so often. Even when he thought he'd finally learned to suppress it, suddenly, unexpectedly, *bang* – there it was again. And Harry would realize once more that it was never truly gone. It was just lying there dormant, somewhere below Life's skin. Like a malignant fucking tumour.

He tried to suppress it. Tried to kill it so many times. But the past was not pencil that could be erased; it was ink – there forever, indelible, though just a little more faded with every passing year.

When Harry could take the thoughts no more, he took in a deep breath and shouldered open the car door. He climbed out onto Pacific Avenue and slowly made his way down the block towards the old heritage home on the south side of the road.

He didn't want to go there; he had to. There was an unspoken code. A duty to perform to old friends. And all that aside, it was a necessary step in the safeguarding of his own future. Yes, there was no doubt about it.

Chad Koda needed to know what was going on.

Thirty-Two

Dressed in a grey workman's suit from the local phone company – and with a fresh strip of gauze covering the stitches Molly had given him to close the gash in his cheek – the bomber stood in the centre of Chad Koda's living room and assessed his setup. Everything was now in place. Perfectly.

Ever since the girl had stumbled into the steel barn down by the river, it felt like he and Molly had been in a constant cycle of assessing and adapting to the original plan. But they were almost back on track now.

Almost.

The notion of it should have brought him some peace, should have made him smile. But it did not.

Too many bad things still needed to be done.

The bomber looked down at the victim before him. Strapped to a leather office chair, duct tape stretched across her mouth, industrial-size zap straps binding each wrist to the corresponding chair leg, was the doctor. Her long straight hair hung over her face as her head drooped forward. She looked like all her spirit had left her.

Like she'd finally succumbed to her fate.

The bomber paid her no heed. He just worked on what needed to be done and whispered the old familiar rhyme to himself:

Tommy Atkins went to war
and he came back a man no more.
Went to Baghdad and Sar-e.
He died, that man who looked like me.

The words made the doctor glance up fearfully. Her dark, wide eyes held a sense of exhaustion and wariness. And when he looked into them, she looked away – as if he were some kind of dog she feared might frenzy at the challenge.

Suddenly, his radio crackled to life.

'All clear,' Molly said.

He keyed the mike. 'Copy. All clear.'

'Requesting sit-rep.'

'Copy the sit-rep. Placing the package. Five minutes.'

'Copy,' Molly said. 'Placing the package. Five minutes.'

He wheeled the doctor into the kitchen area, where she would be seen the moment Koda walked through the front door. He positioned her next to the kitchen island, then removed the toy ducks from his bag. He stared at the small wooden birds, each one dressed in a policeman's uniform. One of them – the duck with the big red 6 on the front – was the same duck he had brought with him to the steel barn down by the river.

For the woman.

The other duck, identical to the first but with a big red number 2 on the chest, was for Chad Koda.

The order was wrong because their plans had gone awry. But it was what it was, and the lack of order made the bomber smile. In some ways, it matched his shambled memories.

He grabbed the metal O-ring attached to the bird and pulled the string:

'These criminals are making me quackers!'

That made him smile. It never got old.

He carefully placed the toys on top of the kitchen island, less than a foot away from the doctor. At chest level. Then he placed the bomb, hidden in the cardboard box, directly behind the two birds.

It was done.

He pulled out the remote activator, which had been constructed from the internal components of a cell phone and a laser pointer, and then the radio came to life once more:

'White male. Approaching from the south. Quarter block.'

He keyed the mike. 'Copy. White male from the south. Quarter block.'

'Up the walkway.' Molly's voice raised in tone. 'He's coming your way!'

'Copy. Up the walkway. Coming my way.'

The bomber looked at the kitchen door that led to the back lane where he had parked the utility van. He would never make it there in time – not if he wanted to reach the observation point and be in visual contact when the bomb activated.

'At the front door!' Molly broadcast. 'Retreat now. *Retreat*.'

The bomber said nothing; he just moved quickly out of the kitchen, into the dining room area, and squatted down on the other side of the hutch. This location was still close to the bomb – maybe too close – but the hutch was made from solid maple wood, and it was heavy. He gripped the activator in his hand and waited for the lock to click and the front door to open.

But seconds passed, and the click never came; instead, all he heard was the hard rap of knuckle bone on the wood.

Three solid knocks. *Rap-rap-rap*.

At first, he did nothing. He only waited patiently to see what would happen next. After a second series of knocks, he left his position and approached the tinted bay window. He remained there, veiled behind the thick bulk of the drapes, and slowly, deftly, parted the sheers. What he saw surprised him. The man standing in the front alcove was a white male with thinning hair. Blue eyes. And puffy, ruddy cheeks.

'Harry Eckhart,' he whispered.

It was an unexpected sighting, and the words felt strange on his tongue.

He said nothing else. Did nothing else. He just stood there behind the veil of tinted glass and curtain, and watched the middle-aged cop knock a few more times, curse, then wheel about and hurry down the stairs.

When Harry Eckhart turned the corner of the walkway and disappeared from sight, Molly came back across the radio:

'White male away. South.'

The bomber nodded as if she could see him. 'Copy. White male away. South.'

After a short moment of silence, the radio crackled to life again, and Molly's tight voice occupied the air. 'Request a question,' she said.

'Go with the question.'

'Did you see his face? Did you recognize him?'

'Yes,' he said softly. 'I recognized him. The man was Harry Eckhart – Target Number Three.'

Thirty-Three

The complex called Portside Court – Solomon Bay's last known address – was a series of two-level duplexes, built on a steep hill-side that dropped rapidly down to the banks of the Fraser River.

As Striker and Felicia turned down Duff Street, Striker glanced out at the view below. Directly ahead was the Fraser River. A kilometre out was Mitchell Island. And to the far west, not more than two kilometres away, was the concrete plant and steel barn where they'd found the frantic rave girl.

Everything felt full circle.

Felicia realized this too. 'Look how close we are to the original crime scene.'

'I don't like it.'

Striker parked the car and got out.

Before heading into the complex, he pulled back the side of his coat and adjusted his holster. Felicia did the same. All geared up, they made their way down a narrow set of stairs that were barely visible under the burned-out street lamp.

Striker scanned the addresses for Unit 17. Within a few hundred feet it became obvious to him that the complex was one giant square. In the centre of it was a darkened playground area that had a teeter totter with no seats and a swing set with no swings. From the unit behind the playground, a couple was arguing – a woman's high-pitched rant and a man's slurred responses:

Bitch!

Fucking failure!

. . . like your goddam mother!

'East Vancouver love,' Striker said.

Felicia didn't laugh. Instead, her face tightened. 'A little too familiar for me.'

She increased her pace, and Striker went with her silently.

Unit 17 was on the east side of the complex. A loose plank raked loudly against the sidewalk as Striker opened the gate. He made sure the gate was left all the way open, in case they needed to perform a tactical retreat. Then he moved down the unlit walkway to the front door.

Inside, a TV was blaring, and the smell of pot smoke was strong in the air. Striker gave Felicia a look to be ready, then knocked five times, hard. Almost immediately, the sound of the TV died. Then a lock clicked and the door opened.

Standing in the doorway was a white man, rake thin, with a complexion as pale as sun-bleached bone. His eyelids were heavy, his face unshaven, and a series of long dirty-blond dreadlocks snaked off his head in uneven clumps.

Striker recognized the man from the Commercial Drive area. The guy went by the nickname Dreadlocks, and had a ton of possession charges in his past.

Dreadlocks nodded at them, then brought a marijuana cigarette to his lips. Took a long drag. 'Yeah?'

Felicia didn't mince words: 'We're looking for Solomon Bay.'

'Solomon?' Dreadlocks spoke the name like it was an absurd request. 'Shit, he ain't here no more.'

'So you know him.'

His eyes narrowed. 'Who's askin'?'

Striker held up his badge. 'I am.'

Dreadlocks' face tightened. 'I ain't talking 'bout this.'

Striker glanced over the man's shoulder. On the table behind him was a litter of drug paraphernalia, a stack of video games, and an even larger stack of porn DVDs and Blu-rays. Striker made out one of the titles, where a busty blonde was scantily clad and holding a bullwhip.

Cindyana Jones.

He turned his eyes from the table back to Dreadlocks and smiled. 'Don't want to talk? That's entirely your prerogative. Of course, it's *my* prerogative to arrest on plain view evidence – and right now I can see grounds for six or seven charges.'

Dreadlocks crossed his arms, almost effeminately, and glanced back at the table. 'I don't see how—'

'What's your *full* name?' Striker ordered.

Dreadlocks hesitated for a moment, then gave it. Striker wrote down all the details, including date of birth. When he looked up again, he offered the man a wide smile. 'Well, sir, today is your lucky day. Isn't it, Feleesh?'

'Totally lucky,' she said.

'Because we're not here for you. We're here for Solomon Bay. But of course, that could change – especially after what I just saw on your table. So if I were you, I would get talking, and fast.'

The cocky look on Dreadlocks' scruffy face vanished, and a nervous expression replaced it. With a trembling hand, he raised his marijuana cigarette to take another puff, then stopped midway as if he had only just realized he was standing in front of two police detectives.

'Go ahead,' Striker said. 'Have a good long drag – if it will refresh your memory.'

Dreadlocks did. When he breathed out in slow, uneven gasps, his entire body seemed to deflate. His eyes turned down and he spoke softly. 'Look, officers, I know him, okay? Shit, he was my roommate for a couple of years there.'

Striker nodded. 'Until . . .'

'Man, of all people, you two should know.'

Striker and Felicia exchanged a glance.

'*We* should know?' Striker asked.

'Yeah, you. The cops. The *state.*' Dreadlocks suddenly became more animated, waving his arm around as if giving a lecture. 'Came in here like gangbusters, man. Martial fuckin' law or something. You're the ones who got rid of him in the first place. And real quick like. Cost me a few hundred bucks in rent before I could find another roommate.'

Striker let the man finish before speaking. '*We* didn't cost you anything. If Solomon owes you money, go get it from him.'

Dreadlocks made a tight face, then let loose a wild laugh – as if this was the funniest damn thing he had ever heard. 'Go get it? From Sunny? Yeah, right. I'll do that – like, *never.*'

Striker found the conversation amusing. 'You find Solomon intimidating?'

Dreadlocks stopped laughing. 'Course I do. Everyone does. Sunny's one of those guys you don't wanna cross, right? He can lose it at times. Scares the shit out of people, you know?'

'Why's that?'

'Cuz he's crazy. One time, my friend asked him if he was Serbian, you know. Like, from Yugoslavia. And it pissed Sunny off like nothing. He grabbed a butcher knife and threatened to slit the guy's throat. And he was serious, man. Sweating, shaking, spit flying from his fuckin' lips – I thought he was gonna do it. Damn near pissed myself.'

'So Solomon can snap.'

Dreadlocks snorted, then wiped his nose with the sleeve of his shirt. 'Shit, he's from Croatia, man. Saw the rest of his family killed over there. That guy's seen and done it all. Serious shit over there. *Serious* shit. He's not a guy . . . not a guy you wanna mess with, right?'

Striker wrote this all down. 'Scary dude.'

'Sure thought so . . . and he was . . . at least, till that cop showed up.'

Striker looked up from his notebook. 'What cop?'

'I dunno. Some guy. Came and took Sunny for a walk. Did it real late one night . . . and Sunny never bothered no one after that. Hell, he never came home again. Just fucked right off, and that was that.'

'You got a name for this cop?' Felicia asked.

Dreadlocks shifted from one foot to the other. 'Look, I don't want no trouble with this.'

'Whatever you say doesn't go past this alcove,' Striker promised.

'For real?'

'For real.'

Dreadlocks looked back uncertainly and his jaw clicked as he ground his teeth. 'Can't remember the dude's name,' he finally said. 'But he was older than you. Late forties maybe. Had a real bad rash on his cheeks. And his eyes were blue. Like *ice* blue. Real fuckin' cold.'

Striker gave Felicia a look and saw that she had made the connection too. Only one cop they knew fit that description. And he did so down to a T.

Harry Eckhart.

Thirty-Four

Harry Eckhart wasn't answering his personal cell or his work phone. When Striker called the General Investigation Unit, he expected to hear that Harry had gone home for the day. But the sergeant in charge told him otherwise; Harry had gone to talk to Vice about a file he was working on.

So he was still around.

Striker wasted no time. He put the car in gear and headed for The Bunker. This was the location the operational squads – Strike Force, the Emergency Response Team, Vice and Drugs – called home, a plain drab concrete warehouse located in the heart of District 3.

Striker checked his watch when they got close. It was just after 19:00 hours now – seven p.m. standard time – and he hoped they hadn't missed the man. They key-carded in to the underground, drove down a couple of levels, and spotted Harry walking towards his car.

'He looks terrible,' Felicia noted. 'Sick.'

Striker could see that. 'Ever since Harry lost his boy, he's never been the same. It took something out of the man he never got back.'

He drove the undercover cruiser ahead.

When Harry climbed into his personal vehicle – an old model Honda CRV – and started the engine, Striker pulled in behind the SUV and gave the horn a tap.

They all exited and gathered between the two vehicles.

'Striker, Felicia,' Harry said. He forced a smile, one that never touched the corners of his eyes, then gestured to the undercover cruiser that Striker had left running in the middle of the driveway, boxing him into the stall. 'I see your parking skills have improved.'

'And I can see your car's still been nothing but lady driven,' Striker retorted.

Harry laughed at that one, and Striker got down to business.

'Listen, Harry, I thought we might take a moment to debrief some of what's happened today.'

'The explosion, or the guy who ran on us?'

Felicia said, '*Other* things.'

Harry nodded, almost cautiously. 'What *other* things?'

Striker took out his notebook and explained. 'Had a little conversation today that turned up something interesting. The name Solomon Bay ring a bell? Guy sometimes goes by the name Sunny.'

Harry offered no reaction. 'Should it?'

'I would think so. He sounds like a guy most people would remember. Real prick. Liked to beat up a woman named Keisha Williams in front of her children. Or at least, he used to – till someone took him for a walk.'

A look of recognition crossed Harry's features, but he did not smile.

'Doesn't ring a bell,' he finally said.

Striker eyed the man, half-surprised at Harry's uncooperativeness. 'You sure on that one?'

Harry said nothing, and Felicia spoke up. 'The description sounded like you.'

The blank expression on Harry's face mutated into one of controlled anger. 'What, you wearing a wire now, Santos?'

She blinked in surprise. 'What?'

Striker just splayed his hands. 'Holy shit, Harry, why the sudden hostility? We're just following up some leads here. You're acting like we're out to get you, or something.'

Harry said nothing at first. He just stood there and his uncommunicative blue eyes lingered on them for a long moment. Then his posture sagged and he bowed his head a little. 'Look, I'm sorry. Been a long day. Hard day. Bad day.' He met Striker's stare, tried to steel his voice but only got out a whisper. 'It's the anniversary of Josh's . . .'

'I understand,' Striker said.

Harry looked away and let out a long breath. 'This is off the record, okay?'

'I wouldn't have it any other way.'

'Yeah, I knew Solomon Bay. He was a piece of *shit.* Real violent. And not just towards Keisha Williams. The guy had a history back east in Ontario. He choked a woman to death after he raped her.'

Striker turned his stare on Felicia. 'You never mentioned that.'

She looked helpless. 'It wasn't in any of the computer databases.'

'And it won't be,' Harry said. 'Because it's from the Barrie Police Department. And they never used PRIME back then. And Solomon was never *officially* charged with anything – no one would testify against him; they were all too afraid.'

'So what happened?' Striker asked.

Harry didn't look away. 'I half-killed the fuck, that's what happened. Took him for a river walk, you know? Made him swim the channel. When the fucker had almost drowned, we stepped in and fished him out.'

'*We?*' Striker asked.

Harry raised a finger. 'I told that sonuvabitch he had a choice to make – he was leaving Vancouver one way or the other. The way he went was up to him.' Harry rubbed a hand through his short, thinning hair and let out a long breath, as if discussing the situation was exhausting. 'That woman – Keisha – she was a single mother of *five* kids. And all of them just little ones. That cocksucker, he really tuned her up bad. Did it right in front of the children . . . But he left her alone after I dealt with him. Left everyone alone. For good.'

Striker waited for Harry to finish. 'So why all the secrecy?'

'What do you mean?'

'Well, why didn't you just tell us all this back at the morgue? You saw Keisha. Saw what had happened to her.'

Harry looked down the parkade corridor at nothing that was there and didn't speak for a long moment. 'I didn't make the connection,' he finally said. 'I didn't even know it was the toy shop that had blown up. I thought . . . I thought . . .' His eyes found Striker's eyes – 'Oh Jesus, was it really her, Shipwreck?'

'It looks like it, Harry.'

The lines in the older cop's face deepened. 'Her kids—'

'Are being taken care of by their uncle,' Felicia said.

Striker flipped through the pages of his notebook. 'What about Sharise Owens? You know her?'

Harry thought it over. 'The cousin, right? Yeah, I remember her. She was the one who called us back then. A doctor or something.'

'That's her.'

'So what about her?'

'There's only two names in the no-contact conditions ordered against Solomon Bay – Keisha Williams and Sharise Owens. One of them is now dead from the explosion at the toy shop, and the other is missing . . . We have reason to believe Dr Sharise

Owens might have been our victim who was tortured in a warehouse this morning, down by the river.'

Harry's expression was one of disbelief. 'And you think Solomon was responsible for all this?'

'He's the strongest lead we have.'

Felicia added, 'He knew both women. There's a restraining order against him. And he's shown a history of violence. He's a perfect suspect.'

'Any ideas where we can find him?' Striker asked.

Harry raised an eyebrow. 'I never heard of the guy again. Not once. And we're talking *years* here.'

Felicia spoke next. 'Harry, you're the only one here who's ever dealt with Solomon. He was a prick, for sure – we all know that – but was he capable of this level of violence?'

Harry said nothing. He just looked away from them and stared down the drive where a white van had entered the underground parkade. A bunch of the ERT guys – the Emergency Response Team – jumped out and started unloading their gear, most of which was long guns and heavy ceramic vests.

'Harry?' Felicia asked again.

The older detective met her stare and his eyes were hard.

'Anyone is capable of anything,' he finally said. 'If they're pushed hard enough.'

Striker found the comment odd, and he was about to ask Harry to clarify the remark when his cell phone rang. He put the phone to his ear, said, 'Striker,' and began crossing the underground in an effort to locate a better signal. When he finally found one, he recognized the caller.

Their weapons expert, Jay Kolt.

'Where the hell you been?' Striker asked. 'Jesus, court ends at four and it's going on seven-thirty.'

The man sounded drained: 'Special meeting in Judge Reinhold's chambers. You don't wanna know.'

Striker understood that. Special meetings were always dreaded, and Judge Reinhold was a prima donna prick who was hated by every man and woman who had ever worn a blue uniform. He had made life hell for many a member.

'I know the day you've had, Jay, believe me, I do, but lives are at stake here. I need to see you. And I need to see you *now.*'

Kolt sounded less than pleased. 'I'm flying out of here in two hours.'

'Fine. Where are you now?'

'Triple 2 Main.'

Striker nodded; Triple 2 Main was the address for the District 2 Courthouse. 'We'll be there in fifteen minutes. Do not leave.' He hung up the phone and signalled to Felicia that it was time to go.

'We'll be in touch,' he said to Harry.

They climbed inside the undercover cruiser and wheeled about. As they rounded the first turn of the parkade, Striker glanced in the rear view mirror and stared at Harry. The man was still standing there, completely still, watching them go. He hadn't so much as budged from the spot.

Felicia caught his stare.

'I get a weird feeling from that guy,' she said.

Striker nodded in agreement. 'He's holding something back.'

Thirty-Five

Still wearing the grey workman's suit and a pair of white latex-free surgical gloves, the bomber stood in the kitchen area of Chad Koda's house and finished taping the entire bay window with thick transparent duct tape. It was a necessary step if he was going to remove the pane and take his place in the preplanned observation point. Now all he had to do was break the outer edges and knock the entire square out onto the rear deck. But before he could begin the process, Molly's tight voice flooded the radio waves once more:

'Target approaching from the south. One block out.'

He closed his eyes. *One block?* He pressed the plunger. 'Are you sure it's him?'

'Follow radio command.'

He sighed. 'Copy. One block out.'

'Exit,' came the reply.

The bomber said nothing. He just stood there going over things in his head. This was too soon. He wasn't ready yet. And still Molly persisted:

'You need to exit. *Now.*'

He said nothing.

'Now!'

He turned down the volume. Grabbed the crowbar. Began smashing out the glass edges of the pane. When he was near completion and the entire window started to tilt and buckle outwards, he gave it one solid push and the whole structure fell on the deck with a loud, hard, flat sound.

Breathing heavier now – as much from anticipation as exertion – he took the crowbar and raked it all around the windowsill, ridding the frame of any remaining glass shards. It was critical. Even one of those shards could kill him if directed the right way from the bomb's percussive force; each one was like a glass arrowhead.

Experience had taught him well.

Sweating, shivering, he stopped. And then he smiled.

Done.

It was *done.*

He turned around and took one final look at the setup before him. The doctor was strapped to the chair, in just the right viewing angle from the front entranceway; the ducks were perfectly positioned on the kitchen island beside her; and, if he moved out to the back patio, he'd be able to discreetly watch the moment unfold from his observation point, then escape in the utility van.

Everything was set.

Almost.

As a final step, he removed a *second* remote – the one intended for the police to find – from his workman's suit and placed it in the doctor's lap.

Molly's voice came across the radio once more – a barely audible yell:

'You must exit the building! Now, now, *NOW*!'

From the front alcove, he heard the excited sound of Koda's dog barking. It was a young, spritely golden retriever. Oddly, this was the one part of the task that bothered him. He didn't want the animal to get hurt. He never liked it when animals got hurt.

Koda's voice penetrated the front door. 'Down, Jake, *down*!'

The dog scratched at the wood and barked again; keys jingled.

Out of time.

He grabbed his toolbox, the crowbar, and the remote activator, and quickly made his way across the hard stone tiles of the kitchen floor. He opened the back door and stepped outside. As he closed the kitchen door, he heard the rattle of the front door as it opened and banged into the wall behind it. Then, the scuffling sound of claws on wood.

The dog was coming.

He hurried across the yard until he reached the laneway where the utility van was parked. He obtained his position directly beside the telephone pole, then waited and watched for the moment to come.

It happened quickly.

In one magical moment, the look on Chad Koda's face turned from relaxed weariness to shocked disbelief. He came to a full stop halfway between the foyer and kitchen, stared at the woman tied to the chair, and then dropped all his mail.

To the bomber, the moment was all-encompassing. No happiness filled him, just a deep sense of satisfaction out of the knowledge that they would be one step closer to the completion of this horrible job.

He gently thumbed the activator and remotely armed the bomb. When Koda hurried forward and removed the duct tape from the doctor's mouth, she began screaming something – fast, garbled words. And Koda's head snapped from the woman in the chair to the two wooden ducks sitting on the kitchen island.

He knew.

He damn well fuckin' *knew.*

The bomber wasted no time. He burst forth from his place of cover and raced down onto the back deck, until he was less than thirty feet from the open area where the window had been removed. Until he was staring inside the room at Koda and the woman and the ducks.

Once there, he breathed in deeply.

Closed his eyes.

And hit the switch.

The fusing system arced. And in one giant blast of light and smoke and swirling debris, Chad Koda, the doctor and the ducks were consumed by the explosion, and the bomber felt himself flailing backwards . . . backwards . . . backwards in the percussive blast of the bomb.

It was *bliss.*

Thirty-Six

Striker and Felicia reached the District 2 Courthouse, located at Triple 2 Main Street. All proceedings had long since ended and the building was now empty, save for the odd sheriff left wandering the halls and the night-time security guards, most of whom were killing time by reading books and chugging coffee.

Striker and Felicia entered the foyer. Lying down on one of the benches was Jay Kolt. On the ground next to him was a brown leather briefcase and, on top of it, a folded trench coat. Kolt saw them coming, let out a groan, and sat up, adjusting his glasses as they approached.

'My friggin' back,' he said.

'Thanks for seeing us,' Felicia offered.

Kolt nodded but did not smile. He got right down to business. 'This suspect of yours, he's using an electrical torture weapon?'

'It would appear so,' Striker said.

'Opened or closed?'

Striker had no idea what the man was talking about, so Kolt explained.

'An open device is essentially a rod with two wires coming off it. One wire is always taped in the victim's mouth. If the victim is a man, the other wire is placed around the testicles; if it's a woman, then the wire is often connected to a pad of steel wool, which is then inserted into the vagina.'

Felicia's face tightened. 'Sick.'

Kolt smiled. 'It's not exactly an aphrodisiac. This completes the circuit for an open device. On the other hand, a *closed* device is essentially wireless, like a cattle prod or a violet wand.'

Felicia shook her head. 'Violet wand?'

Kolt grinned, almost mischievously. 'Small handheld device. Used by S&M lovers to give each other shocks – *that* is an aphrodisiac. A sexual stimulus.'

Striker looked at Felicia. 'That doesn't sound like any of your toys.'

She gave him one of her cross looks – definitely a warning – and he let the joke go.

Kolt continued: 'A picana looks like a long metal stick with two electrodes at one end. The electrodes are of different polarity, of course, and the circuit completes when they're driven into the victim's flesh. Essentially, it's like a longer version of a stun gun, but one that delivers much more voltage – up to thirty thousand volts – all while keeping the amperage down.' He looked directly at Striker. 'Is this more along the lines of what you saw?'

'I'm not sure. I only saw pieces of the device, not the entire thing.'

Kolt blinked behind his thin glasses. 'Then how—'

'The *totality* of the evidence suggested it,' he explained. 'The chair was metal and had straps. The floor beneath it had water stains. And sitting beside the chair was a bucket of water, a crescent-shaped piece of rubber with wires coming off it, a yellow sponge, and an industrial-size battery.'

Kolt nodded. 'Electrical torture.'

Felicia spoke up: 'But why all the gear? That's what I don't get. Why not just use a TASER instead – they deliver up to *two hundred* thousand volts.'

'It's because of the current,' Kolt explained. 'By keeping the amperage down, the torture can go on for hours. Days, even. And with little fear of the victim dying.' He leaned forward with his elbows on his knees and steepled his fingers. 'Odd though, normally the use of a picana involves *two* people – one to apply the baton and the other to regulate the voltage.'

'I only saw one suspect down there,' Striker replied. 'The other person had to be the victim.'

Kolt took off his glasses and began cleaning them with a silk rag from his coat pocket. 'One person *can* operate a picana. It's not unheard of. Just unusual. The operator would have to be very . . . *skilful.*' He put his glasses back on, and continued. 'The thing with a picana is that it's also a very powerful psychological tool. A lot of insurgents use them – like the Taliban. But most of the domestic cases I've seen have been linked to either the cartel or the mafia. Or the high-end gangs from the south or the east – the Tongs, the Triads, the Banditos.'

'What about around here?' Felicia asked. 'There must be some persons of interest.'

Kolt was quiet for a bit. 'A lot of the gangs do use electrical torture,' he said. 'But an actual picana? That is rare. The only one I can think of is the Satan's Prowlers – they were known for using one against the Renegades a while back, but we're talking ten or more years ago, and I believe that was back East in Toronto.'

Felicia nodded. 'Well, one of them might have turned active again.'

Kolt let out a long breath. 'I sincerely hope not. The kind of person that uses a picana is generally either a fanatic or a professional – someone with a specific cause. Definitely not your ordinary everyday criminal.'

Striker wrote all this down in his notebook.

'Anyone come to mind?' he asked.

'Fanatics?' Kolt asked. 'No. But professionals that are *capable* of this? Many. There was a guy named Burns who worked for the Satan's Prowlers back East. Everyone called him Sleeves. He did some time for torturing one of the Renegades. Check him out.' Kolt stopped talking for a moment and eyed Striker up. 'Whoever you're dealing with, this guy has some rather unusual experience. Be ready for it.'

Striker didn't like the sound of that. He wrote 'Burns (Sleeves)' down in his notebook, then his cell went off. He drew it from his belt, put it to his ear.

'Striker,' he said.

The man on the line was Inspector Osaka. His tone was low, his words clipped and direct: 'We got another explosion.'

'Where?'

'Pacific Avenue,' he said. 'Chad Koda's house.'

Thirty-Seven

By the time Striker and Felicia reached Pacific Avenue, it was well after eight. The entire strip was blocked off with patrol cars and police tape, and the red and blue gleam of emergency lights filled the darkening skyline.

Halfway down the block, on the east side of the street, was Chad Koda's residence. As Striker approached it on foot, he was surprised to see that the exterior of the house looked no different from before. The structure appeared to be sound, and no smoke filled the air, indicating there had been no resultant fire. Aside from the shattered windows, everything looked relatively unchanged.

Then he went inside.

The moment Striker walked through the front door, the waxy, smoky smell hit him. In the living room, the sofa's upholstery was destroyed, and in the kitchen, the dining table had been overturned. All the windows on the south and east sides of the house had been blown out, with giant parts of the old plaster imploded, like moon craters in the wall. The remains of a cooking island sat centre stage, looking now like the blown-apart entrance to a World War Two bunker.

Without a doubt, it was the epicentre of the explosion.

Through the strange white smoke that was slowly thinning, Striker looked down the hall and spotted Inspector Osaka. The man walked gingerly towards them, his narrow eyes filled with concern. 'What a goddam nightmare,' he said.

Striker looked past the inspector. Somewhere back there, down near the end of the hall, a dog was barking wildly and scratching at the door. 'That a dog? It's lucky to be alive.'

Osaka let out a long breath. 'Yeah, great. Our only guaranteed survivor is a golden retriever. The Chief will be happy to hear it . . . I locked the dog in the bathroom to keep him out of the way.' He looked around the room, assessing. 'Definitely no gas leak this time. And the second explosion in one day.'

Striker nodded gravely. 'We got a bomber on our hands.'

Osaka pointed to the den area. 'Parts of a fusing system have already been located by the search team – the components were stuck in the rock and stone of the fireplace.'

'I want to see those components,' Striker said.

Osaka muttered, 'Yes, yes,' as if it was a good idea, but the bewildered expression remained on his face. 'Corporal Summer has them now. She's out back, escorting one of the victims into the ambulance.'

Felicia looked from Striker to Osaka. '*One* of the victims?'

'We have two. One male – Chad Koda – may yet survive the blast, though he's in a real bad way. The female – name unknown at this point – did not.' His expression darkened. 'She really had no hope of it.'

Striker looked through the windowless frame and spotted the ambulance driving down the alley. A second later, red emergency lights filled the air and a siren wailed. 'You got a guard on Koda?'

Inspector Osaka nodded. 'Two. From Patrol.'

'How bad is he?'

Osaka shrugged. 'He's alive. And damn lucky to be. From what I know, he's concussed and bloodied and shaken to shit

– the blast knocked him right out. But he seems to have pulled through without his vital areas being hit by shrapnel. It's a miracle, really.'

Felicia looked at all the damage. 'How is that even possible?'

Striker studied the kitchen island. '*This* is how.' He tapped on what was left of the island counter top. 'Two-inch granite. Solid oak cabinetry. The thing's been damn near obliterated, but it took the brunt of the blast. The bomb must have been placed on the other side.'

'Or maybe it was on top and he knocked it off before it exploded,' Felicia suggested.

'Could be.'

Striker studied the scene and was about to say more when he spotted the thick, white tarp on the other side of what remained of the kitchen island. Blood stuck to the kitchen tiles all around it, looking thick and tacky. The entire area was sectioned off by yellow police tape.

Striker stared at the lump under the tarp.

The deceased.

Osaka saw Striker looking at it, and spoke. 'The victim's left side of her neck was torn right open. The explosion almost took her head off.'

Striker nodded. He moved carefully around the island, then crouched down low and gloved up with fresh latex. He snapped the material against his wrists, then carefully pulled back the edge of the plastic tarp. What he saw hit him hard. Damaged as the body was, identification was still possible.

The victim was Dr Sharise Owens.

Felicia made a surprised sound. 'Is it her?'

Striker nodded.

'Dear God,' Osaka said. He closed his eyes and his face tightened. Moments later, he was on the cell with Acting Deputy

Chief Laroche. He moved to one of the back rooms and closed the door for privacy.

Striker was glad for the distance. He took the time to study the body.

The first thing that he noticed was how much of the woman remained intact. Yes, she had taken damage from the percussive force; portions of pulverized flesh made that obvious. But the majority of her body remained whole. There was even a strap still hanging from one of her mangled arms. The condition of her body was surprising, given the force of the bomb. Striker determined she must have somehow been shielded from the worst of the blast.

Maybe by the heavy wood and granite from the kitchen island.

Minus the gaping meaty gash in her neck, Dr Sharise Owens looked identical to the picture the triage nurse had shown him from the hospital personnel records – long straight hair, dyed a lighter brown. High cheekbones. Lean and muscular build. She was even wearing a white hospital coat, though it was now soaked in blood from the breasts down and blackened on the left side.

Striker looked at the doctor's coat. More specifically, at the fabric of the shoulder region. On it was the same medical emblem they had seen before. A caduceus – two snakes wrapped around a staff, wings extending from the top.

Red wings.

Striker pointed at the wings with his pen. 'There it is – we were on the right track after all.'

Felicia nodded. 'The tattoo our rave girl thought she saw.'

Striker examined the body a while longer, then covered it up. He stood up and looked out into the yard, where Corporal Summer was talking to a few members of the search team. On the deck, lying flat, were the remains of the kitchen window. It had been taped up completely, so it still held together well. Striker wondered if the bomber had done this to break the window quietly. It seemed like an awful lot of unnecessary work when a thrown spark plug would also have sufficed.

Perhaps there was another reason.

He detailed this oddity in his notebook.

As he put the book away, Corporal Summer returned from the backyard area into the kitchen. She saw them both and nodded in acknowledgement. 'Detectives,' she said, and there was a weariness in her voice.

With two ongoing explosion scenes to control, assess, and catalogue, Striker understood her lack of exuberance. She must have been exhausted. He turned and faced her. 'You located part of the fusing system?'

She nodded. 'An electrical one.'

Felicia asked, 'Have your teams located any bomb parts at the first scene?'

Corporal Summer shook her head. 'None yet, I'm afraid. But I still have crews sifting through the wreckage. It will take days. My fear is that we lost much of what we were looking for when the Fire Department put out the flames – so much evidence was washed down the sewers. The lab tests will tell us if there were any explosives residues on what was recovered.'

'I know there'll be residues,' Striker said. 'I just want to know what *kind*. Maybe it will give us something to go on.'

'I understand that, and I've put a rush on the testing. Most of it's being sent to private labs. But any true identification will still take at least forty-eight hours. There's just no way around it.'

Striker understood the time issues. He scanned the room. On the eastern wall, where the window had been blown out, was a long black smear. He moved towards it and examined the discoloration. It looked like millions of tiny black dots. Like a shotgun blast.

'Is this bomb residue?' he asked.

Corporal Summer shook her head. 'It's not actually from the explosives – it's carbon powder, a substance left over from the battery.'

'So part of the fusing system,' Felicia said.

'Yes. And it's already been swabbed for the lab.'

Striker looked around the room once more. 'What about this haze? The smoke is the same colour as back at the toy shop, but I thought that military explosives usually give off a black smoke.'

Corporal Summer explained. 'They do, usually; you're right about that. This smoke is definitely a whiter colour. It signifies a cleaner burn – signalling that this was probably some form of commercial explosives.'

'So not HME?'

'No. Home-made explosives would be greyer in colour – usually.'

From the den, one member of the search and canvass crew called out that there were more possible components. Corporal Summer excused herself and left the kitchen. When she was gone, Striker turned to Felicia. Her eyes were focused on the kitchen island.

'Any thoughts?' he asked.

She gave him a dismal look. 'Just the one question we all have – *why*?'

'Learn that and we'll find our suspect.'

'That easy, huh?'

Striker laughed wearily. 'This entire file's like a tangled fishing line. It's knotted and loopy, but if we follow the thread, we should end up on the other side.' He took out his notebook and flipped through the pages. 'At the two explosion scenes, we got two dead women – both black and, more to the point, cousins. We also got one injured male, white, who is the ex-husband of our second victim.'

Felicia nodded. 'An ex-husband who is still emotionally charged over Owens aborting their son. Also, somewhere out there is Solomon Bay – a violent ex-boyfriend with a restraining order against him.'

'Who no one has seen in years,' Striker said. 'And from this morning, we got parts from a picana, some scuba gear, and one gunman who's an expert shooter.'

'Expert?'

'Don't kid yourself, Feleesh. That bastard wasn't too far from tagging me back there in the barn – and that's a *two-hundred-metre* shot. By pistol, not long gun.'

'Which leaves us with what?' Felicia asked.

Striker let out a bemused laugh. 'Take your pick. A mad bomber. A professional hitman. A domestic gone wrong. A hate crime. An abortion issue. And we haven't even touched on organized crime groups yet.'

Felicia's eyes took on a distant look, and Striker continued speaking. 'Maybe we're looking at this the wrong way. Let's stop wondering about possible suspects and look at the victims. Who – and what – are they?'

Felicia listed them out. 'A trauma surgeon, a toymaker and a realtor. Not the most likely of combinations. Not the easiest links to connect.'

'Of course not,' Striker said. He offered Felicia a grim smile. 'Nothing's been easy so far. Why start now?'

He left Felicia's side and took a cursory look around the kitchen and then the den. He stopped hard when he saw one of the craters in the west wall. Stuck within the plaster was what appeared to be a doll of some kind.

Striker gloved up and gently removed the piece.

Felicia neared him. 'What you got there?'

'The remains of a doll.'

Stunned and yet excited, Striker showed her the toy. It had been almost destroyed by the blast. The upper and lower parts were completely gone. All that remained was the torso, which was chipped and covered in debris. It was dressed in the tattered remains of a policeman's uniform.

Striker turned it over, saw that there was a small hole in the back of the doll and the frayed remains of a string hanging down.

'Look at that,' Felicia said.

Striker nodded. 'It looks like a pull-string of some kind.'

'Maybe like one of those Chatty Cathy dolls,' Felicia suggested. 'You pull the string and it talks.'

'I'm not touching that string, not till it's cleared.'

Felicia stared at the frayed rope. 'You think that could have been used as a triggering device?'

Striker thought it over. It seemed unlikely. And even less likely to be used as an explosives base – if the doll had been packed with explosives, nothing would have been left of it.

'It's for something else,' he finally said, but he had no idea what. 'We'll give it to Noodles for a good forensic examination.' He paused in thought before continuing. 'You know, I found another one just like this back at the first crime scene, but since the blown-up business was a toy store, I didn't think much of it. Till now.'

A wariness took over Felicia's stare. 'Was that last one exactly the same?'

'*Exactly*,' he started to say, but stopped when he saw the red number painted on the front of the doll. 'Wait a second . . . the last doll had a big red *five* on the front.'

Felicia leaned closer for a better look. 'This one's a six,' she said softly.

Her words sent a chill through Striker, for their relevance was obvious. The numbers may have been out of order, but the bomber was counting out his victims, one by one. Altogether it told Striker one very important thing:

There were at least four more to go.

Thirty-Eight

Harry parked his car at the corner of Burrard and Pacific and stared at the spectacle before him. Chad Koda's place. Blown sky-high. It was unreal. Explosions going off here and there. People dying in fiery blasts. What the hell was this – Mexico?

Harry closed his eyes.

He had been to Koda's house. He had *just* been there.

His fingers gripped the steering wheel so tightly that the small muscles around his knuckles hurt. He had to will them to let go. So many thoughts rampaged through his head. The past connections were many – too many to discount. A headache was growing behind his temples, a ringing filled his ears. Once, twice, three times – and then he clued in.

He grabbed the cell from the seat and jammed it to his ear.

'Detective Eckhart,' he got out.

'Hi, Dad!'

In two words, the thickening shroud of tension dissipated, and suddenly Harry felt like he could breathe again. 'How you doing there, son? You being a good boy for your mom?'

'Yeah. Mom says I can have ice cream for dessert, if you say it's okay too. Can I? Can I please? *Please?*'

Harry laughed softly. Six-year-olds. Christ. 'Only if you save some for me.'

'I will, I *will!*'

'Put your mother on the phone.'

'Can I play Minecraft?'

'Twenty minutes. No more. Now put your mother on the phone.'

The phone clicked, and for a moment Harry thought the line had gone dead. Then a soft, feminine voice filled the receiver: 'Hey, sweetie. Coming home now?'

'Not for a while.'

She turned silent for a moment, as if sensing his tension. 'Everything okay?'

He took in a deep breath. 'Listen to me carefully, Sandra. Really carefully. I want you to take Ethan and go to your sister's place tonight.'

She let out a worried sound. 'What – why? Harry, what's going on?'

'I'll explain later.'

'But—'

'Later, Sandra.'

She made a nervous sound. 'Okay, Harry, okay. We'll go.'

He could hear the fear in her voice, the jitteriness, and he worried about her driving this way. 'It's all precautionary, Sandra. That's it. Just precautionary.'

'I'll . . . I'll call you when we get there?'

'Yes. Make sure you do. I love you, Sandra. And like I said, I'll explain it all to you later.' He hung up without waiting for a response. When he put the cell on the passenger seat, it dropped from his clumsy fingers. They felt numb. *He* felt numb. Numb all over. Because deep down he knew the truth.

It was happening. Really fucking happening.

The past had finally caught up to them.

Thirty-Nine

It was after nine when Striker and Felicia finally finished going over the details at Chad Koda's house, but it felt like midnight. Striker was sorting through the twenty or so pages of notes he'd written down during the investigation and feeling bombarded by numerous streams of evidence, most of which didn't seem to connect. He was halfway out the front door when they bumped right into Harry.

Striker looked at his watch, then back at the older cop.

'What are you doing here?' he asked.

Harry just swore. 'Goddam press is *everywhere.*'

'Get used to it.'

Harry looked back outside at the stream of reporters gathered at the edge of the yellow line, cursed again, then pushed past Striker and Felicia into the foyer. Once inside, he stopped like he'd been smacked back by some invisible force. Gaped at the destruction.

'Jesus mercy,' he said.

Strewn across the foyer, separating the rest of the house, was a thick slash of police tape, and on the other side of it forensic searchers, dressed in blue booties and matching lab gowns, were conducting a grid search of the room.

Felicia reached out and touched Harry's arm. 'You can't go in there right now.'

Harry just nodded on autopilot, but said nothing. After a long moment, he turned his eyes away from the crime scene and met Striker's stare. 'Is this connected to the toy shop?'

'Why are you here, Harry?' Striker asked.

'Chad Koda was an old friend of mine.'

Striker was surprised by this news. He took a quick glance at Felicia, then back at Harry. 'When was the last time you saw him?'

Harry just raised an eyebrow. 'I haven't actually spoken to Chad in, well, years, I guess . . . but when I saw the explosion on the news, I recognized the house immediately. I headed right up.'

Striker said nothing for a moment, waiting for Harry to continue with more of an explanation. When he didn't, Striker summed it up. 'This is a very strange situation, Harry. You have a direct connection to Keisha Williams, another direct connection to Chad Koda, and through the both of them, an indirect connection to Dr Sharise Owens.'

The words just hung there, and Harry's eyes never left the destruction in the living room.

'How bad is he?' he finally asked.

'Koda? I don't know. Alive. They took him to St Paul's.'

'I'm heading up.'

Without so much as another word, Harry turned and walked back out the front door. He took the front steps two at a time, rounded the sidewalk, and headed up the block.

Striker said nothing; he just stepped onto the front porch and watched Harry step under the yellow line of police tape at the end of the block. The second he did, a swarm of media reporters buzzed around him. Flashes went off; cameras panned; feeds started.

Harry paid them no heed. He pushed aggressively through

the mob, knocking one reporter on her ass and sending a cameraman tripping over the kerb. He climbed into his Honda CRV, did a U-turn, and was gone.

Felicia came up beside Striker.

'That was screwed,' she said.

Striker agreed; he was about to discuss the situation with her further when one of the forensic searchers located something in the living room and called over Corporal Summer. With gloved hands, she opened a clear plastic bag, and the searcher dropped the piece of shrapnel inside.

Striker couldn't help himself. He moved back inside the house, and Felicia followed. They were soon joined by Inspector Osaka at the entrance to the living room, where all three of them met with the bomb specialist.

'What have you got?' Striker asked.

Corporal Summer held up the plastic bag. Inside it was a chunk of green rectangular plastic, less than an inch wide and two inches long. Connected to it was a long wire and a shiny silver box.

'Is that a motherboard?' Striker asked.

She nodded. 'With a transmitter attached. It looks like it came from a cell phone.'

Felicia studied the find. 'So it's a remote detonator, is what you're saying.'

'Part of one.'

Corporal Summer spoke the words with concern, and Striker understood why. 'Hold on a second,' he said. 'If the detonator was found right here in the living room, then where was the bomb triggered from?'

Summer lowered the bag and met his stare. 'Inside the house.'

'*Where* inside the house?'

'Most likely somewhere in this vicinity.'

Striker blinked in near disbelief. 'Then whoever set it off would have been blown up in the explosion.'

'Almost certainly.'

The conclusion drawn from Corporal Summer's words was easy for everyone to see; there had been only two bodies in the area at the time of the explosion – Dr Sharise Owens, who had been strapped to a chair, and Chad Koda, who had miraculously survived the blast.

Inspector Osaka looked uneasy. 'Are we honestly considering whether Chad Koda might have been responsible for this?'

Striker frowned. It sounded ludicrous – and it went completely against their theory that a bomber was out there, using numbered dolls to count off his victims. Still, as outlandish as the notion seemed, it would have been irresponsible of them not to consider and rule out all alternative theories.

'Let's talk it out,' he suggested.

Felicia nodded and went over all they had.

'Chad Koda broke up with Dr Owens years ago after she aborted his child. And he was still quite emotional about that when we talked to him today, so he definitely had motive. Meanwhile, the detonator is right there in your hands, so he definitely had the means. Add in the fact that he miraculously survived the blast, and alarm bells have to go off.'

Striker remained less convinced. 'That's a pretty far leap.'

'It's just a theory,' she replied. 'But remember that doctor at Fort Bragg? He killed his family, then stabbed himself to make it look like he'd fought off a bunch of home invaders to save them all.'

Striker remembered the case. 'You're talking about Jeffrey MacDonald,' he said. 'The man was a medical doctor and a practising physician – he knew how to safely injure himself. It doesn't appear that Koda had the same expertise. Plus, to stab yourself is one thing. It's a *controlled* action. But to half kill yourself in a bomb blast is an entirely different matter. Koda could easily have died here tonight.'

'Maybe he was supposed to,' Felicia replied.

Her words were soft spoken, and they intrigued Striker.

'A murder-suicide?' He hadn't thought of that. But he still remained unconvinced. 'Koda may have had the motive and the means, but do we seriously think he had the *ability* to pull something like this off?'

'Without a doubt,' Osaka said.

It was the first thing the inspector had said with any force. Striker looked at the man in slight surprise. 'He's a *realtor*, sir.'

'And a retired cop. Hell, he was a sergeant in ERT. Red Team.'

The words stunned Striker. This was the first time he had ever heard this information. 'A retired cop? Red Team? How the hell do you know this?'

Osaka shrugged. 'Simple,' he said. 'I worked with the man.'

Forty

The road looked warped. Off-kilter. And somehow tunnelled.

Or was it just him?

The bomber cut the corner onto Denman Street, using every bit of energy he had to turn the steering wheel. It felt unusually stiff and heavy. He came to a jerking stop and parked the van in front of a cheap pizzeria. He jammed on the hand-brake. Crawled between the seats. Crashed down heavily in the empty cargo space. And rolled onto his back.

There was a smell in the cab, something sweet but stale. Like old pineapple. And it made him want to vomit.

That . . . or the pounding in his head.

He reached up, felt the side of his skull. There was wetness there. Stickiness. And the entire area felt numb. When he pulled his hand away, he saw the brown redness of drying blood.

The glass, he realized. *Loose shards.*

Not that it really mattered. He had lived through the blast, and he had felt it once more – that wonderful, heavenly, percussive force. It had shaken the earth around him and ravaged through his body like an invisible wave, reorganizing his thoughts and setting his mind right.

The memories . . . they were slowly falling into place, more and more with every blast:

He was off to war again.

Then his men were dying all around him – chunks of flesh being punched from their bodies by AK-47 fire.

And Father was spinning him round in the air, giving him an airplane ride.

Then Father was leaving. Standing at the car. And he was sobbing, peeking out between the drapes, saying, 'Don't go, Daddy, don't go.'

And Mother was crying, not wanting him to go.

And the helicopter was dropping down – the loud whup-whup-whup of the blades sounding like angry thunder . . .

He blinked out of the memories. The thoughts were confusing. Out of order still. But *better*. He knew that they were better.

And he let out a small laugh.

In the front of the van, a door opened and closed. The engine started. And the vehicle got moving. It rocked about like a boat on rough waters, and the movement made his stomach queasy.

'Are you okay, love?' Molly's voice was soft and nervous. Concerned.

'I'm fine.'

In one moment, her voice went from concern and compassion to anger. 'What the heck were you doing back there? We've been over this! Again and again and again! You could have gotten yourself killed!'

'Molly—'

'You do it again, and that's it. I mean it. I'll end this mission.'

He said nothing back, because her words were empty threats. This mission would be completed. They both knew that.

Life would not be livable otherwise.

Her eyes turned watery. 'What does it matter anyway? We failed again.'

He gave her a confused look.

'Didn't you see the ambulance?' she asked. 'He survived the blast. Chad Koda's *still alive.*'

Her words cut into him. Stunned him. Turned him silent.

How had the man survived? It shouldn't have happened that way. It should have never been possible. And then, like sun breaking through the clouds, he got it.

It was because of *Molly.*

Molly and her damn ethical conflicts. Because of her, they had deviated from the plan. Used less explosives. To prevent further casualties. And in doing so, what had it gotten them? A failed operation.

'I'm taking you to a doctor,' Molly said from the driver's seat.

'No! No doctors!'

'But—'

'*Never again.*'

Images burst through the bomber's head. Flashes of times unknown. The nurse with the dark eyes and the small paper hat. The emaciated doctor who walked like a stork and talked in high bird-like chirps:

There is no choice, young man . . . it has to come off, it simply must come off.

The memory was too much. The bomber rolled over onto his side. Vomited everything he had inside of him. Felt the coolness of the steel cab against his face in this overheated place. Dizzy, his head was splitting . . . splitting in two. Like there was a worm eating through his brain.

Find the calm, he told himself. *Pull back from it. Pull back!*

But he was flailing now. The point of sanity was extending further and further away from him. And soon it would be too far to grasp at all. The clouds were there. Spreading, swirling, thickening.

Ballooning.

There was no doubt about it.

The darkness was coming back on him again – that black wave of memories that took him back to the bad place where all of this began.

Forty-One

It was late by the time Striker and Felicia returned to his sleepy little Dunbar home. Two depressing messages were waiting for him on his cell, ones he had missed in all the chaos.

One was from Rothschild, informing him that there were no leads on the scuba gear found on Mitchell Island. The other was from Medical Examiner Kirstin Dunsmuir, calling to inform them that the fibres pulled from the victim's body at the toy store matched the clothing Keisha Williams had been wearing when she'd left for work that morning. In short, it told them what they already knew – that Keisha Williams was the victim of the toy store explosion.

That evidence was just the final nail in the coffin.

Striker found the knowledge depressing. The woman had five children, all between the ages of eight and nineteen. He'd lost his own parents at an early age himself, so he knew full well the hardships and emptiness it would bring.

As for Dr Sharise Owens, her identity had been confirmed as well. Time of death was estimated to be 19:25 hours. And there was no longer any doubt she had been the woman down by the river – a sample comparison of her shoe matched the footprints in the river silt.

All in all, it was a sad end to a hard day. Solomon Bay had still not been located. Koda was unconscious in the hospital, under police protection. And two women were now dead.

Striker felt like he had failed them all. He wondered if he was right about the big red numbers he had seen on the front of the two recovered dolls. A 6 and a 5. Did that really mean there were four more victims on the bomber's list? He also pondered the significance of the policeman's uniform on the dolls. God forbid the bomber was an ex-cop. What then?

He didn't even want to think about it.

Once inside his home, he sat down on the living room couch and was deep in thought on the matter when his cell went off. When he picked up, he heard Noodles' deep voice, and the newest information the Ident technician gave him was alarming. 'I located the legs to that doll you found at the second blast,' he said.

Striker sat up. 'And?'

'They're just ordinary legs,' Noodles said. 'Wood. They match the police uniform perfectly. But here's the weird thing, I got *three* of them.'

'Three?' Striker closed his eyes. 'Three legs mean there were *two* dolls. You find any of the other pieces?'

'No, and I don't expect to. We're lucky we found these. Everything here is mincemeat.'

'So we got two crime scenes and three dolls for three victims,' Striker said. 'One of which – Koda – has survived.'

'It would appear that way.' Noodles let out a gruff sound. 'Also, I had the doll taken apart. You were right about the pull-string. The toy's got a voice-box inside it. A cheap one.'

'And?' Striker asked.

'And nothing. Thing was completely broken apart from the force. It's irreparable, untraceable. Junk.'

The news was disheartening. Striker talked to Noodles for a bit more, then hung up. As he sat there on the couch, he looked around the room at nothing in particular and felt a bit overwhelmed. He relayed the information to Felicia.

She seemed stunned by the news.

'I need a drink,' she said.

Striker echoed her feelings.

He got up and moved through the living room. Everything was quiet, and the silence felt wrong. It reminded him that Courtney was not home, but a million miles away on the other side of the ocean.

Ireland – it sounded not continents away, but *worlds*.

He cut into the kitchen and grabbed a couple of bottles of ice-cold beer – Miller Genuine Draft. He popped the caps. Gave one to Felicia.

'Thanks,' she said softly.

He just nodded and drank. The beer helped him relax, and it also felt good to have something cool to ward off the nonstop humidity. Wednesday had been one constant heat wave, and the house was stuffy from it. He wished he'd bought another air conditioner to replace the one that had died last summer.

But if wishes were dollars, he would've been rich a long time ago.

Tired and yet overstimulated, they plunked themselves down on the sofa. Tried to relax. It wasn't possible.

'I still can't believe Koda was a cop,' Felicia said between sips. She looked at Striker and her face flushed with embarrassment. 'I mean, I ran that guy a dozen times through the system. It wasn't in there. And the domestic report didn't so much as mention that tidbit.'

Striker cradled the beer between his hands. 'It's not your fault, Feleesh. Koda's not listed in PRIME because he retired about ten years ago – *before* the new system was in place. All his records will be paper.'

Striker guzzled a third of the beer. 'From what Osaka was saying, Koda spent the bulk of his years either being seconded or working for Operations teams – he was a sergeant in Dogs,

Drugs, and the Emergency Response Team. I was in Investigations all that time. So we would never have seen each other unless it was on a call.'

Felicia grew frustrated. 'But even in the Criminal Harassment report, they didn't mention Koda was a former member.'

Striker shrugged. 'That's just cops covering for cops. The author *purposely* omitted that detail . . . We'll have to interview Koda tomorrow morning. When we're fresh.'

Felicia agreed. 'No one gets blown up in their own house for no reason.'

Striker thought it over, then frowned. Feelings of anger, helplessness and urgency intermingled inside his chest. 'There's a connection here somewhere, between all the parties involved, and we'll find it,' he said. 'But that's not what worries me.' He looked up and met Felicia's stare. 'We've got a serial killer on our hands here, Feleesh.'

'A true classification requires three or more homicides,' she started.

But Striker waved her off. 'Don't go all psychology on me. We've had three victims blown sky-high, and it's a miracle one of them even survived. This bomber, he's always using the same MO. He knows the victims' routines – that much is evident by the times and places he's set the bombs. So he's doing recon first. He does surveillance, he sets the bomb, and then he waits for the show to begin.'

Felicia nodded as she thought it over. 'There's got to be a reason for the murders, some motivation *beyond* the violence – otherwise, this guy could have gone after anybody. But we know these parties are connected in different ways.'

Striker let out a heavy breath and stood up. 'We'll learn the motivation as the body count rises.'

'Rises?'

'Make no mistake about it, Feleesh. More bombs are coming. Those numbers on the dolls all but prove it.'

He returned to the kitchen and brought back two more beers. He put Felicia's on the table, then gave her a hard look. 'If there are any more bomb calls tomorrow, remember – no going in till the fire's been put out and the structure's been deemed safe. We could have had a nasty accident there today.'

'I understand that, Jacob. Stop treating me like a rookie.'

Then stop acting like one, he felt like saying. But he knew it would only start a fight. So he opted to go with, 'I'm just looking out for you.'

'It's a fine line between covering your partner and being overprotective.'

'Overprotective?'

'You've been overprotective of me ever since the Billy Mercury shooting six months ago. Okay? Well, it's over. I survived. Move on.'

Striker let out a humourless laugh. 'And you derived all this because I stopped you from walking into a burning building today – one which, I might remind you, *exploded* in the end.'

A cross look spread out on Felicia's face. 'It's more than that, and you know it. You kept me out of the barn this morning too. You went in there and did the whole thing yourself. Yet again. Jacob Striker – Solo Act.'

'Oh come on.'

'I'm serious.'

'First off, you *had* to stay with the girl. We couldn't leave her alone.'

'Sure, but *I* could have cleared the place.'

Striker splayed his hands. 'The girl was afraid of me; you saw that. But she liked you. She had a rapport with you. And for all we knew at the time, she might have been raped. I thought it better to leave her with a female member.'

Felicia just shook her head and put down her beer, half finished. 'You always have an excuse, don't you?'

'Not an excuse, it's the truth. Besides, what's wrong with me looking out for you? I *care* about you.'

'Nothing's wrong with that. But looking out for me and *controlling* me are two entirely different things. When we're at work, I'm a homicide cop – not your girlfriend. You can't lock me away in a box forever.'

'I know that . . . I was thinking more of a wooden crate.'

When Felicia didn't laugh, Striker realized that somewhere along the line, the conversation had turned from relaxed and easygoing to tense and bothersome.

Felicia stood up. 'Look, it's late. I'd better be going.'

'Going? You're not going to stay?'

'I have some things I need to get done at home.'

'At *midnight*?'

She said nothing.

Striker shook his head. 'This is crazy. You know, if you just moved in—'

'We've been over this before, Jacob. A million times.' Felicia let out an exasperated sound. 'We move in together and one of us will be on the first transfer out of Homicide – and it sure as hell won't be you. Not Jacob Striker, the ten-year vet. Not *the man*. It'll be me – the woman who everyone treats like a rookie.'

Striker watched her expression as she spoke. Her eyes were underscored with lines and her face was tight. The more he looked at her, and the more he listened, the more he realized there wasn't really a problem here.

They were both plain exhausted.

When Felicia put on her coat to go, Striker helped pull it around her shoulders. When she turned for the door, he grabbed her arm.

'Hey,' he said.

She turned to face him. 'What?'

'Happy birthday, beautiful.'

A small smile spread her lips. She laughed softly. 'I'd forgotten.'

Striker pulled her close. Wrapped his arms around her waist. Held her tight. Breathed in her wonderful smell. Gave her a soft kiss on the lips and tasted light beer.

'Goodnight,' he said.

'Goodnight, Jacob.'

He walked her out and stood on the porch, with the old planks groaning under his weight. He watched her go. Sometimes, he wondered if working together was such a good idea. He always enjoyed it, but Felicia sometimes seemed at odds with his ways. Maybe they were seeing too much of each other now. Always at work, always at home. He didn't know.

When the taillights of Felicia's Prius turned the corner and were gone from sight, Striker remained on the porch, looking out over the park beyond. Everything was dark, and although the night was as hot as a sweatbox, it looked cold and deep.

For a long time afterwards, Striker did not move. He just stood on the porch and thought everything through. So much for the getaway he'd planned for Felicia's birthday. It was just another letdown in a long day, it seemed. He killed the thought and looked on. Far to the north, on the other side of the park, the lights of the downtown core shone brightly.

Bright whites in a pitch-blackness.

Somewhere in that sprawling metropolis was their madman. An unknown suspect with an unknown motive. And there was only one thing Striker knew about the man with absolute certainty.

He wasn't done yet.

Part 2: Spark

Thursday

Forty-Two

It was early when Striker woke up, barely halfway through till morning. The room was hot and his skin felt sweaty. Sometime during the night, he'd kicked off the bed sheets, and now they covered the floor like another body tarp. The thought was depressing. On autopilot, he reached over to wrap his arm around Felicia, felt nothing there but space, and remembered she hadn't stayed the night.

Felicia at her own home. Courtney in Ireland. Amanda passed away.

Lately, it felt like he was always losing someone.

It wasn't right. A home was supposed to be the one place where a person felt happy and secure, but lately, all he felt was a strange tightness in his chest. An indescribable anxiety tightening and tightening and tightening down on him. He wondered if the time for a move had come. Maybe Rothschild had it right.

New move, new start, new life.

Striker let the thought simmer for a few minutes. When he realized sleep would no longer be possible, he climbed out of bed and started his morning routine – cold shower, hot coffee.

Ten minutes later, he was sitting in the brooding darkness of the porch, drinking java and waiting for the newspaper boy. Had Felicia been there, he could have read it on her Kindle. But she wasn't. So he waited for the newspaper and thought of the case and Courtney.

He grabbed his cell and tried to call his daughter. The line clicked and he heard her digitized voice: *Sorry I can't take your call – I'm busy kissing the Blarney Stone. Please leave your name and number after the banshee wail.*

Striker smiled at her silliness. She was always that way. A lot like her mother, really – at least before the depression had hit her.

He left a simple message:

It's Dad. I hope you're having a good time. I love you.

Then he turned on his portable police radio and switched the setting to Scan. It allowed him to hear all the feeds from each of the four districts. Some of the speciality channels too. But the radio chatter this morning was almost nil: a drunk driver being pulled over on Lakewood; a mental health apprehension by Oppenheimer Park; and a domestic going down on Fraser Street.

All in all, it seemed an ordinary night shift.

Then the prowler call came in from District 4.

Striker turned up the volume. At first, the broadcast brought him no concern. Prowler calls were a dime a dozen. Most often, they ended up being some drunk guy, looking for his house on the wrong block. Once in a while you got lucky though, and it ended up being some toad doing a Break and Enter.

He listened to the call:

An unknown male.

Seen lurking between the houses.

In the Dunbar area.

It was all pretty routine – until Striker heard the address. He blinked, grabbed the radio, and hit the mike. 'This is Detective Striker,' he said. 'Dispatch, can you go again with that address?'

'1757 West 29th Avenue.'

Striker jumped to his feet and hit the plunger again.

'That address is Sergeant Mike Rothschild's house,' he said. 'The man just moved from there two days ago. I'm heading up.'

Forty-Three

Rothschild's last house was less than a mile from Striker's home. It was in the same district, even the same neighbourhood. And because of this, Striker was on scene in less than five minutes.

He parked his car, an old model Saab, two blocks out so that he wouldn't alert the prowler, then made his way in on foot. He hiked along the edge of the park, under the cover of those trees, until he caught sight of the house.

The house was one of the older homes in the area, built on the east side of West 29th Avenue. It sat opposite the Pacific Spirit Regional Park, a 700-acre forest that ran from Dunbar all the way to the university grounds out west.

It was a Vancouver special – one large rectangle, without character or design, built in the early 1980s. The darkness hid the fact that the roof was missing shingles and the white stucco was marred with splotches of grey patchwork, but Striker knew the place well. It was in desperate need of repair, and that was just one of the factors that had prompted Rothschild to put the place up for sale.

Of course, Rosalyn dying had been the real crux.

From the cover of the trees, Striker studied the lot. The house and yard were saturated in darkness. No lights were on inside the house or outside in the yard. The nearest street lamp was two lots down, and the bulb was gone.

Striker watched and waited. He hoped that Patrol would be there soon.

But after a good five minutes, when no signs of movement occurred, his patience ran out. He drew his pistol and made his way across the street. When he reached the driveway, he spotted a broken window.

He pressed the mike. 'We have entry. Ground floor, north corner. I'm going in for a closer look.'

The Dispatcher came across the air: 'Backup is almost there, Detective. Car Echo 21 is en route.'

'Tell them to take the rear lane.'

He headed for the house.

As Striker crossed the yard, he turned the radio volume down to zero. The last thing he needed was radio chatter alerting the suspect. Once closer, he could see that the pane was not actually broken, but the entire window had been removed and placed to the side. He aimed his pistol into the darkness of the basement, then turned on his flashlight and lit up the interior.

Saw nothing.

With Rothschild having just moved to the Kerrisdale area, the house appeared to be empty now. Everything inside was quiet and still, and other than the window being removed, there were no signs of damage. Thoughts of a squatter sneaking inside the house fluttered through Striker's mind – they were always looking for recently vacated buildings – and he was about to ask Dispatch if there had been any similar calls in the area when he stopped hard.

Something stole his attention.

On the window frame were a few small specks. Like tiny patches of dirt that had been raked off the bottom of someone's shoe as they climbed inside.

Striker took a closer look at it, shone the flashlight down.

Within the muck were smaller patches of a whitish-grey powder – similar to what he'd seen down by the docks the previous morning. The sight turned his stomach hard.

Why would the bomber be at Rothschild's place?

Were he and the kids in danger?

Striker got on the air, and his voice was tight and low: 'I want a patrol unit sent to Sergeant Mike Rothschild's new home in Kerrisdale immediately. A two-man car. Station one cop out front and one out back. Tell them to stay with the family until I get there, and to be on their guard.'

The Dispatcher's tone was one of confusion. 'In *Kerrisdale*?' she asked.

'Just do it,' Striker ordered.

'Yes, Detective,' the Dispatcher replied. 'You want a canine unit started up?'

Striker stared at the whitish power on the windowsill. 'Immediately,' he said. 'And make sure he's a bomb dog.'

Forty-Four

The canine handler dispatched to the scene was Frank Faust. He came with his police dog, Nitro.

Striker was happy to hear it. Faust was a twenty-year veteran who'd done ten of those years in his hometown of Berlin, when he'd worked for the bomb squad in the Berlin Police Department.

The man knew his stuff.

Faust was on scene in minutes. His German accent was still strong as he asked for the scene details, and by the time Striker had explained them all, a one-man patrol unit had arrived to assist. The kid who got out was tall and gangly, with a dirty-blond fohawk hairstyle.

Striker motioned him over. 'You got a name?'

He nodded like a bobble-head doll. 'Kevin.'

'Okay, Kevin, listen up. I'll cover right and front; you cover left and rear. Got it?'

The young cop looked exceedingly nervous. 'Is this . . . is this really the bomber?'

'It ain't Martha Stewart.' Striker put on a smile in his best attempt to calm the rookie down. 'Look, just cover your points. Don't let anyone sneak up on us. And be wary of tripwires or IEDs.'

'IE *what*?'

'Bombs. Don't touch anything on the ground, no matter what it looks like. Boxes, cans, toys – not even a shoe, if you see one.'

The young cop said nothing; he just nodded and stared back through large, wide eyes. The quick debrief was over. With the dog leading the way, the three of them made entry through the basement window.

Immediately, the darkness deepened, and Striker shone his flashlight around the room, lighting up all four corners. When everything was clear, he nodded, and they progressed, searching through the basement, and then the upstairs level – living room, dining room, and kitchen. They cleared the bedrooms and bathrooms last of all, and found them to be empty.

Not even a few packing boxes were left.

Faust fed the dog more leash. 'So far so good.'

Striker said nothing back; he just kept scanning the way ahead as Nitro steered them to the garage entrance. Once there, the dog let out a whine. Striker reached out and touched the door. Leaned close to it. *Listened.*

'Hear anything?' the rookie asked.

Striker held up a hand demanding silence.

He gently wrapped his fingers around the doorknob and slowly turned it. Once it clicked, he gently, slowly, edged the door open. Just a quarter-inch. Then he shone his flashlight through the space between the door and frame, looking for the existence of any pull-wires and switches.

He found none.

'Garage looks clear from this angle,' he said. 'But be ready.'

He opened the door the rest of the way, and Nitro went inside. Panting hard, the German Shepherd walked less than ten steps, then came to a hard stop. He raised his tail high in the air.

'We got a positive,' Faust said.

The rookie stepped back. '*Positive?* What does that mean? A bomb? Is there a bomb in here?'

'Be quiet and cover us,' Striker told him.

'I need some light,' Faust said.

The young constable reached out to hit the light switch, but Striker snatched his hand away. 'If that switch is rigged to a detonator, it'll be the last one you ever throw, kid.'

'I . . . I . . .'

'Just watch our backs and *don't touch anything.*'

Striker shone his flashlight across the room – first hitting each of the four corners, then doing a thorough sweep of the floor, and last of all, highlighting the beams of the garage.

He saw nothing, so he turned to Faust. 'The dog is sure?'

Faust looked insulted. 'There's no room for error in this business.'

'So there's definitely a bomb in here?'

Faust shook his head. 'The dog detects *explosives,* not bombs.'

Striker considered this. 'Can he pick up trace elements?'

'He can pick up damn near anything, if the vapour pressure isn't too low.'

Striker had no idea what that meant but took it as good. 'So explosives could have been in this garage, but aren't necessarily here any more. Like with the drug dogs, it can pick up the lingering traces.'

Faust nodded. 'I'm gonna run him round the room a few times, see if he hits on any of the walls.'

Striker held his tongue and let the dog search. As he waited, his cell vibrated against his side. He grabbed it, looked down at the screen, and saw the name 'Mike Rothschild' across the display. He didn't answer for fear of triggering a detonation. Instead, he turned to Faust.

'You okay here?' he asked.

'We'll be fine.'

Satisfied, Striker told the rookie to maintain cover and then made his way back through the house. As he exited the front door, thoughts of his godchildren flashed through his head, images of Shana and Cody – two little kids who had already lost their mother to cancer. For them to lose Rothschild too was unthinkable, and the notion filled Striker with a dark, vacuous feeling.

He tried not to think about the what-ifs.

To the east, the sun was already rising. The roadway was lightening, the blackness being replaced by murky blue tones. At both ends of the street, red and blue police lights flashed, and in between them, a second dogman – Police Constable Hooch with his dog Lancer – was running the tree-line leading into Pacific Spirit Park.

Striker stared at all this as he dialled Rothschild's number. The call was picked up on the first ring, and Rothschild sounded upset: 'Jesus Christ, Shipwreck, what the hell is going on out there?'

'I'm not sure yet, Mike.'

'Well get sure. It's five in the goddam morning, and I got some pre-pubescent patrol cop banging on my door, telling me we need protection. That *my kids* need protection. And Cody overheard him, and now he's all freaking out . . . I mean, really, what the fuck?'

'It might have something to do with the bomber.'

Rothschild's voice grew quieter. 'The *bomber*?'

'He's been in your old house, Mike.'

'What? But . . .' Rothschild sounded confused. 'That makes no sense.'

Striker didn't have the answer. 'Just get your kids together into the centre of your house. In the basement. Away from all the windows. Keep your gun on you and stay alert. We'll talk when I get there.'

'Then get here fast, Shipwreck.'

'As soon as I can.'

Striker had no sooner hung up the phone when the dogman called out from one of the trails leading into the park: 'I got something here!' His dog suddenly darted deeper into the trail.

It gave Striker a bad feeling. The notion of the suspect escaping through the park had already crossed his mind; but any thoughts of catching him were dim at best. The Pacific Spirit Park was 700 acres big – essentially, a forest. It was too large for containment and it had endless places to hide. All they could do was track and hope for the best, and tracking a man like the bomber through the woods was dangerous.

Who knew what he had set up for them?

'Hold up!' Striker called out to Hooch. He drew his pistol and crossed the road. 'You're gonna need cover if you're tracking through there.'

He'd no sooner finished the sentence when a bright flash exploded in the trail, punctuated by a percussive boom that echoed hollowly in the woods. Lancer let out a high-pitched yelp, and Hooch reeled backwards as if hit. He screamed out in alarm. Dropped to his knees. Grabbed his face.

'. . . it burns! I'm on fire – on *fire*!'

Striker raced into the trail and, almost immediately, a strange red smoke began billowing out from between the trees. It stung his face, burned his eyes. He grabbed the dog handler by the back of his uniform and pulled hard.

Hooch let out a cry.

'I got you,' Striker said. 'I got you, Hooch.'

He pulled him out of the woods, back to safety. But the dog handler was panicking now. Screaming. Thrashing. Holding his face.

He was burning up.

Forty-Five

A hundred metres into the woods, from his observation point, the bomber used his binoculars to watch the pandemonium taking place below. The dog had tripped the wire, causing the red phosphorous incendiaries to flash and initiating the ultrasonic noisemaker. The device had been set to maximum frequency – undetectable to humans but painful to dogs.

Judging from the yelp of the police dog and the animal's retreat from the woods, the device was working fine. The dog handler's scream indicated that the oleoresin in the smoke bomb had suffused well into the air. Even now, that red smoke unfurled from the woods in enormous puffs, looking like giant swells of pink cotton candy in the morning twilight. The sight was actually quite beautiful and should have pleased him, but it did not.

The intel Molly had given him was bad. As such, all his recon and planning was for naught.

Rothschild had moved.

But when? And why? Molly had been here not seven days ago, scouting the area, drawing up the plans. It was yet one more strike of bad luck against them. One more unnecessary complication.

Like Chad Koda surviving the blast.

He closed his eyes. Picked at the wound of his left cheek. Struggled to find that calm. Struggled to believe. Moments like this were the difference, he knew. They were what had made them strong. What had kept them alive these past eleven years – their ability to improvise on any mission, no matter what they faced and regardless of the odds.

He and Molly were *survivors.*

Far below the hill from which he watched, in the mouth of the trail, the dog handler was still wailing. More fear than pain. The bomber adjusted the binoculars and zoomed in through the expanding cloud of pink mist. He focused on the big detective who was helping the dogman.

Jacob Striker; the cop he had seen on every news channel.

The man seemed to be an omnipotent force out there, always everywhere you least expected him. The bomber watched him evacuate the fallen dogman, drag him to the front lawn of the Rothschild house, and hold his head under the tap, drenching the man with water to rid the oleoresin. Then, after tending to the dogman, he began flushing out his own eyes.

A soldier.

Had this been Tora Bora or Baghdad again, the bomber would have chosen Striker as one of the men for his squad. But this was not Afghanistan or Iraq.

So he turned away.

Time was wearing thin, and he needed to reposition south before Jacob Striker returned to his car. That was where he needed to be. Down the road, waiting. Jacob Striker required more surveillance. For he was not only a workmate, but a friend of one of their next targets.

He would lead them to Mike Rothschild.

Forty-Six

It was early still, dark and cold, by the time Striker made it to Mike Rothschild's new home on Trafalgar Street. This house was smaller than his last one, and it was older too. Built in the 30s or 40s, Striker was sure. But it was nestled in the heart of Kerrisdale, close to Shana's and Cody's school. And moreover, it was the place of a new start.

Something the family direly needed.

After taking a quick scan of his surroundings and seeing no threats, Striker walked up the rear lane to the backyard. He opened the fence, passed under the sweeping boughs of the maple trees, and glanced inside the garage window.

Nothing seemed out of place. Inside the garage was Rothschild's teenage dream – his prized possession 1963 vintage Ford Cougar II. Ruby red in colour.

A collector's item.

When Mike had gotten it three years ago – a surprise gift from his beloved Rosie – he'd been like a sugar-loaded kid with a new *Star Wars* toy on Christmas morning. It was all he talked about. Now, ever since Rosalyn's death, he spent even more time working on the car, cleaning and waxing and polishing, making sure that not even a trace amount of dust covered the paint. It was a daily obsession. Almost religious to him – as if the slightest bit of grime would not only tarnish the car, but Rosie's memory as well.

And that was unforgivable.

'She's a beauty,' Striker had told him once.

Rothschild's eyes had watered at the comment. 'She was,' he'd said in return, and Striker had realized he was talking about Rosie.

Striker swallowed hard. The memory was not only fresh, but emotionally powerful, so he willed it away. He walked past the garage, triggered the motion detector, and was lit up by the backyard spotlight. Immediately, the kitchen blinds parted, and one of the patrol cops – a tall East Indian male with a turban – looked down at him.

Striker flashed him the badge, came up the porch stairs and walked inside. Before he could ask where Rothschild and the kids were waiting, Rothschild stepped from the living room into the kitchen. His face was tight, as was his posture. A strong-smelling cup of coffee was in his hand.

'Where are the kids?' Striker asked.

'Downstairs. With the other half of Echo 15.'

'They away from the windows?'

'They're safe.' Rothschild scrutinized him. 'What happened to your eyes? They're red.'

Striker blinked as if just remembering the pain. 'Oleoresin, or something similar. It got set off near your old house.'

'By who?'

'Our suspect.'

The notion turned Rothschild's face hard and his eyes took on a distant gaze.

Striker navigated between the piles of moving boxes that littered the kitchen floor and poured himself a cup of coffee. Rothschild, meanwhile, stood there looking lost and confused, rubbing his thumb against the side of his cup.

'What the fuck is going on, Shipwreck?' he finally said.

Striker turned around. 'Why don't you tell me?'

'What the hell's that supposed to mean?'

'You were my first sergeant, Mike. And you're my best goddam friend. So tell me the truth: do you have any connection to Sharise Owens or Keisha Williams – the two women who were killed yesterday?'

Rothschild looked taken aback by the question. 'I would have told you if I did. You know that.'

'You never had any calls where a bomber was suspected?'

'None. Not one in my entire career.'

'What about gangs – one that might have used electrical torture? Specifically, a picana? Like the Satan's Prowlers? Or the Renegades? Or the Basi Brothers?'

Rothschild let out a heavy breath. 'I've arrested tons of gang members over the years – from all those groups. But a fucking *picana*?' He shook his head. 'I've done and seen a lot in my career . . . but nothing like this.'

'What about Chad Koda?'

'*Koda?*' Rothschild raised an eyebrow. He crossed the room and poured himself a second cup. 'Well, there's a name I haven't heard in years.'

'So you do know him.'

'Of course, I know him. He was my first sergeant. Hell, you weren't even on the force yet. That was a good ten years before your time. Why'd you bring him up?'

'Because he was blown sky-high last night.'

Rothschild's face tightened. 'Blown . . . blown up? Like . . . *literally*?'

'Is there any other way?'

Rothschild kept blinking, as if something didn't compute. 'Why? I mean . . . *why*?'

'We don't know. He's in St Paul's right now. Has been all

night. He's unconscious. Blasted pretty good from what I understand, but still has all his limbs intact. He got lucky.'

'Doesn't sound like it. What time did this happen?'

'Long after you'd left. I'm surprised you haven't heard about the explosion – it's been on every damn news channel all night long.'

Rothschild gestured to the unpacked boxes all around the room. 'Do I look like I've had time to watch the news?'

Rothschild crossed the room to the kitchen table where several photos were spread out. The one in the centre was a family photo, taken when Rosalyn was still alive. Not long before her diagnosis. Rothschild looked at it, and his face took on a lost look. 'I came home last night, barbecued up some food for the kids, unpacked more stuff, and started going through *these* . . . When it got to be too much, I crashed down on a mattress on the floor. I slept there all night long – till Patrol started banging down my door.'

Striker turned his eyes away from the picture of Rosalyn, because every time he looked at it, painful memories returned. And not just ones of Rosalyn. Images – feelings – of what he had gone through with his own wife, Amanda, and with Courtney, following her mother's death. Every day had been a struggle back then. And now Rothschild was going through the same hell.

Striker felt for his friend, but didn't know what to do. So he tried to see through the memories and find some clarity. He cleared his throat and changed the subject.

'What can you tell me about Chad Koda?' he asked.

'Chad? I dunno. He was a good guy. Good boss. And he was *smart*. Jaded, sure, but who the hell isn't after all that time?' Rothschild smiled grimly. 'I remember him bitching about the courts a million times a day. He really hated them. "It's a legal system," he used to say. "Not a justice system." How's that for truth?'

'And?'

Rothschild shrugged. 'And what? Koda reached the mandatory minimum and took his leave. Got out of the VPD years ago. Went into real estate. And from what I hear, he does pretty good . . . How is he connected in all this?'

Striker hedged the issue. 'All I know is I got Koda in the hospital, and Keisha Williams and Sharise Owens are dead from two separate bomb blasts. And now, with the suspect being found at your house, Koda is the only real connection I can see here. He knows all three of you.'

Rothschild looked like his mind was a million miles away. 'I just can't see why.'

'He's left a couple of dolls at the scene,' Striker said. 'They've obviously been broken up from the blast, but they might be policemen the way they were dressed. And each one of them has had a number drawn on the chest. That mean anything to you?'

Rothschild just shook his head again. Looked lost.

'Nothing,' he said.

Striker was about to say more when the door to the basement opened and Shana walked into the room. She was dressed in a pair of long-sleeved pyjamas, pink in colour, with princesses and unicorns on them – the perfect motif for any six-year-old girl. Upon seeing Striker, she smiled wide.

'Uncle Jacob!' she said.

She stumbled sleepily across the room and gave him a long, hard hug.

Striker squeezed her back. 'How's my little cupcake?'

'You didn't come over last night.'

'I know. I tried to, but—'

'You had to work.'

Striker smiled grimly. Pretty sad when even a six-year-old knows the same old song and dance.

'Next time,' he said.

'You promise?'

'How 'bout I don't promise, but I bring you some ice cream later?'

The little girl smiled. 'Okay.'

Seconds later, Shana's brother shambled through the doorway. Though Cody was only twenty minutes younger, he had not yet shed some of his childhood insecurities. He clutched his light-blue blankie and rubbed his eyes. He looked at the uniformed patrol cop who had been standing there completely silent the whole time, then at Striker.

'What's going on?' the boy asked.

Striker tussled his hair. 'Police Parade.' When Cody just looked at him through sleepy eyes, Striker told him, 'It's still awfully early, my little man.'

'And the adults are talking,' Rothschild said.

'About what?' the boy asked.

'You two need to go back to bed, son.'

'But Dad—'

'No buts from either one of you.'

Rothschild took both children by the hand and guided them back to the stairwell, where the second member of Echo15 – a short, plump policewoman – was standing. Once the children were being ushered down the stairs, Shana glanced back at Striker and waved.

'Goodnight, Uncle Jacob.'

'Pleasant dreams,' he whispered.

Then they were gone – in presence but not in mind. The image of the little girl remained in Striker's head. Shana was so much like her mother, in personality and appearance. And

Striker wondered how hard that was on Rothschild. When Striker's own wife, Amanda, had died several years earlier, he had seen her every day in his own daughter – every time Courtney smiled, or laughed, and even when she cried.

It had been emotionally exhausting.

It was something he loved and hated all at once, a reflection that constantly filled him with life and yet killed him at the same time. He wondered at what point he had finally got over that. Time seemed a blur.

When Rothschild returned, Striker threw back the rest of his coffee.

'I gotta go,' he said.

'What – where?'

'Koda is the hub in all this. I need to talk to the man.'

'I thought you said he was unconscious.'

'He is.' Striker dropped his cup in the sink and headed for the door. 'Sleeping Beauty's about to get a wake-up call.'

Forty-Seven

Striker drove to the police fleet lot.

He grabbed an undercover cruiser – one of the new Ford Fusions with the reinforced bumper – and made sure the laptop was working and fully charged. He then checked to be sure the trunk was filled with paper evidence bags and latex gloves. Satisfied, he picked up Felicia from the front steps of Cambie Street Headquarters.

'You should have called me,' she said as she climbed in.

'There wasn't time.'

'For a phone call?'

'Hey, I wouldn't have had to call you at all if you'd just stayed the night like I asked.'

Felicia gave him a cool glance. 'Are you really going to use that against me?'

He sighed. 'Look, I'm tired and it's already been a hell of a morning. Nothing but bad news, bad news, and more bad news.'

'Well here's some good. While I was waiting for you, I did some more searching, and guess who I located? Solomon Bay.'

Striker felt a smile return to his lips. 'Where?'

'Oakville Hospital, Toronto.'

'Toronto?'

'He's sick, Jacob.'

'How sick?'

'Sick enough that he's no longer considered a suspect in this file. He's got some strange degenerative disease. An immune disorder. He's been bedridden for over three years now, which is why we couldn't locate any more history on the guy.'

'This all documented?'

Felicia nodded. 'He's not our guy.'

Striker said nothing at first, he just let the information sink in. Ruling Solomon out was necessary, but it left him with an empty feeling. Like someone had stolen something from him.

One more lead destroyed.

He hit the gas and headed for St Paul's Hospital so that they could speak to Chad Koda. Along the way, he gave Felicia a rundown on all that had happened this morning. By the time they arrived some ten minutes later, she was as befuddled as he was about the file.

They headed inside the hospital.

Admitting was unusually calm, even for a Thursday morning. No patients lined up at the front desk. No paramedics or cops gathered in the lobby. No drunks or mental health apprehensions screamed in the waiting area.

Sitting behind the counter was the same girl who had helped them yesterday. When she saw Striker, a nervous look flittered in her eyes, as if she was thinking *Oh God, what now?*

Striker and Felicia passed her by. They took the elevator to the third floor, where the Critical Care Unit was located. As always, the doors were electronically locked. A small round nurse of black ancestry scanned them inside.

'Dis way,' she said softly.

Striker followed her down to Koda's room.

Standing on duty outside the door was a Caucasian cop. Big, bald, and fat with lots of padded muscle bulk. A long vertical scar made his already-hard face appear even more fierce, and

Striker was glad they had posted this guy at the door. He looked like a mixture of an Ultimate Fighter and a Hollywood soldier.

The cop craned his neck at the sight of them and demanded to see their badges. After a quick show of credentials, they went inside.

The recovery room was private, holding only one bed and a chair. Everywhere Striker looked, there were degrees of white – from the faded ivory bed sheets to the cream-coloured curtains to the sterile eggshell of the walls. The only object that held any true colour was the quilt that ran across the lower half of the bed. It was pale blue.

Like Cody's security blankie.

Felicia wrinkled her nose. 'It always smells like bleach in here.'

Striker nodded. 'Cologne of the sick.'

He approached the bed. Lying on his back was Chad Koda. The man's eyes were closed and didn't look like they were moving beneath the lids. A line of stitches ran up the bridge of the man's nose and continued right up his forehead well into his shaved hairline.

It looked like a purple-red zipper.

Striker moved out of the man's earshot, pointed at the scar, and whispered to Felicia. 'Still think he was trying to stage an attack on himself?' When Felicia said nothing, he added, 'An inch more to the right or left, and the metal would have taken his eye out.'

Felicia also kept her voice low. 'If it was a murder-suicide, he wouldn't have cared. Besides, it was just a *theory*, Jacob. Something to consider and rule out.'

'Well consider it ruled out. This bomber's started a countdown. We don't have time to entertain other theories.'

Felicia shot him a look of daggers, and Striker turned away. He was being a dick, he knew, and not because of the case but because Felicia hadn't stayed the night. It was unfair. He got that. But for some reason, he couldn't let it go.

He assessed the man. On Koda's face, surrounding the line of stitches, was a mottling of abrasions that were already turned a bruised-banana colour at the edges. Bruises also marred his right cheek and right chin. Yet the other side of him was completely untouched.

'Two-Face,' Felicia said dryly.

'In more ways than one.'

Striker stepped right up to the bed, until his hip touched the tubular steel railing. Lines were hooked from Koda's left arm and chest; they ran to a trio of machines that sat bedside. One machine was designed to regulate pulse and blood pressure; one was for fluids; and one was for something Striker didn't know.

'Koda,' he said softly, then a little louder. '*Koda*.'

There was no response. Not even a blip on the machine.

Felicia frowned. 'He's really out of it.'

'Koda,' Striker said again, and gently squeezed his forearm.

'Please, you do not touch this man.' The voice came from the doorway, and was heavily accented. Eastern European maybe.

Striker craned his neck and spotted a doctor he did not recognize from any of his previous visits. The man was tall with a thick rug of silver hair and eyes so dark they appeared black.

'I am Dr Varga,' the man offered.

'Detectives Striker and Santos.' Striker flashed him the badge. 'Vancouver Police. We need to speak to this man.'

The doctor shook his head. 'That will not be possible. We sedate this man very much last night. He will not communicate for several hours.'

'Can't you wake him? Just for a few minutes? Time is crucial here.'

Dr Varga shook his head. 'The body of this man does require much rest.'

'I understand that,' Striker said. 'And I wouldn't ask if it wasn't completely necessary. But right now, we have a bomber out there in the city, and this man might be our only key to stopping him.'

The doctor's expression turned from defiance to concern. 'This is an unfortunate thing, I know. But to administer further medications would be negligent. There is too much risk.'

Felicia humphed. 'Tell that to the next victim who gets blown up.'

When Dr Varga offered no response, but merely stood there, looking uncomfortable, Striker pulled out one of his business cards and shoved it in the man's hand. 'Call me the second he wakes up, Doctor.'

'I will do this. Anything else I can do?'

Striker gave the man a hard, unforgiving look. 'Yes. Pray to God no one else is dead by then.'

Forty-Eight

The bomber stood between the two houses on the east side of Trafalgar Street, under the shadows of the roof overhang, and struggled with the tremors inside of him. Deep pulsations racked his head. Bounced around in his skull. It had been this way ever since the explosion at Chad Koda's house – an invisible tide lapping the shores of his mind.

He killed the thought and got back to recon. To planning. He focused on Rothschild's new home. The place had been easy to find – just one single tail of Detective Striker's Saab along the winding, empty roadways of Dunbar.

Right now, security there was omnipresent. A minimum of three cops were on scene at all times – one out front, one in the rear, and one on the upper floor somewhere. He suspected there was one more downstairs, but had not yet confirmed that suspicion. And the more he tried to sort out the information, the more his brain throbbed. A constant, steady thud-thud-thud.

It was maddening, the price he had to pay for sanity.

At his side, the cell phone vibrated. It was the black model – he always carried two.

For personal reasons.

The ringer and LCD display had been deactivated, so as to not attract unwanted attention. But display or no display, he knew the caller. There was only one person who knew this number: Molly. And he was not happy with her.

He answered.

'Bombs-R-Us,' he said dryly.

There was a slight pause. 'Oh bugger, that's not funny – what if someone overheard you?'

He made no reply.

'Do you have a good VP?' she asked.

'Vantage Point is good,' he said. 'Wait – hold on.'

Across the street, a uniformed cop exited the house and walked down the sidewalk. Seconds later, another police cruiser pulled up. The driver handed the other cop a tray of coffees. Two cups. Then the first cop returned inside the house, and the cruiser drove away.

Two cops inside the house, he thought.

Now he knew.

'Are you still there?' Molly asked. 'What's going on?'

His head was pounding, like there was a bass drum set up behind his eyes. 'The vantage point is fine,' he got out. 'The situation is not. It's a tactical nightmare . . . We need to reassess and replan.'

Molly made an unhappy sound. 'Sounds a bit dodgy. Our timeline's already way off.'

'And whose fault is that?'

She hesitated. 'I beg pardon?'

'Intel and acquisitions is your job.'

'What exactly are you implying?'

'That if you were less worried about *how* I set off the bombs and *how much* explosives I used, you might have realized that Rothschild was moving.'

'That's not fair.'

'Life's not fair. All I know is we used less explosives, and now Chad Koda is still alive.'

Molly hung up on him.

A half-minute later, the cell phone vibrated again – not with a phone call but an email message. He opened it up. The header was from: HMPSC – The Hazardous Materials Product Safety Commission.

He read the email:

> Notice: Recall
> Product: Pentaerythritol tetranitrate. Also known as PETN, PENTA and Nitropenta.

The details that followed focused on *distance time-progression* and *linear burn rates*. The news release had been issued by the company's media relations unit only seventeen minutes ago. It told him one important thing: their execution had been fine; the materials were faulty.

It was not Molly's fault.

His cell buzzed again, and he picked up.

'Well?' Molly asked.

'I was wrong.'

'So now what do we do?'

He said nothing, he just thought everything over. Given the timeline they were on, there were few remaining choices. Obtaining more PETN would take time they didn't have and require more risk. Buying other explosives through the black market was even more dangerous. The more he assessed their situation, the more he realized there was no choice in the matter.

'Pick me up,' he finally said. 'It's time to cook.'

Forty-Nine

Striker and Felicia stopped on Denman Street at Striker's favourite coffee shop – an old mom & pop business named Rafello's. The coffee was always strong and the sandwiches were good, and the old couple had been kind to Striker since his first days in Patrol. Striker liked to give them the business. They grabbed a couple of breakfast melts, then ate in the car and went over the bomber's MO.

'Whoever he is, the man is smart,' Striker said. 'Not only does he have the expertise to work with explosive materials, but he knows assembly as well. Add to this the fact he can do surveillance, swim the goddam channel, and has knowledge of various torture devices – in particular electrical – and we can narrow down our search. Military is the first thing that comes to mind.'

'Or some kind of mercenary,' Felicia agreed. 'Possibly a gang hitman or a professional assassin. So much depends on the motive. All that aside, we can't rule out someone with a basic explosives training.'

Striker nodded. 'Like an engineer from a mining company. Or someone in any of the pyrotechnic fields. Even a teacher of explosives would be plausible.'

'*Any* demolitions guy,' Felicia agreed. 'I looked up a few things on Google, and you can learn how to perform surveillance. Hell, there's not only lessons online, but entire courses you can actually take. And not only on surveillance, but counter-surveillance. And as for the associated electronic gadgetry, well you can order that stuff right on Amazon.'

'And the electrical torture?'

'Same thing, I'm afraid. I've never dealt with a picana before, but I looked it up on the net and found directions on how to make one. It's crazy, I know, but I found it.'

The information was disheartening, and Striker shook his head absently. 'So what you're saying is, the MO might point towards a person with this kind of expertise, but a lot of people with the willpower and tools could do this on their own.'

'Unfortunately, yes. It's all just a click away.'

Striker frowned. 'Which is why we keep finding ourselves back at square one, waiting on lab results and following the trails and connections of our victims.' He shook his head and drank some more coffee. 'It's so damn frustrating.'

Felicia agreed. She threw her half-eaten breakfast melt in the garbage and spoke. 'With Solomon ruled out, Koda's our best lead.'

'Well, he's on hold for now.'

She nodded for a long moment, as if debating something. Finally, she crooked her neck to look at him. 'What about Harry?'

'Harry *Eckhart*?' Striker asked. 'He's a cop, Feleesh.'

'I know that, Jacob. But don't forget, Koda was also a cop. And like it or not, Harry's the only other person I can think of who's got some kind of connection to everyone involved.'

'When the first bomb went off, Harry was stuck in a traffic jam on the bridge.'

'I'm not saying he was the actual bomber, Jacob, but he might know more than he's telling us. I'll tell you this: *something's* up with the man. He's been acting downright odd.'

Striker said nothing and thought it over. It was true. Harry did have links to Chad Koda, Keisha Williams, and even Dr Sharise Owens, indirectly. And the man had seemed resistant with the information about Solomon Bay.

But still, Striker gave the idea little credence; he'd known Harry for years. And as hard-nosed and irascible as the man could be, he was a good cop. Always had been. Through the death of his son. Through the breakup of his first marriage. Through everything.

Striker liked the man.

As they both sat there, mulling over the facts, a pair of Harley Davidsons roared by. With their mufflers obviously removed, the motorcycles' loud rumbles shook the street.

Irritated, Striker looked up. The two bikers were members of the Satan's Prowlers gang – the affiliation made obvious by the weeping-skull patch on their jackets. The smaller of the two riders craned his neck and met Striker's stare. He smirked, gave a mock salute, and the bikes drove away.

'Don't you need an IQ greater than three to get a licence?' Felicia asked.

Striker said nothing at first. He just looked at the stereo clock. 'Odd time for them to be out. Early.'

'They're probably still partying from last night.'

Striker said nothing else. The sight reminded him of something else – something their weapons expert, Jay Kolt, had told them:

Some of the high-end gangs use electrical torture, like the Satan's Prowlers.

Striker turned to Felicia. 'Kolt mentioned a biker named Sleeves. Burns was his real name. Or something like that. See what you can find on the man.'

Felicia made an *ahh* sound, then started punching the name into the computer. Two mandatory fields.

Gang Affiliations: Satan's Prowlers.

Surname: Burns.

After a moment, she smiled. 'Direct hit. Brice Burns. Alias: Sleeves.'

Striker looked at the screen and whistled. 'Three pages of files – this guy's a career criminal.'

'He's a dirt-bag, is what he is.'

Striker smirked. Felicia wasn't one to refrain from speaking her mind.

As she began reading through the list of reports and Intel files, Striker put the car into gear and drove around the corner onto Pacific Avenue. Chad Koda's house was just a mile away, and he wanted to visit the scene again, free of all the chaos.

They were still missing something.

He could feel it.

When they arrived, Striker pulled in behind a white utility van that had the Vancouver Police Department crest on the door and a large dent in the rear panel. It was Ident's van.

'Noodles is here.'

Felicia didn't even look up. 'Be still, my beating heart.'

'I need to talk to him about the different scenes. Can you run the bomb call for me before I go on? See if the forensic team's added anything to the file since we last checked.'

Felicia said 'sure' and brought up the report. It was long, filled with numerous evidence pages, police logs, and scanned-in civilian statements which were now in PDF format. Striker read the last supplement link which was marked: Canvass.

'Open that one,' he said.

Felicia did. The page was divided into three columns – one for the addresses that had been canvassed, one for the names of the witnesses living there, and one for whether or not any evidence had been obtained. Out of the eight other homes on the block, only three of them had been occupied during the time of the explosion. Three of the residences had '(PV)' beside their addresses.

PV: *Possible Video.*

Felicia took the initiative. 'You talk to Noodles. I'll check out these addresses.'

'Sounds like a plan.'

They exited the car and parted ways.

As Felicia walked northward down the block, Striker headed for the stairs leading up to Koda's residence. Halfway there, he stopped, turned around, and watched Felicia go.

In her dark women's suit, with her long black hair draping down to her shoulders, she looked professional and pretty at the same time. As if sensing his gaze, she glanced back and caught him. A grin parted her lips, and she mouthed the words 'stop fantasizing'. Then she turned into a nearby lot.

With Felicia disappeared from sight, Striker approached Koda's residence. The look of the house was deceiving. Aside from the blown-out windows and the string of police tape blocking off the front yard, nothing indicated that anything was amiss – certainly not that a bomb had gone off, killing one woman and injuring the homeowner.

In the exterior alcove stood a young constable – a tall white guy with his head shaved. He greeted Striker without interest, but did his job and recorded Striker's badge number for the continuity purposes required. Once done, Striker went past the man.

Inside the foyer, Striker donned a pair of blue forensic booties to be sure he didn't track any trace evidence from one location to the next. In the living room, den and kitchen areas, yellow markers had been set up – cones with numbers on them – and all along the wall and counter surfaces, the black powder traces of the fingerprinting process could be seen. Noodles was still there, standing in the kitchen with his camera. He took a photo, looked at the camera display, and cursed.

'Not working?' Striker asked.

Noodles frowned. 'Damn thing keeps losing focus – must be one of them female models.' He let out a dark chuckle.

'Felicia would have your balls for breakfast if she heard that.'

'She must be a big eater then.'

Striker ignored the comment and shook his head. He stepped into the kitchen and examined the scene. 'You run that white powder from the dock yet?'

Noodles lowered the camera. His expression was one of exhaustion, and his thick white eyebrows drooped. 'Yeah. Turns out it was fairy dust. Got a lead too. First name: *Tinker*. Last name: *Bell*.'

'I need those results, Noodles.'

The Ident tech splayed his hands. 'Everyone needs everything. I got *five* crime scenes on the go – the torture room, the dock, the toy shop, the Break and Enter at Rothschild's old house, and this explosion here. It's a forensic fucking nightmare, and my assistant's at home with the shits.' He raised the camera and took another picture before wiping the sweat from his brow. 'Fucking hot as hell this morning.'

Striker looked at the mess all around them – the cones, the fingerprinting powders, the discarded pile of booties in the garbage can. 'I can't tell what does more damage – the bomb, or you guys.'

Noodles grumbled something incoherent, and Striker left to investigate the other rooms.

Due to the high price of downtown real estate, the house had been designed tall and narrow – three storeys, each floor consisting of nine-foot-high ceilings. Striker climbed to the uppermost floor, which owned nothing but a large bedroom with en suite, a small office, and an outdoor patio area. Outside, red brick was the decor. Inside it was cherry wood and teak.

Even the quickest glance was telling. Koda had amassed a wealth that was well beyond what any cop could dream of. Striker wasn't sure of the house's city-assessed value, but there was little doubt it would be several million.

Six would be his guess.

He searched it all, room by room, and took his time going through the drawers and any papers he found. In the end, the result was the same. There was nothing of evidentiary value to be seized. And, equally surprisingly, he found nothing that connected Koda to his previous life as a cop. No squad plaques. No framed commendations. No retirement badge. Just . . . nothing.

It was as if the man had wiped his previous life clean.

Disappointed, Striker returned downstairs just in time to see Felicia walk through the front door.

'Well?' he asked. 'You get anything?'

She gave him a queer look. 'Something odd.'

'What?'

'I got video of Harry . . . coming by the house here yesterday.'

'Yeah, we saw him.'

'Not after the explosion – *before*.'

Striker frowned. 'You check the tape time? Make sure it matched your watch?'

She gave him a look that said *I'm-not-an-idiot*. 'Yes, it's correct. Pacific Standard Time. There's no denying it. Harry came by here not a half-hour before the bomb went off. It makes me wonder why.'

Striker nodded. 'It makes me wonder why he never told us – he said he hadn't talked to Koda in years.'

The questions hung there for a long moment. Then Striker's cell went off, breaking the silence. He looked down and saw the words 'St Paul's Hospital' on the display screen. He picked up the call and heard a thick, Eastern European accent:

'Detective Striker, if you will please.'

'This is him.'

'It's Dr Varga. Mr Koda is awake now.'

Striker felt his fingers tighten on the phone.

'Do *not* let him go back to sleep. We're heading right up.'

Fifty

A young redheaded nurse who looked no more than twenty swiped Striker and Felicia into the Critical Care Unit. The halls were busier than the last time they'd been there, with pods of nurses and doctors in the middle of their morning rounds. The scene appeared ordinary, routine . . . but something about it felt wrong. When Striker neared the halfway point of the corridor and spotted the door to room 315, he understood why.

No patrolman stood in the hall.

'Where's the guard?' Felicia asked.

Striker hurried down to the room. Dropped his hand near his pistol. Pushed open the door.

Inside, the room was empty. On the bed, the steel rail guard had been lowered and the comforters were folded back. Next to the bed, the blood pressure and heart rate monitors stood unattached. The bathroom door was closed. Striker knocked on it. When no one answered, he opened it up and looked inside.

Empty.

He got on his cell and called Dispatch. Sue Rhaemer answered with a 'What-up, Rockstar?'

'Save it, Sue. I'm in no mood.'

'Pissy.'

'You got no idea. I'm standing here at St Paul's Hospital and Chad Koda is gone. I need you to raise the guard for me.'

'Okay, one sec.' The soft clicks of a keyboard filled the phone, then Sue Rhaemer made a confused sound. 'Weak. Says here that the unit cleared, like, ten minutes ago.'

'Cleared?'

Striker frowned; ten minutes ago was the same time Dr Varga had called to tell them Chad Koda was awake. It made no sense. He was about to get Sue to raise that unit when the door to the recovery room swung open and the doctor walked inside.

'I'll call you back, Sue.' Striker hung up and turned to the doctor. 'Where is Chad Koda?'

Dr Varga frowned. 'Mr Koda is released.'

'*Released?*' Felicia said. 'In his condition? The man was half killed.'

The frown on Varga's face turned into an expression of concern. 'I tried to make him stay. But the man would not listen to reason.'

Striker stepped into the doctor's personal space. 'He's supposed to be under police guard.'

Dr Varga looked confused. 'But . . . he *was* under police guard. The officer released him.'

Striker felt his jaw tightening. 'What officer? *Who* released him?'

Dr Varga looked down at the pad in his hand and searched for the name of the releasing officer. After a long moment, he found it.

'Detective Harry Eckhart,' he said.

Fifty-One

Striker was seething.

The moment he and Felicia exited the hospital, he whipped out his cell phone and dialled Harry's number. It rang three times, then went straight to voicemail. He hung up, dialled again, and got the same response. This time he left a message telling Harry to call him – immediately.

'This is giving me a headache,' Felicia said.

'Nothing like the one Harry's going to have after I throttle him.'

Striker called Dispatch back and got Sue Rhaemer to raise Harry over the air. She said it was no problem and put him on hold while she did this. Almost five minutes later, the line clicked and Rhaemer returned.

'Well?' Striker demanded.

'Okay, don't spaz on me this time, but this guy is weak, man. *Weak*.'

'Weak? What the hell you talking about, Sue?'

'He's not answering the broadcasts.'

'You try all districts?'

'Of course. *And* the Ops channels.'

Striker closed his eyes, felt the tension swelling inside of him. 'Thanks, Sue. I'll be in touch.'

'Rock till ya drop,' she said, and the line went dead.

They headed back for the car. As they walked, Striker turned silent and thought things over. When they reached the cruiser, he snapped his fingers and looked at Felicia. 'I got it – Harry doesn't drive one of the Fusions, does he?'

Felicia thought it over. 'No, he's old school. He likes the older Ford sedans. So what?'

'In the Crown Vics, the GPS is built right into the dashboard, not the laptop.'

She caught on and smiled. 'We can trace him.'

Striker called the Fleet Manager and found out which car Harry had signed out for the day. Sure enough, it was one of the Crown Vics.

Call sign: *Juliet 13.*

With the vehicle ID now known, Striker called back Dispatch. He gave Sue Rhaemer the call sign and asked her to locate the vehicle with the GPS system. She made an uneasy sound. 'You do realize we're only supposed to use GPS in cases of emergencies, right?'

'This *is* an emergency, Sue. You're preventing a homicide – because I'm going to kill Harry if he screws up my case.'

The Central Dispatcher laughed, but said nothing.

'I'm desperate here, Sue.'

'Oh fine, just . . . *chill.*'

Striker heard the woman typing on the terminal. Moments later, when she came back on the line, her voice was rough. 'Okay, listen up. The car's gone mobile. East on Hastings. Three thousand block.'

Striker nodded absently. 'Thanks, Sue. As always.'

He put the car in gear.

'Time for some surveillance?' Felicia asked.

Striker nodded, but did not smile. The fact that they were actually spying on another cop, and a man he had liked for years, did not sit well with him. And thoughts of what it might possibly lead them to left him feeling ill and anxious.

He stepped on the gas and the car surged down the road. He headed east after Harry, searching for evidence, but – maybe for the first time in his career – hoping to come up zero.

Fifty-Two

Harry drove across the Vancouver-Burnaby border and eventually turned left on Gilmore Street. Sitting beside him in the passenger seat, hazy from the medications but conscious, was Chad Koda. The man was looking out the window at nothing in particular and groaned constantly.

Harry stole a glance at him.

Chad Koda looked *bad.* The zipper sutures up the middle of his face were even more noticeable in the daylight, and because the hospital had shaved the top of his head during the process, the entire length of the injury was apparent. It extended from the middle of his nose all the way to the top of his skull.

It was amazing he had survived.

'You gonna make it there?' Harry asked.

Koda made no reply. He just took another T3 and shoved it under his tongue. After a long moment, he cleared his throat.

'I want him dead for this,' he finally said.

Harry let the comment hang there for a moment, then he gave Koda a cool look. 'We need to be calm here. *Smart.*'

Koda gave him a hot look. 'I almost got killed here, Harry. My whole fucking life – *gone.*'

'Your whole life will be gone if you flap those lips to the wrong person.'

'I know what I can and can't say.'

'Not when you're all doped-up on meds, you don't.'

Koda said nothing back, but his pale face darkened.

Harry took a sudden right down a narrow back lane and parked ten feet from the rear of his yard. The garage door opener was on the fritz again, so he got out and left the car parked in the lane. When they entered the garage, Harry closed the door securely behind them. He plugged in the radio. Cranked the volume.

'*Now* we can talk.'

Fifty-Three

With the aid of Central Dispatcher Sue Rhaemer and the GPS , Striker learned that Harry's undercover cruiser was stationary in the Burnaby area. He and Felicia drove there, and within minutes found the old Ford. It was sitting empty in the north lane of Pandora Street, parked alongside a detached garage.

Felicia looked up from the computer and studied the house. She saw the address number on the garage. 'This is Harry's place.' She looked around and saw no one. 'They must have gone inside.'

'Or into the garage,' Striker noted. 'Otherwise, why not park out front?'

He drove the undercover cruiser past the lane entrance, a half block down the road, then put the car into Park and jumped out.

'What are you doing?' Felicia asked.

'Take the wheel and wait for my call.'

'Shouldn't we both—'

'I need you driving in case they bolt again.'

'But—'

'Who's better at driving surveillance?' he asked.

'Well, me.'

'Exactly. You were the one in Strike Force, Feleesh, not me. So just be ready. We're gonna need to follow these guys when they leave. You'll be driving.'

Before Felicia could respond, Striker did a one-eighty and walked down the lane. Like most alleys in the area, the road was extremely narrow, with just enough room for one car to travel down. It was decorated with City garbage cans and blue recycle boxes.

Striker reached the old Ford Harry had been driving and looked inside. On the back seat were some McDonald's hamburger wrappers and a booklet for the Vancouver Police Union. On the floor was a torn-off hospital tag. Along the lateral edge of the band was a red line and the words 'Allergic to Penicillin'. The name on the front was visible:

Chad Heath Koda.

Striker looked around the lane, then at Harry's backyard. No one was there. So he focused on the house. It was a plain model, just a rectangular box. All the windows were dark, upstairs and down, and there was no movement inside.

No one appeared to be home.

Striker approached the lot. As he reached the garage, the soft sound of music filtered through the door. It was quiet, almost inaudible, but there. He moved closer and realized it was a radio – with voices intermingled.

He placed one ear against the door and listened. All he could make out were mumbles, so he rounded the garage. On the west side of the structure was a small window. As Striker neared it, he caught a glimpse of the two men inside.

Harry and Koda.

Having a conversation of some kind.

A *serious* one.

Koda was slowly pacing the room on wobbly legs and looked ready to keel over at any moment. His split-apart face was gaunt and looked freakish. Unreal, like a Halloween mask. Harry was sitting on a milk crate in the centre of the room, leaning with his elbows on his knees. His red and puffy face held only one expression:

Concern.

Striker crouched down low enough to hide under the ledge and tried to eavesdrop on the conversation, but all he could make out was the din of the radio. Gently, he reached up and tried to inch open the window, but it would not budge and he feared making too much noise.

From his pocket, he withdrew his Spyderco knife and flicked open the blade. Wedging it in between the window and frame, Striker gently pried until the window creaked open a quarter of an inch.

Then he listened.

Fifty-Four

'. . . the little fuckin' prick.' The voice was jittery but deep, and definitely belonged to Chad Koda.

'Well, that little prick is their Sergeant-at-Arms,' Harry replied.

'*Used* to be the Sergeant-at-Arms – they fuckin' aced him.'

'When?'

'Who cares? The little shit's using again. And now he needs money, he's *demanding* money.'

There was a pause in the conversation.

'How much?' Harry asked.

'Thirty thou.'

'Call him . . . Just . . . call him.'

'I can't,' Koda replied. 'I don't have his number – he calls me.'

Harry said nothing for a long moment. When he spoke again, his voice had changed. There was a heaviness in his tone. An acceptance.

'I will deal with this,' he said.

Fifty-Five

Ten minutes later, Striker sat in the undercover cruiser with Felicia. They were parked in a T-lane three blocks north of Harry's house, under the cover of someone's garage. Striker finished debriefing Felicia on everything he had overheard Harry and Koda saying. When done, he felt emotionally drained. Like he'd just ratted out an old friend.

'Sounds awfully cryptic,' Felicia said.

He nodded. 'And yet some things are pretty clear.'

'Like?'

'Like they're being blackmailed. And by the sounds of it, by someone dangerous – when they're talking about a Sergeant-at-Arms, they're not referring to the army, Feleesh. It's *gang* related. And that's a pretty high rank.' He scowled as he thought back. 'You should have seen Koda. He was hyped up and raving . . . but he was scared too. You could hear it in his voice.'

'Well, he did just get blown up.'

'He's unstable.'

'And Harry?'

Striker shook his head. 'He sounds very serious.'

Felicia thought things over. 'The big question here is *why* are they being blackmailed?'

Striker looked for connections in both the men. Harry and Koda were old friends. They had both worked for the Vancouver

Police Department. And they had both worked for similar units, though Koda was often seconded. Striker searched for a relevant section and found one.

'Harry and Koda both worked in OMG.'

'The Outlaw Motorcycle Gang section?'

He nodded. 'Yeah. It was broken up long before your time, assimilated into the Gang Crime Unit.' When Felicia said nothing else, Striker continued. 'Our options here are pretty straightforward – we can either confront them and be done with it, or we can do some surveillance on these guys. See where it takes us.'

Felicia thought it over. 'Harry and Koda aren't stupid. They're cops. They know the system. If we confront them, they'll just lie or clam up – especially if they're involved in something dirty.'

Something dirty . . .

The words bothered Striker.

He thought over what Felicia had said, and he agreed. Surveillance was the right choice for now. The only negative aspect was that surveillance took time. And how much more time did they have before another bomb went off somewhere in the city?

How much time before another person was murdered?

Striker let out a long breath. 'This is a dangerous game we're playing.'

'It's not *our* game,' Felicia said. 'It's the system's. And besides, what choice do we have? Oh shit, heads up, they're moving again.'

Striker looked down the road to where Felicia was gesturing. From the mouth of the laneway, Harry's undercover Ford cruiser exited, then sped south on Gilmore. It turned west on Hastings Street and was gone from sight.

Felicia hit the gas in pursuit. Once she had the Crown Vic in sight again, she pulled into the slow lane of Hastings Street and used a transit bus as cover.

Striker touched her arm. 'Not too close.'

'I know how to do this, Jacob.'

'Harry spent three years in property crime – he knows surveillance. He'll spot us if we screw up.'

Felicia cast him a cocky look. 'And as you so clearly pointed out, I spent three years in Strike Force. I *taught* surveillance.'

Striker admired her boldness. He kept his mouth shut.

Felicia sped in and out of traffic, tailing Harry all the way from Willingdon Heights to Grandview-Woodlands. Once there, Harry took a hard right on Semlin Drive.

'He's heading into the industrial area,' Striker noted.

Felicia slowed down and slipped into the A&W burger stand. From past experience she knew that the burger joint had an elevated parking lot from which they could see all of Semlin Drive. They parked in one of the stalls and spied on the two men.

Across the road, Harry pulled in front of an old warehouse. He parked under the telephone wires, and the two men climbed out. They made their way up to the front door.

Striker examined the place. The exterior was made of concrete, chipped and crumbling in places, and further covered by old planks of wood whose green paint was faded and peeling. Unlike the rest of the building, the front doors looked strong. They were made of steel bars and had two separate locks, both of which were shiny and looked brand new.

'No business sign anywhere,' Felicia noted.

'Or a listed address.' Striker looked at the businesses to the immediate south and north. 'Whatever the address for this place is, it's between 317 and 357.' He started running possible numbers through the PRIME database. Finally, he got a hit.

'It's called Hing-Woo Enterprises,' he said. 'There's just two calls listed here – both for complaints on a prowler.' He read through the report. 'Looks like they sell Chinese food ingredients. A wholesale supply company.'

Felicia put on her best Chinese accent. 'Fortune cookie say: you under much surveillance, bad boys.'

Striker grinned.

Out front, Harry and Koda tried the door and found it locked. They knocked, waited, and no one came. Then they took a quick look around back. When they finally returned to the car, Koda's face was tight and pale, and he was talking a mile a minute. Harry said nothing. He just climbed into the car and closed the door. Moments later, the old Ford tore off down the lane.

'Koda looks pretty unhappy,' Striker said.

'Maybe he's allergic to MSG.'

Striker grinned at that. 'Let's go.'

Felicia started the engine. She pulled out of the A&W parking lot and drove down East Hastings Street. She floored it in an effort to catch up to the two men, but no matter how much she increased their speed, the Crown Victoria just kept getting smaller and smaller in the distance.

Harry and Koda were flying.

Fifty-Six

When Striker and Felicia reached Victoria Street, there was no sign of Harry and Koda whatsoever. Knowing they didn't come south, Felicia turned north and raced down the street. Three blocks later, the Crown Victoria was still nowhere to be seen.

They had lost them.

Striker got on his cell and called up Dispatch. 'I need you to check the GPS again, Sue. Where are they now?'

The Central Dispatcher let out a frustrated sound. 'Oh, *lame.* You don't seriously want me to use the system again, do you? You're gonna get me fired, dude.'

'I'll take the heat, Sue. Just tell the brass I ordered you to do it. Told you it was a life or death situation.'

The CD said nothing, and Striker could hear the clicks of the keyboard. After a moment, there was only silence.

'Well?' he asked.

'This is odd,' she finally said. 'Harry's car was there a moment ago . . . but now it's gone.'

Striker narrowed his eyes. 'Gone, as in a weak signal?'

'No, gone like Milli Vanilli – there's *no* signal.'

Striker closed his eyes, swore under his breath. He said goodbye to Sue and hung up.

'Well?' Felicia asked.

'They saw us.'

'Impossible.'

'They saw us.'

Felicia's face coloured.

'It's not your fault,' Striker said. 'Harry's good.'

'But how do you know—'

'They've disconnected the GPS system in the car.' When Striker saw the confused look on Felicia's face, he explained. 'It's not difficult. All you got to do is open the glove box and the wire's right there.'

Felicia slumped back in the driver's seat. 'Great. So now what?'

Striker looked down at the laptop and thought of the warehouse Harry and Koda had visited. He'd run the address and found the attached entity, but he hadn't done the reverse – and that was often a necessary step when using PRIME.

The system didn't always mesh.

In PRIME, it was not uncommon for more than one name to be created for a single entity. Hing-Woo Enterprises could also be called the Hing-Woo Corporation, or simply Hing-Woo. It was a user-based system.

Crap in, crap out.

Instead of running addresses, Striker searched for a name. He typed in every variation he could think of for Hing-Woo Enterprises. Then he hit send and waited for the responses. This time, a second entity came up. Hing-Woo Wholesalers. Like before, the two prowler calls came up – but this time there was also a *third* file listed.

For an Insecure Premises call.

Striker read through it. The details were basic. An alarm had gone off. Police had attended to find the door insecure. And the property representative had been called to attend. It was all very ordinary. Except for one big thing – the name of the property rep: Brice Burns.

'Look at this,' Striker said.

Felicia did. 'Son-of-a-bitch – *Sleeves*?'

'Yep. The biker Kolt mentioned.'

'There's our connection then.'

Striker flipped back through his notebook and tried to connect the dots of information. 'Owens and Williams are killed in two separate bomb blasts, but both women are connected to Chad Koda. And Koda is connected to Harry. Now we know that Koda and Harry are being blackmailed, so it's all one continuous chain.'

'And you're thinking the blackmailer might be this biker, Sleeves?'

He nodded. 'Fits the MO. The guy has organized crime connections. Kolt said he'd done electrical torture before, back east during the biker wars. And now we have him connected to this business Harry and Koda are checking out . . . It fits the bill.'

Felicia clucked her tongue as she thought. 'He is a member of the Satan's Prowlers,' she noted.

Striker read through the computer details. Most of it was typical information – affiliations with other criminal organizations; associations with other known criminals; and a long list of charges and suspected involvements in various other crimes.

But when Striker clicked on the man's entity tab, something else stole his attention. Under the Remarks section, in big red capital letters was a warning:

Satan's Prowlers Enforcer – Sergeant-at-Arms.

'Hey, Feleesh, look at this. He's the Sergeant-at-Arms.'

She looked at the screen, and her voice took on an excited note. 'He's the one Harry and Koda were talking about.'

Striker nodded, then performed another computer search. He ran Sleeves through the Canadian Police Information Centre, requesting a full search of his recorded criminal history and anything connected in the Criminal Name Index. Within seconds, the system came back with a perfect hit:

Brice Burns.

Alias: Sleeves

Violent, Armed and Dangerous, Escape Risk.

Also listed was his 175-centimetre height, his 80-kilogram body weight, and a string of scars, marks and tattoos – his right arm had two dragons fighting over a golden butterfly; his left arm had several naked women bound in chains.

'Charming guy,' Felicia said.

Striker said nothing and read on.

The man's history was extensive. He had a file in the Federal Penitentiary System, a Known Offender number in the DNA database, and a list of crimes going back decades.

Striker searched for a known address, but there was none. In fact, only two addresses were listed – the PO Box for the Matsqui Federal Penitentiary, and the address of the Satan's Prowlers' clubhouse, which was located on Charles Street.

Felicia sighed. 'It's always one step forward, two steps back.'

Striker had had enough of the delays.

'Head out east,' he said. 'Just above Fellows Road.'

'*Fellows?* But no one lives there but—'

'Vicenza Montalba,' Striker said.

The look on Felicia's face was one of disbelief. Vicenza Montalba was the head of the East Van Chapter of the Satan's Prowlers Motorcycle Club. He was a man who was hated by cops, respected by criminals, and feared by his enemies. He was a man who had been damn near untouchable for thirty years. Vicenza Montalba was rich. Powerful. Menacing.

And well known for being anti-police.

Felicia let out a strangled laugh. 'What are you gonna do? Just walk right up there and ring his bell?'

Striker smiled back at her.

'That's the plan.'

Fifty-Seven

Vicenza Montalba's house was a modern square structure, made entirely of white concrete and ten-foot-high tinted windows that were rumoured to be bulletproof for everything up to and including a .300 Winchester Magnum round.

The residence was situated across the Vancouver border, just above Fellows Road on Edinburgh, a relatively unknown strip that overlooked the blackish waters of the Burrard Inlet, and beyond that, the green hills of the North Shore mountains.

It was a beautiful view. A peaceful area.

Probably because Vicenza Montalba demanded it.

Striker parked out front and stared at the house. The rooftop patio, complete with green vegetation and an outdoor terrace with hot tub, was again shielded by a wall of clear bulletproof glass. Atop the walls were numerous security cameras – set there more for the police than enemy gangs – and in the driveway were two Jaguar sedans, a Mercedes coupe, and two black Land Rovers. Brand new.

Striker pointed at them. 'Remember, crime doesn't pay.'

Felicia just grinned back, and the two got out.

As they approached the front gate, the nearest security camera let out an audible whir and panned down on them. Striker took out his badge, held it up for the camera to see. He pressed the intercom button. Seconds later, a man's voice came through the speaker.

'Can I help you, Officer?'

'We'd like to speak to Mr Montalba,' Striker said.

'And this is regarding?'

'That's between me and him.'

There was no response for a moment, but then the black steel gate clicked open and Striker and Felicia stepped inside the lot. Like the outer lands, the inner yard was immaculate. A Japanese rock garden took up the bulk of the yard, with its circular designs running around a waterfall and a cherry blossom tree.

Striker and Felicia used the bridge to cross over the koi pond. When they reached the other side, the front door opened and a man stepped out to greet them.

Striker recognized him immediately.

Vicenza Montalba looked as far removed from the biker lifestyle as was Gandhi from an Outback steakhouse. Sporting a pair of pressed slacks, an off-white dress shirt, and a gold silk tie, he looked more like a stockbroker ready for the Wall Street grind than the leader of an outlaw motorcycle club. His thick greying hair was kept short at the sides and was parted in the middle, and when he smiled, he appeared more fatherly than fiendish.

Striker started the conversation low. He introduced himself and his partner, then got down to business.

'Does the name Sleeves mean anything to you?'

For a brief moment, the fatherly look on Montalba's face fell away and there was turbulence in his dark eyes. 'I know the name well. Mr Burns was disassociated from our club quite some time ago – as I'm sure you're well aware.'

Felicia nodded. 'Mind if we ask why?'

'Let's just say he wasn't keeping up with club protocol.'

Striker nodded. 'Meaning he was using his own product.'

Vicenza Montalba smiled. 'I have no idea what *product* he was using, but I can tell you this, Detective. Mr Burns was nothing but a problem for our club. He had, shall we say, an addictive personality. He was extremely violent. And he brought our club a lot of negative press and unwanted attention. He was relieved from his position *by me* and removed from the club list. Does that answer your question?'

'It does,' Striker said. 'This guy is of special interest to us right now on other unrelated matters.'

'What kind of unrelated matters?'

'Delicate matters – the kind you don't want being tied to your motorcycle club. Believe me on this one. We've been trying to locate Sleeves, but aren't having the greatest of luck. You got any idea where he is?'

Vicenza Montalba shook his head and let out a long breath. 'We have no idea where Mr Burns currently resides.' He fished a business card from his pocket and handed it to Striker. 'If you get any information on the man, I would appreciate a phone call.'

Striker took the card, flipped it over in his hands, played with it. 'Something tells me that would be unwise.'

Montalba offered no reaction. 'Mr Burns has made an awful lot of enemies, Detective. A lot of people are very angry with him.'

'How angry?'

Montalba only smiled.

'Have a nice day, Detectives,' he said. 'I hope you find your man.'

Fifty-Eight

The bomber and Molly stood in the murky greyness of the control room and went over their list one more time. Cooking explosives was never an easy thing to do, and it would be made even more precarious by the fact they'd be using an open-flame method here in the small confines of the command room. Without a fume hood. Or even a proper filtration setup.

There was no choice. It had to be done.

Evaluate. Act. Reassess.

List of supplies in hand, the bomber moved slowly across the room. He sat down on top of the steel table, rolled up his overalls, and removed his leg. The prosthesis was the latest greatest thing – a carbon-fibre shell with an inner plastic mould.

He hated it.

He slid off the liner and let the appendage air. As good as the gel covering was, it always stunk like hot rubber and it made his skin raw. Even worse, the more he walked on the artificial leg, the more he felt every internal screw and rod and butterfly clip shred through his meat. All that steel, always grinding inside.

It was even worse when he tried to run.

'Your leg okay?' Molly asked.

'It's fine.'

She looked at him for a long moment, her round face anxious. 'It doesn't look fine. It's awfully red.'

'Everything's brilliant, okay? Tickety-fuckin'-boo.'

Molly gave him a long furtive stare, as if she had seen this mood many times in their shared past, and said nothing. She looked back at their supply list. Cleared her throat. 'Don't forget the filters. No need to poison ourselves in the process.'

The bomber just nodded. He was about to ask if she preferred charcoal or carbon when he stopped. Something was vibrating in the pocket of his overalls. When he realized it was the phone – the *red* cell – a sick feeling came over him.

Only one person had that number, so he answered immediately.

'Yes?' he said.

He listened to the woman speak.

'Yes,' he said softly.

'Yes,' he said again. 'I understand.'

He hung up the phone and the sickness in his belly intensified – into a feeling so bad it almost matched the darkness of his head. He looked at Molly, who was now frozen in place and staring back at him without expression.

'We need to see him, Molly . . . *You* need to see him.'

'I . . . I can't.'

He looked back at her. Stared hard. Though her face remained frozen and without emotion, there was fear in her eyes. He could see it. And he found the moment so terribly odd. For all of Molly's faith, and despite all her training, and regardless of all the dangers and horrors she had faced these last few years, it had changed nothing in the woman. There would always be the remnants of that scared little girl in there, no matter how hard she tried to kill it.

'There's not much time left,' he told her.

'I can't.'

'You owe it to him.'

'I *can't!*'

He just stared at her. Now there were tears rolling down her cheeks, leaving little faint trails on her skin.

'Not like this,' she said, '. . . not like this.'

He turned away from her. Stared ahead at nothing. And once again, he was hit by a series of memories that had happened somewhere, somehow, sometime in a past that was surely his own. The ball of yarn was fraying a little bit more with each passing day.

Molly looked at him through desperate eyes. 'You understand, don't you?'

He didn't answer, didn't look at her. He couldn't. Instead, he reached out and grabbed the gel liner of his prosthesis and its outer casing.

It was time to put himself back together again.

Fifty-Nine

Striker and Felicia sat in the parked car with the engine running. With no other option available, they put an All Points Bulletin out for Sleeves, flagging him on every critical database, be it police, border, or other emergency personnel services. When Felicia was done, she leaned back in the seat.

'Well, the wait begins.'

'Wait nothing,' Striker said. 'We're getting ourselves a BirdDog.'

They headed for Cambie Street Headquarters.

BirdDog was the nickname cops used for a variety of manual tracking devices. Unlike the modern GPS devices, which were often built right into the vehicle, the BirdDogs consisted of two parts – the main unit, which sent out a signal and could be attached anywhere, and the handheld tracker unit, which acted as a receiver.

The cost per unit was high, but what did that matter? Trackers were a necessary part of most investigations. The department needed them. In all, the VPD owned thirty BirdDogs, and the devices were available for anyone involved in a legitimate file. But there was one important catch – the use of one required a tracking warrant. Otherwise any information gained was inadmissible in court.

Striker and Felicia didn't have a warrant, and for Felicia this was an issue. 'I'm just saying it wouldn't hurt to write up a warrant,' she said as they stepped through the front doors of Cambie Street Headquarters.

It was the third time she'd brought it up.

Striker frowned. 'And I'm *just saying* it's a waste of time. We don't have enough hard evidence to get one yet. And even if we did, I'm not wasting three hours writing one up when we can be out here investigating.'

Felicia shook her head. 'They're going to fry us in court on this one.'

'Like a piece of bacon,' Striker admitted. 'But I'll worry about it later.'

Before Felicia could say more, Striker moved on.

When they reached the sixth floor, they walked down the hall in search of Sergeant, David Connors – or Pooch, as he was better known. The man was a surveillance god, and he regularly taught his techniques not only within the Vancouver Police Department, but at the academy as well.

Striker opened the door to Stolen Auto, and they went inside.

The Stolen Auto section was small – nothing more than a thrown-together row of cubicles in the southeast corner of the building. Piled high in two of the cubicles and spread out against the walls were numerous types of electronic gadgetry – all bait for Theft From Auto projects.

Sitting on the other side of the cubicles was the man they were looking for, David Connors. His long blond hair was braided back over his head, and the goatee he had been trying to grow for two years was still missing patches. Together, the braids and goatee made Connors' head look too small for his body, which was a feat in itself because David Connors had the tiniest build that Striker had ever seen on a man.

'Hey, Pooch,' Striker said.

Connors looked up and frowned. Pooch was the nickname

his old patrol squad had given him years ago, since everyone said he looked like Dawg the Bounty Hunter – if Dawg had failed to reach puberty.

It was a nickname Connors hated.

'Shipwreck,' he grumbled. Then he spotted Felicia. 'Santos.'

Striker grabbed a couple of chairs from a nearby cubicle and slid one over to Felicia. They sat down opposite Connors, and Striker started the conversation.

'You seem to be in your usual bad mood, I see.'

'Why shouldn't I be? It's my last day here before they transfer me out.'

Striker hadn't known the man was moving. It was unfortunate news. Connors *loved* Stolen Auto. It was his baby. And he was damn good at it.

'So where are they sending you?' Striker asked.

'Police Standards.'

'Ouch.'

Both Striker and Felicia made a sour face. Police Standards was just another name for Internal – the place where cops were forced to investigate other cops. It was an assignment no one wanted.

'Who'd you piss off to get sent there?' Felicia asked.

'Just God.'

Striker grinned. 'Well, I've got some more news to brighten your day – we come seeking favours.'

Connors put down the camera he was fidgeting with and looked up. 'Well, now there's a surprise. What do you need?'

'BirdDog,' Striker said.

'Got a warrant?'

'I need one I can use without the documentation.'

Connors frowned. 'Oh boy. I dunno, Shipwreck.' He leaned back in the chair and interlocked his fingers behind his head.

Made a clucking sound with his tongue, as if he was adding things up in his head. 'What is this for?'

Striker thought of Harry and Koda, and said, 'You don't want to know.'

Connors looked away, said nothing.

'I know the rules,' Striker stressed. 'But this is really important, Pooch. Otherwise I'd never ask.'

Connors nodded slowly, then sat forward. 'I got one of the older models left. You can use it – on one condition.'

'That we don't drag you into court?' Felicia said.

'No. That you never call me Pooch again.'

Striker felt a grin come to his face. 'How about *pup*?'

'How about you get no device?'

'Fine, fine. You win.'

Connors reached under the desk and pulled out the unit. 'Make sure this gets back to me when you're done – and don't you dare try using this as part of any criminal charge. Last thing I need is some other cop investigating me when I'm in Internal doing the same damn thing.'

Felicia laughed. 'Think about it, Connors – a breach of the Police Act would actually keep you *out* of Internal.'

Connors looked at her and his face remained hard. 'Am I smiling, Santos? I'm serious here. Don't leave me with my ass in the air on this one.'

Striker took the device from him and smiled.

'Don't worry, Connors,' he said. 'We'll keep you covered. The last thing any of us want is to see you hanging with your ass in the air.'

Sixty

Having the BirdDog was only half of the solution. They still needed to locate Harry and Koda, and that wasn't an easy task. Neither man was answering their phone. They weren't back at the station. They had disabled their vehicle's GPS system. And they were ignoring all radio broadcasts.

After another failed attempt of raising them over the air, Felicia slammed the mike back into its cradle and cussed. 'We should just call Superintendent Laroche and fry their ass for not answering us.'

Striker shook his head. 'All that would do is put Harry and Koda even more on the defensive. Plus I don't want to attract unwanted attention. Believe me, Laroche is the *last* guy we need to get involved there. There's got to be a better way.'

'Better way, schmetter way. What else can we do? Wait outside their house all damn day?'

Thoughts of wasting a half-day setting up on their residences didn't appeal to Striker. He grabbed the laptop from Felicia, hit the chat icon, and sent out a message to every patrol unit that was currently logged on:

If anyone sees Detective Harry Eckhart or retired member Chad Koda, call Detective Jacob Striker immediately.

He then listed his cell phone number. It was unorthodox at best, but at this point he was willing to try anything.

'We'll see if that brings us any luck.'

They didn't have to wait long. Five minutes after sending the message, Striker got the call from the 3/10 report car. 'You looking for Harry Eckhart?' the man asked.

'Desperately,' Striker replied.

'I just saw him. He's gassing up at the yards.'

'How long?'

'Like thirty seconds ago.'

Striker felt a jolt of excitement. The City Yards – the place where the police cruisers were fixed and gassed up daily – was only a five-minute drive from Cambie Street HQ. Two minutes, if he drove like a wild man.

Striker thanked the man, hung up, and raced to the yards.

Once there, he spotted them. Harry was sitting in the undercover cruiser, drinking coffee and waiting with a vacant look on his red puffy face. The passenger seat was empty. A half-second later, the washroom door opened and Koda stepped out, using a paper towel to dab at the stitches running up his nose.

'There they are,' Striker said. 'Play it cool.'

'You're talking to the ice queen, dear.'

Striker hit the gas and pulled up to the pump next to Harry's Crown Vic. He killed the engine and got out. When he grabbed the gas nozzle, he glanced over at Harry and acted like he was surprised to see the man. 'Harry? Shit, I've been calling you all morning. Why don't you answer your cell?'

Harry put on a waxy smile. 'Been a crazy day.'

Striker looked past him at Chad Koda, who had now reached the passenger side of the vehicle. The man looked sick. 'Shouldn't he be in protective custody?'

Koda held his head with both hands as if he was trying to hold his skull together, then spat on the ground. When he looked over at Striker, his eyes were glassy and the whites were rimmed with red. 'I'm done with hospitals. And police protection.'

He climbed into the vehicle.

Beside him, Harry shrugged and forced a smile. 'He's a stubborn ass, what can I say?'

Felicia joined them. 'Hey, Harry.' She looked over at Koda. 'How come he's with you?'

'Me and Chad are old friends,' Harry said. 'I'm just helping him out.'

Striker acted like it wasn't a big deal. 'Protection, no protection, I really don't care. That's your choice, Koda. I'm just glad we bumped into you. How's the head, by the way?'

Koda looked back at him with no expression. 'Cloudy.'

'I bet. How many stitches?'

'Sixty-three.'

'*Ouch.*'

Striker finished gassing up the car and placed the nozzle back into its cradle. He then walked up to Harry's Crown Vic and leaned down on the open windowsill.

'Listen,' he said. 'Me and Feleesh have been doing some investigating here, and we got some stuff we need to run by you two. Some questions that need to be asked.' He glanced down at his watch. 'It's almost ten-thirty and I need some coffee. Why don't we hit Four Chefs?'

Koda's face tightened. 'I got important stuff to do.'

'More important than finding out who's trying to kill you?'

Koda stared back and said nothing.

Striker splayed his hands.

'Listen, Chad, I know you and I got off on the wrong foot, and I'm sorry about that – I had no idea you were a cop the first time I met you. But someone blew up your house and killed a woman in the process. We *need* to do this, and we need to do it now. I've given you a break up till this point because you're a former member.'

'Retired,' he corrected.

'Sorry, retired. Point is I can only extend that leniency so far' – Striker played his wild card – 'I got Acting Deputy Chief Laroche on my back nonstop and he wants to get involved in the file. I'm trying to ward him off as best I can, but you know how he can be. He wants to use this as his bid to get back to DC again.'

The mere mention of Acting Deputy Chief Laroche made both Harry and Koda take notice; everyone knew of Laroche's anal attention to regulations and procedures. It was best for all of them to avoid his involvement. And Striker knew that.

'It will just take a few minutes,' Felicia pressed.

Koda finally relented. 'Right, right. Okay.'

Striker smiled at them. 'Four Chefs then.'

'Four Chefs,' Harry said.

Striker and Felicia climbed back into their own car and left the yards. They drove around Strathcona Park and headed for Clarke Street. As they went, Felicia looked behind them.

'They coming?' Striker asked.

'They're having a conversation,' she said, biting her lip. 'Working on a story, no doubt.'

Striker grinned.

'That's okay,' he said. 'I like fiction.'

Sixty-One

Four Chefs was a small coffee shop tucked away on a dead-end road beneath the Georgia Street overpass. The woman who owned the business had been serving cops for twenty-five years. She was friendly, unobtrusive, and most importantly, gave everyone a police discount.

Striker and Felicia took a seat in the far back, away from the windows, and waited. Five minutes later, the front door opened and Harry and Koda walked in. Felicia waved them over and the two men grabbed coffee before sitting down.

Striker assessed them both.

Koda looked somewhat dazed. It was hard to believe this was the man they had woken up twenty-four hours ago. That man – tanned and rested – had emitted an aura of arrogance and condescension. This man before them now was a shadow of his former self. He gave off an anxious vibe, and seemed constantly on edge – his eyes darting to every exit of the coffee shop. He reminded Striker of a nervous prairie dog.

'So how are you coping?' Striker asked him.

Koda fought to take his eyes off the exit. 'Head's splitting in two.' He popped a couple more T3s and slurped them back with his coffee. 'I'm half deaf and I can't remember anything about the last two days.'

'Nothing?'

'Jack shit.'

Striker nodded. 'Well, it's not really all that surprising, is it? You're just lucky you lived. We're in the waiting process right now for forensics, but in the meantime, Felicia and I have been going through some of the files and we've found something . . . well, *interesting*.' He turned to Felicia, saw that she was ready for their little charade, and said, 'Show them.'

She blinked. 'Show them?'

'Where's the laptop?'

'In the car.'

Striker forced a grin. 'We can't read it from there.'

Felicia's cheeks reddened. She gave him a cross look, then stood up from the table and headed for the front door without a word. Striker watched her go, then jabbed a thumb her way and grinned at Harry and Koda. 'I hate to see her leave, but I love to watch her go.'

Harry looked at Striker. 'Rumour is you've already been there. That true?'

'I've heard the same rumour 'bout you and Koda.'

'Funny guy,' Harry said.

As the sunlight flooded through the windows, it lit up Koda's face and made him squint against the brightness. The light highlighted his sickened condition. The golden-copper tone of his skin was still there, but it looked almost spray-painted on now, with a sicker gauntness lurking beneath. He pounded back two more T3s.

'Those ain't Tic-Tacs, man,' Striker said. 'You'd better slow down a little.' When Koda said nothing, Striker forced a small chuckle and continued the conversation. 'Like I was saying, Chad, yesterday you and I got off on the wrong foot. But I got to admit, your Kardashian joke was a good one – I'll be stealing that from you.'

Koda grinned for the first time. 'It was a good one,' he said.

'Chris Rock level.'

Koda grinned, almost smugly.

Striker took another long sip of his coffee to give himself a moment to think. One moment Koda could remember nothing of the previous few days, the next he recalled the joke he had made to them in the alcove of his home.

Striker pulled out his notebook and went over things.

'Okay,' he said. 'Since my partner seems to be taking a sabbatical, we might as well get started without her . . . This whole case is really strange; anyone can see that. Starts off with a victim down by the river – a woman who we now know was your ex-wife Sharise Owens.'

'Common law,' Koda stressed.

'Granted, but still your ex. Next thing you know, a bomb goes off in your place and not only are you almost killed by the blast, but Owens is actually there with you. She dies in the process.' He looked directly into Koda's eyes. 'Hell, if I didn't know better, given the bad history you two share, I would have guessed it to be a murder-suicide.'

Koda blinked a couple of times, as if he had only now considered the optics of the situation. 'I remember a *little bit*,' he finally said.

Striker smiled. 'Do tell.'

'I came home and Sharise was already there. In my kitchen. Tied to a fuckin' chair. I started walking towards her and . . . and then . . . well, nothing else is there. It's all just one big *blank*.'

'Concussion,' Striker said. 'Maybe it will come back to you later. But let's forget about the actual explosion for now. Do you have any idea why someone would want to blow up your house in the first place?'

Koda's expression went from one of weariness to that of

tension. He wiped away some of the perspiration covering his brow. Cleared his throat. Drank some more coffee and then some water. When he finally spoke, his voice was quiet and sounded faraway.

'I've been over that a million times today. And the answer is *not a clue.* I've had some pretty big real estate deals with some Hong Kong people over the last few years, and a couple of bad law suits as well. But nothing that should warrant *this.*'

'Any of these business associates ever threaten you?'

Koda laughed. 'The angry ones? All of them.'

'With physical violence?'

Koda just shrugged. 'Indirect shit.'

Striker wrote this information down in his notebook. 'Forward me the names of the people in these law suits. I'll need them.' He flipped through the book. 'What about Owens? Could this be somehow related more to her than to you?'

Koda's eyes took on a distant look. 'I hadn't spoken to Sharise in . . . God . . . *years.* Our relationship didn't exactly end well.'

'So I take it. You know Keisha Williams, right? The cousin of your ex? She was also blown up. About eight hours earlier in her toy shop on Granville Island. You see any connections there?'

Koda's face paled even more, turned less tan and more grey. He rubbed his finger down his nose, along the stitches, and swallowed hard. 'I knew her, yeah, of course. But I don't know why she would be targeted for anything. I mean, she's a mother. A family person. A *good woman.* She's been nothing but a toymaker the last ten years; why would anyone want to hurt her?'

Striker looked up from the notebook. 'For the last *ten* years?'

Koda bit his lip. 'Or however long. Figure of speech.'

Striker just nodded. 'This might sound a bit odd to you, but on the note of toymakers, did Keisha Williams ever give you any dolls?'

'Dolls?'

'Yes, dolls. Toys. Like a miniature policeman.'

'No.'

'Would it have any significance to you if we found one at the crime scene?'

Koda's face reddened. He looked confused and worried. 'I don't . . . think so.'

'Don't *think* so?'

'No. It wouldn't.'

'Well, let me know if something comes to mind.'

Koda said he would and Striker asked a few more questions.

During the entire conversation, Harry sat there quietly, drinking his coffee and watching the two men. For the first time, he spoke up. 'Maybe we should get going,' he said. 'You're not looking too well, Chad.'

'We're almost done here anyway,' Striker said. He kept his eyes on Koda, refused to look away. 'What about Mike Rothschild? You knew him from your earlier days with the department, right? You two share any common enemies?'

'*Rothschild?'* Koda asked. The name obviously shocked him.

Harry cleared his throat. For the most part during the conversation, his expression had remained one of calmness and patience, but over the last few questions, that serenity appeared to have escaped him. His eyes narrowed, and his already-crimson cheeks turned a darker shade of red. 'What does Rothschild have to do with any of this?'

'The bomber went for him today. Fortunately, he wasn't successful.'

'Rothschild?' Harry asked, a note of uncertainty in his voice.

His eyes glossed over and a look of disbelief filled his face. He sat back stunned and speechless. Koda, meanwhile, pushed back from the table. He looked blankly around the room.

Shielded his eyes from the bright light pouring in through the windows.

'I don't feel so good,' he said. 'Gonna use . . . gonna use the washroom.'

He stood up. Stepped awkwardly back from the table and stumbled. Righted himself and walked down to the men's restroom.

Striker watched him go, then looked to Harry. 'Maybe Koda should be back in the hospital.'

Harry didn't comment; he just looked at the front door and said, 'Your partner sure is taking an unusually long time to get a laptop.'

Striker sipped his coffee, forced a smirk. 'Probably locked herself in the car again.' When Harry didn't laugh and instead kept staring at the door, Striker went on the offensive. 'So why the game, friend?'

Harry finally looked away from the door and focused on Striker. 'What *game*?'

'I had Koda under guard. *My* order. Who are you to release him?'

A look of something between doubt and concern flooded Harry's features. 'Look, Shipwreck, it wasn't like that. It was *his* decision to leave, not mine. I tried to make him stay there. Under doctor care.'

'But he refused?'

Harry splayed his hands. 'Chad is like that. Said he wanted to get the hell out of there. And how was I to legally stop him? I mean, you tell me, is he being charged with anything? Even detained?'

Striker saw through Harry's veil. This was a fishing exercise. To see what he and Felicia really knew.

He didn't bite.

'Koda's not being charged with anything, Harry. He's the

victim, right? But I still needed to question him in order to find out who the hell is really behind this, and why it's happening. I thought that was fairly obvious.'

Harry looked down into his coffee cup.

'Nothing is obvious,' he said. 'Fact is, I've been over this a dozen times with him myself, and his brain is hash. Guy has no idea why it happened or who would do it. Not a clue.'

'So, basically, you conducted an interview with him yourself. You'll need to put a police statement into the report then.'

Harry acted as if he had never heard Striker. 'If I were you, I'd focus my investigation on the forensic details. See what your bomb girl can give you.'

'I'll keep it under consideration.'

Harry glanced down at Striker's open notebook, and Striker closed it. For the first time, Striker saw a flash of suppressed anger in the man's eyes. He looked back at Striker and his blue eyes were cold.

The dance was over.

'You know, Striker, I remember when you just got on this job. You were cocky as hell then too. A real piss kid.'

'Long time ago, Harry. Life changes. The job changes. Hell, even the people change. Eventually, all dinosaurs go extinct.'

Harry's face hardened. 'You saying I'm old now?'

'I'm saying things change.'

'Yeah? Well sometimes not for the better.'

Striker eyed the man. 'We fighting here, Harry?'

'Course not. We're on the same team, Striker. *I* always remember that.'

Striker said nothing back. He just sipped his coffee and wondered what the hell was taking Felicia so long. As if reading his mind, she walked in through the front door, shook her head in frustration, and sat down with the laptop.

'You run into a shoe sale?' Harry asked.

Felicia gave him a dry look. 'That's some funny stuff, Harry. Don't quit your day job.'

'What took you so long?' he pressed.

She slammed the laptop on the table. 'These things are shit, okay? Someone's bent the entire cradle – the pin was jammed and I couldn't get it to release. If you can do better, then next time you go get it.'

She'd barely finished speaking when Koda exited the washroom. He walked slowly, gingerly, right up to the table. Placed his hand against the edge. Stabilized himself. 'These goddam pills . . . I don't feel so well.'

Harry looked at Striker. 'We finished our little masquerade?'

Striker acted as if he hadn't heard the comment and pulled the laptop across the table. 'Why don't you give me the names of these real estate business partners you were talking about, Chad, and we'll run them through the system.'

The man's eyes took on a lost look. Scared. Confused. Tired.

'He needs rest,' Harry said.

Striker nodded slowly, then muttered 'fine' and closed the laptop. 'Go get some rest then, Chad.' He handed the man his business card. 'Email me the names of your Hong Kong associates and these law suits, and I'll check it out. And call me if anything else comes to mind.'

Koda took the card and nodded. Then Harry stood up and the two men left the coffee shop. The door slammed hard behind them.

Striker turned to Felicia. 'Well? You get the tracker installed?'

She smiled. 'We're in business.'

He let out a relieved breath. 'Thank God. You took so long, Harry started asking questions. You had me worried there.'

She held up her palms. They were clean. 'Had to get the grime off my hands first; otherwise they'd know.' She opened the flap of her coat, pulled out the handheld GPS tracker, then pressed the *On* button. Seconds later, a small map appeared across the LED display and a car icon blipped. The icon was already heading south on Glen Drive.

Calculated speed: 100 kilometres per hour.

'Holy shit, they're *flying*,' Felicia said.

Striker smiled at the sight.

'Let's go,' he said. 'I have a feeling we're about to find out what they're looking for.'

Sixty-Two

The lung compressor in the corner of the room made a soft *shu-shush* sound as the bomber stood motionlessly at the foot of the bed. Dressed in a pair of ordinary blue jeans, a flannel shirt, and sporting a pair of large mirrored sunglasses that covered up most of his face, he stared at the man before him.

He's lost so much weight . . .

The thought pained him. He moved slowly around the bed until he was at the side, and there he delicately traced his fingers down the man's arm. There was hardly any tissue there now, any meat. It was bloody awful. They were so thin. *Child* thin. The full-sleeve tattoos looked like deflated balloons.

Shu-shush, the compressor continued.

He continued tracing his finger up the man's arm, all the way to his chest. So many bumps of scar tissue mottled the skin. On his arms. His chest. His neck and face and head. This, along with his own similar tattoos, was all they shared any more – scar tissue. He had it too. All over his body. Scars and scars and scars.

Little physical memories.

He leaned closer to the man. Whispered, 'I might not be back. Maybe not ever . . . But know this: I'm making things *right*.'

The man on the bed showed no response that he had even

heard the words, showed no response that he was even alive; he only breathed through the assistance of the lung compressor, and that rhythmic *shu-shush* sound continued to break the silence. It filled him with a sorrow so deep that his lungs ached, for he knew full well the outcome of a basilar artery stroke. Of locked-in syndrome. Every voluntary muscle of a person's body failed, and yet the patient remained awake and aware. It was a living hell.

There were no delusions here.

None at all.

But there is always hope, Molly would say.

You can never give up, Molly would say.

We just need to have faith, she would say.

But Molly had not come with him. Like she never came. And there was no loving God up there, watching over them. Or if He was there, He sure as hell didn't care.

No, there was no hope. There was no faith.

Not any more.

Hell, maybe there never had been.

Shu-shush.

His black cell rang. He picked up.

'The GPS is done,' Molly said. Her voice was tight, strained.

He said nothing back.

'Installed and activated,' she said.

Still, he said nothing.

He hung up the phone. He brushed his hand through the hair of the man on the bed. Kissed his forehead. Smelled his pungent body odour. Said, 'I love you . . . I love you *so much*.'

And then the tears finally came – big salty drops, rolling down his cheeks and onto his lips, forcing him to flee the room altogether from what may well have been the final goodbye.

Shu-shush.

Sixty-Three

As Felicia drove their undercover cruiser eastward in pursuit of Harry and Koda, Striker sat in the passenger seat and continued going over all the various connections in his mind. The link between Koda and Sharise Owens was clear. But the link between Koda and Keisha Williams still felt vague.

Striker took out his notebook and searched for the phone number of Keisha Williams' brother, Gerome. When he found it several pages back, he dialled the number. It rang but once, and the man answered. A sadness resonated in his tone, and Striker felt for him. He asked how the children were coping and if the Victim Services Unit had been helpful. The grief in Gerome's voice made it clear that nothing was helpful right now. So Striker got down to business.

'Keisha was the owner of the Toy Hut, was she not?'

'Well, Keisha owned the *business*,' Gerome said. 'Not the actual building.'

'Had making toys always been something she loved to do?'

'Oh yes. Always. We didn't have much money as kids. Our parents were broke. So Keisha used to make us things. She was always good at that, and I think the happiness it brought me made her feel better too.'

'So she made toys all her life?'

'Yes, sir. Mostly from wood. She was good with wood.'

'And she did this as a career? All her life?'

'Well, no, not exactly. She only opened the Toy Hut about ten years ago.'

'What did she do before that?' Striker asked.

'She was a chartered accountant.'

Striker was surprised by this. 'A chartered accountant? . . . Forgive me, Gerome, but I don't get it.'

'Get it, sir?'

'Keisha and the children lived in social housing. She owned second-hand clothes. She looked in all ways like she was – well, for lack of a better word – poor.'

'She *was* poor. The family just got by. Especially after her husband died – Chester had no life insurance, you know.'

Striker shook his head. 'Forgive me, but this doesn't make a whole lot of sense. Why stay poor? If Keisha was registered as a chartered accountant, why didn't she work as one?'

Gerome sighed. 'You tell me, Detective. That was one of the things we used to fight about, Keisha and me. I always told her, "You and the kids got no money. Why don't you go back to your old job? You can buy a place for you and the children." But every time I brought it up, it just created more and more distance between us. Like whenever I told her to get rid of that Solomon guy.'

'Did she work for a company?'

'No. Was all private stuff, much as I know.'

'And where does she keep her records?'

'I dunno,' Gerome said. 'I been going through her stuff myself to see if she had any insurance for the children, but I ain't found nothing so far. If she's got records, they ain't here, I can tell you that.'

Striker thought it over. 'Did something bad happen in the distant past? Something that made her quit her career as a chartered accountant?'

Gerome let out a long breath, one filled with tension. 'I honestly don't know, Detective. She just upped and quit, and that was pretty much that. The topic was off limits around here. She made that pretty clear to me, clear to everyone. Lord, I'll never know.'

Striker said nothing else on the matter. He just thanked Gerome for his time and told him to call if the children were in need of anything. Then he hung up and relayed what he had learned to Felicia.

'Something must have happened,' she said. 'Why else quit a good job like that and live in poverty? It doesn't make sense, even if she loved the other job. I mean, she had children to think about, right?'

Striker thought the same. Something must have happened.

Something bad.

Sixty-Four

Striker and Felicia continued tailing Harry and Koda out into the suburbs.

'Not too close, not too close,' Striker said.

Felicia gave him a cool look. 'They're two blocks east and one block north of us, Jacob. Unless they can see backwards and through the walls of the houses, we're fine.'

Striker frowned. He couldn't help the concern.

'We have to be perfect here, Feleesh. Harry and Koda might chalk up our first meeting in the yards to a fluke, but one more *lucky* meet like that and they'll know we're tracking them. We need to maintain some distance until we figure out some of the other areas they've been searching. Then we can run the addresses and look for some connections.'

'Fine, fine.'

Felicia slowed down another ten K per hour, if only to appease him, and Striker watched the screen of the BirdDog tracker. They navigated deeper into the suburban area of Riley Park, and soon found themselves on James Street. After three more blocks, the car icon on the tracking display stopped moving altogether and the speed read: 0 km/hr.

'They've stopped,' Striker said.

Felicia pulled over to the nearest kerb. 'They on Quebec?'

'Yeah. Right across from the softball centre.'

Her face took on the faraway gaze of deep thought. 'What else is there?'

'Just houses.'

'Maybe they're at a red light or a stop sign.'

Striker shook his head. 'They're mid-block. Just wait them out.'

They gave it another full minute. When the icon didn't start moving again, Striker said, 'I'm getting out and going on foot.'

He shouldered open the door and ran southward down the lane. Two blocks later, he slowed down and started peering in between the houses, one by one. Halfway down the lane, he caught sight of the old undercover police cruiser.

The Crown Vic was parked in front of a small house. The place looked old, was square in shape and covered with water-stained stucco. It had probably been built back in the late 30s or early 40s. Out front, the foliage was out of control. The lawn looked like it hadn't been mowed in years, and the garden was nothing but weed and crabgrass. Standing in the small alcove were Harry and Koda. They were talking to a thin brunette with a narrow face.

Striker looked her over. The woman's hair looked unnaturally black, like a bad home-dye job. She was wearing a red-and-white checked apron which she kept absently smoothing out, and there was a small boy clutching her side.

He was maybe four years old.

Harry and Koda asked the woman several questions, and all the while a nervous expression lingered on the woman's face. Several times, her eyes flitted to the long fresh wound running down the centre of Koda's face and forehead, and at one point the boy pointed at it. She quickly yanked his hand away and gave him a reprimand, before looking back with an expression of embarrassment.

After a long moment, the two men said goodbye and returned to their vehicle. Koda was raving about something while Harry just looked straight ahead, his face communicating nothing.

Striker watched them talk heatedly in the cab, then drive down the road until they were out of sight. When he was sure they were long gone, he turned his attention back to the house.

The woman was still standing in the doorway, looking down the road where they had gone. That nervous, embarrassed look still covered her face. Seconds later, she scooped up her little boy and carried him inside the house.

Striker wrote the address down in his notebook, then added: 'mother and son (4 years old)'. He put the pen away and his cell went off. He answered.

'They're moving again,' Felicia said.

'Run this address: 5311 Quebec Street. See what comes up.'

'Hold on . . .' Striker heard her typing. 'Okay, got it. Let's see here . . . nothing in PRIME, but the Motor Vehicle Branch has a listing there for a woman named Theresa Jameson. Should be about one hundred and seventy centimetres and fifty-one kilos. Brown hair, blue eyes. No criminal record whatsoever.'

Striker listened to the description. It matched the woman from the doorway.

'Hair's a bit off,' he said. 'But it looks dyed. Just hold tight for now. I'm gonna check her out.'

'Be fast – I don't want to lose them.'

Striker crossed the street and marched up the sidewalk. The closer he got to the house, the more run-down the lot appeared. Weeds had pushed through the cracks in the concrete walkway, and thick tree roots could be seen burrowing into the house's foundation – a major structural problem. Add in the water damage to the exterior walls and the place was a rebuild at best.

Striker walked up the front steps and knocked. The moment

the door opened, the fresh smell of baked muffins filled the air. Bran, for sure. Apple too. The woman who answered the door was the same one he'd seen moments earlier talking to Harry and Koda, only now she was holding a bowl of white icing.

'Theresa Jameson?' Striker asked.

'Yes.'

Striker pulled out his badge and offered her a smile. 'Detective Striker, Vancouver Police Department.'

'I just spoke to two cops, not a minute ago.'

Striker put the badge away. 'Oh, I'm sorry, I didn't realize we'd already been by to talk to you.'

'Yes, you just missed them.'

Striker made something up. 'Were they here on the mischief call?'

The woman looked confused. 'Mischief? Uh, I'm not sure. They were more concerned about who lived here now, and how long me and the kids have been living here.'

'Oh,' Striker said. 'Did they take a written statement?'

'No.'

He sighed onerously. 'That figures. No problem though. I'll just make some quick notes and put in a page for you – save you the hassle later on. What exactly did you tell them?'

The woman transferred the bowl of icing to her other arm. 'Uh, just that we'd been living here almost three years now, and that no one rented any rooms from us.' She frowned as she spoke. 'Then they started asking me if I had any *gang* connections. Or if any of my kids did. It kind of scared me, to be honest with you.'

'Did they mention anything specific?'

'I don't understand.'

'Any gang names? Any surnames?'

She shook her head. 'No, no. They didn't.'

When the young boy appeared at her side again, he looked up at Striker and clutched at his mother's apron. Theresa Jameson put the mixing bowl down on a small table just inside the doorway and scooped up the boy, cradling him in her arms. As she did so, she met Striker's stare, and suddenly she looked smaller and more diminutive than before.

Scared.

'Should I . . . should I be worried here, Detective?' she asked.

Striker offered a warm smile.

'Only at your gardener costs.'

Sixty-Five

'We need to learn the history of that house and the people that live there,' Striker said when Felicia picked him up again on Quebec Street. 'There's a reason Harry and Koda stopped there, and it looks gang-related.'

'Just buckle up,' she said. 'They're making ground on us.'

She hammered the gas.

They continued following Harry and Koda with the BirdDog tracker and several kilometres later caught up to them. Once again, the target vehicle stopped, though this time at the White Spot restaurant on Main Street. Striker was not surprised. The White Spot was a cop favourite; it had a central location and none of the cooks there would spit in your food.

'They're gonna be a while,' Striker said. 'Let's head for the Gang Crime Unit, see what they have on this Sergeant-at-Arms biker we keep reading about – Sleeves.'

Felicia shifted irritably. 'We should stay and watch these guys – what if they leave?'

Striker waved a hand dismissively. 'We should head to GCU.'

A cross look took over Felicia's face. 'Don't do that to me.'

'Do what?'

'Wave your hand like my opinion doesn't matter.' She shook her head. 'Sometimes you can be so damn . . . *condescending.*'

Striker looked back, surprised. Once again he'd managed to piss off Felicia without even trying. It was a bad habit of his, he knew, taking the lead and giving orders rather than working in tandem. And all too often he came across as bossy, even though he didn't mean to. He tried to be fair, always. But ultimately, the niceties didn't matter. He was the lead investigator of their partnership and the most senior detective of the unit. And that meant one thing:

All the glory, all the blame.

He tried to smooth things out.

'Look, all I'm saying is I know Harry. Personally. He'll take an hour and a half to eat his lunch. He always does. Besides, the BirdDog will tell us if they leave. If it goes off, we'll turn around. We can always catch up to them if we need to.'

When the look of irritation fell from Felicia's face, Striker softened his voice and spoke again.

'The thing is, every minute counts right now, Feleesh. And I just don't want us wasting ninety of them watching Harry and Koda stuff their faces. Besides, you just know Koda's gonna get food in his goatee – who wants to see that?'

Felicia let out a small laugh, then nodded, if only to appease him.

'Fine, Jacob. GCU it is.'

Striker felt relieved. To do otherwise would have driven him nuts. As far as he was concerned, the Gang Crime Unit was not only their next best bet, it was a critical part of the investigation. The GCU had their own offline-database, which was unavailable to other units. They would definitely have hidden files on the Satan's Prowlers and – if they were lucky enough – this Sergeant-at-Arms, Sleeves.

Striker and Felicia headed for the Bunker.

Like most of the Special Operations squads, the Gang Crime Unit was located in the Bunker, an old warehouse in District 3.

And like the primary headquarters at 312 Main Street, the building was a giant concrete block that was old, outdated, and slowly falling into ruin. The only part of the building that wasn't outdated was the new model security system; cameras stuck out against the crumbling walls of the facility like shiny quarters on a grey sidewalk.

On the second floor, Striker led Felicia down the threadbare carpet, in between the flaking walls of paint. On a blue-painted door at the end of a long, dark corridor was a white wooden sign with red block lettering:

GANG CRIME UNIT.

The door was electronically locked, and the keypad was coded for GCU members only.

'You got clearance?' Felicia asked.

'Yeah, this,' Striker said, and raised his fist.

He rapped hard on the wood, three times, and moments later the door was opened by the very man they were looking for – Delbert Ibarra.

Inspector Delbert Ibarra was one of the few Mexican members of the department and an old friend of Striker's. The two men sometimes went camping together. Once the inspector in charge of Strike Force – the city's best surveillance team – Ibarra was now in charge of the entire Gang Crime Unit. The men and women working under Ibarra said good things about him, and that didn't surprise Striker in the least.

Ibarra was a good man. He put people first.

'Shipwreck, Felicia,' he said. 'Long time no see. I hear you two are working on the bombing.'

'Yeah, lucky us,' Felicia said.

Striker stepped into the room, forcing Ibarra to move back. 'We need your help on this one, Del. I got some nasty suspicions this could all relate back to one of the gangs you've been monitoring – the Satan's Prowlers.'

Ibarra raised an eye. 'Vicenza Montalba?'

'Not him specifically.'

Felicia nodded. 'It's kind of complicated.'

'Come with me.'

Ibarra's demeanour turned from relaxed to serious. He led them down the corridor, in between the rows of cubicles, to a small and secluded computer pod. There, he pulled over some chairs and they all sat down in a half-circle.

'Now what do you got?' he asked.

Striker spent ten minutes filling the inspector in on everything they had discovered, starting with the torture scene in the orange-lit barn and finishing with the links to a Sergeant-at-Arms with the Satan's Prowlers – a man they believed to be Sleeves. He omitted his concerns about Harry and Koda. Once done, Striker leaned forward. 'So why the gang name Sleeves?'

'When you find the prick, check out his forearms. Nothing but tattoos – women chained to women.'

Felicia nodded. 'So you're aware of the man.'

'Oh, I'm *well* aware. In fact his name has come up quite a few times today.'

That got Striker's attention. 'Today? Why?'

'Harry Eckhart's been calling, asking a lot of questions about the man. You guys working the same file or something?'

'What did he want?' Striker asked.

'An address. For Sleeves.'

'Did you give him one?' Felicia asked.

'Don't have one to give.' Ibarra splayed his hands as he explained. 'Sleeves has been in hiding for quite some time now. Word is he's been ousted by the gang for bringing them too much bad press, and for using his own product – though I hear he got himself under control again.'

'What drug?'

'Meth. For the pain.'

'What pain?'

Ibarra splayed his hands as he spoke. 'Sleeves blew himself up pretty badly a few years back. It's a wonder he even survived.'

'Where might we find him?' Striker asked.

'No one knows where he is. And from what I hear, that's probably a good thing. The entire gang is looking for him – and they tend to deal with matters *internally*.'

Striker said nothing as he mulled this over. 'Can you run two addresses through the GCU database for me?' He gave Ibarra the addresses for Hing-Woo Enterprises on Semlin Drive and Theresa Jameson's house on Quebec Street.

Ibarra didn't touch the keyboard. 'Don't have to run the first one,' he said. 'It's a food warehouse now, but a few years back it used to be one of the chop shops for the Satan's Prowlers.'

'Chop shop?' Felicia asked. 'You mean for high-end cars?'

'For enemies,' Ibarra replied. 'Believe me, you didn't want to be taken there. You always left slightly *shorter*.' He grinned darkly. 'As for the house on Quebec Street . . .' He typed the address into the computer, then waited for a response. When he got one, he nodded slowly. 'Ah, there you go. Up until about three years ago, Sleeves was suspected of living there. Rented the basement suite. But he's been gone from there for a long time now. NFA.'

Striker sighed. NFA meant No Fixed Address, and it was about as much as he had expected.

'Any suggestions?' he asked.

Ibarra nodded. 'Yeah, just one. Be careful with this guy. He's a real weasel, Shipwreck. And a former nailer to boot.'

Felicia didn't know the word.

'*Nailer?*' she asked.

'A Prowler hitman. And he's damn good at it. Almost single-handedly took on the Renegades during the biker wars back east.'

'In Toronto?' she asked. The shootings and bombings had made headlines all across the country.

Ibarra nodded. 'That's the one. It's also the reason why the Prowlers transferred him out west – the heat got to be too much. Sleeves became a liability to the gang, especially after that little kid got killed.'

Striker remembered the incident. The little blond boy's image was ingrained in everyone's mind. The wailing mother. The following funeral procession. It was bad. 'Car bomb, right?'

'Two pounds of PETN. Under the driver's seat. The boy was playing on the sidewalk at the time. Never had a chance.'

Striker tried to recall all the details.

'I don't remember them tying the bomb to anyone specifically,' he said.

'They didn't,' Ibarra replied. 'The evidence was never there. But everyone knew who did it – the Satan's Prowlers. Who else would it be? They were the only ones fighting with the Renegades back then. And the Prowlers had just the guy to do it – *Sleeves.*'

'But why him?' Felicia asked.

Ibarra looked at her like she was nuts.

'Because,' he said, 'Sleeves is an explosives expert.'

Sixty-Six

It was the bomber's suggestion they split up.

He and Molly needed certain ingredients to begin the cooking process, and buying too large a quantity of these particular products would bring unwanted attention. As a result, he decided to hit the sporting goods stores and camping supply warehouses while Molly went to the local hardware shops and pharmacies.

Now, as he walked down the aisle of Henan's Sporting Goods store, the PA system droned on through static-filled speakers:

. . . and please be sure to take notice of our centre aisle today, Shoppers, where we have many reduced prices on all your sporting necessities . . .

The clerk on the microphone had a strong guttural sound to his voice. It washed over the bomber insidiously and submerged him in the past. And suddenly he was back there in the war again. In Afghanistan. And it was no longer the store manager on the PA system, but one of his men, yelling for him to *take cover, Goddammit, TAKE COVER!*

His heart raced, his mouth went dry.

How long had it been?

Ten years? Ten months?

Time meant nothing any more.

He stopped walking and closed his eyes. Forced it all out. Focused on the mission, for that was where sanity existed. Peace was hell, and hell was peace. It had been that way for him. Ever since the incident.

Half in this world, half fighting through the past, he floated through the store. Aisle six had the stove supplies, which meant hexamine. And aisle four had a large number of wet-weather fire-starters, which meant magnesium. He loaded up on both, then proceeded to the checkouts.

As he stood there, waiting for his turn at the till, he picked up one of the packages of hexamine. Even though it was wrapped in plastic, the gritty smell always leaked out – that gassy, waxy stink.

He brought it to his nose and sniffed.

At the same time, someone in the lumber section started up a circular saw. Its high-pitched screech of steel slicing through wood filled the air, and a bone-numbing coldness splashed through his body.

Against his wishes, he mind-rioted. Flashed back in time. And suddenly, the doctor was there again. Looking down on him. That tall stork-like figure, telling him *There were some unforeseen issues, young man . . . Complications.*

And then the nurse with the dark eyes and the paper hat was there too, sticking him with her needles, yelling for the orderlies to *Hold him down, Goddammit, HOLD HIM DOWN!*

And he was begging for them to stop.

Screaming for them to stop.

No more surgeries!

Please, no more surgeries!

'NO MORE SURGERIES!'

And suddenly, the image – the recollection – was gone, vanished like his hope had vanished all those years ago. And there was just a young cashier standing there, looking back at him through wide, timid eyes.

'Sir?' she asked. 'Are you all right?'

He looked around in bewilderment. The checkout . . . He was standing at the checkout . . .

The checkout.

'I-I'm sorry,' he tried. But his throat was tight and dry and felt like it was bleeding. All that came out was a croak.

He opened his wallet. 'How . . . how much?'

'Uh, one hundred and seventy-nine dollars. Even.'

He dropped four fifties on the counter – cash, always cash – grabbed his bag of supplies and retreated from the store. In behind him, that god-awful scream of the circular saw continued. Sawing, grinding, chunking through the wood like it was bone.

'Your change, sir. *Your change.*'

But he didn't stop.

Didn't care.

Wasn't listening.

He just needed to get away from there as quickly as possible. Before the past returned once more.

Before another memory swallowed him whole.

Sixty-Seven

Striker amended the CPIC flag they'd put out earlier to include new warnings:

Threat to Police.

And *Explosives Expert.*

Once done, he sat back and looked at Felicia. They were at a crossroads now. They had a decision to make – return to performing surveillance on Harry and Koda, or go their own way in locating Sleeves.

Striker spoke his opinion first. 'I'm getting tired of the cat and mouse game with Harry.'

'Me too,' Felicia admitted. 'But they know this guy better than we do.'

'That may be true,' Striker said. 'But, like us, they have no idea where he's hiding. I mean, think about it – they were calling Ibarra themselves looking for an address. They're in the same position we are. Besides, we have them tracked, so we can always follow the GPS's history later – it's recorded.'

Felicia remained uncertain, and Striker pressed her:

'If Harry and Koda find Sleeves before us, we'll go after them. But right now, this feels like a case of the blind leading the blind.'

Felicia only shrugged. 'I wouldn't mind leaving them so much if we had an idea where we could find Sleeves. But we don't.'

'Actually we do.'

Felicia gave Striker a wary look. 'We do?'

He smiled knowingly.

'I'll tell you on the way.'

They drove from Cambie Street HQ to the Grandview-Woodlands area, with Striker telling Felicia of his plan. Once there, they parked at the corner of Lakewood and Dundas, in a partially hidden lane. From here, the car was almost invisible from the main drive, and yet the entrance to Roebuck's Convenience Store was in plain view. Striker knew the store well; it had been robbed a dozen times over the years, and it was a common area for low-end drug deals to occur.

Which was why they were there.

'So we're looking for Lucky Eddie,' Felicia said.

Striker nodded. 'Today, he will be *Un*lucky Eddie.'

She let out a small laugh. 'Why him?'

'He'll lead us to Sleeves.'

'I still don't see how.'

Striker explained: 'Because District 2 is almost entirely crack cocaine based. Not many dealers here sell meth. And the few who do sure as hell can't afford to buy it in large quantities. But Lucky Eddie can.'

Felicia followed the logic. 'And you're thinking Eddie's wholesaler will be Sleeves?'

'I'm betting on it.'

Felicia nodded. 'One problem though. Meth may not be the drug of choice in District 2, but it's rampant in the downtown core. I can list dozens of dealers who are able to buy large quantities down there. So maybe Sleeves is selling there too.'

Striker shook his head. 'No way. Anyone selling meth in District 1 has to buy their drugs off one of the groups affiliated with the Satan's Prowlers – and that can't happen here. Sleeves has been cut loose by the gang. And even he's not stupid enough to be selling in Prowler territory. It would expedite his death sentence. And besides that, he doesn't need to. He can lie low here and still make a profit.'

Felicia continued poking holes in the theory. 'Granted. But they also sell tons of meth in District 3.'

Striker nodded. 'An area which is controlled by the Seven Nations Gang, the Chinese Scorpions and the Viets. Sure, Sleeves could be selling there too. But if he was, do you think the other gangs would put up with it? – some punk who'd been excommunicated from the Prowlers selling in their area?'

'Probably not.'

'*Definitely* not. They'd have taken action against him immediately. And I've read nothing about that in the Overnights. Have you?'

'No,' she admitted.

Striker continued: 'District 2 is the low end, the free-for-all, mainly because it's a crack cocaine district. That's what sells here, crack. The meth is just an afterthought – but afterthought or not, Sleeves needs somewhere to sell his product. My bet is he's doing it here.'

'Which means he needs a legitimate street trafficker,' Felicia said. 'A guy who has the street cred to move decent amounts of product but isn't a total junkie himself.'

'Which means Lucky Eddie.'

'Who won't be so lucky today.'

Striker grinned. 'Bingo.'

When Felicia still looked uncertain, Striker prodded her. 'Tell you what, I'll make you a bet. If I win, you have to give me a full body massage tonight; if you win, I'll give you one.'

'Sounds like you win either way.'

Striker laughed. 'And you say I have an ego.'

Felicia just smiled at him.

Then the wait began.

It didn't take long. Lucky Eddie was an easy man to spot, mainly because he suffered from Marfan syndrome. Because of this, he was almost 200 centimetres tall and had unusually long arms and legs. When Striker saw the outline of a tall stickman lumbering up to a much smaller individual behind the convenience store, he knew they had found their man.

'Beautiful,' Striker said.

Felicia saw it too. 'He's making a deal right now.'

'*Hold on.*'

Before Felicia could respond, Striker hit the gas. They cut across the main drive of Lakewood and came to a screeching halt behind the convenience store. The swerve of the car and the cry of the brakes caused Lucky Eddie to jump back in surprise, and he dropped his collection of baggies in the process.

Striker jumped out of the car, grabbed Eddie by the arm, and slammed him over the hood of the cruiser. As he handcuffed him, Eddie's customer ran frantically across the park towards Wall Street.

Striker smiled at Felicia. 'Where's the loyalty?'

She looked down at Eddie. 'This will definitely affect your customer approval rating.'

Lucky Eddie said nothing, he just stared back at them through dark eyes that communicated nothing. Striker gave the prisoner a cursory search, clearing the man of knives and guns, and then pulled him off the hood. In behind them, Felicia picked up four dropped baggies, each one containing roughly twenty pills. She held them up and looked at their contents.

'It's jib. Maybe some E too.'

Striker nodded: *Crystal meth and ecstasy*. He turned to Lucky Eddie and smiled. 'Well, this certainly is a dilemma we find ourselves in.'

Eddie's posture sagged. 'You gonna book me or not, Striker?'

'Striker? Wow, you remember me. How thoughtful. And here I thought you'd forgotten.'

'You almost ran me over last time too.'

'*Almost* – that's the key word.' Striker took one of the bags from Felicia. 'Let's see, what charges have we got here? Possession. Trafficking. Evading Arrest. And the last time I checked, you were also out on bail, were you not? So there'll be a breach here somewhere too.'

'It's like a *smorgasbord* of charges,' Felicia said.

Striker nodded. 'And I'm still hungry.'

Eddie scowled at their banter, then looked away. 'So what? Charge me. I'll be out in two months – max.'

'Oh, you'll be out today,' Striker replied. When the drug trafficker looked at him sideways, Striker added, 'It's your lucky day, Lucky Eddie – I don't want to arrest you.'

There was a long pause, then Eddie asked, 'What's the catch?'

'I need some information – an answer to a very important question. One which I know you have . . . Where is Sleeves hiding?'

Recognition and surprise filled Eddie's eyes. But there was also something else there. *Fear.*

'Never heard of him.'

'Actually, you have heard of him. In fact, you're dealing for him right now.'

'Then book me.'

Striker raised an eyebrow. 'Sure, I could do that – or I could take a different approach here. You see, my partner and I just had a conversation with Vicenza Montalba.'

Eddie flinched at the name, and Striker continued.

'Vicenza Montalba is none-too-happy with Sleeves right now. Now if you want, we could always pay Montalba another visit, let him know who's got the balls to sell for the very guy Montalba excommunicated from his criminal enterprise.'

Eddie said nothing but his face hardened.

The reaction made Striker smile. 'Yeah, I think Montalba would deliver a slightly different sentence than the courts, don't you, Feleesh?'

She grinned. 'I'd say Life . . . in some form or another.'

Eddie licked his lips. 'This is bullshit, man, this is fucking *bullshit*!'

Striker lost the smile. He gripped Eddie's collar and got right in his face.

'I'll tell you what's bullshit, Eddie. I got two innocent women murdered and a personal friend of mine who's been targeted by some fuckin' whack-job bomber. You get it? *That* is fuckin' bullshit. All the cards are off the table on this one.'

Felicia nodded in agreement. 'The moment you target a cop, there are no rules.'

Eddie's eyes took on a distant look. 'I never targeted no—'

'We're not messing around here,' Striker said. 'Time is critical. And every minute that goes by endangers a cop's life more. So here's the deal, Eddie: we *know* you have an address for Sleeves. You give it to us, and we let you go and never say a word about this again. You don't cough it up, and we'll charge you with everything I can think of – and then I'll call Montalba myself.'

Eddie looked back, deadpan. 'I call bluff.'

Striker fished the business card Montalba had given him out from his wallet. He held it up for Eddie to see.

'We're talking a cop's life here, Eddie. Your scumbag rights don't count for shit.' He took out his cell and began dialling. 'The moment this call is answered, the deal is off.'

He put it on speakerphone, and the line began to ring.

One, two—

'Okay, okay, *o-fucking-kay*!' Eddie snapped. 'For God's sake, man, Montalba will kill me!'

'That's the general idea.' Striker put the cell away. 'Now where can we find him?'

Eddie let out a long breath, then relented. 'House up on Lakewood. Right behind the 7-Eleven. White, with boarded-up windows.'

'He lives there?'

'He *stays* there with some girl. When he's doing business. Calls it the *bunker*.'

'Where is it?'

'I dunno, man. Serious. He never tells no one 'bout it. He's paranoid.'

'Who's the girl?'

'I dunno. Some chick. She's a freak. Never comes out, never talks to no one.' Eddie shrugged. 'Creepy, if you ask me.'

Striker changed the subject. 'I want his cell number too.'

'Sleeves ain't got no cell.'

'All dealers have a cell.'

'Well he never gave the number to me. He got a pager instead. Like I told you, he's friggin' paranoid, man.'

'Because he's got too many enemies,' Felicia said.

Eddie just shrugged like he didn't much care. 'Look, I don't make no rules. This is just how it is. I call that number, punch in three 8s, and Sleeves brings more product. Same amount every time – twenty dime-bags . . . We got a thing going on here, him and me.'

'Where do you meet?' Striker demanded.

'Men's room,' he grumbled. 'Pandora Park.'

It was not surprising. Pandora Park was a shithole.

Striker took out his notebook, got Eddie talking, and wrote down Sleeves' address. Once done, he called for a jail pick-up.

The wagon arrived five minutes later and Striker shoved Eddie inside the compartment. The drug dealer immediately began whining.

'We had a deal, Striker – a deal!'

Striker turned to face him. 'I said no charges, Eddie, and there'll be none. You'll be released in an hour or so – *after* we catch Sleeves.'

'Just let me go. I won't tell him! I won't say shit! Honest—'

Striker slammed closed the wagon door. Gave the driver the thumbs up. And the diesel engine chugged loudly as the driver headed west.

Striker returned to the undercover police cruiser. Moments later, they were driving south on Lakewood, heading towards East Pender Street. Destination: Sleeves' hideout.

It was only a kilometre away.

Sixty-Eight

'This Sleeves is a real sicko,' Felicia said.

Striker drove as Felicia read through the paperwork. A few blocks later, she looked up from the copies of the confidential files Ibarra had given them back in the Gang Crime Unit. The one she was currently reading was an Intel file from back east, on the death of a seven-year-old child; the boy had been a casualty of the biker wars in Toronto.

The suspect in the bombing was Sleeves.

Seven years old.

It gave Striker a dark feeling.

'Insufficient grounds to charge or even detain,' Felicia continued. 'In fact, *all* these files are only Intel.' She read on. 'They never found any empirical evidence linking Sleeves to any of the bombings. It was all circumstantial.'

'Is it the same MO as the Toy Hut?'

Felicia frowned. 'There's no forensic detail. Just source material. We'd need to get the actual report.'

'Great. Add it to the list.'

Striker had never dealt with the Toronto Police Department before. Didn't even know if they were on the PRIME system. It was yet another task they'd need to perform. He slowed down as East Hastings Street came into view. They were getting closer to Sleeves' basement suite now.

Felicia leaned back from the laptop.

'Something odd here,' she said. 'Sleeves has a record a mile long, a charge or two for every year – except for a twelve-month period where he just plain disappears off the system. Not one report on PRIME or LEIP or PIRS. Nothing.'

'Check the Coronet system. Maybe he was in jail.'

'I did, he wasn't.'

'Something must have happened,' Striker said. 'Guys like him don't take holidays. Maybe he was out of the country. Or in hiding.'

She looked over at him. 'Maybe we should call in the Emergency Response Team on this one.'

'Absolutely not.'

'Why not?'

'First, they're not needed – we're not going in, he's coming out. And second, the moment we bring in ERT, we lose control of the file. They'll call in a negotiator, and the only one on right now is Acting Deputy Chief Laroche. And we've been over that before – Laroche is the last person we want involved with this file. If that happens, we'll lose all ownership of the investigation. Not to mention everyone will know – and that includes Harry and Koda.'

Felicia persisted. 'We at least need a cover unit.'

Striker agreed. 'I'm fine with that. Let's get one. But don't forget, we're not here to arrest Sleeves – we don't have enough evidence for that. We're just gonna put the heavy on the man.'

'What about everything you overheard Harry and Koda talking about?'

Striker shrugged. 'What about it? It's already dubious; you even said that yourself. And it will be nothing but hearsay in court. Harry and Koda are sure as hell never gonna admit to anything. You and I both know they're up to something here, be it a cover-up, revenge, or even their own personal investigation. But we got no real proof of that yet. We got to play this one *smoothly.*'

Felicia relented. She finished reading Sleeves' CNI page – the Criminal Name Index – and a bemused laugh escaped her lips. 'Here's something we can use against him. He got a bench warrant for traffic tickets. We can threaten to make him pay his fines.'

A smile stretched Striker's lips.

'That is perfect,' he said.

Felicia frowned at him. 'I was only joking, Jacob. You don't have to be sarcastic.'

But Striker kept smiling.

'I'm not being sarcastic,' he said. 'Those aren't just traffic tickets Sleeves has got – they're *wild cards.*'

Sixty-Nine

Felicia put them out on a Violent Offender Check in the two thousand block of East Pender Street. The information Lucky Eddie had given them was straightforward. Sleeves was hiding out in the basement suite of a small house that sat just behind the 7-Eleven store.

White house. East end of Pender. North side.

The house was distinguishable because Sleeves had taped black plastic garbage bags over the bedroom window in order to block out the glare from the nearby street lamp.

Once Striker and Felicia had located the suite and the corresponding window, they went to the rear of the house in case Sleeves unexpectedly exited the premises. The position was adequate at best. With the midday sun blasting down from above, there was little shadow for concealment.

Striker got on his cell and called up Niles Quaid, a ten-year Patrol vet who was working the dayshift plainclothes car. Striker had known Quaid for years – he was a good cop who did good work and could keep his mouth shut. Over the phone, Striker filled him in on the situation, stressing that everything was off the record. Within five minutes, Quaid and his partner arrived on scene to assist.

Striker obtained an Ops channel from Dispatch, then they set up.

He and Felicia moved to the rear lane. While keeping cover behind the detached garage, Striker assessed the yard. It was small and open with nowhere that could be called proper cover. Even more problematic was the entrance to the suite. To reach it, one had to cross a long, open walkway, then descend a narrow set of stairs that were sandwiched in by two concrete walls.

'It's a perfect trap,' Felicia said.

Striker agreed. There was absolutely no cover should a gun battle erupt.

With Sleeves justly paranoid and already on the lookout for gang rivals, Striker was concerned about the man shooting first and asking questions later. And judging from the various police files they'd read in the different systems, this had been his standard MO over the years.

'He got any vehicles?' Striker asked.

Felicia looked inside the garage. The window was dirty and hard to see through. She rubbed the pane clean with her elbow. Inside was an old Jeep 4x4 with a cracked windshield. The angle made the licence plate unreadable.

'Might be his vehicle,' she said. 'I better take up a position here in case.'

Striker looked down Lakewood Street. 'Fine. I'll take the east side of the house, in case he takes off on foot.'

He gave Felicia a hard stare.

'What?' she asked.

'No messing around with this guy. He's too dangerous. Just take him down and take him down *hard.*'

'Is there any other way?'

Striker smiled. 'That's my girl.'

He radioed the plainclothes car and told them to cover off the south and west positions. Once everyone was set, he dialled the number Lucky Eddie had given them. Punched in three 8s.

And they waited.

Not five minutes later, the door to the suite opened and the target emerged. Sleeves looked identical to the description listed in the police database: 175 centimetres and a wiry 80 kilos. With blue eyes and short black hair. He wore torn-up blue jeans and a filthy white hoodie with red blocky script that spelled one word:

SNAFU.

Striker recognized it. It was sarcastic military slang for *Situation Normal: All Fucked Up*. He keyed the radio.

'Target's out,' he said.

Sleeves crept slowly up the back steps, his head snapping left and right like a weasel watching for snakes. With one hand tucked deep under the front of his hoodie, he beelined across the overgrown lawn towards the rear lane. When he stepped past the threshold of the carport, Felicia swung into his path, gun out.

'Vancouver Police! Don't move.'

Sleeves startled. Stepped back. Spun about.

Raced for his suite.

Striker cut him off at the door. With all his might, he threw a solid right into the man's cheek. Felt the snap of the punch all the way into his shoulder. Felt the follow-through. Ended up slamming his fist into the porch post.

Sleeves made no noise. He just jerked left, then collapsed onto his stomach. He tried to roll left, but Striker dropped one knee on the man's back, pinning him to the ground. The ex-Prowler started to slide his hand down near his waist, and Felicia stuck her gun in his face.

'Bad move, asshole.'

Sleeves stopped moving. Glared up at her with his hollow blue eyes. 'Your badge isn't a shield.'

'Be quiet,' Striker said as he cuffed him.

He drove the man's face into the grass and searched around

his waist and torso. After a long moment, he frowned. There was nothing on the man. No baggie filled with paper flaps of meth. No gun, no knife. Not even a canister of pepper spray.

He stood up. Told Sleeves not to move. And neared Felicia.

'Lucky Eddie screwed us,' he whispered.

She gave him a questioning look.

'There's no way this guy was leaving without a weapon, not when the entire Prowlers gang is after him.' He thought it over. 'That triple-eight code we punched in . . . it was the wrong one, I'll bet. A fucking warning.'

Felicia scowled and looked at Sleeves. The ex-Prowler was looking right back up at her. But his stare looked somehow detached, as if he were not really there. His face was drawn and gaunt. Then he blinked, and it was as if his mind had returned to his body.

'Take off these cuffs,' he said.

Striker said nothing. He just walked over, leaned down, and grabbed the man's arm. When he lifted Sleeves up, the man went easily. He was surprisingly light. But when Striker spun him around for a better look, he could also see that the man had corded muscle on him – thin and taut like guitar strings.

'Release these cuffs,' he said again. 'Or charge me.'

'I'll decide when and who I charge,' Striker replied. He took a long look at the ex-Prowler and saw small cut marks on his face. The one on his right cheek was from where Striker had punched him, but the one on the left looked relatively fresh. Thoughts of the exploding glass from the toy store flooded Striker's mind.

'Nice cuts,' Striker said. 'You new to shaving or something?'

Sleeves said nothing for a long moment, and when he looked back, his eyes were alert. Full of assessment. 'You almost broke my jaw,' he said. 'I'll remember this.'

Striker wrote down the time and acted like he didn't much care.

'You have nothing,' Sleeves said.

Felicia spoke next: 'You got a bench warrant.'

A look of dark amusement flickered on the man's face, there for a second and then instantly replaced by that distant emptiness. 'You assaulted me over a traffic ticket? Sounds like a reportable breach of the Police Act to me.'

Striker looked up from his notebook and spoke plainly. 'There won't be any reports made to anyone, Sleeves. What's going to happen is this: you and I are going to *cooperate*. I'm going to ask you some questions and you're going to answer them. And then, maybe, I won't throw your ass in jail.'

'You're gonna lodge me in jail? For what? Unpaid parking tickets? Go ahead. I'll pay the fines.'

Striker smiled at the man. 'It's not the money you should be worried about, Sleeves, it's the *time*.'

'What time? I'll be out in an hour.'

'Exactly. And that gives me plenty of time to call Vicenza Montalba, and for him to then contact some of his business associates. I mean, think about it: they'll know *where* you'll be released, and they'll know *when* . . . Suddenly, you're not too hard to find any more. And from what I hear, Montalba's not too happy with you.'

Sleeves said nothing. His face remained expressionless, his eyes once again giving a strange detached stare, as if he was no longer there with them, but somewhere else.

Striker leaned closer, looked at the numerous scars on the man's face and neck. 'I heard you were using your own product, Sleeves. Probably to cover up the pain. I heard you blew yourself up good a few years back. That true?'

The man said nothing.

Striker made a tsk-tsk sound. 'Using. That's a Prowlers no-no, ain't it, Feleesh?'

She grinned. 'Almost as much as selling meth after being excommunicated.'

Striker raised a hand in deference. 'I forgot about that one. That's an even bigger no-no.' He turned back to Sleeves. 'Man, you really like to push the envelope, don't you? Are you trying to die young?'

For the first time since being taken down, the ex-Prowler met Striker's stare, and he spoke plainly.

'I'm not afraid to die.'

He spoke the words so calmly and assuredly that Striker believed the man.

'Just because you don't fear death, doesn't mean you're stupid enough to throw your life away. So what's it going to be, Sleeves? Cooperation or a Prowler phone call?'

For a long moment, Sleeves said nothing. He just stood there and stared back, his hollow blue eyes pointed in Striker's direction, but his thoughts clearly a million miles away. He moved his jaw back and forth, as if trying to get the joint back in place. It made soft clicking sounds.

'What do you want from me?' he finally asked.

'Information,' Striker replied. 'Like, what is your connection to Sharise Owens and Keisha Williams?'

'I've never heard of them.'

'Let me refresh your mind. Owens was a doctor. Williams was a toymaker and an accountant. They were both women in their forties. Black.'

'Never heard of them.'

Striker changed his line of questioning. 'Harry Eckhart and Chad Koda.'

This time, Sleeves' eyes filled with recognition – or was it wariness? His jaw tightened and a dark wild look filled his eyes. 'So that's what this is about – the explosion at Koda's house.'

'So you know about it?'

'The whole city knows.'

Felicia stepped closer. 'The whole city may know about it, Sleeves, but you're the one with a history of bombs.'

'Wasn't me.'

'Like it wasn't you who set the bomb that killed that little boy back east?'

Sleeves glared back at Felicia and his shoulders bulged as he strained against the handcuffs.

'Better be calm there,' Striker warned. 'And while you're at it, maybe you'd like to tell us where you've been the last twenty-four hours. You can start by giving us a list of places and times, then start working on some witnesses who can verify your story.'

Sleeves glanced back towards the house. 'I was here.'

'With who?'

For a long moment, Sleeves said nothing. He just stood there with his cold blue eyes focused on nothing. When he finally spoke again, there was an edge to his voice. A controlled anger. 'Harry and Koda send you?' he asked.

Striker shook his head. 'No one sends me.'

'I want money. One hundred Gs.'

The demand surprised Striker. 'One hundred *grand*?' He laughed softly. 'Sure, no problem. Do you take personal cheques?'

Sleeves did not laugh. 'One hundred grand. The information is worth more.'

'How much more?'

'How much do you value human life?'

Striker looked at Felicia, and she just shrugged. He thought it over for a moment, then stepped closer to Sleeves, purposely invading the man's personal space. 'How do I know you're not full of shit, Sleeves? Or that you won't screw us like Lucky Eddie did? Tell me something about Harry and Koda to get me started.'

The ex-Prowler looked back, unblinking. 'Me and Chipotle . . . we did their burning.'

'*Chipotle?* Who the hell's Chipotle?'

Sleeves laughed bemusedly. 'You don't know a thing, do you?'

'And what *burning*?' Felicia asked.

But Sleeves did not answer her.

'One hundred grand and I will open up your eyes,' he said. 'But be forewarned, you aren't going to like what you see.'

Seventy

With Sleeves handcuffed and in Felicia's custody, Striker snuck away to check out the basement suite. The moment he walked down the concrete stairs and opened the door, the lack of floor space became immediately apparent.

The suite was nothing more than a studio – one room consisting of a small fold-out couch and a kitchenette that didn't even have a proper stove but a simple hotplate and a microwave. Oddly, the place looked not only clean but immaculate. Barely lived in. There were no weapons to be seen and no sign of drugs or drug paraphernalia.

No scale, no packaging products, no drugs score-sheets.

The only thing of interest Striker found were some empty packaging for Duracell D-size batteries and some broken down cell phone pieces – parts that could be used to make a detonator, no doubt, but also a hundred other things as well.

Evidence-wise, it left him with nothing.

Frustrated and a little mystified by the scene, he left the suite. When he returned to the lane where Felicia had Sleeves handcuffed and seated on the ground, Felicia gave him a curious look. 'Well?' she asked.

'Shit outta luck,' Striker said.

Sleeves looked up from his seated position. 'What were you doing back there? You go in my suite? You need a warrant for that.'

Striker ignored the man and jotted down his findings in his notebook. As he did this, Felicia returned to Lakewood to get the undercover cruiser. Once she was back, Striker told Sleeves to stay put or else, then moved closer to Felicia, where the two were out of earshot.

'So what you think?' he asked.

She shrugged. 'Who knows if he knows anything? Besides, we'll never get a hundred grand from Source Handling. Not even with some proof of return. You know how stingy they are. We'd be lucky to get ten Gs.'

Striker nodded and looked back at the ex-Prowler. 'He knows *something*. I believe that wholeheartedly. But he has no intention of telling us. That's why he demanded a hundred grand – he knows we can't get it. He's playing a game. But why? What does he really want?'

Felicia had a tight expression masking her normally pretty features. 'I feel uneasy. I mean, we can't just let him go. He might be responsible for the bombings.'

Striker nodded. 'I agree. But what evidence are we going to hold him on? There's nothing tangible on him and nothing in the suite—and I mean *nothing*. So what you wanna go on? Circumstantial evidence? Similar fact? I'm sure defence counsel would love that.'

Felicia didn't smile. 'He's dangerous, Jacob. What if he is our guy? What if we let him go and he sets off another bomb and it kills more people? I don't want that on my conscience. This guy has no filter – he's killed *a kid* before.'

'Never proved.'

'We fucking know he did it.'

To hear Felicia curse was unusual. Striker could feel her tension. But so what? He agreed with her morally, but legally what could they do? He took a moment to call the Road Boss and fill him in. Inspector Osaka sounded exhausted from all the chaos of the last two days, and Striker had little doubt the man was being grilled constantly by Acting Deputy Chief Laroche.

'I want to put surveillance on Sleeves,' Striker said.

'I'm sure you do,' Osaka replied. 'And so do I. But Strike Force is already working on the kidnapping in District 4.'

'What kidnapping?'

'It's unrelated – an overseas thing from Hong Kong. But a ten-year-old girl is involved and it's life or death. They've even called in Property Crime for this one – I don't have a team to spare.'

Striker nodded absently. 'I wasn't aware of all that.'

'Why would you be? You've been going crazy on the bombings – speaking of which, I'll be expecting a full status report later on.' Osaka sighed. 'It's been a real bad couple of days in Vancouver. Normally, I'd just request support from the Feds, but Special O's way out in the valley today on a gang hit.'

Striker searched for a different solution. He looked down the alley at Niles Quaid's undercover cruiser.

It gave him an idea.

'How about this?' he said. 'I got Niles Quaid here in a plainclothes car. He spent four years in Strike Force, and he was the Road Boss for half of those. Why don't we get him and his partner to do some makeshift surveillance for now?'

'And if they're spotted?'

'So what? If Sleeves thinks he's being watched, so much the better. He'll be careful not to do anything stupid. It's better than nothing.'

Osaka said nothing for a long moment. When it had been so long that Striker thought they might have been disconnected, the inspector okayed the plan, but there was uncertainty in his voice. 'Overtime's approved, Striker. Just keep me informed. I mean it – I got Laroche on my ass every minute of the day right now.'

'Strange. I didn't think he was your type, sir.'

Osaka let out a small laugh, one that sounded more like released tension than humour. 'Just keep me informed.'

Striker said he would and hung up the phone. He then relayed the information to Felicia. Seeing that she was satisfied with the approach, he set everyone up for the operation.

Once done, Striker walked back over to Sleeves. He stood him up and removed the man's handcuffs. The ex-Prowler said nothing. He just headed for the stairs, limping noticeably on the left side. Halfway there, he stopped. He turned, took a long hard look at Striker, and probed into him with those cold blue eyes of his.

Striker met the man's stare.

'Keep moving,' he said.

And Sleeves continued down the stairs.

Striker watched the man close the door and disappear from sight. There was a dangerousness about him, something that put Striker on edge. Even more so than most murderers he dealt with. When Felicia walked over, she stared at the suite and shuddered. Her words echoed exactly what he was thinking.

'That guy gets a one hundred on the creepy scale.'

Striker couldn't have agreed more.

Blue eyes had never looked so dark.

Seventy-One

Harry took the elevator up to Source Handling.

Source Handling was a small section, consisting of nothing more than a few desks and the mandatory coffee machine with a tray of sugar packets and nondairy creamers. The unit's assigned detectives were responsible for investigating the validity of all anonymous tips brought in through the CrimeStoppers programme, and for maintaining and safeguarding the information of police informants, agents, and for all their related restitutions.

Harry walked in through the front door and spotted Trevor sitting at his desk. The man was impossible to miss. Standing almost 200 centimetres and weighing in at 136 kilos, Trevor Eckhart had received every possible gene from their father's side of the family. Harry had taken after their mother's side, and that included the icy-blue eyes and high blood pressure problems.

'Trevor,' he said.

His brother looked up. Trevor had a large head, and when he smiled his unusually full beard and moustache made his mouth look small. 'Harry! Good to see you, man. How's the family?'

'Good, they're doing good,' Harry replied. But the tone of his voice gave away his mood.

Trevor sat back from the keyboard. 'What's wrong? Is someone sick or something?'

Harry said nothing for a moment; he just looked around the room for Clara Sykes, the other detective who worked in the unit. When he didn't see her, he asked, 'Where's your work wife?'

Trevor didn't smile. 'She's off today. What's going on, Harry?'

He closed the office door. 'I need the address for a guy who's been coded.'

'*Your* guy?'

When Harry didn't respond, Trevor shook his head. 'Jesus, Harry, you're really pushing me into a corner here.'

'This isn't about work, Trevor.'

'Even worse then.'

Harry felt his face flush red. And for the moment, he found it hard to meet his brother's eyes. Trevor had always been a good cop. A man of integrity. And it pained Harry to have to ask him for this favour.

But there was no choice.

'I wouldn't ask if I didn't have to; you know that. But this . . . this is becoming a safety issue. For me, and for Sandra and Ethan.'

'A *safety* issue?' Trevor got up and locked the office door. When he returned to the computer, he said, 'Give me the name.'

Relief and shame flooded Harry. 'Gang name is Sleeves. Real name is Brice Burns. List him between thirty-six and forty. I need a contact number, or an address. Something.'

Trevor ran the name through the system. A few minutes later, he had the code. He then went to the safe and grabbed the corresponding file. From it, he took the front page, then jotted down a number.

'This is the only number the guy has,' he explained. 'A cell. And just so you know, it's a *police* cell. So the moment you call it, not only will he know it's the police calling, but there'll be a record of it – so you'd better have a good reason why you're calling him and an even better way of explaining how you got the number in the first place, because you sure as hell never got it from me.'

'Understood.'

'I'm going to purge the file the moment you leave.'

Trevor handed the paper to Harry. When Harry reached out to take the paper, Trevor didn't let go. Harry frowned.

'Trevor,' he started.

But his brother cut him off. 'I don't know who this Sleeves guy is, Harry, but he's got a lot of warning flags on the system.'

Harry said nothing.

'He was coded a long time ago,' Trevor continued. 'Years, in fact. And he was disassociated because of violent crimes.'

'Then why does he still have the police phone?'

'Because he's listed as Under Threat. I don't know why. But as long as that's there, there's an onus on the department to cover him because he was coded. Be careful here, Harry. Be very, *very* careful here. This is a really bad guy you're dealing with.'

'I get it.'

Trevor finally let go of the paper, albeit somewhat reluctantly. When the two brothers met stares again, Trevor's hard expression finally cracked, and his voice softened. 'What else can I do for you, Harry?'

Harry looked back at his brother, and he remembered so many of the times that Trevor had been there for him. During their parents' divorce. Following the death of his son. And the end of his marriage. It was like Trevor had always been the big brother, the responsible one, helping him out of jams.

It shamed him.

'Just be there for Sandra and Ethan,' he said. 'If something bad should ever happen to me.'

Trevor's face paled.

'Something bad? Harry, what's going on here? Jesus, what the hell are you talking about?'

But Harry said nothing else. He just thanked his brother for the help, then left the room and closed the door behind him.

Seventy-Two

They headed for Burnaby, where the lower mainland's largest incinerator was located. Once there, Striker turned onto Penzance Drive and drove down the steep decline until the gravel road became dirt and river mud. The lower road fronted the Burrard Inlet, where gusts of mill steam clouded the view of Mount Seymour Provincial Park.

Felicia pointed to a row of smokestacks and enormous conveyor belts in the distance. Each one stood six or seven storeys high, and spewed out a flow of whiteness.

'Is that the pulp mill?' she asked.

Striker nodded. He pointed to one smokestack that stood separate from the rest. It was thicker, higher, enormous. 'That's where we're going – the incinerator . . . I think that's where Sleeves and this Chipotle guy he was talking about did all their so-called *burning* for Harry and Koda.'

'But burning *what*?'

Striker smiled. 'That's the twenty-four-thousand-dollar question, ain't it?'

Up ahead was a tall billboard sign:

Montreaux Waste-to-Energy Station.

Striker drove into the complex and spotted a roundabout. Here, several garbage trucks were lined up at an on-ramp that connected to a giant, bowl-like incinerator. He drove past them all and parked in front of the main office.

As they climbed out, Felicia asked, 'What exactly does this facility burn?'

Striker shrugged. 'Privately, they burn anything. Publicly, they burn whatever the provincial government sends them – all the non-recyclable trash comes here. As for police, this is where they burn all the old evidence from past files – ones the courts have already deliberated on.'

'So you think that Sleeves was burning evidence?'

'I'm betting on it.'

Felicia shook her head. 'Why didn't you tell me that earlier?'

He gave her a confused look. 'What do you mean?'

Her voice got tighter. 'All this time I've been under the impression they were burning *witnesses*. You know, intimidating them. To stop them from testifying.'

Striker stopped walking and looked at her. 'That crossed my mind too. And I wouldn't put it past the Prowlers. But the more I think about it, the more this makes sense.'

'Why?'

'Because every time old evidence is destroyed, the Emergency Response Team has to escort the driver. It's evidence after all, sensitive information. And the ERT team that's always been in charge of evidence destruction is Red Team.'

'So what?'

'Remember what Osaka said – who was a sergeant for Red Team? Before he retired?'

Felicia thought it over, then got it. 'Chad Koda.'

Striker nodded. 'It's a connection at least. Something to go on. I would have said something to you earlier on, but I've been working things out in my head as we've been driving here. And I'm still not entirely sure. Let's see what we find.'

They got walking again and soon reached the main plant.

Within five minutes, they were being guided around the facility by the site manager, who was a short man with a pudgy face and a crayfish moustache that overgrew his upper lip and disappeared into his mouth. He also had giant overgrown sideburns that would have put Elvis to shame.

'I'd be glad to help,' the manager said.

Striker offered the standard, 'We appreciate your time.'

'Right, right, right.' The manager spoke the words to Striker, but his eyes lingered on Felicia – as they had since the moment she had introduced herself. It was a fact she noticed and was clearly uncomfortable with. 'Just follow me, Detectives. I'll steer ya right.' The manager walked on stoically, constantly patting down the left side of his moustache.

When they reached the control room, the manager stopped walking and made eye contact with Felicia. He gestured to a line of technicians that were monitoring displays on the far wall. 'This is *my* squad. The men I go to battle with every day.'

'Great,' she said.

'They monitor burning times and heat levels – a process which is absolutely critical for plant efficiency. This incinerator gets up to *fourteen hundred* degrees Celsius.'

'Sounds hot,' Felicia said.

'Oh, it's hot, Detective. *Real* hot. Not many things are hotter – unless you want to take a trip to the sun!'

Striker grinned, enjoying the moment.

'Felicia likes hot places,' he said.

She cast him a look of daggers, but said nothing, and the manager continued talking. 'Yep, when my squad here is done with the waste, there's nothing left but metal and ash. We recycle the metals, of course; magnets in Conveyor Line 3 do that – they separate up to *two tons* a day, which makes us only the second plant in all of North America to meet the 14001 standard of the ISO.' He leaned closer to Felicia and explained: 'That's recycle talk for the International Organization for Standardization. Green Planet stuff.'

'You don't say,' she said.

'I'm the emissions chief here. I got to be on top of things.'

Striker grinned again. 'Felicia likes it when men are on top of things.'

She cast him another dark stare, and he smiled at her.

For a moment, the manager was diverted when one of his technicians requested some assistance. He pardoned himself and stepped away. While he was preoccupied, Striker moved closer to Felicia. 'That was so interesting what he said about the ISO.'

'Don't even start.'

'I never realized acronyms were such a turn-on for you. Did I mention I work for the *VPD*.'

'Stop it.'

'In *MCS*.'

'It's not funny, Jacob, this guy gives me the creeps.'

'My favourite sandwich is a *BLT*.'

Felicia let out a frustrated laugh. 'Joke all you want, chowderhead, but I'm pretty sure I saw this guy in *Silence of the Lambs*.'

She'd hardly spoken the words when the manager returned. He splayed his hands and nodded vigorously. 'Sorry for the delay, folks, but that was a close one, boy. Just averted what was damn near a catastrophe.'

'A veritable Chernobyl, I'm sure,' Felicia said dryly.

Striker had had enough of the tour and he stepped forward. 'This facility really is impressive, but what we need to see are your personnel records.'

The wide grin slipped from the manager's face and was replaced by a defensive look. He sucked in his upper lip and half his moustache disappeared. 'Personnel records? Oh boy . . . company's pretty strict with that stuff. You got a warrant?'

Striker said nothing; he just gave Felicia a glance.

She stepped closer to the site manager and placed her hand on his forearm. Gave it a gentle squeeze. 'We understand the need for sensitivity. Believe me, we do. But this wouldn't be for court purposes – it's merely investigative. And it would save me *hours* of work. You'd be doing me a really big service here.'

The defensive look on the man's face fell away. 'Well . . . all I'm saying is we'd have to keep this *confidential*.'

Felicia smiled. 'Of course. We wouldn't have it any other way.'

Minutes later, Striker and Felicia stood in the records office as the manager sat in front of them and navigated through the computer system until he was in the Human Resources folder. He brought up the plant personnel records. 'Everything's electronic nowadays, Detectives.'

Striker read the names, one by one. When he saw the Bs, he put a hand on the manager's shoulder. 'Stop right there.'

On the screen was the name Striker was looking for: Brice Burns.

Sleeves.

Felicia saw it too. 'He was on the payroll.'

Striker got the man to check the Cs as well and found an entry for Carlos Chipotle.

Felicia smiled. 'We got them both here.'

Striker asked, 'What were these guys' roles at the plant?'

The manager read the date. 'Wow, we're talking a long time ago here.' He clicked on a sidebar tab and a mini window popped up. 'Says here they were both Level 3 Operators.'

'Which means?'

'They worked the forklift. Unloaded cargo.'

Striker smiled at that; finally, he was starting to see some light at the end of the tunnel. He looked at the screen and saw that the dates of employment were short – less than sixteen months in all. He pointed at the screen. 'We need copies of all the Vancouver Police Department shipments that occurred on these dates, and we need them now.'

Striker looked up at Felicia and saw the excited expression on her face. It was clear she had made the connection too. They had now linked Sleeves and Chipotle and Koda to the burning facility – Sleeves and Chipotle by way of employee records, Koda by being the sergeant in charge of ERT's Red Team.

They were finally getting somewhere.

Seventy-Three

Once Striker and Felicia pulled up out front of Main Street Headquarters, Felicia stuffed the burn records into a file folder, carried it with her, and the two of them hurried up the front stairs. Striker cut past the Public Service counter and adjoining Ident booth, where a woman was being fingerprinted.

He used his keycard to swipe in to the property office.

Striker found the clerk he was looking for. Larry Smallsy was a tall man with thinning white hair and John Lennon spectacles. Striker had known him for ten years and liked doing work with him because of two things: Smallsy was easy-going, and he operated within the bounds of common sense, not policy and procedure.

'Larry!' Striker called.

The property clerk, seated at his desk, looked up from a far-too-healthy looking bran muffin. 'Hey, Detectives.'

Striker approached his desk. 'I need to see sixteen months of your burn records from ten years ago, and I need them now.'

Smallsy said nothing. He just removed a bag of Wet Wipes from his desk, began cleaning the sticky bran crumbs from his fingers, and bobbed his head. Once his fingers were clean, he got up and wandered down the back corridor.

Striker gave Felicia a nod, and they followed.

As they went, Striker absently assessed the property office.

The place was a dump. Crammed to the roof with box after box of old evidence, infested with cockroaches, and loaded with rat traps in every corner, the place screamed of disrepair.

It matched the rest of the downtown station.

Felicia sniffed loudly, then made a face. 'Everything smells damp and mouldy down here, Smallsy. And there's no room to move. It's a wonder you can even do your job.'

'Yeah, well I'm Larry friggin' Potter,' he said. 'I keep everything organized.'

Up ahead, Smallsy stopped at a long counter that was fronted by numerous shelves of archives. From the uppermost row, he pulled down three ledgers. When he laid them down on the counter and opened them up, Striker saw that the pages of the books were more yellow than white, and coffee stains decorated the edges. He looked at the headings of the books. They were all the same:

Evidence Transfer – Montreaux Incinerator.

Striker grabbed the file folder from Felicia. From it, he removed a wad of papers. He placed them down on the counter top, next to the ledger. He ran his finger down the pages, one by one. When he came across the corresponding date, he stopped. Compared. And found discrepancies.

Felicia made a surprised sound.

'The weights don't match,' she said.

Striker saw it too. The weights logged in at the burning facility were less than the ones shipped out from the property office. In fact, not only were the weights short, but they weren't even close – off by thirty kilos.

'That's far too much to be human error,' he said.

'And far too regular an occurrence,' Felicia added. She scanned down the list. 'What were they transporting?'

Striker pointed to the alphanumeric code in the ledger's right-most column.

24701 – MHC.

He explained: 'The first five digits are the police file number. I'm not entirely sure what the last three letters mean.'

Because the report was so old and could not be brought up electronically, Felicia had to attend Archives. When she returned with the folder and opened it, she was surprised to see how short the report inside it was.

One page, half full of writing.

It stated that a transfer had been done from 312 Main Street to the Montreaux incinerator. Most of the evidence marked for destruction was paperwork – old files, witness statements, Computer-Aided Dispatch call printouts, and such. But part of the evidence marked for destruction had also been drugs.

Striker looked back at the letters in the ledger. 'MHC . . . Marijuana. Heroin. Cocaine.' He looked at Felicia. 'Who authored that report?'

She read the badge number. 'Detective 1160.'

Striker frowned at the words. 'That's Harry.'

He leaned against the counter and rubbed his face as a mixture of excitement and disappointment spilled through him.

'You okay?' Felicia asked.

Striker just shook his head. 'So that's what this has all been about then – *drugs*. Harry and Koda were selling the seized drugs back to the Prowlers and using Sleeves as their conduit.'

Felicia nodded, but the confused look remained on her face. 'This was a long time ago, Jacob.'

'So?'

'So why is all this violence happening *now*? The barn down by the river, the bomb at the toy store, the explosion at Koda's house – why now and not a decade ago? Could it really all be just Sleeves?'

Striker shrugged. He had no idea.

'There's only one thing we really know for certain,' he said. 'Somewhere along the line, something went wrong. And now it's all come back to haunt them.'

Seventy-Four

Tommy Atkins went to war
and he came back a man no more.

The bomber chanted the rhyme under his breath as he stood in front of the makeshift lab he and Molly had set up in the command room.

It was a very basic lab: kerosene-fuelled cooking stoves with charcoal filtration to prevent toxicity; coffee filters in lieu of a filtration kit; a glass carafe instead of an Erlenmeyer flask; and pads of standard triple-ply paper towels used for a drying rack. All in all, it was poor apparatus for the job, but what did that matter?

The HME was near completion.

Looking at it now, the soft, yellow-grey, putty-like material resembled a wad of bread dough, waiting to rise. Like the sourdough Mother had often made for him whenever he was sad. The thought of that light fluffy bread smothered in melting butter filled him with a warm, safe feeling. The dough Mother had made was wonderful. But his was better.

His dough would rise like no other.

Behind him, Molly sat on the steel table, busy sewing the latest uniform – the one that mattered most, the one that had to be precise. She put on a good show, but her normally stable hands trembled with every stitch.

He pretended not to notice and finished chanting his rhyme.

Went to Baghdad and Sar-e.
He died, that man who looked like me.

Molly stopped sewing. Looked up. A sense of loss filled her eyes.

'Did you tell him I loved him?' she finally asked.

He did not bother to turn around. '*Loved* him? He's still alive, Molly. You'd know that if you went to see him.'

'I . . . *love* . . . yes, yes. Did you tell him I love him?'

'No.'

A heavy silence enveloped the small room, and moments later, Molly returned to her sewing as if nothing was wrong. She was whispering to herself now. *Praying*, he knew. To a God who did not care for them now – just as He had not cared for them before.

It angered him to hear it. And he glared at her as she kept praying, praying, praying. He felt like screaming. Raging. Losing control. He closed his eyes. Fought for that elusive calm.

And then the GPS tracker beeped.

He picked it up and stared at the screen. The unit was working well. Everything was going to plan once again. Target 3 was on the move. And the explosives were ready. Had the sight given the bomber even a modicum of happiness, he would have smiled. But it did not bring him joy. So he just put on his workman's overalls. Grabbed the cell, the radio, and the handheld lasers. And packaged up the HME.

'It's time,' he said.

Seventy-Five

It was going on for four o'clock, and they hadn't eaten since morning. When Felicia complained about light-headedness, Striker made a quick pit stop at the local Safeway and grabbed them some grub.

Back in the car, Striker took a few bites of a Soprano sandwich that was stuffed with capicola and hot bell peppers, then downed some Coke. He leaned back against the seat, going over what they had learned, and realized he felt quite a bit better after getting some food in his stomach.

Beside him, Felicia tore a chunk out of her pesto chicken and spoke between bites. 'I'm really getting sick of this game with Harry and Koda. I say we just haul their asses in now, and be done with it.'

Striker swallowed before speaking. 'We've been through this, Feleesh – what actual hard evidence do we have against them?'

'We got a dead woman in Koda's house – the same woman who was victimized down by the river.'

'That doesn't mean he took her there.'

'A polygraph—'

'We can't force them to take a lie detector, and we both know they never will. Harry's no dummy. And Koda's a retired cop, for Christ's sake. He knows everything we got is circumstantial. He'll lawyer up and walk, and we'll have blown our one good chance at charging them with anything criminal. Hell, forget the Criminal Code; if we screw this up, we won't even get a breach of the Police Act.'

Felicia looked down at her sandwich like she had lost her appetite. 'What about the shipping weights to Montreaux?'

'What about them? Harry may have authored the report, but the actual shipment transfers are all *unsigned.* All we have are some really old records from a private burn facility – nothing that actually ties Harry or Koda directly to trafficking. Hell, we can't even prove that's what really happened. All we have are some consistently wrong shipment weights. If it was me under suspicion for it, I'd argue that the scale was improperly calibrated. There's no way to prove it now.'

Felicia nodded as she reconsidered. 'The difference in the shipment weights was almost always exactly thirty kilos – that constant difference would actually support their claim. They could argue that the scale was out that exact amount.'

Striker agreed. 'Knowing Harry, it wouldn't surprise me if that was done on purpose for just such a defence. He's always been extremely smart.'

Felicia swore. She crinkled the cellophane wrap around her sandwich and shoved it back into the bag. She looked out the window. Turned silent.

Striker could tell she was getting rapidly frustrated, and he didn't blame her. He felt it too. He got on the phone and called the plainclothes unit for a status check. Quaid answered on the first ring.

'What's up with the target?' Striker asked.

'Nothing,' Quaid replied. 'Sleeves went back inside his suite and hasn't come out since. Some girl came by and went into the suite with him. I saw her looking out the window a couple of times, almost like she was doing her own recon on us. She's a short thing. Kind of plump.'

'What about Sleeves?'

Quaid made a weary sound. 'Nothing yet. The little prick just – oh wait, hold on a minute.' The line went silent for a moment, then Quaid returned. 'Gotta go. Target's moving. And *fast.*'

The line went dead.

Striker hung up. He turned in his seat to face Felicia.

'Sleeves on the move?' she asked.

He nodded. 'Maybe it'll lead us somewhere.'

'I won't hold my breath.'

Striker frowned. 'It still feels like we're missing a part of the puzzle here. We need more information. On Sleeves. On Harry. On Koda. Even on Williams and Owens.'

Felicia looked back from the window and fixed Striker with a detached look. 'And what about Rothschild?'

Striker felt like he'd been slapped. '*Mike?* What – are you kidding me? He would never get involved in anything like this. I trust that guy with my life. I'd stake my entire career on it.'

'Well good. Because you might have to.' She turned her body to face him. 'There's *something* wrong here, Jacob. There has to be. And you're letting your friendship with Mike Rothschild cloud your vision.'

He laughed. 'You don't seriously think that Mike—'

'All I'm saying is that *everyone* needs to be fully investigated, even if it's just to clear their name. Think about it. Rothschild used to be on Koda's squad, both in Patrol and ERT. And we also know that the bomber was inside his old house – he missed them by only two days. The question is *why.*' She shook her head in frustration. 'We got too many connections here with drugs and bikers. I say we call Gangs.'

Striker tapped the empty Coke bottle against his palm. 'We already have. Del's the best, and he told us everything he knows.'

'Not the Gang Crime Unit,' Felicia explained. 'IGTF.'

IGTF was the Integrated Gang Task Force. They were composed of municipal and federal cops, and had a much broader scope than the Gang Crime Unit. Where the GCU typically dealt with local targets, IGTF worked all across the country.

Even back east to where Sleeves was from.

'That's not a bad idea,' Striker said. 'You got any contacts there?'

For the first time in hours, Felicia smiled. 'Whenever you need information, baby, you just come to momma.' She picked up her cell and started dialling her contact, a detective by the name of Jimmy Sang. Five minutes into the conversation, Felicia's face brightened and she hung up.

Striker could see the excitement in her eyes. 'Well, what you find?'

'*Carlos Chipotle* is the name of another Prowler thug.'

'He was the guy working with Sleeves at the incinerator.'

Felicia nodded. 'Sang says to come down to IGTF right away.'

'He got something good for us?'

Felicia raised an eyebrow. 'I'm not really sure. All he said is, "You're not going to like it".'

Seventy-Six

Detective Jimmy Sang was taking a course on human trafficking at the main detachment on Heather Street. That was good news to Striker and Felicia, and they went to meet him. Once in the cafeteria, Striker grabbed a table while Felicia purchased three coffees.

Not five minutes later, the detective joined them.

'Thanks for seeing us,' Striker said. After the basic introductions were done, he opened the police laptop and got right to the meat of the conversation. 'So what's this information we don't want to hear?'

Sang met Striker's and Felicia's stares. 'Sleeves is suspected in more than just one child death,' he said. 'Ten years ago, one of his bombs killed two little girls and their mother. The children were just nine and twelve years old.'

'In Toronto?' Felicia asked.

'No. Right here in the Lower Mainland.'

The news stunned Striker. He had never heard of this.

He thought back to ten years ago. That was right about the time he'd taken one of his leaves of absence from the police department in order to deal with his wife Amanda's growing depression problems. They'd left town for a bit. Gone down to Arizona for some family support.

Recollections of a bombing just didn't come to mind.

He looked back at Sang and shook his head. 'This file just gets stranger and stranger by the minute.'

'You haven't heard the strangest part yet. The woman and her daughters that Sleeves killed – they were Chipotle's family.'

Upon hearing the news, Striker sat back in his chair and stared at nothing in particular. He closed his eyes and tried to process the ramifications of what Sang had just told him. Finally he sat forward again. 'I'm a bit confused here. I looked all through Sleeves' history and he's never been charged with *any* of these murders.'

Sang took one of the coffees, added four sugars.

'There's a reason for that,' he said. 'Almost no one talks in the biker world, so getting witness statements is damn near impossible. The bomb that went off at Chipotle's house and killed the wife and daughters, it was planted by Sleeves.'

'But *how* do you know?' Felicia asked.

Sang made an uncomfortable face before saying, 'Intel from one of our own. We managed to get a guy inside. On a different matter entirely. But this is what he heard, the talk around the club.'

Striker didn't question the agent's identity. That was information Sang would never divulge.

Felicia pointed to the dates on the computer screen. 'Ten years ago, huh? Interesting. Right after the bombing, Sleeves disappears for almost an entire year – he goes right off the radar.'

Striker suggested, 'Maybe the gang told him to lay low. Maybe he went into hiding.'

But Sang shook his head. 'No. The reason he disappeared is because he blew himself up in the explosion. Pretty bad too. Scars all over his hips and back and arms. Damn near obliterated himself.'

'Too bad he didn't finish the job,' Felicia said.

Striker pulled the laptop over and ran Carlos Chipotle through the system. He frowned at what he saw.

'The bomb call's not in here.'

Sang nodded. 'It happened just across the Vancouver border in Burnaby. So it'll be a federal file. The RCMP. *Mounties.*'

Striker ground his teeth because it was just so typical. The biggest problem with modern-day policing was the lack of free and open communication – different databases, privatized cases, invisible files. Hell, some reports existed only on paper.

For an investigator, it could be maddening at times.

Striker looked at Sang. 'You've got access to Fed paper, right? Can you do a search for us? Get us a copy of the murder file on the Chipotle family?'

Sang stood up from the table. 'Give me ten minutes.'

Striker and Felicia waited. Soon, ten minutes turned into twenty, and twenty turned into thirty. But Sang eventually returned. In his hands was a hard copy of the report. To Striker, it looked like the holy grail. And upon seeing it, a few drops of his frustration ebbed away.

'Thank God,' Felicia said.

'This is just the investigative summary,' Sang warned. 'It's *brief.*'

Striker didn't care; he was happy to have anything. He took the report from Sang, and he and Felicia began poring over it.

The file was straightforward. The murder of the Chipotle family was believed to be a gang-sanctioned killing. A bomb had gone off in the Chipotle basement, killing the wife and two daughters. Carlos – the obvious target – had been in the garage at the time, and as such, had narrowly escaped a fiery death.

Then he had gone missing.

In the report, two things caught Striker's eye. One, Sleeves was never mentioned. In fact, he was not even entered as an entity, much less a suspect in the bombing. And his name did not appear in any of the text pages.

Second, and almost impossible to ignore, was the associated file number at the bottom of the last page. It was a Vancouver Police Department file number – for an investigation into the police-involved shooting death of Carlos Chipotle, which had happened sometime later the same day.

Felicia looked at the number. 'Well, Chipotle didn't go missing for very long.'

Striker said nothing. Carlos Chipotle must have fled the scene, he rationalized, and gotten into a gunfight with police. But where and when and how? Striker read the date and realized that the homicide report would likely be in paper form only. He felt a strange swirl of excitement and frustration all at once.

'Every lead turns into two more,' he said.

Felicia also noted the date. 'Archives?' she asked.

Striker didn't have time to answer her question; his cell phone rang. He looked at the screen, saw the name Niles Quaid on the display, and hoped to God they had discovered something pertinent. He answered the call.

'Niles, what you got for me?'

The man's voice was tight, his tone low.

'Sleeves is gone,' he said. 'We lost him.'

Seventy-Seven

Harry and Koda pulled into the parking lot of the A&W burger stand and left their undercover cruiser parked by the north wall. Once out of the car, Koda began pacing the lot. His hands trembled as he popped another T3 into his mouth and chugged back some Red Bull. Harry took a long look at the can, then at Koda, and shook his head.

'You're already jittery enough,' he said. 'You really need to drink that shit?'

'I'll drink what I drink.'

'I still don't think you should come. Given all that's happened.'

Koda threw the can on the ground. 'I told you, I'm fucking *coming.*'

Harry offered no response. He just gave his SIG Sauer a firm tug and made sure the pistol was snug in its holster. Then he opened the back of the police car and grabbed his second piece, a smaller snub-nose forty-cal he'd seized off a gang member at the Pink Palace strip club two years ago. He tucked it in the back of his waistband, then draped the tail of his coat over the butt. He turned to Koda. Smiled. Offered the man a sense of calm.

'Nothing's going to happen, Chad,' he said. 'We're just here to find out what really happened back at your place . . . and to *negotiate.*'

Koda grabbed a second can of Red Bull from the car and picked at the stitches on his nose.

'Got to be ready for anything,' he said.

The parking lot off-ramp led to the north alley of Hastings Street. Together, Harry and Koda walked down to the roadway, then crossed Semlin Drive to the Hing-Woo warehouse. The doors were closed and locked, just like before, and the lights were out. Everything was quiet. They circled the building into the rear lane and waited under the overhang of the loading bay.

Koda opened the can of Red Bull. 'Smells like goddam soy sauce back here.'

'It's a Chinese food warehouse.'

'Fucking stinks. Always fucking stinks around here – where the hell is that rat anyway?'

'He'll come. He needs money. Now relax.'

Koda turned on him. '*You* fuckin' relax – it wasn't your goddam house he blew up! Your ex-wife he killed! He's coming back on us, man. I keep telling you.'

Harry eyed Koda carefully. 'You let me do the talking, Chad.'

Koda drank some more Red Bull and mumbled under his breath. Harry did not react. Ignoring the man, he took out his cell phone and dialled the number his brother Trevor had given him back in Source Handling.

Sleeves answered immediately.

'*What?*' came the response. Out of breath.

'Where are you?' Harry asked.

'Close by.'

Harry closed his eyes. '*Where* is close by, Sleeves?'

'I'm on Hastings Street.'

'Well, we're in the loading bay. Like we said.'

'I know. I can see you.'

The line went dead.

Harry didn't like the sound of that. He swept his eyes around the alley, searching for possible bombs, and saw nothing. He looked at Koda and said, 'Be ready.'

Then they waited.

A minute later, Harry spotted saw the small, wiry outline of the man called Sleeves. He was at the west end of the lane, and he did not move. He took a long moment to scan his surroundings, then slowly, cautiously, moved forward, checking out every nook and cranny as he went. When he reached the loading zone, his eyes found Koda's face, then his scar.

He smiled darkly. 'Nice zipper – I got one in my pants.'

Koda trembled. 'I should fucking kill you—'

Harry intervened. Placed a hand against Koda's chest. Firm. Decisive. Controlled. 'We're here to talk. Nothing more.' He looked back at the ex-Prowler. 'Right, Sleeves?'

The grin left the man's face. 'You sold me out.'

'No one sold anyone—'

'Hundred grand. That's what it'll cost you.'

Harry held up his hand. 'We'll talk money later. But first, there are some ground rules. Rule one: You take the cash, you leave town, and you never come back. Rule two: You never contact either one of us or our families again. Rule three: You never demand money again; this is a one-time payment. And Rule four: you never breathe a word about this to anyone. As far as you're concerned, nothing ever happened – and I mean *nothing*.'

Sleeves' eyes turned hard. 'The payment just went up. *Two* hundred grand.'

Koda took a half-step forward. 'Are you completely insane?' he spat.

Sleeves was unmoved by the man's emotional state. 'Either

you pay, or I'm sure Striker will – with a little help from Crown Counsel.'

Koda's face flushed until his stitches looked like black train tracks on red desert sand. He threw his can of Red Bull on the ground and balled up his fists. 'You twisted little fuck! You think we'll be the only ones going down? We'll *all* be fucked!'

Harry made no verbal reply, for he understood the situation perfectly. If Sleeves went to Striker, it would mean jail time for all of them. And jail time for Harry would mean the death of his family.

It was unacceptable.

Harry drew the snub-nose from the back of his waistband.

Took aim.

Pulled the trigger.

In one quick moment, a sharp blast of thunder filled the laneway, echoing off the tall walls of the warehouses around them. The bullet caught the ex-Prowler in the stomach. Sleeves let loose a spit-filled gasp, wobbled where he stood, and then collapsed to his knees on the cement pad of the loading bay. His mouth dropped open, his eyes turned wide. He touched his stomach with his hand, pulled it away, and stared at the redness that now also spilled from his hoodie.

'You shot . . . you shot . . . *you fucking shot me!*'

Harry stepped forward, took aim once more, and pulled the trigger again. Sleeves' head snapped backward, and blood and brain matter exploded all over the cement behind him. His body slumped to the left and landed on the loading bay with a soft, almost-inaudible thump.

For a moment, everything was quiet.

Then Koda sucked in a deep gasp of air.

'Holy fuck, holy fuck, *holy FUCK!*' He gaped at Harry, then spun and looked all around the lane. 'The noise, the noise, the *noise* – we gotta go!'

Harry paid him no heed. He stepped up to the fallen man, took aim once more, and blasted off two more rounds.

One for each kneecap.

'Satan's Prowler style,' he said.

Then he turned and exited the alley.

Seventy-Eight

The rush-hour grind of Hastings Street was bad, and it was further bogged down by the road construction which seemed to be taking place at two-block intervals. Everywhere Striker looked there were men and women wearing orange reflective vests, sweating from the nonstop summer heat and exhaust fumes. He drove past two of them, all the while scanning every main street and alley they crossed.

'You see Sleeves anywhere?'

'No.' Felicia cursed. 'How the hell could they lose him?'

Striker made no reply. He was trying to focus on the situation at hand and not to let the frustration swell up on him. The plainclothes unit had lost visual continuity of Sleeves back at William MacDonald Elementary School. The ex-Prowler had cut through the school grounds and failed to exit on the other side. The area had since been cleared, with negative results.

Sleeves was gone.

Striker turned south on Victoria. Less than a half-block later, Felicia looked down at the BirdDog tracker and made a *hmm* sound.

'Interesting,' she said.

Striker cast her a glance. 'What?'

'Your plainclothes friends lost track of Sleeves somewhere around the elementary school, and look at this' – she held up the handheld tracker – 'Harry and Koda are just a few blocks away.'

Striker studied the screen. 'They're back near Semlin again – at the old chop shop, I'll bet. The Hing-Woo.'

Felicia nodded. 'Maybe meeting Sleeves.'

Her words ignited him. Striker cranked the wheel, hit the gas and raced around the Franklin Street bend. He turned up Semlin, stopped out front of the Hing-Woo warehouse, and hopped out with the handheld tracking device in hand. When Felicia joined him, he approached the front door of the warehouse and tried the handle.

Locked.

He went to look through the iron-barred window, paused. Sniffed. Then looked at Felicia.

'You smell that?' he asked.

She nodded. 'It's . . . *gunpowder*?'

Using one hand to hold the tracker, Striker drew his pistol with the other and slowly made his way around the building into the side lane, where the stink grew worse. Ten steps later, he saw someone sprawled out in the loading zone, surrounded by a brownish-red puddle. He stopped hard.

'Heads up, Feleesh, we got a DB here.'

She drew her pistol. 'Copy. I got you covered.'

Striker swept his eyes around the lane, checking for threats. But all he saw were some old wooden pallets. An empty loading zone. And some broken bottles of soy sauce in the corner.

'Cover me to the west,' he said.

'Copy, west.'

Striker approached the body.

As he closed the distance, it quickly became apparent that half the victim's face had been blown away from the gunshot. Both knees had also been shot out. Striker reached the body, leaned forward, and saw the hoodie – it was a dirty white colour with red block lettering across the front:

SNAFU.

'Ah fuck me, this is Sleeves.'

Felicia came up beside him, gun nestled between both hands. 'I'll call it in.'

As she got on her cell and alerted Dispatch, Striker scanned the lane one more time. When he saw nothing, he started west, then stopped. He looked down at the handheld tracking device and saw that the red-car icon representing Harry's undercover Ford cruiser was still stationary.

And it was right *behind* him.

He turned around and approached the mouth of the lane, and saw no sign of Harry's undercover cruiser. Not on the side street. Not in the laneway. And not in the vacant lot where the old car dealership had been torn down.

For a moment he thought the GPS was buggered, or that the mount had dislodged from the vehicle. But then he looked across the way and saw the elevated parking lot of the A&W burger stand.

Up there.

Felicia got off her cell. 'Patrol's a block out.'

Striker never took his eyes from the parking lot. 'Put your back against the wall and hold the area, Feleesh . . . There's something I need to see over here.'

Seventy-Nine

Harry cut through the front door of the A&W burger stand, trying to get his breath.

Did that happen?

Did that really just fucking happen?

The words raged through his mind. His head felt light. He tried to slow his breathing. Tried to stop the trembling of his hands. But the shakes were hitting him hard now. Really hard.

Did that really just fucking happen?

Koda urged him on. 'We gotta go, we gotta go, we gotta *move*!'

Harry said nothing. In front of him, rows of people blocked the way. The line-up to the till was twelve deep. And all around him, most of the tables were already full of people eating hamburgers and French fries and onion rings. All he could smell was grease and vinegar and gravy.

'Move, Harry, we gotta *move*!'

Robot-like, on autopilot, Harry moved across the tiled floor and pushed his way through the east-side door that led to the parking lot. The thick glass made the door heavy, and when it swung open, hot humid air blasted in his face.

He started for the car.

Slowed.

Stopped.

Something tugged at the back of his mind . . . something Sleeves had said during their cell phone conversation:

I'm on Hastings Street.

It made Harry wonder: Why had Sleeves been looking for them up on Hastings Street when the meeting place was in the alley behind the warehouse? The more he thought about it, the more obvious the answer became – because Sleeves had seen their cruiser parked in the A&W parking lot.

Up ahead, Koda was reaching for the vehicle.

'WAIT!' Harry said. 'Don't touch that car!'

Koda stopped. Wheeled back. 'Jesus, *what now*?'

'We got to make sure it's not rigged or nothing.'

The thought of another bomb going off made Koda's already-white face turn an even sicklier pallor, and he reared away from the vehicle.

'You check it,' he said.

Harry offered no response. He approached the undercover cruiser, got down on his hands and knees, and looked beneath the frame. The search took little time. Seconds. And he found something. There, on the top of the leaf spring, was a device – though it was not the one Harry was expecting to see.

He reached under, tried to pry it free, and broke the base of the device right off the mount. He looked at what he was holding and felt a coldness wash over him. Not a bomb, but something equally frightening – a Vancouver Police Department BirdDog.

They were being tracked.

Eighty

Striker hurried up the steep incline of Semlin Drive and turned into the A&W burger stand. Inside, the foyer was jammed with the dinner rush. People were lined up at the tills, sitting in booths, and even waiting for an available washroom.

The radio chirped at his side, and Sue Rhaemer began broadcasting that a dog was heading down to the shooting, along with several more patrol units. Moments later, Inspector Osaka came across the air, his voice thick with disbelief that there had been yet another death on his watch this week.

'Car 10 heading up,' he said.

Striker blocked it all out. Made his way into the crowd. Assessed the people:

Chinese girl. Tight shorts, bikini top.

Black male, tall, shaved head.

Three white kids, computer geeks.

All non-threats.

He pushed further into the crowd, heading towards the parking lot. Halfway there, through the maze of people, he spotted the two cops he was looking for – Harry and Koda. They were in the parking lot just outside the burger shack. Koda's Halloween face was lost and stressed. Harry's expression was one of tension and seriousness.

Harry was looking right back at him.

'Hold it right there!' Striker called out.

He headed for the door.

Eighty-One

One moment Harry was standing there in disbelief, holding the GPS unit and realizing with all certainty that this was definitely Vancouver Police Department property. The next moment, he was eyes-locked with Jacob Striker.

'Motherfucker,' he said.

He panicked. Stuffed the GPS base into his pocket. Then spun away from the restaurant. Immediately, his eyes found Koda. The man was standing there with a stunned look on his wrecked face.

Harry quickly formulated a plan. He grabbed the keys to the Crown Vic and the snub-nose pistol he'd used to kill Sleeves and stuffed them into Koda's hands. The man's face filled with apprehension.

'What the hell—'

'Get out of here,' Harry ordered.

'But—'

'Go now!'

Koda's eyes flitted over Harry's shoulder, then narrowed with understanding when he saw Jacob Striker coming through the restaurant. Gear in hand, he spun away from Harry and raced for the driver's side of the car.

Seeing Koda go, Harry wheeled about. He beelined towards the restaurant door to intercept and delay Striker from reaching the Crown Vic. All the while, a hundred thoughts raced through Harry's mind – all the standard questions he'd need answers to:

Why were you there?

Why did Koda take off?

Do you know Sleeves is dead in the alley?

Did you hear the gunshots?

The questions were endless. And halfway there, another idea surged to the forefront of his mind, one which would cover their tracks entirely.

Burn the car.

Harry stopped walking in the direction of the restaurant, spun about, and raced back towards Koda. After five steps, he caught sight of Koda, sitting there in the driver's seat – and the sight of the man made him come to a halt.

Koda was sitting there, frozen, with a terrified expression on his face. He was staring at the object that had been placed on the dashboard of the cruiser.

A doll of some kind.

Suddenly, Koda let out a strangled cry. He shouldered open the car door. Tried to get out.

But he was far too late.

A strange, wind-sucking sound filled the air, and was followed by a piercing flash of light. In one quick blast of smoke and fire and tearing metal, the Ford Crown Vic cruiser exploded – killing Chad Koda in the process.

Eighty-Two

Striker raised his hands without thinking.

The flash came first – one giant burst of light, followed by the fracturing sounds of the windows. A percussive force powered through the A&W restaurant, driving wood and rock and dirt and glass shards with it. One moment, Striker was hurrying to get outside, the next thing he knew he was spinning across the floor like a small toy flung by some giant child. He rolled and flipped, and slammed into a nearby wall. Stunned, he instinctively reached for his pistol. Drew it. Tried to focus.

All around him, people were crying. Crawling. Screaming:

'I'm bleeding, I'm bleeding!'

'A bomb! It was a fucking bomb!'

'. . . an ambulance, we need an ambulance . . .'

'. . . she's not breathing, someone—'

The screams and cries all mutated into one loud din that Striker could barely hear through his deafened ears. Dizzy, reeling, he grabbed on to the nearest booth and hauled himself to his feet. The tiles beneath his shoes felt like moving mush; and the world shifted.

Out in the parking lot, the undercover police cruiser was nothing but a fragmented, flaming shell now. Dark smoke poured through the lot like some form of unfurling, gaseous molasses. And on the ground, not twenty feet from the blast, was Harry.

The man tried to get up.

Fell.

Tried again.

Striker reached into his jacket pocket for the portable radio, found it wasn't there. Swearing, he got his legs moving. He navigated through the chaos in the restaurant. Past two girls who were standing there like frozen statues. Around an old lady who was on her knees, sobbing. He reached the exit door. Stared through the broken glass panes into the parking lot.

And then he saw the woman.

She was small but stocky. Dressed in coveralls – just like the man he'd chased yesterday by the toy store. She moved quickly into the parking lot, in a semi-crouched position, and she moved with *purpose*. From behind her back, she suddenly pulled something out and zoned in on Harry.

Gun.

She had a gun.

Striker kicked open the broken frame of the door. Raised his SIG. Fought to stabilize himself.

'Police – don't move!'

The woman did not so much as flinch. She dropped lower, kept moving towards her target, and took one quick glance in Striker's direction – assessing; clearly assessing. Then she raised her gun and took aim.

But not at Striker.

She aimed at Harry.

Eighty-Three

With the world shifting all around him, Striker opened fire.

The first bullet hit the cement wall of the neighbouring shop; the second ricocheted off the burning husk of the police car; the third shattered the brick wall behind the woman. It startled her. Stopped her dead in her tracks. And she turned her eyes towards him.

Saw that he had her lined up.

'Don't fuckin' move!' Striker ordered.

In between them, Harry crawled behind a cement parking barrier.

When the woman saw this, her face darkened. She could not reach him now. And her hands tightened on the pistol.

'Don't do it,' Striker warned.

He put one hand against the door frame to stabilize himself and fought to steady his aim.

'Drop the gun! Drop it right now—'

He'd barely finished the sentence when the male appeared. He came from the south end of the lot, and was dressed exactly the same as the girl – a pair of workman's coveralls with an orange vest.

Like a flag-person.

The man raced across the lot, firing at Striker as he came. Quick double-taps.

Striker dropped down and hit the ground as the shots rang

out. *One-two, three-four.* They ricocheted throughout the foyer. Clattered off tile and steel. Shattered more glass. And caused the remaining customers to wail and scream in terror.

In the parking lot, Harry returned fire.

Striker needed cover. He rolled onto his belly. Tried to lift his head above the window partition and engage the enemy. But it was impossible – bullets continued to spear through the restaurant in a constant stream of suppressive fire.

Five-six, seven-eight.

He was pinned down. Unable to reposition.

Couldn't get a shot off.

And then he spotted Felicia. He had no idea where she'd come from or how long she'd been there. But suddenly she was at the broken remains of the northeast window, using the wall as cover and emptying her clip on their enemies.

Her unexpected presence changed the firefight, forcing the enemy to reposition. They slid in behind one of the lot's cement parking barriers and returned fire – though now on Felicia. Two streams of bullets punched through the window like sideways rain.

'Down!' Striker yelled. 'Everyone stay DOWN!'

Felicia dropped low and rolled for cover as more glass shattered all around her; Striker seized the moment. He rolled out. Extended his arms. Took aim. And returned fire.

Two shots, one hit.

And the man in the orange work vest let out a surprised cry. He stumbled backwards. Fell. Landed on his ass. And still, he kept firing – one constant, steady rhythm of gunfire, with each bullet plunking into the wall behind Striker.

Again, Striker rolled for cover.

And then, as quickly as the gun battle had started, it ended.

And there was only silence.

Striker looked at Felicia. Saw blood on her hand.

'You hit?' he asked.

'Just glass. *Go.*'

Striker clambered to his feet. Peered out from cover. Scanned the parking lot.

Out there, the police cruiser was in flames, and Harry was on his hands and knees, struggling to cross the lot. Disoriented, Harry took aim and tried to get a shot off. But before he could so much as pull the trigger, one of the shooters lined him up and fired.

The bullet hit him square on.

Harry let out a cry and crumpled to the ground.

Striker ran to assist him.

He took hold of Harry, saw that the kevlar vest had saved him by taking the round, and dragged him back to the paltry cover of the A&W restaurant while Felicia provided cover. Once inside, Striker spotted his portable in the debris. He snatched the radio up, stuffed it into his jacket, and raced back outside. With his equilibrium slowly returning, he made it to the far end of the parking lot where there was a five-foot-high concrete wall.

Felicia caught up and they both looked over the wall.

Below, the laneway was empty. Straight ahead to the north, the lot that had once been the used car dealership also appeared vacant. So was the road to the east. When Striker looked west – towards the crime scene where the dead body of Sleeves still lay behind the Hing-Woo – all he saw was the red and blue gleam of police lights. As quickly as the gun battle had begun, it was now over.

Their enemies had vanished.

Eighty-Four

'Where the hell did they go?' Felicia asked.

Striker grabbed his radio, keyed the mike. 'We got another bomb explosion,' he said. 'And shots fired. Two shooters – male and female. Caucasians. Dressed like city workers in reflective vests and overalls. Last seen running south from the A&W parking lot on Hastings.'

He took a moment to get his breath.

'Should I call in ERT?' the Dispatcher asked.

'Yes,' Striker replied. 'And a dog. And some ambulances to the restaurant, Code 3. Casualties unknown.'

Striker let go of the mike and scanned the area to the south one more time. There was *nothing*. The two shooters had just plain disappeared. It made no sense. Pistol in hand, he walked down the off-ramp into the rear lane with Felicia paralleling him. Once his feet touched the pavement, he spotted what he was looking for and pointed:

'Right there. Blood droplets.'

Felicia nodded. 'Heading east.'

They followed the trail. Twenty steps later, Striker and Felicia stopped when the blood droplets ended abruptly. Suddenly the suspects' vanishing act made sense. Striker pressed his mike:

'They're using the sewer systems.'

At Striker's feet was a manhole cover, partially unseated.

When he crouched down to look at it, he saw more blood. He looked up at Felicia.

'Stand back.'

When she got out of the way, he grabbed hold of the rim. He readied his gun. Yanked open the manhole cover. And they both stuck their pistols down into the hole.

Leading down from street level was a series of metal rungs embedded in the cement tube. At the bottom, there was only darkness. Striker broadcast the find and stared into the void below. Images of the two shooters escaping flashed through his mind, and it ate away at him.

He took out his flashlight and readied his pistol.

Felicia saw this and let out a startled sound. 'Whoa-whoa-*whoa* – you're not going down there.'

'I need to see where they're going.'

'Send in a dog first.'

'The dog's ten minutes out, they'll be long gone by then.'

'So let them go.'

'I'm not losing them again.'

Before Felicia could object a third time, Striker stepped down on the rung. The metal felt thin and weak under his shoe and the contact made a hollow scuffing sound in the cement tube.

He dropped lower and lower into the darkness.

When his feet touched the bottom, he immediately crouched down low and shone the flashlight in both directions. To the immediate west was a steel door that was padlocked. To the east was a long, narrow passageway that darkened quickly but seemed to turn south at the end.

Striker took one step that way.

Suddenly, a loud whistling sound filled the tunnel. High in pitch. So sharp it hurt his ears. Then a series of red lines shot out all across the path. Some of them were vertical, some horizontal, and some crisscrossed. One look at them and Striker knew exactly what they were:

Laser tripwires.

'Jesus Christ,' he said and stepped back.

Going down that way would be suicide.

Up above him, Felicia called out a warning. 'I'm coming down to back you up!' She stepped on the first rung, but Striker waved her away.

'No! Don't come down! Get out – get out now!'

Eighty-Five

Cradling his left arm, not allowing the shoulder joint to move, the bomber stumbled down the long, winding corridors of the sewer system with Molly by his side. The bullet had tagged him. Torn through the upper-left shoulder. And something inside that joint had broken.

He could feel the bones grinding.

'We got them,' he said through the haze. 'We got them both.'

'Keep moving,' Molly said.

'. . . them both . . .'

'Come on. *Leg it.* We have to keep moving.'

He looked left at her, and suddenly, she was no longer Molly, but one of his squadmates dragging him across the Green Valley plains. And he was watching his body bleed out.

From somewhere high above him, he could hear the sharp zings of the bullets flying by, and he could feel every ounce of the lead and steel and copper that had torn through his body from the exploding bomb. It was hot – the metal was so goddam *hot.* He was on fire.

The inside of his body was *aflame*.

'My leg,' he said. 'Don't let them take my leg.'

'No one's taking your leg.'

'The doctor . . . don't let him take—'

Molly shook him. 'You're not back there, you're here. Look at me, *look at me*!'

And then, suddenly, the world changed again. And the soldier looking back at him was gone. And in the man's place was Molly. 'Get up,' she was saying. 'You've got to get up! Get up! Let me help you. LET ME HELP YOU!'

He struggled back to one knee, then managed to stand. The world tilted on him. The tunnel seemed to be moving in impossible, unnatural circles. Like some demonic carnival ride. And the air was hot. Stuffy. Rank. His shoulder *seared* with pain. So much so that he feared he'd black out.

But instead of losing consciousness, the reverse happened – a sharp, distinct clarity swept into him. And he laughed out loud because everything was finally okay again.

He was moving.

Seeing action.

Operating.

For the first time in as long as he could remember, he felt completely, undeniably, one hundred per cent wonderful.

He felt *alive.*

Eighty-Six

It was six-thirty p.m. by the time the bomb tech climbed back out of the manhole. He was a federal cop Striker had never seen before, and a smug look covered his olive-skinned face. In his fingers was an array of pen-like devices.

Striker studied them. 'They real?'

'They're just trips,' the technician said. 'No actual explosives down there.'

'None?'

'Not a one.'

Striker cursed and closed his eyes in frustration. The thought of the two shooters escaping down the tunnel made his guts tighten.

'I can't believe this.'

'It was a scare tactic. To prevent anyone from following them.'

'Well, it worked.'

'Of course, it did. You'd have been a fool to go down there. And don't go assuming that, next time, the circumstances will be the same – next time they might really be rigged and ready to go.'

Striker tried to hide the bitterness from his voice. 'Point taken.'

He turned away from the bomb tech for a breath of fresh air. With the tunnel now clear of explosives, the dogman was next to go inside, and behind him went two young constables Striker did not recognize. They started the dog track.

Striker turned away in frustration. It was useless, he knew.

The shooters were long gone.

He approached the bomb tech again and told the man to bag and tag the laser tripwires for forensics. Then he stared at the A&W parking lot, and then at the alley behind the warehouse. Everywhere he looked, it was barely controlled chaos. Two crime scenes. One with the dead body of Sleeves; the other with the dead body of Chad Koda.

Due to the high number of witnesses in the restaurant at the time of the explosion and subsequent gunfight, Inspector Osaka had commandeered a city bus to take them all down to police headquarters for proper interviewing and stress counselling. Over ten detectives had been called out to assist. Victim Services as well.

With the adrenalin fading, everyone was operating on fumes.

Witnesses aside, there were also seven victims of the blast. Each one had been injured by some form of flying shrapnel, and each had been taken to one of several hospitals. Fortunately, none of the wounds were considered critical. There had been no deaths here today.

Other than Sleeves and Koda.

'Jesus H. Christ,' Inspector Osaka said. His dark eyes were underscored and his white wavy hair was out of place. He approached Striker and shook his head in frustration. 'You got to get these guys. They're blowing up the entire city!'

'We're doing our best, sir.'

'Well it's not good enough! Do *better*. I got three bomb blasts in my city, an unresolved kidnapping in District 4, and a media frenzy. The public is panicking and so is Laroche – he's on my ass every second of the day and is threatening to pull me from the road!'

'We're doing our best, sir,' Striker said one more time.

Inspector Osaka let out a long heavy breath. He closed his eyes. Pinched the bridge of his nose. Nodded slowly. 'Just . . . keep me informed every step of the way.'

Before Striker could respond, the inspector turned away and marched up the road to face the ravenous media horde. Striker watched him go. Inspector Osaka was a good man. But no matter how this thing played out, he was in for a shit storm with his superiors. That was just the way life went in the VPD. All par for the course.

He turned around and got to work.

Ten minutes later, Striker was busy diagramming the scene and trying to figure out timelines when Felicia walked back from the other side of Semlin Drive. She held a bandage against her left hand, where she'd cut herself on the glass, and looked tired.

Striker examined her hand. 'It gonna need stitches?'

She shook her head. 'Nah. Sleeves' body has been taken to the morgue for autopsy. Noodles is processing the scene right now. He's none too happy.'

Striker didn't much care if Noodles was happy or not. He was just glad Felicia wasn't cut too bad. He looked at his diagram, then at the explosion scene, and made sure he had everything right.

In the parking lot, Corporal Summer was busy working on her third bomb in two days. Her young, pretty face looked older and harder than it had the previous day. With so much debris to sort through, she had sent tech requests to all other departments – New Westminster, West Vancouver, Delta, Abbotsford, Port Moody, and to her own Fed bosses with the RCMP. It was necessary. Yellow police tape cordoned off two entire city blocks.

This amount of work was staggering.

Behind the yellow tape of Semlin Drive, Inspector Osaka was busy debriefing the media. He still looked like a Japanese Colonel Sanders, but one that had just finished battle in World War Two. All around him, swarms of reporters and soundmen buzzed: newspaper, radio, TV – the works. As far as they were concerned, the city was under siege and every child's life was in immediate danger.

Considering the magnitude of this nightmare, Striker thought Osaka was handling himself extremely well.

'Are you okay, Jacob?'

He blinked. Looked back at Felicia. Saw her staring at him with concern.

'I'm fine.'

'You're *shaking*.'

He looked down at himself. Saw it too. 'Adrenalin dump.'

She touched the side of his face. Turned his chin. Scraped away some crusted blood with her fingernail.

'Glass or shrapnel?' she asked softly.

'I'll take glass for two hundred.'

He forced a smile, fought to keep it, couldn't. Thoughts of Chad Koda's charred body in the car kept resurfacing in his mind. He looked back at the parking lot and a dark sombre feeling overtook him. Whatever problems Koda had brought upon himself, it sure as hell didn't warrant this.

He turned to Felicia. 'We need to check out the car bomb.'

She nodded silently.

Together, they walked back to the parking lot. Once at the mouth of the lot, the smouldering mass of steel became more apparent. From it, a thin smoke rose into the air. Not white like before, but *greyer* in colour. Inside the burned-up shell, the blackened, unidentifiable body of Chad Koda had yet to be removed. A horrible meaty smell filled the air, and Striker wasn't sure if it was from the burger stand or Chad Koda's burned-up body.

Felicia covered her mouth.

Striker did not. He just took all this in, somewhat numbly, and images of the explosion returned to him in quick, jarring patches. Like broken video clips. He sensed Felicia's eyes on him – her unwarranted concern – and was relieved when Corporal Summer approached them from the side.

'I'm concerned,' the bomb investigator said without preamble. 'This is a completely different signature from before.'

Felicia stopped covering her mouth. 'Meaning?'

'Usually, a new signature suggests a new bomber.'

Striker shook his head. 'It's the same two as before – I saw them firsthand. Hell, I tagged one of them.' He explained what had transpired, and Corporal Summer listened intently. When Striker was done talking, she nodded, but the concern never left her eyes.

'Still,' she said. 'It *is* unusual for a bomber to change method halfway through. Here . . . glove up and check this out.'

Once Striker and Felicia snapped on some latex, Corporal Summer called over one of her technicians and took from the woman two evidence bags. From the first one, the Corporal withdrew a blackened piece of U-shaped steel.

'You can touch it,' she said. 'It's already been swabbed for DNA – not that we expect to get any. If we're lucky though, we will get some residue samples.' She held up the bracket – a broken mount for the BirdDog tracking unit – and made a concerned sound. 'Someone had GPS on our police car.'

An *oh-shit* feeling flooded Striker, and he fessed up. 'The GPS unit was ours.'

'Both of them?'

Striker and Felicia exchanged glances, and Striker spoke:

'What do you mean, *both*?'

Corporal Summer opened up the second evidence bag. Inside it was another U-shaped bracket, twisted and blackened. 'We've already identified the manufacturer. This one comes from a company called Lowry Systems. It's the base part of one of their handheld tracking systems – GPS.'

Striker found it difficult to accept what he was hearing. 'So just to be clear here, this car had *two* GPS tracking systems on it.'

'From two different companies, yes.'

Striker mulled it over. 'That would explain how the bombers found them.'

Felicia took the bracket and analysed it. 'Where would they get a Lowry GPS unit from?'

Corporal Summer shrugged. 'Anywhere. So much has changed the past five years. Global Positioning is nothing new any more. God, you can bid for one of these things on eBay.' She took back both brackets and put them into their corresponding evidence bags. Then she directed Striker and Felicia to the corner of the parking lot where they examined a piece of V-shaped steel that was roughly the size of a large cooking pot. 'This was the base, what held the explosives.'

Striker crouched down to examine it. The V-shape would direct the explosion upwards, making the explosion more focal and directed. Striker looked up at the corporal. 'Was this shape used to increase the damage to the victim – or to limit casualties?'

'Only the bomber knows that,' Summer replied. 'But that's not what concerns me. What does is the actual *size* of the base. What it signifies.'

'And that is?' Felicia asked.

'They've switched to home-made explosives.'

Striker thought this over. 'And you're sure of this?'

'Positive. If they'd used this much professional grade, nothing would be left of the car. We'll have to get the lab to test the residue samples to be one hundred per cent certain. But this much is true – a commercial or military explosive would never require this size of a base. The bombers are using HME now. I'd stake my career on it.'

Striker thought of the smoke pouring from the car. 'That would explain the greyer colour of the smoke, would it not?'

'Completely.'

Felicia interjected: 'These are all nice tidbits. But it doesn't explain the most fundamental question of all – *why the change*?'

Corporal Summer hazarded a guess. 'It could be something simple. Maybe they ran out. Maybe their black-market supplier fell through. Who knows for sure? Maybe they underestimated their need.'

Felicia shook her head. 'I can't believe that. Not these two. They've been completely prepared for every job. I mean, think about it: electrical torture, scuba gear, laser tripwires – we're talking *organized* here. There has to be a reason for the switch. These are professionals we're dealing with, not some hacks.'

Striker nodded. He had to agree.

He looked at the leftover blackened shell of the undercover police cruiser that was still smoking in the parking lot. Aside from the actual frame, almost nothing remained.

'This is going to sound like an odd question, but I don't suppose you found any dolls in that debris?' he asked. 'Like a miniature policeman.'

Corporal Summer gave him a curious look and shook her head. 'No. Anything that was in that car has long since been burned up.'

Striker nodded half-heartedly. 'Let me know if you find anything.'

Before she could respond, he turned around and headed for the exit. Harry was still on scene, being treated by a paramedic in the back of one of the ambulances.

Hard questions needed to be asked of the man.

Eighty-Seven

Striker and Felicia made their way out of the A&W parking lot and headed across Semlin Drive towards the primary crime scene where Sleeves had been executed. Behind the yellow row of tape, a gaggle of reporters were squawking out his name: Detective Striker. Detective Striker! *Detective Striker!*

He ignored them all.

Two uniformed patrolmen guarded the entrance to the lane, one at each end. In between them, Noodles was busy snapping pictures.

Striker took a moment to examine the bloodied spot of pavement where Sleeves had died. 'If someone had told me three hours ago that Sleeves was going to be dead, I'd have thought this nightmare would be over.' He met Felicia's stare. 'But he's not the bomber, Feleesh. He *never was* the bomber. We've been chasing a lie.'

Felicia had a confused look on her face.

'Maybe not,' she admitted. 'But he was part of this in *some* way. He had to be – at least through his gang affiliations.'

Striker thought of the Satan's Prowlers. Then of Sleeves. And finally of the latest name that they'd been hearing a lot of lately – Carlos Chipotle. The more Striker thought it over, the more something bothered him.

'Something doesn't mesh here.'

'What?'

'The Satan's Prowlers. They may be an outlaw motorcycle gang, but they still have their own set of rules to abide by – and they take them very seriously. Disrespect your colours and you can be killed; no Blacks or Jews in the club; never bring the gang unwanted police attention—'

'And no women, either,' Felicia said. 'Women are just property to them.'

Striker nodded. 'Exactly. But there's one rule the gang follows that's above all the others – no family members targeted. And no children.'

'Not ever,' Felicia agreed.

Striker reasoned it out. 'I've heard of some ex-members getting burned to death and others having their dicks cut off, but never once have I heard of the gang going after another member's family – and especially not the children.'

Felicia shook her head. 'Where are you going with all this?'

Striker met her stare. 'Not only did Sleeves blow up Chipotle's family, but the Prowlers actually *sanctioned* the killing. Why? What could this man possibly have done for the gang to break their most fundamental rule? To implement such a horrific penalty? I can think of only one thing.'

Felicia let out an excited breath. 'Being a *rat*.'

Striker nodded. 'I'm starting to wonder if Chipotle was selling information on the side. Or acting as a police informant. If that was the case, we have an interesting turn of events here. With Sleeves and Chipotle both dead, it works out rather well for the Prowlers, doesn't it?'

'It does,' Felicia admitted.

'And look at the style of shooting. Kneecapping someone before the final headshot is a Prowler trademark.'

'But a commonly known one,' she pointed out.

'What do you mean by that?'

She shrugged. 'For all we know, someone *wants* us to think it was the Prowlers who did him in. I mean, who else benefits from Sleeves being dead? I can think of *two* people – one of them was killed when that car blew up and the other is being treated in the ambulance.'

Striker looked at her in surprise. 'You don't seriously mean Harry?'

'Once again, Jacob, friendship is like a veil to you.'

'Feleesh—'

'Harry was right here in the area when Sleeves took one. We know that – we got him on GPS. Plus, he's been hiding Koda from us ever since the first bomb went off. And we know he was selling drugs back to the Prowlers.'

'We *believe* he was selling—'

'Oh bullshit. If it walks like a duck and quacks like a duck, it's a duck.'

Striker said nothing. Processing the thought was difficult. He'd known Harry for so long, almost his entire career. And he'd seen the man suffer through some very hard times – the accidental drowning of his first son; the divorce from his first wife.

It had been more than most men could have handled.

And through it all, Harry had been a rock of integrity. A good man. To see him acting this strangely was shocking, no doubt. And to think that he might have been selling seized drugs back to the gang was an even greater blow.

But *murder*?

Striker couldn't believe that.

He looked down the lane to where the last ambulance was parked, its red lights flashing against the darkening sky. 'I'll go talk to the man.'

'And what then?' Felicia said.

'What do you mean?'

'You gonna take him down to the station for questioning?'

'I don't even know what his medical status is yet.'

'What if it's good? You gonna do a full interview? Taped? Even a polygraph?'

Striker said nothing for a moment as he thought it over. Taking witnesses and suspects down to the station was standard protocol, but this wasn't some crook or civilian they were dealing with here, it was *Harry*. Another cop. And an experienced one at that. Like all cops, Harry would be willing to provide a field interview no doubt – but allow himself to be transported to one of the interrogation rooms?

That would be a problem.

Striker met Felicia's stare. 'If I demand that Harry attends the station and he says no, we back ourselves into a corner. Then what?'

'Read him his rights. *Force* him to come in.'

Striker splayed his hands in frustration. 'You keep saying that. But on what *grounds*, Feleesh? What law has he broken? Right now we got a pair of assassins out there who just blew up a car and killed Koda. For all we know, Harry might have been caught in the crossfire.'

'They fired on him, Jacob.'

'And he's going to argue mistaken identity; you know that. He'll say the suspects were going after Koda. He'll play the victim.' Striker took in a slow breath and sorted his thoughts. 'Fact is, Harry doesn't have to cooperate in the investigation at all. It's his right not to, and he knows that. He's got twenty-five years on the job, Feleesh. More than both of us. We're not dealing with some piss kid rookie here. We show our hand too soon and we lose it all.'

She stared back at him with doubt. 'All I'm saying, Jacob, is prepare yourself for what you might have to do. Harry's not your friend. Not any more.'

Striker looked down the lane at the awaiting ambulance and felt a hardness form in his gut. This file was getting more complicated all the time. He couldn't wait for it to end.

'Jacob?' Felicia asked.

'I'll go talk to the man,' he said.

Without another word, he marched down the long dark corridor towards the awaiting ambulance, feeling every bit as injured as the man inside.

Eighty-Eight

Striker reached the back doors of the ambulance, opened them up, and saw Harry sitting on a gurney. He was holding an ice bag to his head and staring off into space like a wax figure. His complexion was two shades darker than normal and the flesh of his face looked bloated. Upon seeing Striker, he nodded slowly but his eyes remained vacant.

'You okay there, Harry?'

'What?'

'Are you all right?'

'. . . fine . . .'

The paramedic, a short plump thing, handed Harry another ice pack and shook her head admonishingly. 'He should be going to the hospital for further assessment, but he's a stubborn ass.'

Harry put the ice pack against his head and waved her away. He stared at the floor, as if his head was too heavy to lift.

Striker stepped forward. 'You're lucky you had on Kevlar, Harry. Or today your number would have come up.'

He said nothing back; he just winced and took a slow, deep breath.

Striker softened his voice. 'Listen, Harry, I hate to do this to you, but given the circumstances and all, I need to ask you some questions. You wanna come down to the station?'

When Harry lifted his head to meet Striker's stare, his blue eyes were cold as ice. 'The *station*? *Y*ou fucking kidding me here? What the hell happened to a field interview?'

'I'm just suggesting it might be easier downtown.'

'What, you gonna tape me too? Maybe put me on the poly?' When Striker didn't answer, Harry's face darkened. 'I'm the *victim* here, Striker. Not to mention a fucking cop. What, do I need to lawyer up now too?'

Striker took in a slow deep breath, if only to allow the conversation a pause. He closed his notebook. Put it away. Then played his best card. 'Do you know a man called Brice Burns – also goes by the alias Sleeves?'

Harry let out a laugh that held no joy. 'Of course I do. I've arrested him a half-dozen times. You know that.'

'What can you tell me about him?'

'That he's dead, for one.'

The words caught Striker off guard, but he said nothing. He allowed Harry a moment to realize what he had said. When Striker spoke again, his words were slow and direct.

'How do you know this, Harry? I never mentioned the identity of the person who was shot back there. Not once.'

Harry sat up straight. Met Striker's stare. And spoke coldly.

'You didn't have to tell me,' he said. 'I watched Koda shoot him.'

Eighty-Nine

Before returning to the undercover police cruiser, Striker spent over thirty minutes obtaining a proper statement from Harry, but in the end, no matter how much he prodded the man, the answers remained the same – vague and without logic.

According to Harry, Chad Koda had asked him to stop by the A&W restaurant for a hamburger. While there, he had suddenly informed Harry that he needed to step out for a minute to meet with a contact about a possible real estate venture regarding the car dealership lot.

Koda had left the restaurant, crossed Semlin Drive, and entered the laneway behind the Hing-Woo warehouse. Finding the situation odd, Harry had followed. When he reached the mouth of the lane, he heard the gunshots. Then he had spotted the two men.

Koda, standing holding the gun; Sleeves, dead on the ground.

The moment had stunned Harry. Frozen him. And before he'd realized what was happening, Koda had fled to the A&W parking lot. And that was where the car had exploded and they had suddenly come under fire.

Back in the car, Striker read and re-read the statement over several times.

When he finally finished, he passed the statement over to Felicia. She read it over and came up with the same conclusion.

'He's blocked every investigative lead we could have taken. His reason for being with Koda. His connection to the event. Even any possible gunpowder residue we could swab from his hands – it's all redundant now. And with Sleeves and Koda both dead, there's no one to rebut his version of events.'

'He's tied it all together perfectly.'

She looked at him hopefully. 'Will he take the poly?'

Striker laughed. 'Says he's already done his duty by providing the statement. Any more follow-up, and he'll call the union to lawyer up. Says he's been traumatized enough by what's happened and that he's concussed by the explosion – which is also a perfect excuse for having the entire statement stricken from the record anyway.'

'He's a master manipulator.'

'Hey, according to Harry, he's the victim here.'

'Stop it, you're breaking my heart,' Felicia said dryly.

'Well, like it or not, an attempt was made on his life, and there's an onus on us – legally and ethically – to protect him.' Striker shook his head as he thought back to the shootout in the parking lot. 'Harry was lucky today. If he hadn't been wearing that vest, it would all be over for him. Hell, the bombers probably think they got him.'

The moment he spoke the words, Felicia looked over, and they both knew what the other was thinking.

'If they already think he's dead,' Felicia said, 'then let's keep it that way.'

Striker nodded. 'It makes sense. We already have to give a press release for Koda's death, why not just add in Harry's name while we're at it?'

'We can retract it later,' Felicia said.

'And it will keep him safe, at least for a while, until we can figure this whole mess out.'

'There's just one problem,' Felicia said. 'He'll have to agree with it.'

Striker thought that over and nodded. 'That won't be a problem,' he finally said.

'You don't think?'

Striker shook his head. 'No. Because he's not doing it for himself. He's doing it for his son. He's doing it for Ethan.' He looked at Felicia and his grin widened. 'You set up what you need to with Laroche and Media Liaison. Leave Harry to me.'

Ninety

Following a lengthy discussion with Harry, Striker got the man to agree with the plan. He would allow them to release his name as one of the officers killed in the line of duty; what he would not allow is police protection. No guard. No safe house. No nothing.

'You're being foolish,' Striker said.

'We can protect you,' he said.

'We can even relocate you,' he said.

But Harry knew the routine well. And the man was adamant.

'I'll make my own way,' he said.

It left Striker with no other recourse. He returned to the undercover cruiser and informed Felicia of Harry's response. Upon hearing it, she shook her head and her eyes flared with anger.

'It makes him look guilty, if you ask me,' she said. 'He wants to be out here. In the field. So he can see what's going on.'

Striker did not disagree. But this was the best they could do in an imperfect situation. He said nothing more; he just leaned back in the seat, closed his eyes, and went over the file in his head. Nothing seemed to fit. And his mind felt overworked now.

He was tired.

Felicia spoke up. 'I checked the lane, by the way. Where Sleeves was killed.' She closed the laptop, clearly frustrated. 'There's nothing – we got no video surveillance and no witnesses. It's an investigative dead end.'

Striker opened his eyes. 'Let's switch gears for a bit. Focus on Chipotle. He's the other end to this equation.'

Felicia agreed wholeheartedly.

'Head to Source Handling?' she asked.

Striker nodded. 'It's time to see if this guy was coded.'

Without full authorization, Striker and Felicia couldn't access the coded files of the Source Handling Unit. This was standard and a necessary safety measure. Regardless, it left them with only two options – contacting Trevor Eckhart, or contacting Clara Sykes.

Due to Trevor's obvious conflict of interest with having Harry for a brother, Striker chose to contact Detective Sykes. She lived in the fisherman's village of Richmond known as Steveston – a twenty-minute drive to Cambie Street Headquarters – and she took every one of those minutes getting down there.

Not that it mattered much. Clara Sykes spent less than two minutes searching through the database before saying the one word Striker had been fearing all along:

'Purged.'

The coded information was gone.

Striker swore out loud and felt himself deflate. It was disappointing, though not exactly surprising – the information on Chipotle was a decade old. Striker thanked the detective for coming in after hours and trying to help them, then he and Felicia left the Source Handling Unit and returned to Homicide.

There they printed up every file ever created for Carlos Chipotle. There were many. They also attended Archives in an effort to locate the Vancouver Police file for Chipotle's homicide. When Striker found the folder, a jolt of excitement hit him – one that quickly turned to frustration when he found the folder to be empty. He threw it on the shelf and cursed.

'Missing,' he said. 'Gone – just like the coded information.'

Felicia didn't give up. 'I'll check the fiche.'

She left the room and Striker continued searching through the files. When Felicia returned ten minutes later, an equally dejected look smeared her features.

'Nothing?' Striker asked.

'Zilch.'

Striker laughed out of scorn. Missing source papers, missing homicide reports – it was beyond coincidental. Someone had taken them. He knew it. There was simply no other logical explanation.

He grabbed all the folders he could find that were Chipotle-related and realized with all certainty that their day was done. He gave Felicia a weary stare.

'Let's get the hell outta here,' he said. 'Read this stuff at home – over an ice-cold beer.'

For the first time in hours, a smile found Felicia's face.

'You had me at *ice cold*,' she said.

Ninety-One

On the way home, Striker drove in a circuitous route and cut through the Kerrisdale area. He stopped in at the Stone Cold Creamery and bought a two-litre carton of ice cream for Cody and Shana – blue bubble gum, their favourite.

Once back in the car, Felicia stared at the odd blue colour of the dessert and made a wary sound. 'This stuff looks like it was made in Chernobyl.'

Striker grinned. 'Looks like your attempt at risotto last week.'

'Hey, at least I try – what have you ever tried to make for us?'

'I do all my cooking in the bedroom.'

'Yeah? Well next time you need to preheat the oven a little more.'

Striker laughed; the banter felt good. Getting away from the work for a bit felt good. He could suddenly breathe again.

They drove to Rothschild's new residence and parked out front. The engine died with a rattle. Carton in hand, Striker climbed out and approached the front door. Rothschild opened it before he could so much as knock, and in behind him, two tiny faces peered out.

Cody and Shana.

Striker held up the ice cream container. 'Hey, little ones. Who wants a sugar high?'

Shana's tight expression vanished and was replaced by one of glee, while Cody let out a scream of delight and began chanting the words 'ice cream' over and over again, and marching in a circle around the boxes in the living room.

'Oh man, you're gonna get them all hyper,' Rothschild said.

'Who cares?' Felicia said with a grin. 'Jacob and I can always leave.'

Rothschild just laughed softly. 'You're an evil woman.'

Striker ignored the banter and walked into the kitchen. He pulled extra-large bowls from one of the opened packing boxes, gave them a quick rinse under the taps, and then began doling out the cold blue concoction in huge overflowing spoonfuls. Once the treats were served, they all retreated to the living room and found a place to sit down – Striker and Felicia on the couch with the two children nestled between them, and Rothschild perched down on a green plastic moving crate.

The blue bubble gum flavour turned out to be a hit, even for the adults. They ate well. Striker chatted about SpongeBob with Cody, and Felicia talked about Selena Gomez with Shana.

A half-hour later, bedtime came.

Shana was the first to get up.

'Thanks, Uncle Jacob,' she said. She gave him a quick hug, then looked uncertainly at Felicia but gave her one too.

'Thanks, sweetie,' Felicia told her.

Cody did the same, then followed his sister down the hall, whining the whole way about having to go to bed so early.

Striker watched them go and felt a strange mix of emotions. Amusement and yet anxiety, love and yet worry.

'They're nice kids,' Felicia said.

He nodded.

While waiting for Rothschild's return, Striker looked around the room at all the moving boxes, then at the fireplace mantel where a picture of Rosalyn had already been placed. The image reminded him of Keisha Williams, and all the hell her children were going through right now. Suddenly the joy of the moment was gone, replaced by a deep melancholy.

'They all deserved better,' he said.

Felicia gave him a tender look, and before too long Rothschild returned. He sat down with them, spooned up the last of his blue bubble gum ice cream, and then sat back with an almost wary look on his face.

'Well?' he asked. 'Do I want to know?'

'Know what?' Striker asked.

'Where's the investigation at now?'

Striker really didn't want to get into it any more this night, but the man was owed a full debrief. Together, he and Felicia spent a good half-hour filling Rothschild in on all that had transpired during the day's events. With each word, Rothschild's face took on an even deeper expression of disbelief.

'This is a friggin' nightmare,' he finally said.

Striker let out a humourless chuckle. 'You think?'

'Nothing seems to fit,' Felicia said.

Striker agreed. There were not only pieces of the puzzle that didn't seem to fit, but pieces seemed to be missing as well. It almost felt like two entirely different puzzles had been dumped together, making one big jumbled mess for them to sort through.

It was maddening.

Together, the three of them discussed many of the aspects of the case, and tried to sort things out. But the more they talked, the deeper their sense of frustration grew. When it was finally time to head home, Striker couldn't wait to go.

The tank was empty now. He was running on fumes.

Ninety-Two

When Striker and Felicia finally got home to Striker's place and closed the door behind them, the clock on the living room wall read 10:17.

It felt *hours* later.

Striker dropped his coat on the floor beside the coat rack, stacked the Chipotle folders on the coffee table in the den, and then grabbed a couple of ice-cold beers from the fridge. Felicia took her beer and pressed the bottle against her cheek. 'God, that feels good.' She rolled it against the side of her neck and shivered. 'I need a shower.'

She wandered down the hall and disappeared into the bedroom.

Striker took a long swig of his beer and grabbed the first stack of papers. He read. In a few of the files, Chipotle had been charged. In a few more, he had been listed as a suspect. But in most of them, he was simply labelled as a Known Associate.

Striker read the vast array of offences – *Living off the Avails, Running a Common Bawdy House, Theft Over, Robbery, Trafficking, Murder.*

The list went on and on.

It was almost fifteen minutes later when the bedroom door opened and Felicia returned. Striker looked up at her and suppressed a chuckle. She was wearing a pair of red socks, black

Lululemon yoga tights, a yellow T-shirt, and had her hair pulled back with a purple scrunchie.

She caught his smirk and crossed her arms.

'What?' she demanded.

'You look like a rainbow exploded.'

She raised an eyebrow and walked into the room. 'Might I remind you that *I'm* the one living out of a suitcase here – everything else I have is dirty.'

'Which is why you should just move in.'

Felicia stared at him with a mischievous look on her face, but said nothing. She came over to the couch, shoved him hard against the backing, and straddled his hips. 'If you hate the colours so much, why don't you take them off me?'

Striker wrapped his arms around her waist and pulled her close enough to kiss her.

'Taste the rainbow?' he asked.

She laughed. 'Now that's just plain dirty.'

She kissed him gently at first, then harder and with an open mouth, her tongue sliding against his lips, tickling his tongue. Striker reached up, removed the scrunchie from her ponytail, and her long dark hair spilled around her shoulders. Striker wrapped his fingers in it, pulled her close, breathed her in.

'I love you,' she said.

'I know,' he replied.

She smirked as she pushed herself down against his hardness.

Striker held her there. Reached up and pulled the yellow T-shirt from her caramel skin and threw it on the floor. With both his hands, he grabbed her breasts, and felt her breathing quicken.

She pulled slightly back from him.

'Bed?' she asked.

He just nodded and smiled and felt good. For a small brief

moment, his worries and concerns all melted away, and it was no longer a world of bombs or bullets or dirty cops. There was just him and Felicia and their cosy private bedroom.

Nothing else really mattered.

Striker had no idea what time it was when he woke up, but he came to with a jolt. His pulse was racing, friggin' skyrocketing, and all he could see was the fiery image of Chad Koda in the police cruiser, Harry sprawled out helplessly on the ground, and the two shooters encroaching on them.

Closer, closer, *closer* . . .

He blinked away the lingering nightmare. Told himself it was just a dream, a mishmash of bad memories.

But it did little good.

Covered in a thin film of sweat, and with his mouth dust-dry, Striker climbed out of bed – gently so as to not wake Felicia – and walked down the hall to the washroom. He poured himself a glass of tap water, then hopped in the shower for a cool rinse. When he got out, it was obvious that sleep would not come. So he wrapped a robe around himself and returned to the living room to go over the Chipotle files.

To his surprise, Felicia was already going through them.

'You're up,' he said.

She smiled. 'No, you're still dreaming, I'm afraid.'

'I tried not to wake you.'

'You're like a baby elephant rampaging through the house.' He sat down beside her, and she handed him a file. 'Get reading.'

Striker did. Twenty minutes later, when he had found nothing relevant, and was considering going back to bed, Felicia made an excited sound. She held up a thin folder for him to see. On the tab was an old file number, and beside it someone had written: *Lottery Ticket Thefts – 7-Eleven.*

'Look what momma found,' she said.

Striker saw it. 'I read that file already; Chipotle's listed as a suspect. So what? It's a minor theft.'

'You read it, did you? Well, you obviously read the electronic file on the *computer* and didn't look in the folder.'

Striker gave her a curious look. 'What you find?'

She pulled out the paperwork from inside. It was about an inch thick, and divided into two sections by a pair of paper clips. She handed Striker the first section, which had a front page detailing the address of the 7-Eleven store where the lottery tickets had been stolen during a standard smash-and-grab.

Striker shrugged. It was just a printout of the exact same report he'd read on the computer.

But when Felicia showed him the second section of the report, something clicked. For one, the address was different. For two, the role code was wrong. The numbers there were 4169. Not a theft, but . . .

'A *homicide*?'

Felicia nodded. 'It's the police shooting of Chipotle. Someone put it in the wrong folder – one file number away.'

Striker smiled. 'You're a god.'

'God*dess,* darling. God*dess.*'

Felicia spread the pages out on the coffee table.

The first thing Striker noticed was that the report was oddly *basic*. The synopsis told the elementary details of what had occurred: Chipotle had been killed in a shootout with integrated forces. The shooting had happened on the Vancouver-Burnaby border, just up from the Fraser River. And Chipotle had ended up dying on the same day as his wife and daughters, who had been blown up only a few hours earlier by the bomb Sleeves had set.

This had all led to speculation of Chipotle's death being a suicide-by-cop mission from a grieving father suffering from cocaine psychosis. To reinforce that belief, the subsequent autopsy revealed cocaine levels of .643 mg/L.

Striker read that number and whistled.

'That a lot?' Felicia asked.

'Enough to kill Keith Richards.'

He flipped past the synopsis, then through the rest of the pages – the investigative summary, police statement pages, witness statements, and so forth. The shooting seemed pretty straightforward.

Gunman called in.

Police attended.

And Chipotle started shooting.

It was exactly what Striker had expected. And then he spotted one ordinary detail that changed everything – the name of the cop responsible for shooting Chipotle.

Striker read that name and slumped back against the couch. Slowly, horrifyingly, the information sank in. And connections started falling into place.

Chipotle had been killed, not by a standard hollow jacket round, but by a bullet from a police-issued sniper rifle. That rifle was registered to a member on the Emergency Response Team. To Striker's one-time mentor and now closest friend.

Mike Rothschild.

Part 3:
Detonation

Friday

Ninety-Three

The room was hot, so unbelievably hot, and yet he could not stop shaking. His teeth chattered, his body trembled, he couldn't catch his breath. He lay stretched out on a cot that Molly had unfolded, staring at the blue and red pipes that crisscrossed the low ceiling of the command room. The pipes hummed loudly, constantly, like the distant rumble of a coming freight train.

To his left, a pot of water began boiling over onto the kerosene stove. Molly removed it, poured the water into a bucket, and a puff of steam filled the air. She grabbed the antibiotic ointment and sanitized the scalpel, then turned to face him.

Her approach made him shiver. And for the briefest of moments, she looked like the tiny nurse with the paper hat.

'It's okay,' she said. 'It's just me.'

He tried to lift his head off the table, struggled. 'The news release . . .'

'Chad Koda and Harry Eckhart are dead.'

The bomber closed his eyes, as if in relief. He let his head fall back to the table.

'Done,' he whispered. '. . . it's almost done.'

Molly said nothing, she just got to work.

She removed the tape and packing gauze from his shoulder, then applied another coat of lidocaine cream before using the scalpel to scrape away the remaining grime, which was still embedded in the entry wound. She rolled him onto his side and did the exact same to the exit wound. Once complete, she added a final rise of saline and covered both wounds with gauze.

'You're killing me,' he said.

'Oh hush,' she said softly. 'You're lucky it was a through-and-through. The clavicle may have broken, but the bone didn't splinter through the subclavian.' She felt his wrist, and smiled. 'Your pulse is still strong. But you need rest.'

He tried to catch his breath. 'You need to put lidocaine—'

'I just did that. *Rest.*'

He looked at her, confused.

'I can do this job on my own,' Molly said.

'*No.*'

He struggled to sit forward. As he did, the room tilted on him, and he had to grab on to the wall with his good hand. Small beads of sweat trickled down his neck and back, and he felt like he was floating there in the room, kind of hovering above the cot. An apparition.

So hot . . . so goddam *hot.*

'You need rest, love.'

He struggled through the haze. 'I'm finishing this mission – with or without you.'

Molly said nothing. She just nodded and grabbed the medical tape. Firmly, almost roughly, she began tightening the tape around the shoulder joint and clavicle in order to stop it from moving.

He let out a pained sound as she did this, but that was okay. Everything was okay.

The operation was almost done.

Ninety-Four

For Striker, the night had been a long one.

After seeing Rothschild's name on Chipotle's homicide report, he'd made the decision to bring Mike and the kids over to stay at his place, and had gone and gotten them himself. It was the only action that had made sense. After all, if the bombers had found Rothschild's old house, how long before they found his new one too?

Safety was everything.

Once the family was at his own house, Striker felt better. They all got back to bed at sometime after three, and the remainder of the night had been uneasy and restless.

Now, just five o'clock, Striker lay in bed, listening to the creaks and groans of the old house. With Courtney on the other side of the world, it felt like his home was half empty. And to be honest, ever since Amanda had died, the place had never felt whole again. There was always a sadness in his heart. A deep ache that would never go away.

He tried not to think about it, but it was always there.

The relationship he had with Felicia helped. It helped greatly. Striker loved her. But that didn't change a thing. Loving another person with all your heart didn't nullify the love you had felt – and still felt – for another.

Life could be hard.

From down the hall, Cody called out amid his dreams. Striker was sure the boy was half-asleep, but his thoughts played havoc on his mind. Knowing he wouldn't be able to sleep until he checked on the boy, Striker climbed out of bed. He snuck down the hall and peered into the guest bedroom.

The room was still and covered with different shades of black and grey. Rothschild was asleep on the left half of the bed, snoring like an old bear, and Cody and Shana were on the right, snuggled together like a pair of Pringles chips.

Safe and sound.

For now.

Striker returned to his bedroom. He slowly eased back into the bed and grabbed the comforters. Then Felicia spoke: 'The house alarm works fine, Jacob. You don't need to check on the kids for a tenth time.'

'Sorry. Didn't mean to wake you.'

'You're lucky we got dental.'

'Why? You gonna knock my teeth out?'

She laughed softly. 'No. But you've been grinding your teeth all night.'

Striker said nothing, but he reached up and felt his right jaw joint. He'd suffered from TMJ for years; it was probably one of the reasons he got so many headaches. The joint was sore as hell.

'I must have kept you up all night.'

Felicia rolled over to face him and smirked. 'I didn't mind for part of it.'

Striker tried to smile but couldn't. As good as Felicia was at compartmentalizing things in her mind, he was equally bad. The case was *always* there. Breaking through his defences with glaring brightness, like sun through cloud.

'The Prowlers are some bad people,' he said. 'But do you honestly think they'd go after a cop? They usually respect our professional boundaries. And why would they care anyway? I mean really, so what if Rothschild shot Chipotle? The guy was already on the gang's hit list. It makes no sense.'

Felicia rubbed his chest. 'It's just one more theory we have to work through.'

'Yeah, well, my mind's not working through it very well.'

She smiled weakly. 'That's because you've had only eight hours' sleep in three nights. Close your eyes and get some slumber. We can worry about it in the morning.'

'Sure, sure,' he replied.

But fifteen minutes later, he climbed out of bed, then threw on a pair of old blue jeans and a wrinkled baseball shirt. With Felicia fast asleep again, Striker returned to the den to read through some more of the files.

He had to.

They were missing something.

Ninety-Five

The work was agonizing. Even the most minimal of movements tore his shoulder apart. But the bomber pushed through the pain. Performed the required task. And now it was done.

The bomb was set.

He retreated across the road to a small hole in the hedge bushes of the neighbouring yard. It was a perfect place of concealment – hidden, dark, with a full view of the target residence. It also had the wooden backing of the fence to support him, and he needed that.

Sweat dripped from every pore of his skin, so much that the remote detonator felt slippery in his hands. He tightened his grip, slumped back against the fence, and smelled the putrid stink of his own body odour. He smelled like something that had gone bad.

Old meat in the sun, as his former sergeant often said.

High above, the sky was slowly lightening, the stars turning more and more invisible in the softening blue. The moon was all but gone now, dropped down to her nightly bed, and in the east, the morning sun was rising like a waking fiery beast. The sight made him smile.

It wouldn't be long now.

They were one step closer to the completion of their mission.

One step closer to retribution.

Ninety-Six

Striker read through an Assault report – a CBH, or a Causing Bodily Harm – in which Chipotle was one of the main suspects in a gang swarming. As Striker read, he put on a pot of coffee. He leaned against the counter, waited, and listened to the machine percolate. Soon, the rich aroma filled the entire kitchen.

As if on cue, Rothschild walked sleepily into the kitchen. He was wearing a red-and-green striped robe, was unshaven, and his silvering hair was sticking out all over the place. He took one look at Striker and nodded.

'So that's what your ugly mug looks like in the morning.'

Striker nodded. 'If I had a few more wrinkles, people would think I was you.'

Rothschild shouldered him aside to get to the counter. Not bothering to wait till the pot was finished brewing, he poured himself a cup. The burner made a hissing sound when the percolating coffee hit it.

Striker did the same, and the two men sat down at the table with the stacks of file folders in front of them.

'How'd you sleep?' Striker asked.

Rothschild rubbed his eyes and an almost defeated look filled his face. 'Dreams of Rozzie.' He gave Striker a tired look. 'I sure miss her . . . Does it ever stop?'

'Do you want it to?'

Rothschild said nothing, he just shook his head in a *no* manner.

It suddenly occurred to Striker how similar their lives had been. Both of them had spent too many hard years living for the job; both had lost their wives to tragedy; and both were still struggling with the notion of raising their kids.

Striker sipped his brew. The memories were harder to deal with than the investigation, so he changed the subject back to the police-involved shooting of Chipotle and began firing questions at his old friend.

Rothschild soon conceded the point.

'Yeah, I shot Chipotle. So what? It was a goddam gunfight. Everyone was shooting. Bullets were flying everywhere. Mine was just the one that finally found its target – I had the sniper rifle.' He took a long sip of his coffee and made a bitter face. 'It's old fuckin' news. I still don't see how any of this is relevant.'

Striker splayed his hands. 'It *has* to be relevant, Mike. It's the only thing that connects you to the Prowlers. And to Koda and Harry too.'

'Harry? He was never part of the Emergency Response Team. How the hell is he connected?'

Striker thought of how the two bikers – Sleeves and Chipotle – were linked to the two cops – Harry and Koda – by way of the drugs. Then he thought of how Chipotle and Koda were also linked to Rothschild through the Emergency Response Team and the shooting.

The whole thing was a tangled web. Two separate files that were connected, though only through the people involved.

'It's complicated,' Striker finally said. 'But there's no denying one thing – the bomber was at your *house,* Mike.'

Rothschild nodded. 'He was also at the Toy Hut, and I got no connection to the shop or that woman he killed.' He stood up from the table looking stressed out. 'I need some air.'

He topped off his cup with another splash of coffee, then walked down the hall to the front door. He disabled the alarm, opened the door, and walked out onto the porch.

Striker got up and followed him. By the time he stepped onto the porch, Rothschild had already lit up a cigarillo. The sweet burning smell of wine-tipped tobacco filled the morning air. As much as Striker hated to admit it, he loved the aroma. It reminded him of his father.

At his feet, on the front-door mat, was the morning newspaper. It was all rolled up in an elastic band. Striker picked it up, unrolled it, and read the headline:

Mad Bomber Blowing Up The City
How to Protect Your Family

'Oh Jesus, you gotta be kidding me,' he said.

The header was your typical media scare tactic, implemented to sell more papers, and it drove Striker crazy. The editors often unleashed their stories with no concern for the public anxiety it would create. All this would do now was put even more attention on the file, and more pressure on the bombers to achieve their task.

It would speed up their attacks.

'You see this, Mike?' he asked.

'What? Yeah, sure.'

Striker looked up and saw that Rothschild had wandered down to the roadside, where he was enjoying his smoke and watching the sun rising in the east. Next to him was a marked cruiser, and inside it was the patrol cop on guard.

Striker looked farther down the road.

Ten feet away was another car – an old Honda Civic, parked by the kerb. The vehicle was covered with leaves and the right front tyre looked half flat. Striker had never seen the car before, and something about it bothered him.

'Hey Mike, move over here.'

'Huh?'

'Get away from that car.'

Before Rothschild could so much as respond, Striker realized what was bothering him. It was the maple leaves on the hood – they didn't match the cherry blossoms of the tree above it. On autopilot, Striker swept his hand down to his gun, felt nothing – not even a holster – and realized he hadn't geared up yet. He felt naked without the gun. Exposed.

He started down the porch steps.

'Get away from that goddam car!'

Ninety-Seven

Tiny, invisible strings pulled at the bomber's consciousness as he waited, hidden in the dark crevice of the observation point. Like a slowly coming night, the darkness was pressing in on him, forcing out the light. And his body was weakening as fast as his mind. Thoughts of the big homicide cop kept charging into his mind, and he found that oddly intriguing.

Jacob Striker was the one cop he had no desire to kill. But desire or not, some things were unavoidable.

Collateral damage was often necessary.

He stood there with so many thoughts rampaging through his head. And he fought to stay alert. It was hard. His mind felt off. Like he was losing control. Like he was slip . . . slip . . . slipping away into a semiconscious state . . .

And then the haze cleared.

And Target 4 was spotted.

There, coming down the walk.

The goddam cop.

The bomber took a quick look at the sedan. At the little wooden duck with the red number 4 painted on its chest. It was sitting on the hood. He willed his fingers to relax on the remote detonator, tried to calm his nerves. The plastic device was slippery in his sweaty grip, and his fingers felt clumsy. He flicked the switch. Armed the bomb. And the wheels became hot.

The cop came. Ten feet.

Five feet.

Two.

One.

And the bomber pushed the activation button:

Click – spark – *combustion.*

The driver's side of the car exploded in a fountain of flame and light and smoke, showering the cop with metal shrapnel and sending him reeling twenty feet from the percussive blast.

It was done.

Target 4 was eliminated.

Ninety-Eight

Striker and Rothschild stood on the front porch, Striker drinking his coffee and Rothschild sucking back a second smoke.

'Man, you really need to relax a little,' Rothschild said. 'You really scared the shit out of me back there.'

'I needed you to get away from that car. And fast.'

'It's your *neighbour's* car.'

'Well something looked off about it. The leaves on the hood.'

'The leaves?' Rothschild let out a soft laugh that was filled with cigarillo smoke, and shook his head. 'Look thirty metres down – there's a maple right there. The owner just moved the car a little, probably because it's got a flat . . . The stress is making you paranoid, man.'

Striker was about to respond to the comment when his cell went off. Being five-thirty in the morning, Striker felt an immediate concern. A call at this time likely meant one of two things – it was a call from Courtney in Ireland, where it was now one-thirty in the afternoon, or it was more bad news from work. Without looking at the caller ID, Striker stuck the phone to his ear. Listened. And all the wind left his lungs.

'Are you sure?' he asked.

'Yes,' the patrolman told him.

'Are you one hundred per cent positive?' he asked a second time.

'Yes,' came the answer again.

Striker nodded and said, 'Get the drains screened . . . we'll be right down.'

When he hung up the phone and turned around, Rothschild was staring at him, frozen to the spot. The cigarillo dangled precariously from his lips and a wary look smeared his face.

'What the hell's going on now?' he asked.

Striker spoke the words almost mechanically. 'Terry Osaka was killed this morning.'

'What?'

'Ten minutes ago. Just outside his house . . . Another bomb.'

Rothschild looked stunned. For a moment he just stood there and stared. Then he shook his head, threw down his cigarillo, and said, 'I'm coming with you.'

'Absolutely not,' Striker said. 'You stay here with the kids. They need you now more than ever. I'll let you know what we find.'

'I really should—'

'You can't, Mike. Not even if you want to. Not until we know how you're connected in all of this. Until then it's a conflict of interest.'

Rothschild's face took on an almost hurt look, but he nodded. Striker gave the man no time to argue. He spun about and beelined back inside the house to gear up and wake Felicia. They needed to get down to that crime scene before the fire trucks did. This time it had to be processed right.

Terry Osaka had not only been a workmate, but a man Striker considered a friend. To think of him dead was too much to process at the moment, so Striker buried the grief swelling up inside of him and focused on what needed to be done.

Go after the man's killers.

It was the right thing to do. The only thing to do.

Terry would have wanted it that way.

Ninety-Nine

It was just six a.m. when Striker and Felicia arrived on scene at Rosemont Drive, and the sight shocked them. Already, neighbours had spilled out into the street and the fronts of their yards to witness the spectacle of the burning car. The press was also already there, standing flush with the single strip of yellow police tape that blocked off the entire road. One of the reporters, a tall African-American woman with wild, star-shaped hair, recognized him.

'Detective Striker, Detective Striker!' she called.

'No comment,' he said, and pushed past her.

To his dismay, the firefighters had beaten them to the scene and were busy hosing down the smouldering wreckage of Osaka's personal vehicle – some type of a sedan, impossible to recognize now. They had used their fire engine to block video coverage from the opposite end of the street.

Striker appreciated that.

In between the smouldering wreck and the fire engine was a soaked white sheet, under which lay an unidentifiable lump. As Striker got closer, he could see two feet sticking out. One of them was wearing a dress shoe, the other only a sock.

'Osaka,' Felicia said softly.

The sight hit Striker hard. Deep in his belly, a sickness developed, a feeling he couldn't quite define. Something between degrees of rage and loss.

'This should never have happened,' he said.

To the left of the fire engine, the reporter with the star-shaped afro snuck through the police tape. Felicia swore out loud, then ran over to deal with the woman. Striker watched her go. When Striker saw that she had the situation well in hand, he turned his attention back on the crime scene.

Up ahead, he spotted Corporal Summer. She was rushing around the scene, setting up screens over the drains so that the firefighters didn't wash away all the trace evidence. Striker ran over to help her. When they were done, she stood up and wiped her brow and looked at him with a lost expression distorting her features.

'Jesus Christ,' she said. 'Osaka.'

Striker pushed away the grief. There would be plenty of time for that later. Right now time was critical. 'What have we got here, Summer?'

The corporal regained her focus. She raised her hand in the air and whistled loudly, signalling for one of her techs to bring over what they had discovered. A large man in white Tyvek coveralls walked over carrying a twisted steel container. Striker wasn't wearing latex so he didn't touch it.

'That's the base?' he asked.

Corporal Summer nodded. 'It is.'

'Jesus, that's a ton of explosive.'

'HME again.'

Home-made explosive . . . the notion concerned Striker. Not only because of the bomber's apparent skill in creating the material, but because they were smart enough to realize that all other routes of acquiring a commercial or military grade product would now be flagged.

'And look at this,' Corporal Summer said. She held out a plastic bag, containing the remnants of what appeared to be a doll in a policeman's uniform. 'Is this what you were talking about?'

Striker took the bag from her and nodded. It was the same kind of toy found at the Toy Hut and at Koda's place – a ten-inch wooden doll in a policeman's uniform. Just like before, the head and legs had been blown away in the explosion, making Striker believe that those two areas must have been structurally weaker.

On the doll's torso was another number. In red paint.

A number 4.

The sight left Striker chilled.

A 6, a 5, and now a 4. There was no more doubting the fact that this was a countdown of sorts – a taunt from the bombers.

But what was the significance? And furthermore, who were the remaining numbers left for? Although only one number had been found at Koda's, there had been three legs there, so therefore, two dolls. No doll had been found in the carnage of the exploded police cruiser, back at the A&W parking lot, but that didn't mean one hadn't been there – the vehicle had burned for a long time. And there was no doubt that the same people had set that bomb.

So had it been placed there for Koda, the resultant victim? Or had it been placed there for Harry? For both of them? Striker went over everything in his mind for the umpteenth time. It was entirely plausible that Harry and Koda were targets 3 and 2.

But if so, then who was target 1?

Only one person came to mind, and it was one that left Striker feeling sick to his stomach.

Rothschild.

He got on the phone with Dispatch and made sure he had units stationed outside his house. Then he looked back at Corporal Summer and cautioned her. 'The doll is holdback evidence, you understand?'

She nodded. 'What doll?'

'Exactly.'

She returned to work, and Striker let her go. Thoughts of his own preoccupied him. Too many of them. And he was still deep in thought when a strong voice with a French drawl called out from behind him. 'Striker. *Striker!*'

He knew it at once. Acting Deputy Chief Laroche.

Striker turned around to face the man.

'Sir?' he said.

The Acting Deputy Chief looked tired and stressed, but focused. As always, his thick black hair was pristinely combed back over his head and his white commander's dress shirt was without crease. He came to within a foot of Striker.

'What is the status of this investigation?' he demanded.

With forensic techs and patrolmen running all around them, Striker gave Laroche a five-minute rundown of everything that had occurred from the torture scene down by the river, up to and including the death of Inspector Terry Osaka. He left out as much as he could regarding the details of Harry and Koda, and also of the dolls he had found.

It was necessarily prudent to do so.

The Acting Deputy Chief was often like a spinning top, knocking down everything around him with his misguided, erratic decisions. It wasn't entirely his fault, Striker knew. Laroche always meant well, in his own twisted way. But over the years the man had become more of a manager and politician than a cop. As a result, it was best to placate him with the bare minimum of facts and leave him in the dark on the full details.

'And that's when we got here,' Striker finished.

Laroche's face remained hard. 'You've been in two gunfights in forty-eight hours. If this was any other day, I'd put you on stress leave and send you for crisis counselling. But we got bombs going off all over the goddam city and cops are being targeted.'

Laroche's posture sagged, and suddenly, unexpectedly, his expression softened. His face looked *fragile.*

'Sir?' Striker asked.

Laroche cleared his throat. 'Terry was . . . a good friend of mine. I knew the man for twenty goddam years.'

'He was a friend of mine too, sir.'

Laroche nodded. 'Just keep me informed – every step of the way.'

'I'll do my best.'

'Do *better.*'

Striker made no reply, and seconds later the Acting Deputy Chief spotted Corporal Summer. Without so much as another word to Striker, Laroche spun away from him and cornered her by the car wreckage. With the conversation ended, Felicia walked up to Striker and gave him a dubious look.

'What was that all about?' she asked.

'A difficult situation just got a whole lot more complicated,' Striker said. 'Laroche is on the case.'

One Hundred

Harry hadn't slept a wink all night. Bad dreams and an even worse reality. Eventually, he had gotten up and spent the bulk of the night drinking coffee in an all-night café and listening to the police scanner for more news.

Wish granted.

It had come.

He parked his undercover cruiser on the east side of Kerr Street, directly across from the Fraserview Golf Club. A sense of horrified disbelief swept over him. In the far-off distance, he could see the red gleaming lights of the fire engine and the greyish smoke that poured from the shell of a vehicle. Half-dazed, in disbelief and stupor, he walked up the road until he was flush with the yellow police tape.

'Media point's on Killarney,' the young cop guarding the scene told him.

Harry barely glanced at him. Keeping his eyes focused on the chaos ahead, he took out his wallet and showed the badge. The young cop nodded, took down the badge number, and lifted the tape for him to enter.

But Harry did not budge. He just stood there and watched Striker and Felicia and the RCMP bomb specialist cluster together with Acting Deputy Chief Laroche. His eyes fell to the white sheet that lay a few feet from the smouldering wreckage.'Is it true?'

'Detective?'

'Is that really him?'

The young cop nodded hesitantly. 'Inspector Osaka is what they're saying. But it's all hush-hush right now. I really don't know too much about it.'

Harry did not respond. He just stared at that white, wrinkled, dirty sheet. At the uneven lump in the centre of it. And he felt his world come further apart. A dizziness hit him. Spun his head like a top. And the road looked like a tarmac on a blistering hot day – distorted, wavy, blurred.

With the heavy bass strum of blood pulsating through his temples, Harry turned away from the scene and walked back to the undercover cruiser. He tried to sort things out in his head, but couldn't.

When Keisha Williams had been targeted, he'd *thought* he'd known everything. Even more so when Koda's ex-wife had been whacked. But now, if these people had gone after Terry Osaka as well, then he and Koda had gotten it wrong. All wrong from the very start.

Sleeves hadn't been setting the bombs.

But who then?

One Hundred and One

The explosion from the car bomb had sent Inspector Terry Osaka flying over twenty feet from the scene of impact, taking off his left arm in the process. A jagged piece of aluminium, almost eight inches long, had embedded itself through the man's left eye, leading the on-call coroner to believe that death for the inspector had been mercifully instantaneous.

With the body now removed from the scene, Striker performed a cursory search of the area. In the grass, a half-foot away from where the body had been found, were a series of – what appeared to be – fingermarks.

Claw marks in the grass.

Striker looked at them for a long moment, and he prayed that the coroner was right about Osaka's death being instantaneous. To think that the man might have been trying to pull himself back to his house while dying was too horrific to consider.

Striker killed the thought. He refused to let grief derail his logic. The loss here was overwhelming and personal. So it was critical that he maintained a professional distance. Catching the bombers was all that mattered now, and the first step in finding them was interviewing Osaka's wife.

Striker looked at the small rancher on the far side of the road. It was so quaint. So *Mayberry*. White paint, blue trim, on a small ordinary lot with a white picket fence. It was the North American dream – one that had mutated into a nightmare at sometime before five a.m. Somewhere within those walls, Mrs Osaka was in shock. In grief. And probably being counselled by the Victim Services Unit.

How the hell had it ever come to this?

With Felicia still preoccupied with the neighbourhood witnesses and the ongoing canvass, Striker headed for the front door of the Osaka house.

It was the last thing he wanted to do.

Five minutes later, Striker sat on a cushy sofa with floral patterns and glanced numbly around the living room. It was small, barely big enough to hold the sofa and loveseat, and modest. Only a few photographs decorated the room – kids that looked like grandchildren. They made Striker realize that he didn't really know too much about Osaka's personal life.

Across from him sat Mrs Osaka.

Pearl, as she introduced herself.

Her face was so pale that she looked Caucasian. Her eyes were swollen from crying, and her hair still looked matted and out of place – as if she had not yet had time to drag a brush through it. On the coffee table in front of her sat an untouched glass of saki, and next to it was a Princess Cruise Lines brochure, where retirees were laughing on deck.

Striker glanced at it, and Mrs Osaka noticed.

'Terry wanted to see the Panama Canal,' she explained. Her voice was but a whisper. 'He'd been planning on doing it when he retired. He was just . . . just six months away.'

Striker tried to meet her stare, but the woman's eyes remained fixated on the happy couple on the brochure. He spoke anyway. 'I knew your husband, Pearl, for twenty years. He was a good man.'

The words seemed to wake the woman, and her eyes took on a pleading look. 'Terry *was* a good man. He was a really, really good man. So why? *Why?*' Her voice broke and she cupped a hand over her mouth.

Striker refused to look away. 'That's what I'm going to find out. You got my word on that. I'm going to catch the people responsible for this.' He gave her a moment to gather herself, then continued. 'Can you think of anything that might be related to this, Pearl? Anything odd that might have happened recently or even years ago? Maybe a file that went bad, or a personal vendetta someone had against him? Some threats that were made but never reported?'

Mrs Osaka straightened her back. Folded her hands in her lap. Looked down. And for a moment, Striker thought he had lost her again.

'There is nothing,' she finally said. 'I can think of nothing . . . All Terry ever did was work hard and be a good cop. If anything, he worked *too* hard and *too* much – like with this case you're on now. He'd been working on it day and night. He wasn't able to sleep or relax. It was always with him, always. *Always.*'

Striker wanted to comfort the woman but wasn't sure what to say. Just as he was searching for a proper response, his cell phone buzzed with a work email. It surprised him because he had most of the departmental sludge forwarded to his backup folder.

Only external emails found their way to his cell.

'Is that important?' Mrs Osaka asked.

'I'd better just check it,' he said.

He hit the email button. There on the screen was a message that left him cold:

You seem like good honest cops, Detectives. Not like Osaka. There's been enough bloodshed. Please don't make me kill you too.

The message was unsigned, but the sight of it made Striker's pulse quicken.

'Is everything all right, Detective?'

'Just forensics,' Striker said.

He put the cell away and stared at the woman before him. Her expression was one of despondency. Of pure loss. And it pained him. He wished there were something he could say to ease her grief. All he could come up with was:

'Your husband was a dedicated man, Pearl.'

She let out a sad laugh. '*Too* dedicated . . . This job was hard on him. He was slowly breaking down from it, and he didn't even see it.' As the woman spoke, a sense of anger began to creep into her tone. 'The department can't expect a man to work morning to night every single day, Detective. Leaving at six, not getting home till two. Those are crazy hours – crazy. They make a person ill. Make them unclear. And they make mistakes.'

Striker said nothing back.

Morning to night?

Leaving at six?

The words rang untrue. Sure, they'd all been putting in tough hours this last week. And yes, Osaka had been held over on many of the calls. But on all those days, Striker hadn't seen the inspector signed on until his shift had started. And that was at noon. He met the woman's stare again. 'What hours did you say your husband was working on this file?'

'*All* hours. He left the house every morning before six and he sometimes didn't get home till after one or two in the morning. It was ridiculous.'

Striker wrote this down in his notebook. 'Did he say what part of the investigation he was working on so early? Or where he was going?'

'Well, no, not really. Terry didn't like to talk about his work.

He thought it would worry me, and he was right about that – it did. But he did mention White Rock once or twice.'

'White Rock?' Striker asked. That was far out of Vancouver's jurisdiction, almost a half-hour drive into the valley. 'When was that?'

'Well . . . just yesterday.'

'Do you know what he was doing out there?'

Mrs Osaka shook her head. 'I just remember him mentioning that because it was such a far way to go, and he was so tired.'

Striker took note of the woman's words, and he wrote it down in his notebook, then spent another half-hour conversing with the woman, going over all other possible leads. But nothing seemed to hold any value. And when he was done, there was only one thought in his mind.

White Rock . . .

What the hell was Osaka doing way out there?

One Hundred and Two

When Striker left the Osaka house, Felicia was standing by the front kerb waiting for him. The muscles under her skin were tight, and it made her face look hard and serious. Upon seeing him, she beelined up the walk.

'I got a message,' she said.

'From the bomber?'

She nodded, half surprised. 'You get one too?'

'We need to trace the email ASAP.'

Felicia frowned. 'Already done.'

'Through Ich?'

She gave him an irritated look. 'Of course, Ich.'

'And?'

She shook her head. 'The message was sent through an offshore proxy. It's completely untraceable. You can't even reply. It won't connect.' She opened her email app and showed Striker the message she had received.

It was the exact same.

'I don't get it,' she said. 'Why send this at all? What, is he taunting us?'

Striker thought it over. It didn't seem that way. If anything, it was almost like the man was genuinely warning them off. The idea that they would ever stop the investigation was ludicrous – a break from reality. It told much of the bomber's mental state.

'Nothing makes sense any more.'

Striker looked at the scene behind them, where Corporal Summer was now taking complete control of the latest bomb scene. Patrol was busy canvassing, forensic techs were filtering through the debris, and the Media Liaison unit was busy dealing with the constantly amassing press.

They could do no more here.

'Come on,' Striker said. 'Let's get the hell out of here. We got a wildcat to see.'

They headed out east to the 2800 block of Pender Street with Striker at the wheel. That was where E-Comm was located. While en route, Felicia went through the CAD call remarks of the Osaka bombing, looking for anything unusual.

'Interesting,' she said after a while. 'Listen to this: not five minutes after Osaka was killed in the blast, a witness reported seeing a white van racing south on Kerr Street.'

'They get a plate number?'

'No . . . Then, ten minutes after that, one of the Alpha units tried to pull over a white van in the Marpole area. But it bolted on them.'

'Any plate?'

'No.'

'A make or model?'

'Again, no. It was a good block ahead and going fast.'

Striker frowned. 'Get the analyst to put that information into the Overnights. I want Patrol to see it. Have checks done on all generic white vans spotted between the hours of midnight and five a.m.'

Felicia agreed; she got on the phone and got things done.

When they reached E-Comm, the Emergency Communications Centre, Striker and Felicia entered the security foyer. Striker flashed his badge to the guard inside the booth, then they obtained a pass key.

Before heading on, Striker grabbed a bottle of Coke from the dispenser. Once on the main floor, they located Sue Rhaemer. The woman was seated in District 2 Command, west side of the facility. She was leaning forward in a high-backed office chair, wearing a set of earphones complete with a voice-activated mike. She was busy scanning three huge monitors that were full of information.

Felicia pointed at her. 'Didn't I see her in the last *Star Trek* movie?'

'I think it was *The Matrix*.'

As they finished their conversation, Sue looked over and spotted them. She yelled out, 'Hey, dude and dudette!' and pumped her fist in the air.

Striker just smiled at her. Sue was more than uninhibited. She'd played electric guitar in her own band – the Femme Fatales – wore low-cut shirts and push-up bras, and teased her bleached, platinum-blonde hair like Samantha Fox.

Now midway through her forties and wearing plus-size clothing, her dream of gyrating on the hood of a Jaguar in a Whitesnake rock video may have passed, but she was still known to frequent the back of a few Buicks. She wore that rumour unabashedly and made no apologies for it. It was for reasons like this that Striker couldn't help but like the woman. Sue was genuine.

He approached her work station, backed up by Felicia. 'You got my list there, Bananarama?'

Sue scowled. 'Bananarama? *Puu – leeeze*.' She spun her chair around. 'My stage name was *Wildcat*, not Bubbles or Candy. Now where the hell's my Coke?'

Striker handed her the bottle, and Sue unscrewed the cap. She took a couple of swigs. Let out a sigh. 'Sweet sugar bliss.'

Striker prodded her. 'The GPS history on Osaka's car.'

She put down the bottle. 'Fine, fine, okay. But this is the last of it, Striker. The *last*. You know the protocols. You're going to get me in some serious trouble here.'

'You're helping us save lives.'

Sue said nothing back. She just logged into the GPS tracking system, located Osaka's vehicle number, and brought up the history. 'This is just the basic hourly rundown. You want the full history, you need to retrieve the unit and hook it up to a computer.'

'I just need a list of all of his GPS coordinates over the last few days, in particular the morning hours. Places where he'd been – especially ones out in the valley.'

Sue ran her finger down the monitor, scanning the electronic list. She stopped a third of the way from the bottom and made a noise. 'Hmm, look here . . . and here. Two times in two days. Same place, out in the valley.'

Striker leaned closer and looked at the list. 'Where is this? White Rock?'

'Yeah. But way, way, *way* down south. We're talking Zero Avenue here – right down by the US border.'

Striker looked at the times Osaka had been there. 09:00 hours. Both times. And on two consecutive days. He turned back and looked at Felicia. Her eyes were focused on the screen with the same intrigue.

'That's odd,' she said. 'Why would he go all the way out there when there's so much chaos going on right here in the city?'

'There's only one way to find out,' Striker said.

It was time for a road trip.

One Hundred and Three

The holiday rental Harry booked was a small yellow house with wood siding. It sat on the edge of the Fraser River in the quaint, historical town of Fort Langley, a fifty-minute drive from Vancouver's downtown core. Harry had found the place online, and immediately knew it was the perfect hiding place for his family. The B&B was far enough from the city to be removed, yet still close enough to be reachable.

It was no solution, but it would buy him time.

Harry finished unloading the last suitcase from the car and carried it up the walkway. Ethan went with him the entire way, skipping more than running, holding Harry's free hand. When they reached the foyer, Ethan bounded ahead to the TV and put on the Teletoon channel. Soon enough, he was deeply enmeshed in the wonderful world of *The Smurfs*.

Harry's wife Sandra stood by the sink in the kitchen, staring out at the river's edge. Her hands were folded over her stomach and a nervous expression marred her face. She glanced at Harry, then back at the river. 'The currents look bad,' she said, and her voice broke.

'Sandra—'

'I'm not comfortable here, Harry.'

'It's necessary. For now.'

'But *why*?'

'Because no one knows you're here.'

A mix of fear and resentment filled her eyes. 'I can't take much more of this,' she said. 'Cryptic phone calls. Moving to secret locations. Press releases of your death – my God, Harry! I'm scared. I'm scared for Ethan.'

Harry grabbed her by the shoulders. 'You and Ethan are precisely why I've done all this,' he said. 'Look, Sandra, I can't explain it all right now. You have to trust me on this one. But I will tell you. Later. *I promise.*'

For a brief moment, her worry mutated into anger, and she gave him a hot look. 'Sometimes, I wonder why I listen to you.'

Harry raised a finger. 'Poppa Smurf always says . . .'

Her cross look broke, and a small smile found the corners of her mouth.

Harry pulled her close, held her tight. After a moment, she relaxed a little, and rested her head against his neck. Even though her muscles lost their rigidness, her breath continued to flow in uneven shudders, so Harry didn't let go.

'It's just precautionary,' he said one more time.

'But *why*?' she said back, and the look in her eyes told Harry she would no longer be denied. 'You're not protecting us by keeping us in the dark.'

'Cops are being targeted, Sandra. Ones I'm associated with. And that puts not only me, but you and Ethan at risk. I won't take any chances. Not with my wife and son.'

A knock came on the front door, and Harry pulled away from her. The door swung open and standing there was Trevor. Before either man could speak, Ethan screamed out, 'Uncle Trevor!' The boy jumped off the couch and raced across the room. He slammed into his uncle and gave Trevor a long, hard hug at waist level.

Trevor dropped to one knee and was still taller than the boy. 'How ya doing, champ?'

'*The Smurfs* are on! We're going to live out here for a bit.'

'I know. I'll be living with you.'

'Awesome!'

Sandra heard the words and she stiffened. She turned to her husband and that look was back on her face again. 'Trevor is staying? Harry, this is scaring me.'

'I told you, Sandra, it's just precautionary.'

She said nothing; she just nodded, then walked over and gave her brother-in-law a hug. 'It's good to see you, Trevor.'

'Likewise, as always.'

Sandra grabbed one of the smaller suitcases and took it up the stairs. Trevor carried the larger one and went with her.

With his wife and brother gone from the room, Harry took the time to assess the place. Everything was bright and clean and smelled like lemon Pledge. Not bad for a safe house. He studied all the exits – one front door, one kitchen door, a sliding glass door to the patio. Then he realized that Ethan was looking at him. Intently.

'I don't want to be away from you,' the boy said.

For a moment, Harry could see Joshua in him. And as much as it saddened him, it also made him love the boy even more, were that possible. He knelt down, gave his son a hard hug, and didn't want to let go. Once again, he touched his son's chest. Right over the heart.

'No matter where you go, no matter where I am, I will always be right here, Ethan. Never forget that.'

The boy looked back through large wide eyes and smiled.

'I love you more than anything, son.'

'I love you *more*.'

Harry smiled at the boy's words and felt tears come to his eyes.

'That's just not possible, son.'

One Hundred and Four

It was well after eight a.m. by the time Striker turned onto Zero Avenue and paralleled the Canada–US border. He glanced at the stereo clock twice, disbelieving the display. 'Day already feels long – just like yesterday and the day before.'

Felicia nodded. 'Well, that's what happens when you start around five in the morning.'

Striker drove on.

The GPS coordinates from Osaka's cruiser translated to the 17000 block of Zero Avenue. It was an odd area. Half the land was made up of large patches of wilderness, and the other half was a mix of ten-acre lots. Paralleling the area were even larger squares of farmland. Flats and rolling hills. Everywhere Striker looked, zoning permits had been put up.

Condo developments were in the works.

Striker turned into a narrow cement driveway that opened up on a wider roundabout. Standing at the mouth of the oval was a large wooden sign that said: 'Sunset Grove Care Centre'. Behind the sign was a rectangular, one-level structure, made up entirely of brown stucco and brown brick.

'This is it?' Felicia asked.

Striker nodded. 'According to the GPS unit we've arrived. Osaka came here early in the morning, each of the last two days.'

'Well, let's go find out why.'

They parked the car and got out.

The doors to the main foyer were electronic, and they swished open as Striker and Felicia approached. Inside, a cooler air hit them, and the soft sound of Billy Joel's 'Piano Man' played over the speakers. The facility smelled of green pea soup.

Felicia read a plaque on the wall. 'Hmm. This is a long-term care facility.'

Her words struck a chord with Striker, and the name started to sound familiar. 'Sunset Grove . . . I think the Police Mutual Benevolent Association contributes to this place. For cops who get sick.'

He approached the reception desk. The nurse working there was early thirties, black, and had her curly hair tied back in a bun. Striker flashed her the badge, explained that they were here on some follow-up matters for their boss, and the woman smiled.

'For Inspector Osaka?' she asked.

Striker forced a smile and said yes. 'You know him?'

'Oh yes, he's a very nice man – he's been here two days in a row now.'

'I wasn't aware of that,' Striker said. 'Do you know why he was here?'

'Well, visiting, of course.'

When Striker said nothing else, the nurse reached across the desk and grabbed the sign-in book. She turned it slightly so he could read the writing, then flipped the pages back a day.

'There's his signature. Room 17. Mr Hurst.'

It took Striker a moment to recognize the name. Hurst was a man he'd known years ago and had long since forgotten. He looked down at the line, spotted Osaka's signature, then pushed the book back to the nurse. 'Can we visit him?'

'Of course you can. I'm sure he'd love the company.' She

pointed down the hall. 'East Corridor, just that way there. But be warned . . . he's not doing all that well today.'

Striker nodded but asked nothing more. He turned around and spotted Felicia, who was still reading the information on the welcome plaque. He gave her a nod, muttered, 'We got someone to talk to,' and the two of them headed down the long corridor.

As they went, the lighting grew dimmer. The walls were brown, just like the floor – just like the entire exterior of the building. The drab colour made everything appear darker, especially the sections where the natural light of the front windows couldn't reach. Striker wondered why they'd used it.

They passed a few lifting cranes and a series of walkers and motorized wheelchairs, then reached Room 17. The name plate on the wall was Salvador Hurst.

'Salvador?' Felicia asked. '*Sal?*'

Striker nodded. 'Used to be a detective with the Drug Unit. Long time ago, though. He got seconded to the Feds for about eight years and I never saw him again. Had no idea he was even in here.'

He gave a rap on the door and went inside.

At first Striker thought they had entered the wrong room, or maybe that the nameplate was wrong. Yes, it had been eight years since he had seen Sal Hurst, but the man he remembered was a strong, solid cop with South American good looks.

The man on the bed did not even resemble that man.

This man was thin – so awfully thin. The skin hung off his body like drapes. Underneath his flesh, there was no fat, and even less muscle. His eyes were just sockets now, his cheeks all bone, and his hair was not only white and thin, but missing in patches. His breaths came in slow, erratic wheezes.

'Sal?' Striker asked.

The man on the bed did not move.

'*Sal,*' he said again, a little louder.

The man's eyes opened part way, and then narrowed. 'I . . . *know* you,' he said. The words were weak, and they seemed to take everything out of the man.

Striker stepped forward and introduced himself. 'And this is Detective Felicia Santos. She's with the VPD too.'

Hurst just blinked.

'We're here because of Terry Osaka,' Striker said.

A flicker of happiness filled the man's eyes. 'Terry . . . he was . . . just here . . . some day.' He looked at the box of chocolates on the side table, all of which remained. 'Take some.'

Striker did not. Instead, he pulled over a chair and sat closer to the bed. 'I haven't seen you in years, Sal. Not since you left for the secondment.'

Hurst's eyelids closed for a moment, then opened again. '. . . didn't last long . . . got *sick*.'

Felicia sat down next to them. 'Is that why Terry was here, Sal? Just to visit you? Or was there another reason?'

Hurst took a few laborious breaths before responding. 'Old friends . . . *squadmates*.'

Striker nodded. 'We know that, Sal. But did he come here for any other reason, other than to say hi?'

Hurst just rolled his head lazily back and forth, as if shaking his head no. As he did this, Striker saw the sweat marks on the pillow. 'Just . . . saying hi,' Hurst got out. 'Terry was always . . . a good guy.'

Striker nodded slowly, then cast a glance over at Felicia, who merely shrugged. She took a moment to ask Sal a few questions. But the answers she received were inevitably more of the same, and she didn't want to tire the poor man. One thing here was clear. Hurst was ill. Probably dying. And he looked like he had little time left. It seemed that Osaka had been merely paying his final respects.

Striker stood to leave. 'It was good to see you, Sal.'

'Say . . . say hi . . . to Terry.'

Striker nodded and forced a smile.

'Get some rest, Sal,' he said.

One Hundred and Five

They took Highway 99 back to the city. The road curved gradually through the flatlands, then dipped down into the City of Richmond. Coming this way, the scenery was less appealing visually, but it shaved twenty minutes off their commute. Once back in Vancouver, Felicia spotted a Starbucks on Oak.

'I need a caffeine jolt,' she said.

Striker didn't disagree. The thought of a hot cup of Joe was stimulating, and he pulled over. The Starbucks didn't have a drive-thru, so he parked on the main drag out front. When he opened his door, Felicia's cell went off. She looked at the screen and said, 'I need to take this – my contact with the Explosives Branch.'

Striker nodded and retreated from the car.

Felicia had contacts everywhere. It was one of the best things she brought to the partnership – her ability to liaise and schmooze with the best of them. Her contact at the Safety and Explosives Branch of the British Columbia Government was a perfect example of this. And they needed that information badly.

Striker went inside the Starbucks.

When he returned five minutes later, Felicia was still on the phone. He put her drink – a vanilla-caramel latte, size Venti – in the cup holder, then passed her one of the egg-white wraps he had bought. She took it, sniffed it, and made a face. 'Doesn't smell like a lemon scone.'

'Want me to throw some icing sugar on it? *Eat.* You need the protein.'

She just gave him a sideways glance and took a bite.

Five minutes later, when Striker was half done eating his own egg-white wrap, Felicia hung up her cell and turned to face him. 'Okay, some interesting stuff here. As it turns out, there was a major recall on PETN the other day – the same explosive your love crush thinks the bombers used to blow up the toy shop and Chad Koda's place.'

Striker let the 'love crush' comment go. 'Did your contact say why?'

Felicia nodded. 'I don't understand all the jargon, but in basic terms, the product was unstable.'

'We need to get a list of all the places where that batch was sent.'

'Already requested, they're working on it now.' Felicia took a bite of her wrap. 'And just so we're clear, next time I prefer lemon scones.'

Striker said nothing. He was too busy thinking about the bombers' MO. Now it made sense why they'd switched to home-made explosives. It had been an unforeseen roadblock in their plan – and one they had adapted to with seeming ease.

'So PETN on the toy shop and Koda's house, then HME on the two vehicles.'

'Looks like it.'

Recollections of the bomb that had killed Osaka made the egg in Striker's stomach feel off. Already, he missed his old friend. And try as he did to treat the bombing like it was just another case, it was not possible. Not only because Osaka had been his friend, and not only because Osaka had been a cop, but because the man didn't deserve an end like this. One thing Osaka had always been was a good man.

He deserved better.

Striker threw the wrapper in the garbage. 'I still find it strange that Osaka went all the way out there to visit Sal.'

'He was a good friend. And the man's not well.'

'I understand that. But why *now*? In the middle of the investigation? Was there not a better time to do it? I mean, think of the hours he'd been putting in with all these bombs going off. Plus the kidnapping in District 4. He must have been running on fumes. Then, two days in a row, he gets up early and drives almost an hour into the valley, just to say hi to an old friend? The timing seems off.'

'You heard the nurse. Sal's not doing well. Maybe he wasn't saying hi, maybe he was saying goodbye.'

'I get that,' Striker said. 'But I talked to the nurse. Sal hasn't been doing well for *months*. I don't know . . . to me, the timing doesn't make sense. Not when we have a mad bomber running around the city. Visiting Sal could have waited a few days.'

He put the car into gear and pulled into the fast lane.

'Where to?' Felicia asked.

Striker sighed. 'White Rock was a bust. But there's something going on with Osaka, otherwise he wouldn't have been involved. We need to obtain all his old files – especially ones from about ten years ago.'

'Why? Where was he working ten years ago?'

Striker gave her a dark look. 'The Police Standards Section. *Internal*.'

One Hundred and Six

The bomber lay back on the heavy steel table. He was thirsty.

And cold.

So cold.

When Molly wiped him down with more lidocaine, it chilled his overheated skin and stung him at the same time. He flinched when she began removing the packing gauze from the entry wound in his shoulder; it slithered out of him like a bloodied snake and turned the steel bowl pink.

'If you're going to vomit, let me know.'

'. . . so cold.'

Molly washed the wound with saline, then injected him with another dose of meds – some antihistamines, some plasma and antibiotics – before patching him back up again.

'You need rest,' she said.

'. . . out of time.'

'Lay still. You're tearing your wounds open. Lay *still.*'

'The operation . . . we're almost done.'

Molly held up the bowl of gauze and pointed to the white pus within the blood. 'It's *purulent*. Infection's setting in fast. Your body needs time. It needs to rest.'

He refused to look at her.

'You're making this personal,' she said.

He heard that, and he laughed. 'Personal? It always was

personal, Molly. We were kidding ourselves to think it wasn't.'

'Maybe so . . . but you're *enjoying* it.'

'Feelings and emotion have nothing to do with it. The world is black and white, not grey. You're either guilty or innocent, right or wrong, alive or dead . . . You used to see that once, a long time ago.'

The bomber closed his eyes. Despite what he had said, Molly was right, he knew. At least on some level. He *was* enjoying this. More than anything, he wanted to stay active. In the moment. *Engaged.* Whenever inactivity returned, bringing with it the passivity and the silence, so too did the awful, awful memories.

It was a strange notion – that peace would be hell, and hell would bring peace. But that was the way it was now. The way it had always been.

Ever since that first explosion in Afghanistan.

The one that took his leg off.

He fought to get up from the heavy metal table and stared at the grey cement walls of the command room. Overhead, the red and blue pipes began making noise again, their rumbling call something between the hiss of snakes and the thunder of a storm.

On the only other table the room offered was the last wooden duck, dressed in a policeman's uniform.

Number 1.

The most crucial of all.

He reached over and picked it up. Stared at the little white duck. And he smiled weakly.

It was time.

'Where's my uniform?' he said.

One Hundred and Seven

When Striker and Felicia made it to Cambie Street Headquarters, it was going on for eleven. They took the elevator to the seventh floor and walked down the hall to the Deputy Chief's office.

As Striker turned the corner, he spotted Laroche. The man was on the phone, barking more than talking, and absently brushing his fingers through his thick black hair, trying to keep every strand in place. In front of him, spread out across the mahogany desk, were several inter-office memos.

Striker read a few of the headings: *Global TV. News 1130. The National.*

All media outlets.

Before being demoted from the Deputy Chief position, Laroche had been known as *Deputy Drama Queen* by many of the men. Now some of the street cops called him the *Superintendent Starlet*. It was probably unfair – one of the man's responsibilities was, in fact, assisting Media Liaison in dealing with the press. But the fact that Laroche so *revelled* in the spotlight rubbed a lot of people the wrong way.

Striker included.

'Sir,' Striker finally said to get the man's attention.

Laroche looked up. A less-than-pleasant expression spread across his face. There was a certain thinness in his features, the kind brought on by extreme stress, and Striker could see that Osaka's death was affecting the man.

Laroche didn't say hello, didn't so much as nod. He just finished his phone conversation, then hung up – slammed the receiver so hard, the strands of his perfect hair fell out of place.

'Press is all over this goddam thing,' he said.

Striker was not surprised. 'Of course they are. We got bombs going off all around the city. Cops have been targeted. Civilians too. And we still don't know who the bombers are.'

Laroche's face tightened. 'As always, Striker, thank you so much for the wonderful goddam news. Jesus Christ, are you any closer to solving this thing?'

Striker moved out of the doorway into the office. He grabbed a chair for him and Felicia, then sat down and told the Acting Deputy Chief more of what they knew. 'This might all come back to a police-involved shooting – one that took place ten years ago, involving a Satan's Prowler member and an integrated ERT squad.'

Laroche's dark eyes took on a distant look. 'Ten years . . . you're talking about Carlos Chipotle.'

Striker was surprised Laroche even knew of the man. 'We are.'

'Chipotle was a psychopath and a cokehead.' Laroche slumped back in his chair with a bewildered look on his face. 'What makes you believe this might be related?'

'It's one of the few links that exist between all the parties involved. We're still in the middle of the investigation. We'll let you know what we uncover.'

Laroche's face remained slack for a long moment, then his eyes turned suspicious as he realized they were here for a particular reason. 'What do you need of me?'

Felicia spoke first. 'Clearance.'

Striker clarified: 'We need authorization to read Osaka's files

– the older ones from when he was working in the Police Standards Section. Osaka was working there at the time of the Chipotle shooting. Those files are essential to this case.'

'Which files do you need?'

'All of them.'

'*All?*' Laroche said nothing for a moment, then he nodded his head in submission. 'PSS files are classified. So I need not remind you that whatever permissions you're given, the information in those files will be for your eyes alone.'

Striker nodded. 'Understood.'

Felicia said the same.

Laroche got on the computer and began typing. A minute or two later, he was obviously done, because he sat back and shook his head like he was expecting something bad to happen. He looked up at Striker, and his pale face was tight and grave-looking. 'Why do I have a feeling you're about to single-handedly sewer my career for the second time, Striker?'

Striker just smiled.

'What can I say, sir? Misery loves company.'

One Hundred and Eight

The Police Standards Section, once located in the same building as Cambie Street Headquarters, had recently been moved outside the walls of the department in order to offer the appearance of impartiality. In truth, it made no difference. The investigations were still done primarily by Vancouver Police Department sergeants, with the help of their assistants.

And that was the way it had to be.

Lately, a select portion of special interest groups had been fighting the system, trying to replace the police sergeants with civilian investigators who would then take charge of the investigations.

Striker couldn't see it happening. Not with all the requirements of the courts and the union and the ability to scour through secret police files. A purely civilian investigation team seemed nothing more than a self-serving, special-interest pipe dream . . . but there was little doubt that *some* changes would be coming.

It was inevitable.

They parked out front. To most onlookers, the building looked like any other business. No department insignias decorated the tinted glass doors, no signs or inscriptions guided the way. The building was small, plain, and newly built.

A modern facility for a modern force.

Striker and Felicia went inside and found their way to the

records room, where they began searching through the files. By the time they were done, almost a half-hour later, they had removed and photocopied twenty-three investigations, several of which were linked to other departmental files.

Felicia looked at the pile. 'This is a ton of work to go through. Osaka must have been single-handedly working a dozen files back then.'

'He was a busy man. We'll start with the most relevant files and go backwards from there.'

Together, they started sorting through the folders.

When Felicia picked up one, she looked at it, then shook her head as if confused. 'This one is linked to the Chipotle shooting – I thought the investigation had already been done by Homicide?'

'This is the internal investigation,' Striker reminded her. 'Everything they do here is *separate* from the other police files. It has to be, or else there would be no impartiality. Look around and you'll find lots of duplicate investigations. The difference is that these reports focus solely on the officer's actions, not the suspect's.'

Felicia just nodded as if making the connection; they now had access to secondary independent reports.

Rather than leave the office, they took the paperwork to one of the unused meeting rooms, and locked the door behind them. The desk inside was oval and long, designed to seat twenty people. Striker took his position at one end, and Felicia the other.

Then they got to work.

Twenty minutes later, Striker was skimming through some of the attachments – Civilian Statements, primarily – while Felicia was reading the Chronological Timeline that Osaka had entered on his own investigation into the Chipotle shooting.

'One thing about Osaka,' she said. 'He was *thorough.*'

Striker nodded. 'Public image. He had to be on a file like this. The shooter was Rothschild – one of our own guys. Nowadays, the Vancouver Police Department wouldn't even investigate the call. We'd send it to an outside agency, probably Abbotsford or Delta.'

'For impartiality.'

He nodded. 'Optics are everything.'

When Striker finished reading the complete narrative of the shooting, he re-read the bombing report on Chipotle's wife and kids. After a long while he looked up and frowned. 'Everything appears to be on the level. At exactly nine o'clock in the morning, Chipotle's house is blown sky-high.'

'From a bomb Sleeves set.'

Striker nodded. 'The wife and two daughters are killed, and no one can find Chipotle anywhere. Then, at two in the afternoon, a civilian calls in. She sees a man with a machine gun down by the river. He's crying, screaming, aiming the gun at people.'

'And she calls 911.'

Striker ran his finger down the timelines on the page. 'First, Dispatch thinks it's just some crazy guy wandering around. They send Patrol. But then they realize it really is an automatic weapon, so they call in the Emergency Response Team.'

Felicia knew the file well, and she chimed in:

'But the Vancouver ERT unit is already on another call in District 1. And this call is right on the Vancouver-Burnaby border, so they order in the Integrated Unit.'

Striker held up his finger. '*But* . . . they're still short on bodies for a full team. And with the information about an AK-47, there's no time to waste. So they throw together an impromptu team using reserves. They lock down the block and the river, but by now Chipotle's gone inside one of the houses. They try to call him out. But he's having none of it.'

Felicia looked at the medical section of the report which held the cocaine levels. 'Not only is he grieving, but he's all coked-out. Completely irrational.'

'And he blames the cop several times for selling him out after he "gave them the information they wanted".' Striker read back through the narrative. 'He blames the police for the death of his wife and kids.'

The words hit him like a hammer. He stopped reading and looked over at Felicia with a sick look on his face. 'So, essentially, what we have here is an agent, regularly selling information about the Prowlers back to the police, and then accusing his handlers of selling him out.'

She winced. 'It sounds bad.'

'Does it get any worse?' He took a moment to write this information down in his notebook, then continued: 'So the stand-off with Chipotle goes on for over an hour with no progress made whatsoever. Koda is the sergeant at the time, and he makes the decision to breach.'

'And Chipotle opens fire.'

'*Massive* gun battle.' Striker turned to the conclusion. 'In the end, the fatal bullet comes from Mike Rothschild's rifle; this was verified by ballistics. Mike is cleared of any wrongdoing and receives the highest award for bravery the department can give – the Award of Valour.'

'As he damn well should,' Felicia said. 'They *all* should. Their lives were on the line out there. And the shooting was basic. I don't see why it went to a full internal investigation anyway.'

Striker turned past the conclusion page. At the end of the report was one page of miscellaneous notes:

Injuries – Police Constable Davies.

'Oh boy,' Striker said. 'This is why . . . Chipotle wasn't the only one who got shot that day – that prick tagged one of our own.'

Felicia wasn't aware of this, and the news made her eyes narrow. 'Who?'

'Some guy named Archer Davies . . . I've never heard of him before. Maybe he was a Fed cop, I'm not sure. Regardless, he was the breacher for Team Red that day. Not a full ERT member, but a *reserve*.'

'Did he survive?' Felicia asked the words almost regretfully.

Striker turned the page and saw nothing else. 'He must have survived – he's listed as Injured, not Deceased. Plus there's no link to a second homicide report. Either way, we got two people shot at this call – Archer Davies and Carlos Chipotle. It's an avenue that needs pursuing. Write it down.'

Felicia did. When she was done, she looked up with a sick expression. 'This is gonna sound bad, because it's terrible that this Archer guy got shot . . . but I still don't see how it necessitates a full *internal* investigation into the shooting of Chipotle. Once again, we know that Rothschild was the one who shot him. And we know that Chipotle was all coked-out and blasting away with an AK-47 – that much is indisputable.'

Striker nodded. 'The problem here is one of *timing*.'

'What timing?'

He pointed to various segments in the report. 'Carlos Chipotle was shot at 14:23 hours – that time was taken directly from the CAD call. Chipotle died not two minutes later at 14:25 – also taken directly from the CAD call.'

'So what's the problem?'

'The problem is this: at 14:24 hours, one of the units went over the air telling everyone, and I quote, "He's giving up. He's coming out! Hands clear."'

Felicia made an *oh-shit* sound, and Striker continued.

'When the incident was over, no one would admit to going over the air with that remark, but the dispatcher heard it because she typed it into the CAD call.'

'Can't they just check the radio number?'

Striker shook his head. 'No. Don't forget, this was *before* the radios went digital. Back then, everything was analogue. A radio was just a radio. There was no way of linking which unit was broadcasting at any one time. So not only were the radios not encrypted, but people could say whatever they damn well wanted to over the air.'

He skimmed back through the report pages until he found the police statement of Constable Mike Rothschild.

'In his statement, Rothschild says he heard someone say: "He's coming out! *Heads up!*" When Chipotle stepped into the doorway, he still had the AK-47 in his hands. Rothschild says he feared for the safety of his squadmates and he took the shot. End of story.'

By the time Striker had finished speaking, Felicia's expression had darkened.

'As much as I hate to admit it, Jacob, the optics are bad here. *Real* bad. In fact, if someone didn't know any better, you know what it looks like?'

Striker nodded gravely.

'A police execution.'

One Hundred and Nine

The bomber and Molly drove south, dressed in matching paramedic uniforms. Molly was uncertain and edgy; she had been prepared to wait and reassess their plans. But he would hear nothing of it. He was determined to find Target 1.

Today.

His body was against him now. He could not deny that. He felt overheated. Exhausted. Weak. So unusually weak. But that was all okay, he told himself, because they were finishing this entire operation. And despite the failings of his body, a part of him felt good inside. Really, really good.

Then his phone went off.

The *red* cell.

The ringing sound made his heart flutter, made his stomach clench and his throat dry up. It brought him back an immediate sickness that only the red phone could bring. He put the cell to his ear and heard the nurse's voice. It was full of regret and concern.

'It's time,' she said.

He listened with fear creeping over him.

'Yes,' he said softly. 'Yes.'

'Yes,' he said again, almost a whisper.

To his left, Molly looked straight ahead as she drove, refusing to so much as glance in his direction.

When he finally hung up the phone, his face was slack and his skin looked not only pale but bloodless. There was a haunted look in his eyes, a hollow, gaping darkness he could not hide. He began to shake. Shake as if his fever was finally reaching unlivable temperatures.

Molly took notice. 'Is everything okay?'

He said nothing.

She reached over and touched his arm.

'It's time,' he said softly. 'He's *dying*.'

One Hundred and Ten

It was twelve noon by the time Striker and Felicia finished reading the PSS files at Internal. The time spent had been worthwhile – it had brought them more leads, and, with it, a dozen more questions. Most troubling to Striker was the notion that the police-involved shooting of Chipotle could wrongly be viewed as a police execution.

It gave them a possible motive for the bombers.

Files in hand, they grabbed a coffee from the next-door café and returned to the car.

Once seated in the passenger seat, Striker spoke his thoughts aloud: 'The Chipotle shooting connects Chad Koda and Mike Rothschild because they were involved in the call. And it connects Osaka because he was running the internal investigation on the file. But it still leaves out Harry and the two women.'

Felicia thought it over. 'That car bomb was *remotely* armed,' she said. 'The bombers could pick and choose when to detonate. With Koda in the car, he was the obvious target. But with Harry also so close, they might have been trying for both of them. God knows they came in shooting at Harry afterwards.'

Striker thought it over, said nothing, and Felicia continued.

'As for Dr Sharise Owens, she was Koda's common-law wife at one point.'

'So what?' Striker replied. 'I don't see them blowing up Pearl

Osaka or going after the Williams children, do you?' When Felicia said nothing, Striker continued. 'Some of this just doesn't make any sense. Think about it. If someone was going after cops for revenge, why wait ten damn years to do it? There's only two reasons I can think of – either they were in jail, or they were in an institution somewhere.'

'Well, lots of Prowlers have been in and out of jail over the last decade. They could have been biding their time.'

'I don't buy it.'

'Why not?'

'Because,' Striker explained, 'the Prowlers usually contract out their killings. Or they use their underlings to do it. That's how Sleeves got into the gang in the first place. Which blows the whole jail-time theory right out the window. Why wait ten years when they can order one of the prospects to do it whenever they want?'

Striker took a long sip of his coffee. He tasted bitterness, and wished he'd added some cream and sugar. 'Let's look at some other angles. Bring up this breacher who got shot – Archer Davies.'

Felicia ran the name. 'There's nothing in PRIME.'

'Not even the report for when he was shot?'

She scanned the various reports they already had. 'Maybe they lumped it in with the Chipotle shooting.'

Striker shook his head. 'They shouldn't have. Every victim requires his own file. Given the cross-border issues, there'll probably be some overlap.'

Felicia groaned. As always, jurisdictional issues and separate databases made for the creation of extra work. At times it felt mind-boggling. 'Why a *federal* report for the Davies shooting? He was a Vancouver cop.'

'That's precisely why. The investigation had to be impartial. That required an outside agency.'

'Right, right.' Felicia scanned through the reports, both paper and electronic. After a moment, she looked up. 'We got all the reports here except for the shooting of Archer Davies. It registers nothing on the screen.'

Striker was unsurprised. 'It'll be a Fed file and likely paper.'

'Which means more red tape.'

Striker felt her pain, and he had reached his fill of the bureaucracy. He relented, took out his cell phone, and began dialling the one number he wanted to avoid.

'You calling the Burnaby detachment?' Felicia asked.

Striker shook his head. 'Deputy Chief.'

'Laroche?'

Striker just nodded reluctantly and forced out a weak grin. 'Why does it feel like I'm selling my soul?'

One Hundred and Eleven

Improper procedure or not, the moment Acting Deputy Chief Laroche got on the phone with one of his RCMP counterparts, the federal red tape was cut. Within minutes, the two reports – *Carlos Chipotle: Homicide* and *Archer Davies: Attempted Murder* – were pulled from federal archives. Because they were both in paper form and there was no electronic copy to send, the reports had to be sent by fax to Laroche's office.

Striker and Felicia drove there to pick them up.

Striker was relieved to be getting them so fast, but miffed as well. He looked at Felicia as they walked up to the main foyer elevator. 'Why is it the moment the brass needs information, the report is expedited? Yet whenever I – the actual investigator – need something, there's walls of red tape to climb?'

Felicia smiled. 'Karma?'

He shrugged. 'Maybe you're right. God knows I've pissed off someone up there.' He pushed the button for the third floor. 'We'll hit Personnel first. See if they have a folder on Archer Davies.'

Felicia agreed.

Moments later, they stood in the Human Resources archives reading through the file. The bundle was thin, consisting of a record of employment with the City of Vancouver, a list of mandatory courses the man had passed to be exempt from Block

3 of the Academy, a statement from his Field Training Officer, advising that Davies was fully competent, and a Deputy Chief release, ending his probationary period early by six months.

'That's unusual,' Felicia remarked.

Striker agreed. It was unusual, but not unheard of with interdepartmental transfers – especially for employees who brought with them a needed skill set.

Like being able to use C4 explosives to breach barricaded entranceways.

They left Human Resources and headed for the Deputy Chief's office. Laroche's secretary gave them the reports that the RCMP had faxed over – the shooting of Archer Davies and the police-involved shooting of Carlos Chipotle.

Striker felt the thickness of the bundle and nodded approvingly. These were the *full* reports, and he and Felicia wasted no time. They took the paperwork into the hall, found a corner, and began reading.

The first thing Striker noticed was the call code. The file was marked not as a Homicide, but as an Attempted Murder. It told him one very important fact – that Archer Davies had indeed survived his wounds.

'We need to talk to this man,' he said.

Felicia nodded eagerly. 'One more avenue to follow.'

Striker continued reading. The report was long and included photographic evidence of the crime scene, a detailed map of the house where the shooting took place, and dozens of printed-out PDF files, which were mostly civilian witness statements. Once done, Striker handed Felicia the last page and waited for her to finish reading.

'Well?' he finally asked.

She stared blankly at the papers and did not smile. 'It's pretty much what we already know.'

'It damn well *mirrors* Osaka's report.'

'Almost. Unlike Osaka's report, this one is pretty poorly written.'

Striker shook his head. 'I disagree with that completely.'

Felicia gave him an odd look. She fanned out a few of the pages on a nearby filing cabinet and started quoting lines. 'Chipotle acted erratically . . . He displayed hostile actions . . . Police responded as required . . . Don't you see? The author doesn't explain *how* Chipotle acted erratically, or *what* his hostile actions were, and he doesn't even go into detail about how many rounds were fired in the mayhem. Someone should teach this guy a thing or two about detail.'

Striker grinned. 'On the contrary, I think he knows his details perfectly. In fact, I think he's expertly written this report without really saying all that much. Pretty hard to counter it in court, if it ever went that far.'

Felicia took a hard look at him. 'You think the author was *purposely* vague.'

'I'd bet my career on it.'

'Why?'

'Look at the badge number. Who authored the report?'

Felicia looked down at the header, and a shocked sound escaped her lips. The first two letters were VA, meaning the author was not a Mountie but a member of the Vancouver Police Department. 'Badge Number 1176? Isn't that—'

'Chad Koda.'

Felicia stacked all the papers together. 'The more we research this file, the more circular it gets.'

'And the more frustrating.' Striker punched the elevator button and waited for the booth to arrive. 'We need to speak to someone who was on scene at ground zero. This breacher, this Archer Davies guy. Hopefully, he hasn't moved out of province.' He looked back at the report. 'Where does it say he lives now?'

Felicia shuffled through the pages until she reached an updated Entities section, one that listed names and addresses for court subpoena purposes. She skimmed down the list and, after two pages, let out an excited gasp. 'You're not gonna believe this. The last known address for Archer Davies is down on Zero Avenue.'

'In White Rock?'

Felicia nodded. 'The Sunset Grove Care Centre.'

One Hundred and Twelve

It was one-thirty in the afternoon when Harry pulled back into town in his brother's personal vehicle, a new-model Dodge pickup truck. Black. He drove down Camosun Street and parked out front of Striker's house, directly across from the park. By the time he had rammed the gear shift in Park and shouldered open the door, one of the patrolmen guarding the house was already fast approaching him.

'Can I help you, sir?' the young cop asked.

Harry did not recognize the man. He was tall and thin, and had a look of no-nonsense about him. Harry flashed the badge and the man nodded.

'Detective Striker isn't here,' the cop said.

'I know that; I'm here to see Rothschild.'

The patrolman looked at him somewhat uncertainly, and Harry realized it was probably because of his appearance; he was unshaven and dishevelled today, wearing yesterday's clothes – all gifts from a night spent sleeping in the truck.

'Long shift,' he finally said.

The cop just nodded.

Harry opened the wooden gate and stepped into the yard. He hiked the cement walkway, climbed the porch steps to the front door and knocked three times. Moments later, he heard the sound of footsteps inside and sensed someone looking through the peephole.

A lock clicked, a chain rattled, the door swung open.

Mike Rothschild stood in the doorway. It had been a while since Harry had seen the man, maybe eighteen months, and the time had not been kind. The lines on Rothschild's face were cut deep into his flesh, like little dugout trenches on a battlefield. Like Harry, the man looked worn thin.

Rothschild took a half-step onto the balcony. 'What are you doing here?'

Harry did not smile. He just took a step forward and met Rothschild's stare.

'You and I have to talk,' he said.

One Hundred and Thirteen

The first thing Striker did upon returning to the Sunset Grove Care Centre was head for the front desk. Seated there, glossing over the newspaper with a steaming cup of coffee in her hand, was a new woman who looked terribly serious. Her hair was pulled back into a bun so tight that it tugged at her eyes and made her face look like she'd had one too many lifts.

Striker showed the front-desk clerk his credentials, then grabbed the sign-in book. As he flipped backwards through the pages, Felicia watched eagerly beside him. The book was relatively new, and he reached the first page quickly. He looked at the clerk. 'Do you have the previous book?'

Her eyes flitted up from her paper. '*Previous* book?'

'For signing in.'

She stared back through steely dark eyes. Said nothing. And then finally moved off her stool as if this required all the energy she had left in her body. She slowly wandered over to the filing cabinet that sat behind the front counter, scoured through the top drawer, and eventually returned with another binder made up of imitation black leather.

'It cannot leave the front desk.'

Striker offered no comment. He took the book, snapped it open to the end, and began turning back the pages, one by one. He found Osaka's name only three pages back. And this time the signature was not beside Sal Hurst's room number, but beside another name they were looking for.

Archer Davies.

Felicia smiled. 'There it is. Archer Davies. Room 12.'

Striker looked up at the woman behind the desk. 'Did you ever have any dealings with Inspector Osaka?'

'No.'

Striker thought of the nurse he'd spoken with during their previous visit. 'Did anyone else?'

The woman glanced down at the book. 'Room 12 is Nurse Janet's rounds. She's in today. Probably somewhere down the hall. Ask her; she would know.' She looked back down at her newspaper as if the detectives no longer existed.

Striker paid the woman no heed. He closed the book and slid it back to her, then proceeded down the hall. A nervous tension filled him, and for some reason the hall looked longer and narrower than it had the first time he'd been here. Everything felt dark and heavy.

He reached Room 12 and went inside.

A man occupied the bed. He was hooked up to an air compressor of some kind, and a soft intermittent *shu-shush* sound filled the room.

One look at the man and any person could tell he was not well. His face had an aged appearance. The colour of his skin was off, like cream gone bad, and the skin rimming his eyes was a faint purple colour. Beneath the stubble of his face, and under the faded tattoos of his arms, the meat and fat were gone, eaten away by time and sickness. It gave his body the appearance of a deflated balloon, one that had long since lost its resiliency. Compared to this man, Sal Hurst looked ready to run a marathon.

Felicia neared Striker, whispered: 'He looks like he's already dead.'

Striker thought the same. Any previous hope of questioning this man had been wishful thinking at best. Felicia moved up to the bed and gently placed her hand on the man's left arm.

'Sir?' she asked. '*Sir?*'

But no response came.

'Can I help you?' a voice said from behind Striker.

He turned around and found himself standing face-to-face with a tall thin brunette who was wearing a pale-blue uniform and a pair of matching clogs. In her hands was a clipboard with some charts on it. Striker flashed her the badge.

'Are you Janet?' he asked.

'Yes, I'm the nurse in this wing.'

'We're here to speak to this man. Is there any way you can wake him for us?'

The nurse just smiled sadly. 'I wish I could,' she replied. 'But that's completely impossible, I'm afraid . . . Mr Davies is in a coma.'

One Hundred and Fourteen

For the bomber, the drive to the Sunset Grove Care Centre was one of nervousness and fear. With every passing mile, an indescribable desperation grew within him. He felt like there was an unknown organism eating him from the inside out. Sucking away his strength. Devouring his hope.

When they reached the parking lot, Molly kept the motor running and did not move from her seat. It was her usual passive-aggressive way of telling him she wasn't coming inside. He offered no reaction to it. She had never come in to see him. Not once in all the time he had been here.

Why should she change now?

He fumbled for the latch, found it, and opened the door. Outside, the air was hotter than it had been in the van, and it seemed to beat down on him relentlessly as he crossed the blacktop and approached the entranceway. When he walked inside the front doors of the care home, the interior air washed over him and was a cool relief. Compared to the bright glare of the midday sun, the foyer was masked in darkness, and he took a moment to let his eyes adapt. Splotches of dark browns impeded his vision.

The world felt distorted. Off-kilter.

The fever was worsening.

He moved towards the south corridor, walking on feet that

felt swollen and oddly light. Drops of sweat rolled down his brow and neck, tickling his overheated skin in the cold draught of the air conditioning.

'Sir? . . . Sir? . . . *Sir!*'

He stopped. Looked left. Saw a very serious woman.

'You *must* sign in.'

'Of course.'

He floated left. Fumbled with the pen. Scribbled something in the book.

'You don't look well, sir. Is everything okay?'

'Tickety-boo.'

He put down the pen. Turned towards the south hall. Headed down it.

Ten steps later, he reached Room 12 and came to a hard stop. Standing at the foot of the bed, talking to Nurse Janet, was the one man he had been battling ever since this nightmare had begun – Homicide Detective Jacob Striker.

The cop had finally found them.

One Hundred and Fifteen

'How long has he been like this?' Striker asked the nurse.

'As long as I've been here,' she said. 'And that's going on two years now. But I think it's been longer. He was transferred here some time ago – I'd have to check his records.'

Striker nodded. He looked down at the pale man lying there, at all the tubes running from his arms to the machines standing bedside, and he noticed something. Where the man's left hand should have been, there was only a mangled stump of flesh.

'Is something wrong, Detective?' the nurse asked.

He explained: 'I've read the police reports. I know Archer was shot. But this,' – he pointed to the stubby remains of the man's left arm – '*this* was not in the report. What happened? Did it get gangrenous?'

The nurse shook her head. 'We didn't remove it. That was a result of the explosion.'

Striker and Felicia shared a glance. 'What explosion?'

'Perhaps I'd better get the file.' The nurse left the room, and they were left with nothing but the soft *shu-shush* sound of the air compressor. She returned a few minutes later with a green folder and continued speaking as if the conversation had never stopped. 'Ah yes, here it is. The bullet entered the spinal cord at the T11-12 level' – she glanced up from the papers – 'that's the middle of the back.'

'We understand that,' Striker said.

'Autopsies . . . of course you do.' The nurse carried on. 'The bullet left him paralysed, of course. But that was not the reason for the coma. That was brought on by the trauma from the explosion.'

'Again, what explosion?' Felicia asked.

The nurse flipped through the pages. 'It says here an explosion occurred during the incident, but it doesn't say exactly what.'

Striker gestured for the report. 'May I?'

The nurse gave him an uncertain look, but then conceded. Striker took less than five minutes perusing the material, and by the time he was done, he understood things more clearly.

'Archer was the lead guy and he was trying to breach the door,' he said to Felicia. 'That's the only thing that makes sense. They were attempting entry and something went wrong. The C4 exploded – that's what happened to his left arm. And somehow in the mayhem he got shot.'

'It's also why he had the stroke,' the nurse explained. 'The force, the trauma, the resultant high blood pressure – it all added up and was just too much for his body to handle as time went by.'

'How serious was the stroke?' Felicia asked.

'A basilar, I'm afraid. There's none more debilitating.'

'I don't understand,' Felicia said.

'It's why he can't breathe on his own any more. Why he can't even blink.'

Felicia made a horrified sound. 'You mean to say he can think perfectly normal in there, but he can't even *blink*?'

The nurse's expression was glum. 'It's one of the reasons the doctors put him under – the coma was induced. For humane reasons.'

Striker listened to everything the nurse said, and he felt sick for the man. He wrote down the name and practitioner number of the doctor in charge – a woman he had never heard of. Then he looked back at the nurse. 'Does anyone come to visit him? A wife or kids?'

'Oh yes, he has a wife. And a son and a daughter too.'

'How old are they?'

'Young. Fourteen or fifteen, I would think. To be honest, they don't come all that often. The wife comes more, and even she is here only once a month. It used to be more, a long time ago, but over time . . . well, she's been away more and more.'

Striker nodded. 'I'd like to talk to them.'

'I can't give out their personal information.'

Striker understood the rules and regulations with regards to privacy. 'Call the wife, please. Ask if she doesn't mind seeing us. If she's willing, we'll meet her at her place, wherever that is.'

The nurse said she would do this, then turned to leave the room. Striker stopped her with a few words: 'Is that it, by the way?'

She turned back. 'Is what it?'

'Is that all the people who come to see him?'

She shook her head. 'Actually, there is one more. A man – he comes every day without fail. Has for almost two months now. It's just so sad. He just sits there, inside the room, and he talks to him. Sometimes for hours.'

'Who is he?'

'Tom Atkins,' she said.

'Tom Atkins?' Striker asked. The name sounded familiar for some reason. Had he read it in one of the reports? He wasn't sure. 'Is that the name he gives you?'

'Well, he never actually gives me any name. I never really speak to him – that's just the way he signs the guest book.'

Striker gave Felicia a quick glance, then focused back on the nurse. 'This man . . . what does he look like?'

The nurse's face tightened. 'I actually don't know for sure. He's fiercely private. And I think he might also have injured himself in some way. He always covers himself up. Wears a kangaroo jacket sometimes. Or a baseball hat and sunglasses.'

Striker turned to Felicia. 'Call Dispatch. I want plainclothes units here now.'

Felicia nodded and was already dialling.

The nurse was clearly taken aback. 'Is . . . is everything all right?'

Striker ignored the question. 'This man . . . when was he here last?'

'Well, just . . . just yesterday.'

'You *saw* him?'

'Yes, I spoke to him. He's quiet, but he's really very nice. Really.'

'Does he have an address or a telephone number? How do you get in contact with him if there's an emergency?'

'I . . . I call him. His number's right there in the file. On the back page.'

Striker opened the folder and turned to the back. There, in red ink, was the name *Tom Atkins*, followed by a 778 number. A cell phone. He called up Info and got the operator to do a search on the number.

'Prepay,' came the reply.

In other words, *untraceable.*

Striker was not surprised. He turned to the nurse. 'When exactly did you last speak to this man?'

'Just . . . just a half-hour. After trying to get a hold of Mrs Davies but having no luck, I called Mr Atkins. I told him how sick Mr Davies was, and that now would be the time to give his final respects. He was quite concerned and said he'd be right down.'

The words made Striker's hand drop near his pistol. He looked at Felicia, who was now just hanging up her cell. 'You hear that?'

She nodded. 'Got two plainclothes units on the way.'

Striker was about to ask if the plainclothes units were Fed or city cops when a loud, strident beeping noise filled the room. Upon hearing it, the nurse rushed over to the bed, then out of the room and down the hallway. She was calling for one of the doctors.

Striker didn't need to ask what was going on. The answer was obvious.

Archer Davies had flat-lined.

One Hundred and Sixteen

The time of death for Archer Davies was 14:35 hours.

Twenty-five minutes later, at exactly three p.m., two plain-clothes units arrived – federal cops from the RCMP.

Striker was grateful for their presence. He quickly debriefed them on the investigation and told them his suspicions – that this so-called Tom Atkins might really be one of the bombers. As he did the debrief, Felicia scoured the databases for any Tom Atkins that might be related to the files.

She could find none.

'It's got to be an alias,' she said.

Striker agreed. For the moment, the name didn't matter. He got the plainclothes units set up. He placed two men inside the room, one man out of sight in the south corridor, and one man outside the facility in an unmarked car.

Then the wait began.

When the clock struck three-thirty and the man listing himself as Tom Atkins had still not arrived, Striker's sense of excitement slowly gave way to concern. When the clock struck four, his concern collapsed into full-blown disappointment. He signalled to the plainclothes unit that he was heading down the hall, then left the room and found the nursing station. Waiting there nervously was Nurse Janet.

'Is everything going okay?' she asked.

'How often have you called him?'

'Mr Atkins? Uh, probably eight or nine times this last month.'

'Does he always arrive on time?'

She nodded. 'Like clockwork.'

Striker cursed. 'He knows we're here.' He said nothing for a long moment, he just stood there and went over everything in his head. 'Contact him again.'

'Call him?'

'Do it on speakerphone.'

The nurse made no move to do so. Her face took on a tight look.

'I wouldn't ask you to do this if it weren't absolutely crucial,' Striker said.

The nurse placed a hand over her heart. 'What . . . what do you want me to say?'

'That Archer Davies has little time left, and that Mr Atkins must come down immediately if he wants to have any hope of saying goodbye. Tell him time is of the utmost importance. Minutes count.'

The nurse said nothing, but she nodded. And after taking in a deep breath and trying to stabilize her nerves, she walked over to the nearest phone, picked up the receiver and began dialling. Moments later, the call was answered.

'Mr Atkins?' the nurse asked.

'Put the cop on the phone, Janet.'

'I-I-I'm sorry?'

'Put. The cop. On. The phone.' His words were spoken slowly. Rhythmically.

Striker took the receiver. 'I'm right here.'

'So you are then. Good. Listen up. I've killed a cop before – one besides Koda and Osaka. And if I'm forced to, I'll do it again. Without hesitation.'

Striker asked the man, 'What's your real name?'

'Do you know, Detective, what happens when a bomb goes off at your feet? I'll tell you. A half-pound of explosives will tear off one limb. A full pound will take off two. And a bomb with three pounds will take off everything. No one survives that.'

'Listen to me—'

'Soft tissue goes first. If you're a man, the testicles are often torn right from the body. Not that it matters much. The percussive force destroys them internally regardless. As for the ladies – like your lovely Spanish partner there – it's not uncommon for the breasts to be blown right off. You might want to suggest to Detective Santos that she start wearing her bulletproof vest from now on. Kevlar helps disperse the percussive force.'

Striker waited till the man finished talking. When there was finally silence on the phone, he asked the one question he needed an answer to.

'Why are you doing this?'

'Walk away, Detective. You have no idea what you're dealing with here.'

Then the line went dead.

One Hundred and Seventeen

The bomber stood in the woods to the west of the facility, almost directly on the US border, and stared through his binoculars at the man on the bed in Room 12. He looked like he was in there alone, but he was not, of course. The detective was in there with him, and so was at least one plainclothes cop. He couldn't see them, but they were there.

He *knew* it.

Shivering in the shadows of a giant oak tree, he focused on the man in the bed and a strange stirring sensation slowly overpowered his numbness. It made him want to run. To break free. Like a wildebeest kicking loose at a lion's claws. So many odd emotions intermingling.

Anxiety. Desperation.

Grief.

Archer Davies was dead.

Slowly, inevitably, the shield that he had built around himself these past ten years disintegrated. Crumbled like the walls of Babylon. And for the first time since he was a little boy, he panicked. How he longed to go inside that room. To hold that man's hand one last time. To lay his head down on the man's chest. And to just tell him that he loved him. That, more than anything.

Just to tell him he loved him.

The black cell vibrated in his pocket, and he let it ring. It would only be Molly, and fuck her anyway right now. She had never come to see him. Not once. It was unforgivable. All this violence they had committed, all her goddam faith, and yet in the end she could not face mortality – not even a death that was not her own.

The more he thought about it, the more angry and lost he became.

Tommy Atkins went to war
and he came back a man no more.
Went to Baghdad and Sar-e.
He died, that man who looked like me.

The words seemed to lack punch now as he chanted them.

With the tears leaking out his eyes, he took one final look at the man on the bed, and realized that his final goodbye would never come now. The detective had made sure of that.

'Goodbye,' he whispered.

It was all he could do.

One Hundred and Eighteen

When the line had gone dead, Striker knew it was time to change tactics. Tom Atkins – or whatever alias the man was using – would never return to the care hospital now.

Striker got on his cell and called up the regional RCMP brass who had lent them the plainclothes units. After a lengthy discussion, the RCMP Superintendent agreed to maintain surveillance of the Sunset Grove Care Centre, just in case the bombers returned. With the place now secure, Striker and Felicia headed out to speak with the Davies family. According to the hospital documents, Archer's wife's name was Lilly, and she lived in White Rock with her two children, Logan and Rachel.

It was just a ten-minute drive down the road.

The lot was small, as was the house on it, which was composed mainly of blue wood trim and old white stucco that was now a dirty beige colour. The place looked like it had been built in the 60s. So did the old Ford jalopy in the driveway.

They parked and climbed out.

Striker reminded Felicia, 'I've already instructed the care home not to call Mrs Davies until I tell them to do so. So whatever you do, don't mention Archer's death. Right now we need to get information from this woman. We need her calm.'

'Of course.'

'And be ready for anything.'

Felicia just nodded and adjusted her holster.

They knocked on the front door, and minutes later were inside the living room with Lilly Davies. She wore ironed slacks and a cream blouse. She was clearly of Eurasian descent, and a Japanese strictness flowed through her in everything she did, from the way she offered them tea and cookies to the way she sat – her back board straight, her hands cupped in her lap, her head held high.

'Thanks for seeing us,' Striker said.

'Especially without any notice,' Felicia added.

The woman smiled politely. 'It is no problem, Detectives. Though I still don't quite understand the connection here . . . how is this related to my husband?'

Striker avoided the details. 'We're not entirely sure, Mrs Davies. We're checking out all the possible links we have – family, police, you name it.'

Lilly Davies nodded as if she understood but the confusion remained in her eyes.

'Are your son and daughter here?' Felicia asked.

She shook her head. 'Logan is visiting my sister right now. In Toronto. And Rachel is at work – at The Sizzle.'

'Is that a restaurant?' Felicia asked.

'Yes. She waitresses there. Like me. Actually, I got her the job.'

Striker nodded. 'You like working there?'

Lilly Davies offered a weak smile. 'It helps us get by, especially with both children fast approaching college.'

Striker nodded. 'I know the feeling.'

He looked at the fireplace mantel, at pictures of the kids. Both were good-looking, with much of their mother's Japanese features in them. In the photos, they both looked to be around fifteen or sixteen. The boy was dressed in a school basketball uniform; the girl in a dance costume of some kind.

Striker pointed to the girl. 'When was the photo taken?'

'That? Oh, just last Christmas. Rachel's dance class.'

'And your son obviously loves basketball.'

'Well, hockey was his first love – just like figure skating was Rachel's. But after Archer's injury, well, we just couldn't afford it. Hockey and figure skating are very expensive sports.'

'They're nice-looking kids,' Felicia said.

Lilly smiled politely.

Striker moved past the niceties and got down to business. 'I'm sorry to stir up bad memories, Mrs Davies, but could you tell us a little bit about your husband – his history, and how the two of you met?'

Lilly Davies nodded. 'I met Archer during one of his leaves.'

'From the police department?'

'No, from the RLC.'

That made Striker pause. 'RLC? You mean the Royal Logistics Corps?'

'Yes.'

'Who's the RLC?' Felicia asked.

Striker cast her a glance. 'They're part of the British Army. We got a couple of guys on the job from over there. They're good men. Smart. Tactical. Well trained.' He turned back to Lilly. 'So Archer was from the UK?'

'Oh yes, he never could lose the accent.' She laughed softly. 'As I said, he was taking a leave when we met, in fact. He was here visiting his brother – the poor man passed away from cancer a few years after Archer was injured.'

'I'm sorry,' Striker offered.

Lilly kept talking as if she hadn't heard the condolence. 'One thing led to another, and before you knew it, Archer was taking all his leaves here. And then we were married. He left the RLC and joined the Vancouver Police Department. With his military experience, he was fast-tracked into the Emergency Response Team. As a reserve.'

'Did he miss the old job?' Felicia asked.

Lilly nodded emphatically. 'Oh yes. He did a great deal. But his squadmates came over to visit him a few times. And that made him very happy.'

Striker asked, 'You two ever go back there?'

'Oh no, never. Archer loved his squad, but he had no love for the UK, and he hated London. Called it a dirty little town.' She looked down for a moment, and the teacup trembled between her hands. 'I often wish he'd stayed there and brought me over instead. Then he never would have joined the Vancouver Police Department.'

Striker nodded. It was understandable. 'These squadmates of his—'

'They called themselves *The Untouchables*.'

'Why?'

'Because, back then, they'd all served several tours, and yet none of them had ever been killed. Not even injured.'

'And now?'

Lilly's face saddened. 'They're almost all dead now. I don't know the details . . . I don't *want* to know the details.'

'And the ones who still live?' he pressed.

Lilly sighed. 'I don't know. I haven't heard from any of them in years. Not since the first time they came to see Archer, and that was . . . well, I don't even know when.' She looked at the photos on the mantel shelf. 'Logan and Rachel are almost grown up . . . if only Archer could see them now. He'd be so proud of how they turned out.'

For a moment, Striker thought the woman might break down on him; so he changed the subject. 'When your husband worked for the Vancouver Police Department, did he ever confide anything in you?'

'Confide?' She spoke the word with caution.

'Tell you any secrets. Anything you think we should know at this particular point in time?'

Lilly shook her head, confused, and Felicia spoke next.

'Ms Davies, the reason we're investigating your husband isn't because he's suspected of any wrongdoing. Quite the contrary, I think he was an impressive cop with a strong moral compass. What we're investigating is the latest string of bombings that have been going off in the Lower Mainland . . . We believe there's a connection to your husband.'

'To *Archer*?' Lilly Davies' face flushed with the words. It was the first glimpse of true emotion that Striker had seen in the woman.

'We don't know the reason yet,' she continued. 'But there are many connecting factors here. And they all seem to lead back to your husband. Is there anything he was working on he told you about? Anything off the books?

Lilly's face remained white. 'No. No, he never told me anything about his work. Nothing at all. He kept his work very private.'

'I see. Does the name Tom Atkins mean anything to you?'

'Tom Atkins? Why, no. I've never heard that name before.'

Felicia nodded but made no reply.

Striker began questioning the woman next, particularly on Archer's ex-army squadmates. Had any of them been in trouble with the law since they'd left the service? Were any of them unbalanced? Suffering from post-traumatic stress disorder? And so on. The answers to his questions were all a resounding *no*. Lilly didn't know anything about these people, and she hadn't seen them in years. The same thing went for the Vancouver Police Department. No cops came around.

Not ever.

'That was the saddest thing,' Lilly added. 'After Archer was hurt, no one came by to visit him. It was as if he had suddenly ceased to exist. As if he had become taboo or something. He was new at the Vancouver Police Department – I know that – and not many people knew him. But it still hurt him deeply. And it added to his depression, to his blood pressure, and eventually, he had the stroke.'

Striker listened to the woman talk, and after a moment, she finally broke down and cried in front of him.

'I'm sorry,' he offered again. 'I really am so sorry.'

The words felt small and hollow, but he could think of nothing else to say.

One Hundred and Nineteen

Striker and Felicia were on the highway in ten minutes, heading back for the City of Vancouver. Felicia kept herself busy checking messages and emails; none were file-related, so she saved them all and hung up her cell. Only when Striker had pulled into the fast lane and hit one hundred and twenty K per hour did they speak again.

'Something back there just doesn't add up,' he said.

Felicia looked up. 'With Lilly Davies or the care centre?'

'With Lilly. Archer was injured *on the job*.'

'Yeah?'

'So when cops are injured in the line of duty, not only do they get insurance money, but the Police Mutual Benevolent Association steps in. They help the families out financially. Granted, it's nothing mind-blowing, but it's enough to live comfortably. Plus, Lilly should be getting a partial pension from the British Army.'

'Again, so what?'

'So where is all the money? She lives in an old house, she drives an old beater, she has to work as a waitress just to make ends meet, and even still, she can't afford for her kids to play hockey or figure-skate. White Rock may be nice, but it sure as hell isn't expensive like West Vancouver or Kitsilano. She should be doing fine financially.'

Felicia looked out the window. 'Maybe she's made some bad business decisions or investments.'

'I want to know why. Call up the land title office. See if she owns that house. And then call the PMBA. I want to see what kind of funds she's getting.'

'If they'll tell us – that's confidential information.'

'I know the secretary-treasurer. She can find that information. Just tell her it's me and that these are exigent circumstances.'

'You say everything is exigent.'

'If a guy blowing up the city isn't pressing enough, the courts can hang me for it. Besides, our bomber has been visiting Archer. They're connected. Make the call.'

Felicia agreed. She took out her cell and began dialling, and Striker increased their speed to one hundred and forty K per hour. By the time they had reached the Knight Street Bridge, Felicia was still on the cell and running names on the laptop.

Several kilometres later, she finished the phone call. She hung up and turned slightly in her seat to face him. 'Okay, you were right about the land title. Lilly rents the place. The house is actually owned by a family that rents a half-dozen other houses in the neighbourhood.'

'Any crime connections?'

'No, the family is clean. But that's not the interesting part. The interesting part is the pension and the PMBA money – Lilly's only getting half of it.'

'Half?'

'The rest of it is going overseas. To the UK.'

Striker stopped hard at a red light on Broadway and looked at her. 'You got to be kidding me.'

'A *first* wife, by the sounds of it. And a first family.'

'He has other kids?'

'Two names are listed.'

'Is one of them Tom?'

Felicia shook her head. 'No. Oliver and Molly.'

'A boy and a girl,' Striker mused. 'Just like our bombers . . . If Archer had kids real young, these could be them. What's their surname?'

'They took their mother's maiden name – Howell.'

'Oliver Howell and Molly Howell,' Striker said. 'It sounds so ordinary.' He gave Felicia a queer look. 'Did you run a full search on the names?'

'On Oliver and Molly Howell? Of course. On all the systems. There's nothing.'

He nodded absently. 'What about Tom Atkins?'

'Negative too.'

Striker swore. 'I know I've heard that name somewhere before. Run another search. Hell, *Google it.*'

Felicia started up the web browser and performed the search. The very first link on the page was to the online encyclopedia, Wikipedia. She clicked on the link and soon found herself reading up on the name Tom Atkins. After a long moment, she let out a sound somewhere between surprise and disbelief.

Striker caught it. 'What did you find?'

'A direct hit.' Felicia summarized the passage. 'The name *Tommy Atkins* is a slang term for any soldier in the British Army.'

Striker cocked an eyebrow her way. 'Are you shitting me?'

She shook her head. 'In World War One, in the trenches, British soldiers were often referred to as "Tommies".'

Striker couldn't believe his ears. 'The cocky bastard. He's *laughing* at us.'

'So Oliver Howell is Tommy Atkins?'

'We're about to find out.'

Striker pressed his foot down hard on the accelerator and the car surged forward just as the light turned green. Their destination was Main Street Headquarters. Striker couldn't wait to get there. He had a few phone calls to make. First to Interpol, and, failing that, the British Army. If Oliver and Molly Howell were in any way associated with the armed forces, Striker was going to find out.

For the first time since this investigation had started, he felt as if they were on the edge of a major discovery.

One Hundred and Twenty

Feeling like a bag of shit, Harry parked the pickup truck behind Main Street HQ and walked down the lane. Because of the press release, informing the world of his death, he was supposed to lay low till things calmed down.

But he had never been one to sit idly by.

High above, swooping lines of telephone wires crisscrossed the sky, and a drunk from the Empress Hotel was yelling out the top-floor window. Harry ignored the racket, swiped his keycard, and walked inside the south entrance where Stores was located. Ahead of him, a couple of rookie cops were leaving the counter with their new gear – uniforms, bulletproof vests and new holsters. The uniforms meant little to Harry; he was more concerned about the global positioning devices the department owned.

Harry approached the service area. Behind the counter, the desks were overflowing with mounds of supplies and stacks of paperwork. Harry reached out, rang the bell, and waited. After a minute or two, he rang it again.

'Yeah, yeah, yeah – hold on!' came the call. 'We're unloading back here.'

The caustic tone of the woman's voice told Harry it was Desiree Wentworth, and he frowned. The Stores clerk was about as sweet as cyanide and just as deadly. Standing only 152 centimetres and weighing in at damn near 118 kilos, there was a reason everyone called her *A Street Car Named Desiree.*

Harry waited for almost five minutes until she finally rounded the corner. 'Hot as a fuck in here,' she said, then eyed him up and down. 'Harry Eckhart? I thought you were dead.'

'Long story.'

Desiree didn't mince words. 'Well, welcome back to the land of the living. What ya want?'

'GPS records.'

'For what?'

He held up the base of the GPS device – the unit he had broken off the Ford cruiser before it had exploded in the A&W parking lot. 'Found this in the back lane. Not sure if it fell out of my car or someone else's. Can you check the database?'

Desiree grabbed the device from him, yanking it from his fingers. Harry felt his hands ball into fists. Had any street toad done that, he would have busted their jaw . . . but this was the VPD, and around here you got more flies with honey.

He watched patiently as Desiree searched through the database for the part number. When she located one and cross-referenced it through the system, she found what she was looking for. She didn't even bother to look up.

'Not yours.'

'You sure?'

'You change your name to Connors? Leave it here. I'll see that it's returned.'

Without so much as another word, she approached the front counter and muttered, 'Closing time.' She slammed down the window partition, leaving Harry standing there, staring at a grey steel barrier.

He barely noticed. All he could think of was the name she had spoken. Connors . . . that meant David Connors. The man had just been transferred to the Police Standards Section. To Internal. And the thought of it turned Harry cold.

They know, he thought. *The department knows.*

And they were coming after him.

One Hundred and Twenty-One

When they got back to HQ, Felicia continued with the task of figuring out where their suspects had managed to obtain the explosives. While she was following the PETN trail, Striker began making phone calls on Oliver and Molly Howell.

The task was not an easy one.

Time differences were always an issue with federal and international files. It was six p.m. Pacific Time when Striker finally got through to a sergeant in the National Central Bureau of Canada's Interpol branch. After almost a half-hour of runaround time and dead ends, he gave up.

He hung up the phone and dialled the operator. Soon he was connected directly with the City of London Police and speaking to a weary-sounding but polite female staff sergeant.

Striker told her what he required and why.

'The information you're asking for is protected,' she explained. 'I can't just tell you this over the phone. Not without proper verification.'

Striker nodded absently. 'I understand that completely. We can do this one of three ways. You can send the information to my Vancouver Police Department email account, you can send it via CPIC – the Canadian Police Information Centre; but that will take time – or you can verify my badge and identity through the main switchboard and call me back on this line.'

'How time-sensitive is this information?' the staff sergeant asked.

'Extremely. Lives are at stake here. Minutes count.'

'I'll call you right back then.'

The staff sergeant verified that she had Striker's correct name, badge number, and position, then she hung up. Striker did the same and then waited by the phone. After ten minutes, he was getting edgy. After twenty, he was downright annoyed. After thirty, he turned on the Internet, opened Google, and typed in:

Time: London, UK.

The response came back: 01:59 a.m.

Then the phone rang, and he picked up on the first ring.

'Striker,' he said.

The staff sergeant identified herself once more. 'Sorry about the delay, Detective. There was a problem transferring the call – it got dropped several times.'

'The distance, I guess.'

'That – and I made some other calls first.'

'To?'

'The British Army.'

The words made Striker's heart skip a beat. 'The army?'

The staff sergeant made an uncomfortable sound. 'Look, Detective, I'd be lying if I said the information here isn't of great concern to us. These two individuals – Oliver and Molly Howell – have *outstanding* service records with our country's military. You do realize they're both members of the Royal Logistics Corps.'

Striker's stomach knotted up. 'I knew their father was a member of the RLC, and had my worries their paths might have turned out similar.'

'They're both war heroes, Detective. *Highly* decorated. I'm sure I don't have to tell you how extremely sensitive this information is.'

'I'll be as discreet as is legally possible.'

'Legally possible . . . That doesn't sound well on this end. And considering the urgency of your call, I'm assuming the worst.'

'Have you Googled Vancouver?' he asked.

There was a pause. 'I have indeed.'

'What was the first thing that came up?'

The staff sergeant made an uncomfortable sound. 'The bombings.' When Striker made no reply, she cursed and said, 'Bloody hell, this is awful.'

'Tell me, Staff Sergeant, what exactly did they do in the RLC?'

There was another brief pause and the sound of pages being flipped before the staff sergeant spoke again. 'Molly is a demolitions tech and a sharpshooter.'

Striker thought back to the woman firing at him in the A&W parking lot – her pinpoint accuracy, her use of suppressing fire just above his head, designed to keep him down and out.

'Jesus Christ,' he said. 'And the brother, what about him?'

'Oliver Howell is a Commando-trained Ammunitions Technician . . . a Warrant Officer – Second Class.'

Striker closed his eyes and felt a rush of concern. *Ammunitions Technician* was just a fancy title for a man with a deadly job. Oliver Howell was the one thing that Striker had feared most.

A bomb hunter.

One Hundred and Twenty-Two

The first thing Striker did was flag every single database available for Oliver and Molly Howell. He then notified the airports, ferries and the US border. Following all this, he contacted Acting Deputy Chief Laroche.

Laroche listened intently, then said, 'We need to debrief.'

For once, Striker agreed with the man.

The brass and their advisors all met in the briefing room on the seventh floor of Cambie Street Headquarters. Occupying the centre of the meeting room was a twenty-foot-long mahogany desk. Laroche took one look at Striker and Felicia, then offered them the head of the table.

'Finally, we can begin,' he said. 'Detective Striker, why don't you give us a rundown of everything you've learned these past three days. Bring us up to speed on where we stand.'

Striker did as asked. And the more he told the story, the greater the disbelief on their faces grew. When he was done explaining, Superintendent Stewart was the first to speak. 'But why? What do these people want?'

'That's the problem,' Felicia said. 'They haven't asked for anything.'

Striker nodded. 'Which makes the motive pretty clear in my estimation – *revenge*.'

Constable Lincoln Johnstone, the Media Liaison Officer, and

Heath Ballantyne, a civilian who acted as the department's public image consultant, let out simultaneous grumbles. Johnstone's eyes took on a faraway look. 'This is going to be a difficulty with the media.'

'A difficulty?' Ballantyne whined. 'It's a public relations *nightmare*. Two crazed bombers hell-bent on blowing up people around the city – you think the press has had fun till this point, you just wait. *Christ.*'

Through the back and forth arguments, Laroche remained silent, listening, thinking. He looked at Striker and Felicia all the while, and when the ruckus was calming down, he asked, 'What do we know about their history?'

Striker spoke first. 'They're both members of the Royal Logistics Corps.'

'Bomb hunters,' Felicia added.

The look on Laroche's face hardened. Johnstone made an exasperated sound, while Ballantyne just let loose another string of profanities.

'Are you certain of this?' Laroche asked.

Striker gave him a hard look. 'Completely.'

Felicia nodded her support. 'The military angle also explains how they acquired the explosives . . . They've been here in Canada for several months now, under the guise of visiting our own army to assess their bomb-defusing techniques. I've called some contacts on the matter.'

'And?' Laroche pressed.

'It's interesting,' she continued. 'During times of war, most countries just blow up any Improvised Explosive Devices they locate. But not the Brits and Canadians. We *defuse* them in order to save the components. It creates a trail leading back to the manufacturers. The information gained from dismantling the bombs is invaluable, but it also costs a lot of lives. The soldiers who do this, they're of a different breed. They have to be in order to handle the constant unbelievable stress.'

'It's a wonder they don't all have PTSD,' Ballantyne commented.

'Many do,' Felicia said. 'The job has a high mortality rate. In fact, Oliver Howell was blown up once himself and hospitalized for it. I haven't been able to get access to the army medical records yet, but we do know this – both Oliver and Molly are highly decorated war vets who have seen several tours in Afghanistan and Iraq. Quite frankly, they're the worst possible enemies we could have in this case.'

Striker turned in his seat to face her. 'Does the army stock PETN?'

She nodded. 'I spoke to their Ammunitions Officer. Not only do they stock PETN, but theirs was one of the batches that was recalled.'

'Was any missing?'

Felicia frowned. 'There's no way of checking. The company who makes the product gave the army a full credit for the batch. Rather than waste time and money shipping the product back, they detonated it with other explosives. As a result, there's no way of checking inventories, although I don't think it's a big stretch to conclude that this is where the bombers got their supply.'

Striker thought things through. 'The faulty batch explains how Koda survived the explosion at his home. It also explains why the bombers switched to home-made explosives halfway through the mission.'

For a moment, the room turned silent. Then Laroche spoke.

'What else can we do to prevent further casualties?' he asked.

Striker gave them a rundown of what had been done so far – police databases, the border, and all modes of international travel had been flagged. The RCMP had undercover units set up on the Sunset Care Centre as well as Archer Davies' second family. And here in Vancouver, Patrol was already guarding Rothschild and his family.

This seemed to satisfy Laroche for the moment. 'Then the only remaining question is our line of action with regard to public knowledge . . . Do we inform them?'

Striker was the first to speak. 'You go public with this information, and you might sewer any chance we have of catching them.'

Media Liaison Constable Johnstone agreed. 'We have to consider the fear aspect. These are well-trained military officers. Informing the public will cause mass hysteria. We can't tell them.'

'We *have* to tell them,' Ballantyne countered. He looked directly at Laroche when he spoke. 'If you hold back this information, and a bomb goes off killing innocent civilians – and, God forbid, children – the department will be *liable*. Not to mention your approval rating will plummet to an all-time low. It could take years to recover from something like that. A decade.'

Striker couldn't believe his ears. Were they really talking about public approval ratings at a time like this? It was all he could do to hold his tongue. He gave Felicia a hot look, and she returned it.

After a long moment of discussion, Laroche turned away from the table. He walked to the window and stared outside. Behind him, Ballantyne and Johnstone argued back and forth over the right decision, while Felicia and Striker waited with feigned patience. After a long moment, the Acting Deputy Chief returned.

'We have a duty to inform the public.'

Striker balled his fingers into fists. 'This is a mistake,' he said.

'All you're going to do is create more fear, speed up the bombers' plans, and make the investigation more difficult for us.'

But Laroche acted as if he had never heard the rebuttal. He turned to Media Liaison Johnstone and nodded.

'Go get your scribe,' he said. 'We have a speech to write.'

One Hundred and Twenty-Three

The house was warm and smelled of fresh-baked scones, and that Beatles guy Mommy loved so much was singing about Jude over the speakers again. Outside the sun was shining brightly in the deep blue sky. Everything *looked* wonderful. Like it was a perfect day. But to six-year-old Oliver, there was no day worse.

Daddy was leaving again.

'Don't go . . . please, Daddy . . . don't leave me!'

He stood at the front-room window and gaped at the man he had not seen for so long he could almost not remember – not since the last time he had left in his uniform for that Green Valley Mommy had told him about, where he went to save the world.

Beside Oliver, Molly was breathing hard, crying. She had her hands pressed up against the window and her breath was fogging up the glass.

'Don't go, don't go, *Daddy, don't go*!'

Her cries echoed his own.

Oliver banged on the glass as hard as he could with his little fists, but it made no difference. Daddy kept walking. He reached the taxi cab, adjusted his hat, and looked back towards the house. For a moment, they saw each other, and now the tears began to fall.

'*Don't go*,' he said, all but a whisper.

Daddy did not move for a moment, he just stared back and his face became awfully hard and his eyes looked like wet glass. He gave them a quick salute.

'I love you two,' he mouthed, and touched his heart.

From the kitchen, came Mother. Her apron was covered in flour, and she gently wrapped her arm around both of them, then guided them away from the window. 'Come on, dears, I've made your favourite treat – scones with cream and strawberry jam.'

'No!' Oliver yelled.

He spun away from her. Ran back to the window. Placed his hands and face against the glass. Big tears rolled down his cheeks.

Outside, the cab was already driving away. And Oliver let loose a wild, agonized sound as it left. He sobbed and sobbed and sobbed some more, while Bert and Ernie talked on the TV and the smell of fresh-baked scones spread throughout the living room.

Don't go don't go don't go . . .

'DON'T GO!' Oliver yelled.

He reached out and grabbed for nothing that was there.

'I'm not going anywhere,' Molly said.

Her voice – her *tone* – startled him. Woke him. And he looked around the room in a haze. It was as if someone had suddenly screamed in his ear while he was meditating, and he now realized he was horizontal with the ground. He tried to sit up, and the earth shifted beneath him.

He fell back down.

'Lie down, Oliver. Lie down . . .' Molly stared at him from above, her round face tight, her eyes distant. She brushed a hand through his hair. 'Jesus almighty, you're *soaked,* Oliver. You're burning up.'

He tried to sit up again; she pushed him back down.

'Rest!' she said.

'Target's away . . . left turn, south . . .'

'There is no target, Oliver. You're here. With me.'

'. . . bomb's *hot* . . .'

Molly stood up. Walked to the corner. And opened a small red medical cooler. From it, she withdrew a cloth and three cold packs. She sat back down and used a rag to gently mop the sweat from Oliver's brow, then she broke the chemical seals on the ice packs and placed one against his forehead and two under his armpits.

'*No!*' He tried to take them out.

'Leave them.'

'. . . is cold.'

'Leave them.'

'My leg. Leave the leg . . .'

Molly said nothing. From the steel table across the room, she grabbed the remaining bottles of antibiotics and antihistamines, and injected Oliver for the third time of the hour. Wanting the medications closer, she crossed the room, grabbed hold of the steel table and tried to pull it across the room. But it was too heavy, so she left the table where it was and laid her supplies down on the red medical cooler.

She turned on the relay system, then the monitor, and watched the news. What she saw turned her blood ice-cold. She changed the channel several times, but it made no difference. Everywhere she looked, the news was the same.

'Our pictures . . . they're everywhere, Oliver.'

'. . . doctors . . .'

'They know who we are.'

'. . . took my leg . . . my *leg*!'

Molly stood up uneasily, almost hesitantly from the table.

'We're all out of options,' she said softly, and there was a tremor in her voice. A note of finality and despondency and regret. 'I have to finish the mission without you.'

One Hundred and Twenty-Four

It was eight o'clock on a Friday night and the city was in an uproar. During the news release, Media Liaison Officer Johnstone had informed the press that the investigating officers were Detectives Jacob Striker and Felicia Santos. As a result, their office phones had been ringing off the hook. Striker had over twenty-three messages waiting for him.

He turned off his ringer and swivelled in his seat to face Felicia. 'This is ridiculous. The brass really screwed us on this one.'

The look on Felicia's face mirrored his own. 'They've made everything so much harder. Now it feels like one long waiting game.'

'Cat and mouse.'

'More like Whack-a-Mole, if you're Harry,' Felicia suggested.

Striker couldn't find a smile. 'Any calls on him?'

'Not a one. The undercover guys have had no sightings. And I even called his brother, Trevor. But no one's heard or seen a thing.'

Striker stood up. 'Come on then. If we can't find the bombers, let's go where the bombers might find us.'

'Rothschild's new place?'

'You got it.'

Twenty minutes later, they drove through Dunbar and headed

for the Kerrisdale area, where Rothschild's new home was located. Striker wanted to test the protection detail, so they parked three blocks south of Trafalgar and made their way in on foot.

Striker went straight; Felicia walked a parallel lane. The purpose of doing so was to either spot the protection team or have the protection team spot them. When Striker neared Rothschild's backyard, he peered inside the garage window and spotted Mike's prized possession – the old Cougar. From what Striker could see, there were no undercover operatives near it. When Felicia also reached the garage, Striker reached for the doorknob, turned it gently—

And a deep male voice called out:

'You'd already be a dead man, Detective.'

Striker stopped turning the knob and smiled; the protection team had caught him before he'd caught them. That was good. He and Felicia turned around, but they saw no one in the lane.

'Good work, guys,' Felicia said.

Striker searched for the source of the voice but all he could see were backyard fences, dark shadows which lined the inter-house walkways, and bushes and trees in every yard.

'Felicia and I will be staying in the house tonight,' he said.

'Cool,' came the reply. 'We've been bored back here. Tell Felicia to have a few drinks and put on a show for us.'

Felicia offered a weak grin. 'You couldn't handle it.'

Ignoring the banter, Striker walked up the back porch steps. At the midway point, he was lit up by the motion detector light. Squinting against the glare, he unlocked the patio door.

Inside, the kitchen was filled with a table and chairs and a half-dozen unpacked moving boxes. Striker opened the fridge and was pleased to see a row of Sleeman's Original Draught bottles lined up along the shelf of the door. He took two beers, twisted off the caps, and held one out to Felicia.

She took it and clinked her bottle on his.

'To catching these guys,' she said.

Striker smiled back.

'Bombs away,' he said.

One Hundred and Twenty-Five

Harry sat in a black pickup truck, parked a half-block back from where Striker and Felicia had parked their undercover cruiser. An hour earlier, Harry himself had tried to go home, but he'd done some of his own reconnaissance first. It had taken him less than ten minutes to spot one of the undercover operatives watching his place.

Strike Force, he thought.

There to take me down.

He killed any thought of an Internal investigation and stared down the road in the direction of Rothschild's place. Striker and Felicia were spending the night here. And that was good news.

It worked perfectly for him.

He grabbed a wire brush and the GPS tracking device. It was one he had purchased from Best Buy – nowhere near the quality of the BirdDog devices the department owned; those were several thousand dollars apiece. But so long as Striker and Felicia didn't take the tunnel into the Richmond area, this consumer model would work just fine.

Harry got moving. He lay down beneath the undercover cruiser, reached up with the wire brush, and vigorously raked it along the uppermost part of the frame. When the metal was shiny clean, he hit the 'on' switch and attached the unit. He gave the device a firm tug, felt the magnet hold, and was satisfied with the result.

He returned to his vehicle and backed up a few blocks into a T-lane near Balsam. When he turned on the tracking device, it worked fine. A small red icon filled the centre of the display.

Striker was all set to be tailed.

Somewhat relieved, Harry let out a long breath. Tracking other cops . . . the whole thing left a bad taste in his mouth. But so be it. This was no longer about good and evil, or right and wrong. It was about *survival.* And Harry would be damned if he was going down without a fight.

One Hundred and Twenty-Six

The night was hot and dark.

Striker sat in the dimness of the kitchen. His body was tired, and his conscious mind begged for sleep. But every time he tried to doze, his subconscious kicked in, sending a wave of adrenalin surging through his body and giving him a wicked case of restless legs. Sleeping fully clothed with a holster attached to his belt didn't help him get comfortable, but that was how it had to be. They were up against some highly trained operatives right now.

He needed every advantage he could get.

Out of habit, he ejected the magazine from his SIG and unloaded the bullets. He checked each round for irregularities. When he found none, he reloaded the SIG and shoved it back into its holster.

He thought of Courtney. And like he had done a hundred times this week, he took out his cell and dialled long distance to Ireland. The connection took so long he thought the line had been dropped, but then it rang. Once, twice, and then a third time. On the fourth ring, the call was picked up.

'Dad!' she said.

Her voice did something to him, choked him up a little, and he had to take in a deep breath. 'Hey, Pumpkin. How's the trip going?'

'Freakin' *awesome* . . . but I miss you though.'

'I miss you too.' He thought of her spinal injury, and frowned. 'You keeping up your exercises?'

'My Kegels? Yeah, I do them every day.'

'Very funny.'

She laughed out loud. 'What time is it there anyway?'

'Two in the morning.'

'You should be in bed. Are you eating well? Felicia better be taking good care of you.'

'She feeds me bacon cheeseburgers twice a day and took out extra life insurance on me. So it must be love.'

'I'm serious, Dad. Eat well. Food is medicine, right?'

Striker smiled at her concern. Ever since he had lost Amanda, Courtney had taken on opposing roles – half filled with teenage angst, half filled with motherly concern. She'd been through a lot these last few years – too much for a sixteen-year-old girl – and despite his grumblings, Striker was glad that she had met Tate. And glad that Tate and his parents had taken her away for a while.

The break would do Courtney good.

'I tasted real Guinness for the first time,' she said. 'And I loved it.'

So did your mother, he thought. It was her favourite drink.

'You're underage, Pumpkin.'

'Not here – so long as I order it with food.'

'Just don't go crazy.'

Courtney prattled on about how she was enjoying the trip. Striker listened to every word. She told him about the Cliffs of Moher, the Lakes of Killarney, and Dublin city. And all the while, Striker wished he could reach out across the distance and hug her through the phone.

Feeling a little more cheery, Striker stole another beer from the fridge as Courtney filled him in on the famed O'Connell

Street. Bottle in hand, he exited the kitchen and wandered onto the back porch. Three steps later, he stopped hard.

The motion detector light did not activate.

Striker waved his hand in front of the sensor. When nothing happened, he reached over, grabbed the light bulb and turned it. The connection was secure, but the bulb did not light up. He ran his finger along the motion sensor and felt a thin strip of something. He pulled it off and found himself holding a black piece of electrician's tape.

'. . . and then we went to St Patrick's Cathedral!' Courtney said.

'Gotta go, Pumpkin,' he said softly. 'I love you.'

He abruptly ended the phone call and put his beer down on the porch railing. He drew his pistol, scanned the backyard, saw nothing. He dialled Dispatch and asked them to raise the rear guard of his protection team. Ten seconds later, the response chilled him:

'He's not answering.'

'What about the rest of the team?'

'They're still accounted for.'

Striker thought of their positions. None were near the back-yard. 'Keep trying on the rear guard. Tell the others to be on high alert. Something's wrong here.'

When the Dispatcher said she would, Striker shoved the cell back into his pocket. For a moment he considered retreating inside and waiting for cover. But the thought of losing the bombers again was too much. He started down the porch steps and heard Felicia's voice behind him. 'What's going on?'

'Motion detector's been deactivated – you got your piece?'

'Of course. I got you covered.'

Striker nodded, never taking his eyes off the yard. He moved down the back steps onto the concrete patio and stopped at the edge of the house. Using the corner for cover, he looked down the walkway between the houses and saw no one there.

'Clear,' he whispered. 'Watch back and left; I got front and right.'

'Copy, I got back and left.'

Striker moved forward along the cement path that led across the backyard, all the way to the fence and garage. As he went, he strained his ears for any indicating sounds, but aside from the gentle hush of the warm summer wind, the night was quiet and still.

He reached the garage. Stopped. Looked in through the glass.

Everything was black because a shade had been pulled down over the window.

He reached out. Gently wrapped his fingers around the doorknob. Turned. And slowly opened the door.

Inside the garage, everything was dark. But one thing became immediately obvious. The front hood of the Cougar was up.

Striker held up a hand to get Felicia's attention. Then he readied his pistol and turned on his flashlight.

In a quick burst of illumination, the centre of the garage was suddenly lit up and exposed. The air was oily and musty, and the window on the far side of the room had also been covered with black plastic. The Cougar, sitting with its hood lifted, was parked ass-end in. As a result, it occupied both parking stalls.

On the ground, by the front tyre, was an array of tools – a wrench, a screwdriver, a pair of vice grips, and some wire-cutters. Also there was a small handheld device that looked like a walkie-talkie.

But all that was background to what sat in front of it – a small white doll dressed in a policeman's uniform. It had a big red number 1 painted on its chest, and the sight of it told Striker all he needed to know:

The bomber was here.

'Cover left!' he ordered Felicia.

Striker swung right, taking quick aim, and within seconds saw the shape of a woman scampering on the ground. She was wearing a pair of dark overalls and had her hair pulled back into a short ponytail. When Striker saw her face, there was no doubt in his mind. This was the woman he had been searching for – the same one who'd been shooting at him back in the A&W parking lot.

Bomber number 2.

Molly Howell.

He took aim. 'Vancouver Police – don't move!'

The woman said nothing. She gave no response, verbal or otherwise. She simply looked up at him, her face filled not only with shock, but cold calculation. Her eyes flitted from Striker to the area behind the car – as if searching for Felicia. When they turned back again, they dipped down and left.

'It's over,' Striker started to say.

But before he could finish, Molly dove across the pavement.

Striker darted to the side, avoiding her attack. But then, in one horrific moment, he realized that she wasn't jumping at him – she was jumping beside him.

For the *detonator.*

He levelled the gun, took aim, and opened fire. Three shots. All direct hits.

Two to the body, one to the face.

And Molly Howell – criminal to some; decorated war hero to all – collapsed. She flopped over sideways and landed in a tangled position with both legs twisted beneath her body. Her dull brown eyes remained open and lifeless.

It was over for her.

Molly Howell was dead.

One Hundred and Twenty-Seven

Oliver lay on the cot and felt sweat dripping off his body. An ache ran through him like a hot liquid in his bones, radiating from his neck all the way down to his tailbone.

He was in the dark greyness of the command room. He knew this. But he kept finding himself *back there* again. In the Green Zone. And it was happening – it was happening all over again.

His squad was being led to their doom.

It all started with the Afghan cop – that tall, burly, black sergeant from the Afghan National Police. Smoking his Egyptian cigarettes, he led them all across the Helmand plain. He was eager, nervous.

Excited even.

'Dis way, dis way,' he said several times. 'On da plain. You see. On da plain.'

Oliver followed. He wiped his brow with the sleeve of his uniform as they went. Early still, a chilly dew covered the tall grass of the fields, but soon it would be stolen by the arid heat of the day.

'Hold up,' he commanded.

They had neared their destination.

At the end of the trail was the bomb the cop had found – an Improvised Explosive Device buried deep within the rocky sand. It seemed to be a standard IED – one pound of HME, a pressure-plate release pad, and tied to a dummy bomb beside it.

But looks could be deceiving. Especially when dealing with the Taliban.

Oliver assessed the scene and didn't like it. The work area was narrow, less than four feet wide, and flanked by drainage canals. Beyond that, tall sweeping hills backed the plains. It was an enemy haven – concealment below and cover above.

'I don't like it,' Oliver said. 'And I don't like this man.'

'He's a cop,' the point man said. 'He's ANP.'

'Means nothing. They got sleepers everywhere.'

Oliver frowned. The situation was bad. He wanted nothing more than to retreat. But orders were orders in the Green Zone, and if he didn't deal with the IED now, it would end up taking out another soldier later on.

It *always* did.

Reality dictated. There was no choice.

'Cover me,' he told his men.

Then he started the long walk.

Voices from the past haunted him.

The cop, the cop, shoot the goddam cop!

The words blasted through Oliver's head, a desperate scream no one else could hear. He sat up with a jolt, and suddenly, he was back in the command room. On the cot. In the stark hotness of the dark grey room.

Out of one nightmare, into another.

For as the haze dissipated, the soft sounds of the monitor filled his ears. A jumble of words that caught his attention:

. . . bomber . . .

. . . shootout . . .

. . . hero cop . . .

And then the most horrible words he had ever heard in his life:

. . . believed to be Royal Logistic Corps Warrant Officer Molly Howell.

Oliver forced his stiff neck left and gaped at the monitor. One look at the image was all it took. Standing there in the camera feed was the cop – the big Homicide detective, Jacob Striker. And next to him were two large men in jumpsuits, loading a body hidden beneath a white sheet into a van.

The Body Removal Team.

'Molly,' Oliver said. His voice was soft and weak and tiny. '*Molly*.'

A sob filled his throat. Choked him mute. And like a slow pressing tide, Oliver felt himself slipping further and further away, into that dark fog of pain and medications, with only the image of his sister in his head. This time, he did not fight the feeling. This time he allowed himself to be enveloped by the thick, churning darkness. Within seconds, it overpowered him completely.

It was done.

He had passed the point of no return.

Part 4: Shockwave

Saturday

One Hundred and Twenty-Eight

Police had located the rear guard of the protection team by the time that Mike Rothschild arrived on scene at his own home; the guard had been knocked over the head and rendered unconscious, but – aside from some bruises to his skull and to his ego – he was no worse for wear.

Striker found the situation odd. Why had Molly Howell not just killed the man? Why take a chance like that when a bullet to the head or a blade to the throat would have been so much more effective? After all, dead men didn't return to consciousness and call in alerts.

Clearly, there was a difference in beliefs between the two bombers.

And it appeared as if he was left with the more dangerous of the two.

Pondering all this, Striker sat on the back porch, staring intently at the toy seized from the crime scene and absently rubbing his thumb along the red number 1 painted on its torso. To his surprise, the doll was not an accurate depiction of a policeman, but the personification of a duck, complete with legs and arms, and dressed in a policeman's uniform.

It was strange. Such an odd thing for the bomber to leave behind. A policeman made sense to Striker, because there were so many connections there.

But a duck?

It was just so . . . *odd.*

Striker heard an engine growl, looked up and spotted Rothschild's Toyota minivan just outside the strewn-up police tape at the south end of the lane. The man parked, then came walking in with purpose. The lines of his face were deeper than normal this morning.

'Up here, Mike,' Striker called.

Rothschild looked over the fence and spotted him. 'The whole world's gone insane!'

Striker did not respond. He just watched Rothschild enter the yard, stop at the entrance to his garage – which was now taped off as the primary crime scene with a patrolman standing guard – and peer inside. After a long moment, Rothschild shook his head in disbelief, then walked up the back porch steps to Striker's side.

'So she was actually in there, huh?'

Striker nodded. 'Planting a bomb under your hood.'

'She pull on you?'

'Went for the detonator.'

'Son-of-a-bitch.'

Striker looked to the east, where the sun was breaking through the strange mist that had flooded the woods of the park. 'The woman gave me no choice . . . I opened fire.'

'You scratch my paint?'

Striker didn't laugh. Black humour was usually the key to warding off depression, but today it didn't feel so good.

Rothschild took a seat beside Striker in one of the patio chairs. 'They take your piece?'

'Yeah. Noodles seized it and brought me a new SIG. No flash-light attachment or grip though. Laroche wants me off the road till I meet up with the Trauma Team, but me and Felicia are fighting him on it.' He jabbed a thumb over his shoulder.

'They're in there right now with Noodles and the coroner. It's a nightmare.'

Rothschild said nothing. He just looked at all the golden streams of police tape stretching across the backyard, the laneway, and the garage. 'I can tell you this much – next time I paint the house, it won't be yellow.'

Striker smiled for the first time. 'How about white and blue?' he said, and held up the toy duck.

All at once, Rothschild's face changed. 'Where'd you get that?'

'Crime scene. Molly Howell brought it with her. They've been leaving one of them for each victim, but we don't know why. ' Striker turned it over in his hands and examined the toy. Its body was wood, its beak plastic. The toy was solid. Well built. Striker stuck his finger through the metal O-ring and Rothschild stiffened.

'You sure—'

'It's been checked already.'

Striker gave the O-ring a yank and the bills flapped open and the duck began speaking: *'These criminals are making me quackers!'*

Rothschild reached out and took the duck from Striker. He held it in his hands, stared at it in wonder and partial disbelief. 'This is more than a toy, Shipwreck. It's Chief Quackers.'

Striker looked hard at Rothschild. 'You've seen this before?'

'Of course, I have. It used to be our goddam mascot. In ERT.'

'Mascot?'

Rothschild's eyes took on a faraway look and he explained. 'Was about ten years ago, I guess. I was on Red Team. That was when Chief Ackers was in charge. Guy was a self-righteous prick. Condescending. Arrogant as hell. He interfered with everything. No one liked the man, and we couldn't wait to get rid of him.'

'I heard about Ackers. He only lasted one term.'

'Yeah, the union stepped in on that one, thank God.'

Rothschild turned the duck over and over in his hands as he spoke. 'Anyway, Ackers was always bitching about the team's stats and saying how we weren't keeping track of our calls, and how it was making him look bad at the meetings.'

'CompStat?' Striker asked. It was the monthly meeting where city-wide statistics were discussed in public forums.

'Yeah, goddam CompStat,' Rothschild replied. 'Anyway, one day, Koda comes walking into the bunker – he was our sergeant back then – and he's got this little white duck in his hands. Got it from someone he knew, his wife or something, I can't really remember. But he pulls the string and it starts speaking about how these criminals are making him quackers. And one of the guys says, "Holy shit, it's Chief Ackers." Then someone else yells, "No, it's Chief *Quackers.*" And before you knew it everyone was laughing because it was, like, a total slag on the chief and all. Next thing you know, it ended up being our team mascot . . . Chief Quackers . . . God, I never thought I'd see him again.'

Striker looked at the duck for a long moment and felt some of the pieces fall into place. 'They've been leaving one of these ducks for each victim.'

'Like a calling card?'

Striker nodded. 'Calling card, signature, taunt – call it whatever you want. The point is they're doing it to let the victim know *why* this is happening.'

Rothschild shook his head. 'But I was part of that squad and I still don't fucking know why.'

Striker took back the duck and stared at it for a long moment.

'Doesn't matter if you know why or not,' he finally said. 'Oliver Howell thinks you do.'

One Hundred and Twenty-Nine

The memory of losing his leg was so vivid to Oliver, like it had just happened yesterday – or to Oliver's messed-up mind, like it had happened ten years ago, or ten minutes.

It made no difference.

The tall beefy black cop from the Afghan National Police had led them to the site of the IED, and it was in the worst possible location – down a narrow strip of dirt, flanked on both sides by canals and high sweeping hills. As Oliver made the long walk towards the bomb, the unusual tension from his squad was palpable.

He absorbed it right through his skin.

He reached the bomb site and felt himself sweating on the chilly valley plain. He scanned his eyes across the hills, east and west, searching for any sign of the enemy. But all he saw was cold blue sky. Sweeping rocky hills of unforgiving terrain. And crevice after crevice, cave after cave.

The favoured ambush spots of the Taliban.

With time running thin, Oliver dropped low. Opened his case. And pulled out the tools required for the job – wire-cutters, alligator clips, and a paintbrush of fine horsehair. He lay prone across the dirt and rock, and used gentle sweeping motions to brush away the pebbles and dirt until the rectangular form of the pressure plate became visible.

This was the first bomb, and that was a good start. But the wand had picked up *two* signals. So he angled himself to the right and performed the same actions once more until a second plate was uncovered, this one a pressure-release pad.

Finding the plate was always a relief. And a smile broke Oliver's lips. The operation was going smoothly thus far. And he felt good. Positive. Optimistic, even.

And then he saw the line – one long piece of dead wire snaking off to the east canal.

It was a goddam trap.

Oliver shoved himself back, spun about, and scampered to one knee in an effort to run. But the blast came. Light exploded, followed by a swelling of darkness as the earth rose up beneath him like some giant creature breaking out of hell. An invisible force tore through his body, and was followed by a thunderous wave. Suddenly he was *airborne.* Floating, spinning, rolling through the sky. When he finally landed, a wave of agony ripped through his body. He lay there, on the dirt of the path, feeling every inch of his being throb and spasm as he stared out, not thirty feet into the field, and saw the ground being torn apart by gunfire rounds and mortar.

'Sandman down – SANDMAN DOWN!' Someone was screaming. One of his men.

Oliver could barely hear the man.

He managed to turn his head. To look back down the trail. And he saw his squadmates running his way.

High-calibre rounds rained down from the rocky terrain above. East *and* west. AK-47 fire. Mowing them down. In the constant drone of gunfire, half his men were ripped apart. Shreddings of meat and tissue and blood exploded from their bodies. The few who survived the assault grabbed him. Lifted him from the ground.

'The path,' Oliver whispered weakly. 'Stay on . . . *the path.*'

But no one could heard him, and suddenly more bombs were going off. Loud, thunderous booms. One explosion to the east – a one-pounder that tore off the bottom half of his point man's legs. And one to the west – a definite two-pounder that obliterated two other men completely.

And for Oliver, everything just sort of *slooowed* down.

Greyed out.

Muted.

Even the high-powered chain guns of the Black Hawks seemed soft and distant as the rescue birds came sweeping in from the hills and rained fire on their enemies. To Oliver, none of it mattered now. There was only pain and spasm, and a deep dark hollowness that was sucking him down like an animal in a tar-pit trap, covering his head in suffocating blackness.

He couldn't *breathe* . . .

Back in the command room, Oliver's eyes snapped open and he gasped for air.

His mouth was dusty dry, his tongue felt too large. Sounds from the monitors hit his ears. Talk of bombs and police. And for a moment, he thought it was the ANP cop again, and he reached for his assault rifle. When he found no long gun there, he forced himself to sit up. And all at once, reality spilled over him like a cold wave.

The news was still on.

Molly was not there.

And she would never be coming back.

Oliver let out a wail.

A mixture of emotions hit him. His squadmates, gone. His friends, gone. His father and mother, gone. And now Molly . . . she too was gone. *Molly.* He wanted nothing more than to break down and give up.

But he did not. The soldier in him would not allow it.

Thirsty, exhausted, throbbing with pain and fever, he forced himself to his feet and shuffled like an old man across the room to the costume Molly had created. Her last one. He grabbed the uniform, then a SIG P224, because it allowed for the attachment of night sights, a tactical light-laser attachment, and above all, a sound suppressor – which would definitely be needed for this job to be successful.

Hot yet cold, and slick with a chilly sweat, Oliver placed the compact SIG behind his waistband, then stumbled and had to grab the wall for support. The fever – and perhaps the infection – was still going strong. A microscopic symphony in his veins. But so what?

Oliver knew sickness; he had been ill many times before. Been *deathly* ill. And he knew that without rest, this injury would kill him. But that was okay. He had the uniform. He had the gun. He had the plan. After that, nothing really mattered any more.

He didn't plan on surviving the day.

One Hundred and Thirty

Striker pulled Felicia from the house.

'We're going,' he said.

'Where?'

'Anywhere but here.'

'But Laroche—'

'We have a bomber to find.'

Felicia looked at him curiously, almost cautiously, then smiled.

'Let's go,' she said.

Moments later, they were marching up Trafalgar Street towards the undercover cruiser. As they went, Striker explained what Rothschild had told him about the toy duck. Felicia listened intently, biting her lip with every detail. When Striker was done speaking, Felicia made a point:

'So that gives us one more connection to Williams,' she said. 'She was the toymaker who gave Koda the duck.'

Striker agreed. 'It's how she was connected to the squad, yes, but I think her main role was hiding Harry and Koda's drug money through her accounting practices.'

'But why kill her? The drug crimes are only indirectly connected to the shootings. Unless . . . maybe Oliver doesn't know that. Maybe he thinks it's all connected.'

Striker shook his head. 'It wouldn't matter anyway. From everything we've seen with this man, it's obvious his mind is fractured. His belief system is polarized. He treats everything as if they were *absolutes*. There are no degrees of right or wrong here, no grey areas – only black and white. Either you're culpable or innocent. There is no in-between. So for Keisha Williams to be funnelling away the money, she was involved. Period.'

'It still leaves us with nothing for Dr Owens.'

Striker nodded and sighed. 'The very person whose kidnapping started this whole call.'

They reached the undercover cruiser and Striker used the remote to unlock the doors. Once inside, he took a moment to think things over, then had an idea. He turned to Felicia. 'Maybe we're looking at this the wrong way.'

'How so?'

'We keep assuming that, because Sharise Owens had once been in a relationship with Koda, that this was her connection to it all. But that doesn't make sense. Harry and Osaka had wives too, and yet none of them have been targeted.'

'Or tortured, for that matter.'

'Exactly. Dr Owens worked at St Paul's Hospital. But the nurse said she'd been there for, what?' – Striker flipped back through his notebook to find the answer – 'seven years. *Seven*. Yet she's been a trauma surgeon for twelve. Do we know where the rest of those years were spent?'

Felicia shook her head, and Striker continued.

'The shooting down by the river . . . it took place on the Vancouver-Burnaby border. So when Archer was injured, what hospital would he have been taken to?'

'Burnaby General.'

Striker put the car into Drive and headed that way. 'We need to read that medical report.'

One Hundred and Thirty-One

They walked down the dim corridors of Burnaby General Hospital without speaking, Striker deep in his own thoughts and Felicia checking her iPhone emails. When they reached the Health Records Office, they went inside. The woman behind the counter had dyed auburn hair and far too much blue eyeliner on. She looked up from her newspaper, snapped her gum, and said, 'Can I help you?'

'I sincerely hope so,' Striker said.

He explained the situation.

After a quick system check, the clerk confirmed the existence of the medical report for a patient known as Archer J. Davies. As expected – and much to Striker's chagrin – she would not release the documents without the proper authorization, and that meant one of two things: obtaining a warrant, which would require writing an Information to Obtain, or giving the hospital a Release of Medical Documents form, signed by the deceased's closest living relative.

There was no time for writing an ITO at this point, so Striker spent an uncomfortable ten minutes on the phone with Lilly Davies, explaining the need for police access to the medical records. After getting her consent, he spent another half-hour waiting for the papers to be faxed.

'We're wasting so much time,' he griped.

'We're *saving* time,' Felicia countered. 'It would take us four hours to write an ITO – and that doesn't include getting some judge to approve it.'

He knew she was right, but he grumbled anyway. Moments later, the clerk motioned them over to the counter. In her hands was a deep red folder marked:

Trauma Surgery Report.

Striker wasted no time. He signed the form and grabbed the medical report. With Felicia peering over his shoulder, he sat down in the same chair he had been waiting in and opened the report. The first thing he noticed was the author's name.

Dr Sharise Owens.

It gave him hope for a new lead.

Together, they started reading through the medical report, skimming through the Procedural Summary and finishing with the full Operative Narrative. Once done, Striker sat back and looked at Felicia. The glum look on her face told him she had learned the exact same thing he had.

Nothing was amiss.

'It's all standard procedure,' she said. 'A very detailed and thorough report. In fact, it looks like she went *beyond* the call with this one – probably because Archer was a cop.'

Striker nodded. He went to snap the folder shut, then paused. He looked at Felicia. 'What are the odds that Koda's common-law wife would be the trauma surgeon working at this hospital when the call came in?'

Felicia thought it over. 'Low?'

'Definitely low.'

He got up and approached the front-desk clerk again. Her hair had fallen out of place and she was struggling to pin it back again. She gave him a queer look when he asked her for a copy of the shift schedules for the night of the shooting.

'That was, like, ten years ago,' she said.

Striker nodded. 'They still should be archived, shouldn't they?'

She gave him an exasperated look, but nodded. She muttered something about archives, then disappeared around the corner. When she returned some ten minutes later, she had a ten-by-fourteen photocopied page in her hand.

'This is it, Your Highness.'

Striker smiled and thanked her for it.

He and Felicia analysed the page. In the left column were the shifts and times. In the right was a list of doctors' names, each one followed by their practitioner number. Next to Sharise Owens' name were the letters 'CO' in brackets.

Striker showed it to the clerk behind the counter. 'What does this mean?

'CO?' she asked. 'Called Out.'

'So this was not her normal shift?'

'That's what called out means.'

'Interesting,' Striker said. He looked at the shift schedule, then at the medical report Felicia was holding. He asked the clerk, 'Tell me . . . how come there are no recordings in the medical file?'

'Recordings?'

'Last time I checked, there were audio tapes made as well.'

The woman gave him another queer look. 'Audio tapes are standard procedure on autopsies, not surgeries.'

Striker shook his head. 'They were with Dr Owens. The woman was meticulous. I've seen the copies she keeps back at her office.'

'Hold on, let me check.' The clerk spoke the words with irritation but she swivelled her chair around and began typing on the keyboard. After a while, she made a *hmm* sound. 'There's something here that says "micro".'

'Those would be the audio tapes,' Striker said. He explained the situation to the clerk. 'Everything may be digitally recorded nowadays, but ten years ago it was all put on mini-tapes.'

'I can't give you those.'

'I'll take a copy.'

'Hold on.'

She started to turn away from the computer, then stopped. Chewing her gum harder and faster, she leaned back towards the computer, studied the screen, and frowned. 'That's odd . . . Is this the second set of copies the police have acquired?'

Striker shook his head. 'Not that I'm aware of. Why?'

'Someone else obtained a copy of these tapes just two months ago.'

'You got a name?' Striker asked.

She nodded.

'Tom Atkins.'

One Hundred and Thirty-Two

The police property office was open from seven to five, Monday to Friday, and closed on the weekends. Harry needed to get in there to seize the burn records from Montreaux. Being Saturday, it left him with two options – get Car 10 to come down and open the office, or call the property office supervisor at home.

Knowing he was supposed to be nonexistent since the press release and also on paid leave pending the investigation, Harry avoided contacting Car 10. Instead, he called up property office clerk Larry Smallsy and gingerly explained that he needed some stored records for a walk-through warrant. Upon hearing the request, Smallsy made a tired sound. 'Geez, can't it wait, Harry?'

'Not on a walk-through.'

'Then just call Car 10.'

Harry cleared his throat. 'The road boss is Laroche . . . I'd rather keep him out of this, if you know what I mean. The only reason I'm writing the warrant is to cover my ass on a mistake I made last week. Last thing I need is King Tight-ass finding out.'

Smallsy laughed at that. He understood it well. 'Fine, fine, fine. I only live in Kits. I'll be right down.'

Harry was relieved. He waited on the south side of the property office – away from the main traffic of the report writing room.

Fifteen agonizing minutes later, Larry Smallsy buzzed himself through the back doors. He plodded down the hall, adjusting his John Lennon spectacles and sipping a frothy latte. When he was close enough, Harry could smell the hazelnut flavouring.

'I really appreciate this, Larry.'

Smallsy just unlocked the door and guided him inside. He walked down the corridor, in between the tall stacks of boxes that columned the passageway. When he reached the back end, he put his paper cup down on the counter and looked up at the array of binders that lined the shelves. 'Which one do you need, Harry?'

'There's a few of them – burning records from a decade back. From Montreaux.'

'Man, between you and Striker, you guys are bleeding me dry.'

Harry stiffened. 'Striker?'

'Yeah, he came in and took a bunch of these too. Five binders in all. He legally seized them.'

Harry felt ill. 'Which years?'

Smallsy showed him the dates and then gestured to the top row, where a large portion of the shelf now sat empty. Harry saw this and fell slightly back against the counter.

Gone, he thought. *Fucking seized.*

'Hey,' Smallsy asked. 'You okay?'

But Harry said nothing. He just turned around and left the property office without another word.

One Hundred and Thirty-Three

The audio recordings Dr Sharise Owens had made were on one single tape, yet it took three-quarters of an hour for the clerk to have it copied by the tech out back. When Striker complained about the lengthy delay, she shot back, 'You're lucky we can do this at all today – only one guy knows how to transfer the files and burn the disc, and he's not normally in on Saturdays. You should count yourself lucky.'

Properly chastised, Striker sat back down and waited for the CD.

When the clerk finally returned, she held a single bubble-wrapped envelope. Striker signed the Medical Information Release form, stating that he was now in possession of the material, then took the envelope and left the hospital with Felicia by his side.

Once in the car, Striker removed the CD from the envelope and powered on the radio. He slid the disc into the tray and nothing happened. When the LCD mini-screen flashed the message 'UNREADABLE FORMAT' he swore.

'What the hell now?' he asked.

'Wrong format,' Felicia replied. 'It's probably an MP3 or a FLAC or something. This radio's ancient. Plays only regular audio.' She loaded the CD into the laptop and waited. Seconds later, the Windows Media Player initiated and the voice of Dr Sharise Owens came over the speakers.

At first it struck Striker odd to hear her voice, this woman whose disappearance and death had triggered the investigation. Over the cheap speakers of the laptop, she sounded eerily faraway and tinny, but her voice was also filled with confidence and professionalism:

'This is Dr Sharise Owens, regarding file number 71139. My practitioner number is 15572 and the patient's name is Archer Jeffery Davies, Medical Number 4050 030 9019.' She then gave the date and location of the writing.

As they listened to the feed, Striker opened the written file. Together, they compared the written report with the audio. For the first twenty minutes, everything matched perfectly, and Striker was growing antsy. When the tape timeline hit 21 minutes, 42 seconds, everything changed.

Striker blinked, then looked at Felicia. 'You get that?'

'Get what?'

'Roll back the feed.'

Felicia used the mouse to drag the cursor back a full minute. Dr Sharise Owens' voice took over the air once more:

'The bullet round is of the frangible type, which has caused an array of soft tissue complications, most pertinently in the nervous and cardiovascular systems. The entrance wound, a three-inch opening, has destroyed the spinous processes of the eighth and ninth thoracic vertebrae and the subsequent vertebral bodies; the bullet's exit caused fracturing of the inferior third of the sternum and the subsequent splintering of the ninth and tenth ribs anteriorly . . . This is indicative of a high-calibre, high-velocity round.'

Felicia listened to the woman's explanation, then nodded. 'She's telling us it was a high-velocity, high-calibre round.'

Striker's eyes darkened. 'It's not the calibre or speed that concern me, it's the *type* and *direction*.' He pointed to the written report. 'Carlos Chipotle was firing an AK-47. Full Metal Jacket rounds.'

Felicia made an *oh-shit* sound. 'Non-frangible.'

Striker nodded. 'The only guys there with frangible rounds were *us* – the cops.'

'Which means Archer got tagged by one of our own guys.'

Striker nodded. 'And where does the report list Archer Davies' entrance wound?'

Felicia searched the report. 'The sternum.'

'Exactly. But given the size of the posterior gunshot wound, that would be impossible – the entrance wound is always *smaller* than the exit wound.'

Felicia suddenly looked ill. 'But if the exit wound was on the front side of Archer's body, then that would mean—'

Striker nodded numbly.

'They shot him in the back.'

One Hundred and Thirty-Four

Striker wanted a list of every cop on scene at the Chipotle gun call where Archer Davies had been shot. To do this, he and Felicia stopped in at Main Street Headquarters to use one of the desktop computers. They were linked in to the mainframe and could bring up information that the mobile laptops could not.

Being Saturday, the office should have been busy with cops sorting out the Friday night files, but today it was almost empty.

Striker walked right down to his desk. He brought up the call, read for a bit, then leaned back in the chair and felt like he was going to get sick. He gave Felicia a dismal look.

'What?' she asked.

'The bullet that struck Archer Davies entered through his mid-spine and came out his chest; that much is undeniable. Judging from the ballistics report, it's also true that the bullet was fired from a police *sniper* rifle. In the report, there's only one ERT sniper listed.'

She understood the significance of that.

'Rothschild,' she said.

Striker nodded. 'Carlos Chipotle was all coked-out with an assault rifle in his possession. So containment was essential. If Chipotle managed to escape with a weapon like that, who knows what might have happened? There's a school just four blocks down the road, and a Community Police Office a mile north of there.'

'What's your point?'

'My point is this – in order to contain him properly, there should have been *two* snipers on the scene. Both in elevated positions. Was Rothschild the only one – or was there another?'

Striker focused back on the computer and began paging through the information. For a Man With a Gun call, it was surprisingly and disappointingly brief, but the information that was there offered clarity.

He read through it:

11:45: The call comes in. A witness reports a man with a machine gun down by the river.
11:51: The first Patrol unit arrives on scene.
11:57: The entire block is cordoned off.
11:59: A request for the Emergency Response Team is made by Car 10.

Striker scanned ahead for the next important time:

12:28: The Emergency Response Team is delayed due to an ongoing incident in the downtown core.
12:29: A city-wide message is sent requesting all Patrolmen qualified as carbine operators to head towards the area.
12:47: With the assistance of the Burnaby RCMP and the New Westminster Police Department, a makeshift team is assembled with Chad Koda as the lead sergeant. Constable Mike Rothschild is the lone sniper. His position is a two-storey elevation from the southeast.

Striker paused. *This* was what he had been searching for, and upon seeing it he frowned. The breaching team had come in from the southeast – under cover of the sniper. So for Archer

Davies to be shot in the back, and on a thirty-degree angle, the bullet could only have been fired by one person.

Mike Rothschild.

Striker scanned through the list of badge numbers, looking for any other officer that had arrived with a long gun, be it another ERT sniper or one of the patrolmen carrying a carbine.

But there were none.

'Goddammit,' he said. 'There must have been another shooter there – someone other than Mike who could have fired that bullet.'

Felicia's face softened. She reached out and touched his arm for support.

'I'm sorry, Jacob, but Rothschild was the only cop there with a long gun. You have to face it . . . Rothschild shot Archer.'

One Hundred and Thirty-Five

Oliver stood on the corner of Cambie and West 2nd, directly across from Vancouver Police Headquarters, with his bag of supplies in hand. He wore the police uniform his sister had created for him, and knew that it was an exact replica, right down to the buttons. Feeling the sweat from his brow trickle under the line of his hat, he wiped his brow and flagged down the first marked patrol car that turned the corner.

A short fat mug of a cop with a horseshoe balding pattern rolled down the passenger window. 'Need a lift there, fella?'

'Yeah. Leaving early today and I gotta get myself back to Kerrisdale.'

'Hop in.'

Oliver threw his bag on the floor, then jumped in the passenger side and slammed the door. The cop hit the gas, turned south on Quebec Street, and gave him a sideways stare. 'Never seen you before – you from the odd side?'

'Yeah.'

'Call-out?'

'Uh-huh.'

'You're sweating up a storm, buddy. You sick or something?'

'Yeah. Sick.'

'Man, you look it. Don't breathe on me, huh?' The cop guffawed, then grabbed his iced cappuccino from the cup holder and sipped. 'So where exactly we going here?'

'Just get me to Arbutus and 41st . . . then I'll show you.'

The balding cop nodded and they drove on.

As they went, Oliver crossed his arms, slowly, gingerly, to take pressure off the fractured bone in his shoulder. He leaned back in the seat and tried to get comfortable. It wasn't easy. The cop had the air conditioner going full bore and the draught felt like pins and needles on his skin – painful, yet oddly soothing. Were it not for the man's constant yammering, Oliver would have zoned out completely.

They reached Arbutus and 41st.

'Where now?' the cop asked.

Oliver blinked. Tried to focus. He saw a green Starbucks coffee shop and the blue glare of a Bank of Montreal sign. He got his bearings. Then pointed. 'Turn left here, then down the lane.'

Soon, they found themselves at the end of a long back alley. Oliver deftly unzipped the bag. Inside it was his SIG P224. The suppressor – seven inches long and nearly as big as the gun itself – was not yet unattached.

The cop finished his iced cap and gestured to the backyard of a tiny rancher. 'This your place?'

Oliver didn't answer the man. Instead, he pointed at the floor near the gas pedal. 'That thing yours?'

When the cop glanced down, Oliver drove the man's head forward with as much force as he could muster. The cop's face slammed into the steering wheel and his nose broke with a soft crunching sound. He screamed. Jolted back. Raised his hands in a pathetic display of defence.

Oliver drove his elbow into the man's face and almost knocked him out. Then he pulled him closer, pinned his face down into the seat, and slammed the base of his pistol onto the back of the man's skull – once, twice, three times – until the cop moved no more.

Breathing hard, shaking, exhausted from the moment, Oliver closed his eyes and fought against the soft beckoning call of unconsciousness.

It was done.

It was done . . .

The beginning of the end was here.

One Hundred and Thirty-Six

The drive from Main Street Headquarters back to Striker's house was one of deep thought and consternation. Felicia kept herself busy reading and re-reading the CAD call they had printed out, the reports they'd gathered, and all the history brought up on the numerous police databases. Striker drove on autopilot. Before he knew it, they were stopped behind a marked patrol car outside his house. He sat there and listened to the motor idle. After a while, he killed the engine.

Felicia opened the door. 'Well? You coming in?'

He nodded. Exited the car. Went inside.

Sitting in the den with his feet on the coffee table was Rothschild. He was nestling a Coke.

'Hey,' he said.

Striker sat down in the recliner facing Rothschild. Felicia sat down in the love seat that was angled between the two men. Striker spoke first. 'The Chipotle shooting years ago . . . how many snipers were on that call?'

Rothschild looked taken aback by the question, and he gave it some thought. 'Just one,' he finally said. 'Me.'

'No carbines?'

'Not that I recall.' His eyes took on a faraway stare. 'It's been ten years, man. A long time.'

'I know that. But think hard. Were there any other long guns there? Something that would fire a .223?'

Rothschild was silent a long moment, then answered. 'I don't think so. I mean, we called for one, but I don't think any arrived. Why don't you check the CAD call? Everything should be documented in there.'

'We've checked, Mike. No other long guns are listed.'

'Then what's the problem? Why all the questions?'

'Do you remember Archer Davies?'

Rothschild's face darkened. 'Of course I do. He got injured, went back to England or something. Chipotle shot him.'

'Not Chipotle, Mike. *You.*'

Rothschild's face hardened at the words and his eyes got wide. 'What the hell you talking about, Shipwreck? That's not even funny.'

Striker did not look away. 'I'm being serious here.'

Felicia nodded. 'There's no doubt about it, Mike. The bullet that felled Archer Davies came from your sniper rifle. A .223 round.'

Rothschild froze for a moment, then shook his head in disbelief.

'Not possible,' he said. 'The autopsy—'

'Chad Koda had it doctored,' Striker said. 'He knew what had happened, Mike. He knew it was your bullet that tagged the man. And he covered it up. There's no denying this fact. It was your bullet. You shot him.'

Rothschild's face turned from red to white, and he looked helplessly around the room. 'I . . . I never . . . never knew . . .' He stood up awkwardly, on legs that looked rubbery. He went to place his bottle of Coke on the table, tipped it over, and pop spilled all over the glass surface. Swearing, he grabbed the bottle, stood it up, and walked aimlessly around the room. He stopped by the fireplace mantel. Placed a hand over his stomach. Looked sick.

'It gets worse,' Striker said.

Rothschild looked back with concern. 'What could be worse?'

'Archer was shot in the back, Mike. You need to tell me how that happened.'

Felicia nodded. 'And since the only time his back was towards you was when the team was making entry, that would mean that the bullet was fired *before* the explosives went off. Even before Chipotle started shooting.'

For a moment the words just hung there, and the confused, sick look on Rothschild's face remained. Stunned as he was by the news, he nodded as if he realized what they were getting at – how the situation looked. Like a premeditated cop-on-cop shooting.

'That's *not* how it happened,' he said.

'Then explain it to me,' Striker said. 'Cause I want to believe you here, Mike, I really do. But nothing's adding up.'

Rothschild took the CAD papers from Striker, sorted through them, and then frowned. 'The problem is right here. Page seven. They've listed my position as southeast; fact is, I was *north*.'

'North?' Felicia said.

Rothschild nodded. 'Think of the terrain.'

Striker did, and as the layout developed in his mind, he cursed himself for not seeing it sooner. 'That house is on Blanche Street . . . where the land there slopes down towards the river.'

'And it's steep as hell,' Rothschild replied. 'You *can't* get an elevated eye from the south – only a ground eye.'

'Which would put the squad directly in your sights.'

'Exactly.'

Felicia nodded as she saw it too. 'So you repositioned north. You should have broadcast it.'

'I *did* broadcast it. North was the only option. And it was still bad. The entire side of the rancher was nothing but windows.

And with the midday sun shining down, there was one hell of a gleam. Breaching from that end would have been squad suicide. So they came in from the south, and I did what I could to cover from the north.'

'Sounds like a less than perfect situation,' Striker said.

Rothschild let out a frustrated sound. 'It was a cluster-fuck. A thrown-together squad of reserves. Only Koda and Archer had any experience. The rest of us were just a bunch of novices. When things went bad and Chipotle started firing through the windows, the whole team fell apart. Half of them spun about and raced for cover, and before you knew it, Archer was exposed. The breach went off, and Chipotle was out there firing at everyone . . . it was fuckin' *chaos.*'

As Rothschild spoke the words, his breathing grew deeper, faster.

'I *had* to engage,' he said. 'Otherwise Chipotle would have mowed them all down. So I fired – three, four, five times, I can't remember. I just fired and fired and fired till he stopped shooting, until he went down . . . And then we found out about Archer.' He looked up and now his eyes were watery. 'I thought – we all thought – that Chipotle had gotten him. No one knew it was us . . . that it was *me.*'

'Chad Koda did,' Felicia said. 'Or he found out soon after.'

Striker nodded. 'And so did Oliver Howell. He thinks this was all one giant cover-up. That's why we're all here, Mike . . . Oliver Howell thinks you murdered his father.'

One Hundred and Thirty-Seven

Striker and Felicia left Rothschild and the kids under the protective care of Patrol and headed down Kerrisdale's main drive. Striker needed some time away with Felicia. A place where they could be alone to organize all the jigsaw pieces of this puzzle.

So much, there was so much.

He stopped at the local Starbucks on 41st, the one across from the Bank of Montreal, and purchased a pair of coffees and two pastries. 'Any kind,' he told the clerk. 'Just throw them in the bag.'

Food in hand, he returned to the car.

They drove down to Maple Grove Park and watched the children laughing and giggling and jumping into the public pool. For a brief moment, memories of taking Courtney here returned to Striker – the time she had first learned to swim, the time she had finally gotten the nerve to jump in by herself – and he smiled at those memories.

They calmed his mind.

'We have to go through this one more time,' he finally said to Felicia. 'In detail. So we have it right.'

She agreed. She put down the file she was re-reading, then grabbed her pad of paper and a pen.

'From the beginning,' she said.

Striker nodded. 'Essentially, what we have here are two files that are connected. And sadly, I think it all started with the death of Harry Eckhart's first son.'

'Joshua?'

Striker nodded. 'When the boy died, Harry broke down. He got into financial trouble, did some dumb things – who knows what. But in the end, he needed money, and he needed it bad.'

Felicia nodded. 'And since he was in charge of burning the drugs, he started selling some of them back to the Satan's Prowlers, through Sleeves and Chipotle.'

'Exactly. But the operation got too dangerous to do alone.'

'So he brought in an old friend,' Felicia said.

Striker nodded. 'Chad Koda. Which was a perfect fit because, aside from trusting the man, Koda – through his ex-wife Sharise Owens – connected them to Keisha Williams.'

'And Williams is how Koda got the toy duck.'

Striker held up a finger. 'Williams was killed for more than just her job as the toymaker,' he said. 'Don't forget, she was also a chartered accountant. Her real role here was to move the money.'

'Risky work,' Felicia said. 'She rolled the dice. She lost.'

'Came up snake eyes,' Striker said.

'You think Harry and Koda manipulated her?'

Striker shrugged. 'Who knows how she got involved. But once she started moving that money, it was over for her. She was involved. Culpable.'

Felicia scribbled all this down furiously, using mostly shorthand. 'For all we know, she might have thought it legitimate in the beginning. After all, these were two cops she was dealing with, one of which was living with her cousin. Which also ties in Dr Sharise Owens.'

'Partly,' Striker said. 'But we'll get to her later.'

He picked up some of the paperwork they'd obtained from

the Source Handling Unit, skimmed the pages, and then nodded. 'Next, we have Archer Davies. The man's an ex-soldier from the British Army. He's moved to Canada to start a new life with a new woman. He joined the VPD, and soon had his own source.'

'Carlos Chipotle.'

Striker opened the man's file. 'Yes, Chipotle – a man who quickly finds himself in hot water when the gang catches him double-dipping. He owes the gang money and he can't pay. And these are the Prowlers we're talking about. They don't mess around. So if Chipotle can't come up with the money quick, they'll kill him. And he knows that.'

'And he can't come up with the money.'

Striker nodded. 'So where does he go? To the VPD. To *Archer* – offering information about Harry and Koda's little operation in exchange for protection and indemnity.'

'Big mistake,' Felicia said.

'The biggest. The Prowlers find out. Before you know it, Chipotle's family is blown sky-high by Sleeves and Chipotle's on the run.'

'Which leads to him being grief-stricken, coked-up, and flaunting a machine gun down by the river.'

Striker nodded sadly. 'And Archer ends up getting injured – which is real bad because it looks like Harry and Koda have worked something out to silence him, fearing what Chipotle might have told him.'

'And Archer eventually dies from his wounds.'

Striker heard that and stopped talking. Turned silent for a while. The more he thought it over, the more surreal it all felt. So many links in this nightmare chain. He took a moment to sip his coffee and watch the children frolicking in the pool. Their high-pitched shrieks of joy and excitement. Their laughter.

Their *innocence.*

After a moment, he looked over at Felicia. 'You got all that?'

She read it all over and nodded slowly.

'Yeah,' she replied. 'Make one hell of a novel.'

One Hundred and Thirty-Eight

Oliver needed to discard the dead cop.

He drove slowly along Crown Street, searching for a good dump site. To the east was the sprawling suburbia of the Dunbar area, but to the west was the wilderness of the Pacific Spirit National Park. He pulled up next to a natural hollow that was three feet deep and filled with reeds and further covered by shrouds of bush.

This was the place.

From the cop's tool belt, Oliver took the gun – a SIG Sauer P226 – the radio, the pepper spray, and the handcuffs. He then glanced at the police laptop. On the screen, the small GPS icon flashed in the bottom right-hand corner of the task bar.

He was online.

Oliver immediately undocked the laptop and threw it into the bushes. Then, with his shoulder screaming in pain, he dragged the cop's body out the passenger side of the vehicle and dropped it into the hollow where it was quickly hidden by bush and reed. Someone would find the body, he knew, and probably within days. But so what?

It would all be done by then.

Ten minutes later, after a quick stop at Tim Horton's coffee shop, Oliver made his way towards Striker's house. The smell of the freshly brewed coffee filled the car. Four large cups – double cream, double sugar – sat in a cardboard cup holder on the passenger seat, along with a second tray of chocolate milks, a couple of egg salad sandwiches, and a large box of miscellaneous doughnuts.

He drove down Camosun Street until he saw the undercover police car out front of Striker's house. He pulled over and attached the Black Knight suppressor to the SIG Sauer pistol. Once secure, he laid the pistol on the passenger seat and covered it with the box of doughnuts. Then he pulled up in his marked patrol car, rolled down the window, and smiled.

'Got some coffees,' he said. 'Compliments of the boss man.'

The patrolman in the other car was a dead ringer for Ricky Gervais. He smiled. 'Thank Jesus. I'm falling asleep here and the day's not half over.'

Oliver handed him one of the paper cups. 'I hope I bought enough. All I got was four coffees, plus my own.'

'That's perfect – all we got is four.'

Oliver sipped his own coffee. 'Where's the rest of them?'

The Gervais cop removed the lid from his cup. 'House and lane. Want me to call them?'

Oliver shrugged. 'Tell whoever's inside to come grab theirs. I'll drop the rest off to the mates out back.'

The Gervais cop took out his cell, made the call, and a short moment later, the front door opened. The cop that emerged from the house was tall and thin with long bony arms. He crested the cop cars, then nodded at Oliver. 'You from the odd side?'

Oliver wiped away the sweat from his brow. 'Yeah. Call-out.'

They both nodded.

The cop accepted the coffee and thanked Oliver. When he sat down in the passenger seat, next to the Gervais cop and said, 'Fuck, I hate guard detail,' Oliver acted. He drew his pistol and shot the driver first, then the passenger. Two quick blasts. Both head shots.

Thwip-thwip!

And it was done.

Oliver watched the cop in the passenger seat slump forward against the dashboard. He felt nothing. It was all immaterial now. Just one more road block dealt with on the way home.

He exited the cruiser, climbed on top of the dead cop in the driver's seat, and drove the car thirty feet down the road. He parked out of view, on a side street, and then walked down to Striker's house.

The front door was unlocked.

Inside, watching cartoons in the den, were the two children. The boy – Cody was his name – did not so much as glance back when Oliver entered the room. The Girl – Shana – turned and studied him for a moment. Her eyes fell to his uniform and a relaxed look spread across her face.

Oliver smiled at her. 'Shift change, little ones. Where's your father?'

'What?'

'Your father. Your *dad*.'

'He's out killing bad guys,' the boy said, and he made a pretend gun with his fingers, which he started shooting.

The girl rolled her eyes. 'He went out.'

Out? The word made Oliver's jaws clench. 'When's he getting back?'

'Who knows?' the girl said. 'He never tells us anything.'

Oliver steeled his nerves and refused to allow his emotions to get the better of him. *Evaluate. Act. Reassess.* If Rothschild was not here, he would simply go to Plan B: Why run after Rothschild when he could simply make Rothschild come to him?

Oliver smiled at the children. 'Well, too bad for Dad. Because I brought doughnuts and chocolate milk!'

The boy finally turned away from the TV set. '*Awesome.*'

Even the girl smiled.

Oliver looked at the children and their happy eager faces. He allowed them to dig into the treats he had brought. As they ate, he offered them a wide captivating smile.

'Who wants a ride in the police car?' he asked.

One Hundred and Thirty-Nine

Striker sat in the car, staring at the SIG Sauer, and frowned. This pistol Hal had given him didn't feel right. It didn't have the special order, rubberized grip he was accustomed too. And it was brand new. The slide had barely been broken in. He ejected the magazine and expelled the last round from the chamber.

Felicia sat beside him, finishing the last of the notes she had made on the file. When done, she let out a long breath and looked back at Striker, ready to continue going over their chronological sequence of events.

'So where were we?' she said. She glanced back to the last line. 'Archer is shot in the gunfight – blown up by the breach – and everyone thinks it was Chipotle who tagged him.'

Striker nodded absently as he racked the slide a few times; it needed oil. 'At some point, either during the battle or just after it, Koda figured this out – or at the very least, he suspected it.'

'You think?'

'One hundred per cent. How else does Sharise Owens end up being the surgeon called out? Something had to happen there.' He removed the slide from the base of the pistol and put it on the dashboard. 'Besides, it makes sense from Harry and Koda's standpoint. Think about it – Koda's in charge of this whole botched takedown, and because he and Harry are already worried about being investigated for the trafficking operation, the *last* thing they want is more heat coming their way for a cop-on-cop shooting . . . this slide needs oil.'

'I got some in my bag – hold on.' Felicia went to the trunk and returned with some gun oil and a clean rag. She handed it to Striker. 'So Harry and Koda get Owens to doctor the report.'

Striker oiled the rail guides as he spoke. 'You can see why – the shooting was an *accident.* As far as Harry and Koda were concerned, it was a good choice of action: Archer would be taken care of. Rothschild would get a commendation. And a public investigation into a cop-on-cop shooting would never occur. So they got Owens to alter the report. Just a few amendments here and there . . . but ones that changed everything.'

'But she made mistakes.'

Striker nodded. 'Not destroying her original tapes was one of them. She may have been an excellent doctor, but she wasn't used to being a cover-up artist. And she screwed up in the written report as well – she changed the locations of the entrance and exit wounds, but she didn't change the wound sizes. That discrepancy alone proves that the entrance and exit locations were reversed.'

Striker looked up and saw Felicia grinning at him.

'What?' he asked.

'Everything's connected. Except for one thing – we know *why* Oliver and Molly Howell did this, but we don't know *how* they found out.'

'Actually we do,' Striker said. 'They can request any report we have – so long as it hasn't been stolen or misplaced or destroyed.'

'Through the Freedom of Information Act.'

Striker nodded. 'Exactly. Well, Oliver got them. And when he compared the police reports, the medical reports, and the medical tapes, he realized pretty quickly the same things we did – that everything didn't mesh.' Striker grabbed the slide and re-attached it to the base of the pistol. 'From there on, everything snowballed.'

Felicia took back the gun oil. 'So when Oliver kidnapped Sharise Owens down by the river, it wasn't so much about torture as it was about information.'

Striker agreed. 'It was an interrogation session – to corroborate what he already suspected. And what she told him only reinforced his belief that this was one massive cover-up.' Striker racked the slide a few more times to get the oil moving.

Felicia went quiet for a long moment as Striker continued to rack the slide.

'But why Osaka?' she finally asked.

Striker stopped playing with the slide. 'He was the Internal Investigator in charge of the shooting.' Striker frowned. 'Fact is, Archer was shot by one of our own men. And mistake or not, Osaka dropped the ball on that file. There were reasons for the mistake – this was at a time when Osaka was already dealing with the Stanley Park Six incident. The man was *swamped.*'

'Stanley Park – what a hell file that was.'

Striker nodded. 'The worst. But Osaka did an excellent job on it. And as a result, four months later, he got promoted – and not just to sergeant, he jumped *two ranks* to inspector. You know, that was only the second time in the department's history that anyone has ever jumped two ranks.' Striker grabbed the pistol one more time and starting doing a function test to be sure it wouldn't misfire in a time of need.

Felicia looked at him. 'You're not implying that Osaka dropped Archer's file in order to get promoted, are you?'

Striker shook his head. 'God, no. Osaka was a man of the highest integrity. I don't think he had any idea that Archer was shot by one of our own guys. I mean they had a coked-up biker with an AK-47 shooting at them. Archer got hit. It all seemed pretty straightforward.'

'But Oliver thought the shooting was intentional.'

Striker nodded. 'He still does. He thinks the squad murdered his father. He also thinks the department knew about this and covered it up to avoid public embarrassment. And he thinks that Rothschild was the worst of the lot because he was the man who pulled the trigger.'

Felicia continued writing down the information. After a long moment, she put down the pen, shook out her fingers, and scanned through the six pages of notes. She blinked as if relieved and horrified all at once.

'It all fits,' she said.

'It does.'

'You don't seem overly happy about it.'

Striker reloaded the magazine with bullets and frowned. 'Why should I be? So many people have died over this file – and I've got a really bad feeling about what's ahead.'

'How so?'

'Oliver Howell is a soldier, Feleesh. He's been through hell. He's seen war. And now he's on a personal vendetta.' Striker loaded the magazine into the pistol, held it with two hands, and looked down the sights.

They were good.

Felicia looked at him with concern. 'You're worried he won't go down without a fight.'

Striker nodded slowly.

'It's a suicide mission,' he said sadly. 'It has been from the start.'

One Hundred and Forty

The sun beat down upon the graveyard, turning the green grass a dying yellow-brown colour and bleaching the tombstones white. Despite the brightness, the sweltering heat of the past week had suddenly evaporated and the air was oddly cool. When the wind hit Harry, he shivered.

In the northeast section, under the tall overhang of a dogwood tree, was the grave of his little boy – Joshua William Eckhart. The Boy Who Had Died.

Harry stood at the foot of the grave.

He had been standing there for a long time now. How long, he had no idea. But long enough that the joints of his knees ached. So far, all he'd done was stand there. Stand there and do nothing, say nothing, think nothing. He just listened to the cool wind ruffle the white flowers of the dogwood trees, like it was the ghost of his boy trying to tell him something.

The headstone had Joshua's name on it with the words 'Beloved Son' beneath. It was surrounded by four sculptured angels. Each one faced a different direction – north, south, east and west – and each one brandished a sword.

The stone-and-granite artwork had been demanded by Kelly, Harry's wife at the time – as if spending vast amounts of money they didn't have would somehow diminish the grief and culpability they both felt.

Harry had given her everything she needed back then. And it had been a mistake. The money they spent had done nothing to assuage their loss. All it did was put them another twenty-eight thousand dollars into debt, and start the ball rolling on what had been their financial doom.

By the time everything was done – the funeral, the procession, the headstone, the flowers and the videos, and all the extra medical bills – Harry had found himself owing almost a hundred grand. With Kelly not working and barely communicating in her stark depression, there had been no hope of paying off the debt. At the time, Harry really hadn't cared. All he'd known was a grief so overwhelming that suicide had been a daily thought.

It had been a dark time. Such a dark time.

Kind of like now.

He blinked, coming out of the sad reverie, and almost immediately the tears slipped from his eyes. He would have traded his life for Josh's a thousand times over. Put a bullet through his own head, killed another person – hell, he would have done damn near anything to have him back.

'I love you,' he said. 'I love you *so much*.'

Harry started to shake because he knew now what he had to do. For his other son. For Ethan. The Boy Who Still Lived. And that meant he would probably never be back here again.

This was the final goodbye.

Harry wiped his eyes. He knelt down. He kissed the headstone. And then he got up and left the graveyard.

He never looked back.

One Hundred and Forty-One

It was exactly twelve-thirty, and Striker and Felicia had just grabbed a couple of green apple & cheddar sandwiches from the Kit's Coffee House on Broadway. He sat back in one of the outdoor patio chairs, unwrapped the cellophane and took a bite. The flavours were odd but good, and as he swallowed, his cell rang. He looked down at the screen and saw Rothschild's name.

He answered. 'What's up, Mike?'

'They're gone, they're fucking gone, *he took my kids*!'

Striker's throat clenched and the world around him ceased to exist. He dropped the sandwich and jumped to his feet.

'Where are you?'

'Your house. My kids, Striker – he's got my fucking kids!'

'Just calm down, Mike, calm down. How do you know—'

'I went out for a smoke. Ten minutes – just ten fucking minutes.'

Striker tried to keep his voice steady. 'Mike, listen to me. There's a patrol cop out front. Go out there and talk to—'

'The car's down the road . . . they're dead, the cops are dead, they're all fucking dead!'

Striker's blood turned ice cold. 'Call it in.'

'*No!*' Rothschild screamed. 'Do *not* call it in.'

'Mike, you have to—'

'He'll kill them, he said he'll kill them.'

'You talked to him?'

'He called, he fucking *called*.'

Striker felt the world collapsing all around him, and suddenly he was racing back to the cruiser with Felicia running after him. 'Don't move, Mike – we're coming right now!'

But the line was already dead.

One Hundred and Forty-Two

With Felicia providing cover, Striker raced up the steps of his porch, kicked open the front door, and moved inside.

Too late. The house was empty.

Rothschild and the children were gone.

'We have to call this in,' Felicia said. Her voice was unusually high and tremor-filled.

'Just give me a goddam second,' Striker said.

He stood in the horrible stillness of the den and fought not to grip his gun too tightly. Behind him, the sound of Felicia's heavy gasps filled the room, broken by only the deep steady tocks of the grandfather clock – each one a reminder that precious seconds were being lost.

Striker paced the room, tried to think.

In here. In my house . . .

He took the children from my own house . . .

He stopped pacing, scanned his surroundings, looked for any evidence left behind. When he saw nothing, he walked back outside and looked there. On the welcome mat, trapped in the rough wool-like tendrils, was another dusting of that same whitish powdery substance he had seen in the mud by the docks and again on the window ledge at Rothschild's former home.

Striker knelt down, studied it.

Once again, it looked like concrete. But *greyer*. With tiny bits of white in it. He reached down, picked some of it up, rubbed it between his fingers. It looked and felt like nothing more than dirt and dust.

He took out his cell phone and called Noodles.

'Did you get an answer yet – from the lab?'

The man was lost. 'Huh? On what?'

'That goddam white substance!'

'The powder, oh yeah, we got the results.'

'Well, why the hell didn't you call then?'

'Because it was *nothing*.' Noodles made an exasperated sound. 'Jesus Christ, Shipwreck, it's just fucking dust. *Dust*. That's it. What the hell is up your ass today?'

'It's not like any dust I've ever seen before. What else did they tell you?'

'Nothing, that's it – just dust.'

Striker hung up on Noodles and dialled the lab himself. Being Saturday, they were still open, but the technician who had done the actual testing was not available. Striker managed to get hold of the head boss. He explained the direness of the situation, and within sixty seconds, received a phone call back from the primary technician. The woman seemed perplexed by the severity of the situation.

'It was just ordinary dust,' she explained.

'Then why the strange white-grey colour?'

'Well, that's because it's been exposed to quite a high heat, and for a long time, I would say – it's all in the report we forwarded yesterday.'

'We don't have that report yet,' Striker said. 'And minutes are critical. Now what kind of heat and what kind of times?'

The woman made an uncomfortable sound. 'That, I can't really tell you with any certainty. But it would have to be *quite* hot.'

'How hot? Like as hot as a foundry or something like that?'

'I wouldn't think so. Some of those foundries can reach sixteen hundred degrees Celsius. That would be *exceedingly* hot. Plus, you would then find contaminants within the dust – bronze or magnesium, copper or tin, steel or—'

'I get it,' Striker said. 'Then where?'

The tech made a frustrated sound. 'Well, *any* factory setting where industrial machines are hard at work, especially ones that have boilers or an ongoing distillation process – oil refineries; garbage incinerators; recycling plants; heck, even some food processing plants. The list is really endless.'

Striker felt his hopes deflating, felt the seconds ticking away. 'I'll call you back – stay by the phone.' He hung up and turned to Felicia. 'Location-wise, if you had to make a guess, where would you think this guy would be hiding out?'

'Geographically speaking?' She turned silent for a moment. 'It would have to be somewhere relatively close by. He's hurt. He's got two little kids with him. And his sole focus lies here in Vancouver.'

Striker nodded. 'I agree completely.'

Felicia flipped back through her notebook pages. 'That Alpha unit had a white van take off on them just ten minutes after the Osaka bombing, remember? It was racing west on Southwest Marine Drive. From Collingwood Street.'

Striker mapped out the area in his head. 'There's nothing west of there but the Shaughnessy Golf Club, the Musqueam Reserve, and the university grounds. After that, it's all ocean.'

'And I don't recall there being any factories on the reserve,' Felicia said. 'Same thing goes for the golf club.'

Striker nodded. 'But there are some on the university grounds.'

Felicia continued flipping back through her notes. 'And wasn't that the way the bomber fled from Rothschild's house?

On Thursday morning? He ran into Pacific Spirit – that park is how big?'

'Seven hundred acres,' Striker said. 'And he did so without a getaway vehicle.'

'So either he hid in the woods and waited us out – which seems highly unlikely given that we had police dogs tracking him – or . . .'

'He's hiding out somewhere on the university grounds.'

Striker grabbed the laptop and used Google to bring up a map of the University of British Columbia. He scanned the grounds for any possible locations where Oliver might be hiding. By the time he was done, he had narrowed it down to three possible areas – the Food Systems buildings, the Applied Sciences grounds, or the UBC Hospital. Each one of them had numerous boilers and areas of constant high heat temperatures.

He called back the technician. She answered on the first ring and Striker didn't even say hello. 'The university hospital, the Food Systems, or the Applied Sciences buildings – do any of those match?'

Her response was defeating. 'There would be contaminants,' she explained. 'Especially in the dust from the Applied Sciences buildings and the hospital. As for the Food Systems, that would depend on where the dust came from – it's quite a big facility.' She turned silent for a moment as she thought it over. 'Then again, because of the type of machinery involved and the health regulations required, I can't see the dust coming from there either.'

Striker ground his teeth. There was also the issue of the heat being *constant.* He closed his eyes. Struggled to calm his thoughts. He felt like an overheated boiler, ready to explode from the growing pressure.

A boiler . . .

And then he realized where.

He snapped his eyes back to the map of the university grounds, but did not see what he was looking for. No icons, no writing.

But it was there. He knew it. That one place out west, on the university grounds, where heat was a constant factor. Where no one would ever find Oliver. And where the dust he tracked would have no telltale impurities within it.

A place where it was *always* hot and humid. A place where the pipes could reach a hundred and eight degrees Celsius.

He stood up and met Felicia's stare.

'He's in the steam tunnels.'

One Hundred and Forty-Three

Harry drove towards the southwest section of Vancouver. The more he thought about his situation, the more he realized there was but one way out. In order for his family to have any hope of a peaceful future, it was going to require a violent present.

When he reached the Marpole district, the GPS icon on his tracking display was a steady red colour. It told him that Striker and Felicia were in the 4400 block of Camosun Street. Just across from St Patrick's High School. They were stationary.

By the time Harry had reached 41st Avenue and started westward, the icon was flashing.

Striker and Felicia were on the move.

He pulled over for a moment and watched the red icon move past the school and down Imperial Drive. Soon the car was racing west, out towards the university grounds, at speeds of one hundred and forty K.

Three times the speed limit.

Harry watched the icon race into the centre of the campus and stop in the middle of the Thunderbird thoroughfare. Speed equalled zero. He sat there anxiously, waiting for them to move again; when they did not, he put the car in Drive and headed for UBC.

Something important was happening.

One Hundred and Forty-Four

The steam tunnels of UBC had long been a place of urban legend among the campus populace. Tales of students making it into the secret entrance were abundant, as were the horror stories of those who had entered and never come out again. Some writings even claimed that there was a serial killer lurking below the streets.

Most of it was gobbledygook, but the fact was the tunnels *did* exist. The University of British Columbia, being one of the few remaining steam networks left in North America, still used the terribly inefficient system to pipe in heat from the steam plant to all the old dorm buildings and the administrative offices the university owned.

For anyone who had access to Google – and the knowledge of where to look – the main entrance was no secret.

While Striker waited for UBC maintenance staff to answer his call, Felicia found the information they needed on the Internet. She lowered her phone and stopped walking down Thunderbird Avenue. She turned to talk to him.

'Okay, there's a few entrances,' she said. 'Three are somewhat hidden and off the track, but the main one is just ahead.' She pointed to what appeared to be a rather large manhole cover that sat less than twenty feet off the main drive, in a square recess of concrete. 'That's it right there.'

Striker grabbed a tyre iron from the cruiser and neared the

manhole. He looked down. The lid was seated properly, fitting snugly into its receptacle, and there were no signs of tampering. He jammed the tyre iron in between the rim of the cover and the manhole receptacle and applied some pressure. The round plate of steel gave a little and, seconds later, lifted altogether.

Striker removed it.

'This is it,' he said. 'Where they went.'

'There are other entry points,' Felicia started, but Striker cut her off.

'No. You don't understand. These covers are normally *locked.* We should never have even been able to get in here . . . Someone went in before us, and it sure as hell wasn't a maintenance man.'

Felicia looked into the hole. Everything below was a sea of darkness. 'Maybe we should call in the Emergency Response Team.'

Striker shook his head. 'They show up and this entire thing is over.'

'He might have *bombs* down there, Jacob.'

'Might nothing – you can damn well bet on it. And he'll set them off the moment he sees ERT.' Striker drew his pistol and double-checked that the magazine was secure. 'I'll go in alone.'

'Don't be an ass.' Felicia drew her own piece.

Striker didn't respond. He just swung his leg into the hole, stepped on the first rung of the ladder, and climbed down into the murky darkness below. Seconds later, Felicia followed him.

They were in.

One Hundred and Forty-Five

Having no access to night-vision goggles, Striker and Felicia were left peering through a crimson darkness. The underground was a series of long cement tubes, running north and south and east from their location. All along the top of the tunnels, a series of red lights dimly illuminated the way.

Striker took out his flashlight and shone it in all three directions. Within twenty feet, the way south led to a gated door that was locked. That left them with two options. He shone his flashlight on the ground, scanning the area for footprints in the dust. As he did so, Felicia let out an excited sound.

'Look here,' she said.

Striker did. Mounted on the wall was a strange-looking sensor, obviously new. It was blinking every so often – a deep red light.

'What the hell is that?' he said.

'Looks like part of a relay system,' Felicia said. She looked down the tunnel and then above them. 'We're underground and this is thick cement. Oliver probably can't get a signal down here without one. He'd need it for any type of radio communications or Internet devices.'

'Or to trigger a bomb,' Striker said.

He looked around further.

On the side of the wall, running down the entire stretch of tunnel, were two large red pipes and two large blue pipes. They were *hot* – Striker could feel heat radiating off them – and they were covered in a thin film of dust. In the dimness of the tunnel, it was difficult to tell if it was the same kind of dust found at the crime scenes, but as Striker analysed it, something else caught his eye.

A long scratch mark ran down the entire length of pipe. It had been ground right into the red paint and gave off a silver gleam from the metal below.

'Check it out. Looks fresh. Rothschild's police knife maybe.'

Felicia noticed the scratch. 'Or Oliver leading the way. Believe me, he knows we're coming, Jacob.'

'I know that. But what choice do we have?'

Striker began following the scratch down the eastern tunnel. Within thirty feet, the passage angled left, then after another ten feet, left again. Before Striker knew it, he had no idea which way they were heading. The place was a giant underground labyrinth, and it was getting progressively hotter with every step. When they turned another corner, Striker lost his balance and put out his hand. It touched the red pipe next to them, and he pulled it away fast.

'Fucking *hot*,' he said.

Felicia said nothing; she just listened. There was a rushing sound in the tunnel. A soft but constant rumble.

'That's the steam in the pipes,' she said. 'You can imagine the pressure.'

Striker looked at the pipes for a long moment. 'If Oliver sets off a bomb down here, we're gonna be like lobsters in a pot.' He took out his cell phone and tried to get a signal. When it failed, he cursed. 'I thought he had relays down here?'

Felicia just shrugged like she had no idea.

Striker turned to face her. 'You have to go back.'

'What?' She gave him a stunned look. 'Without you? No way.'

'There's no choice. If Oliver blows us up down here, we'll cook to death, Feleesh. You, me, Rothschild – the kids. You got to get that steam turned off, and as fast as you can.'

'But—'

'There's no choice. We're out of time.'

Felicia said nothing for a moment. She swore, then gave him a quick hug and a kiss.

'Be careful,' she said. 'I'll be back as fast as I can.'

Then she turned and hurried back down the tunnel.

Striker watched her turn the bend and disappear from sight. Alone and sweating from the growing heat, he tightened his grip on the SIG and headed deeper into the crimson darkness of the tunnel.

One Hundred and Forty-Six

Five minutes later, Striker hiked down a long sloping corridor. As he went, he passed by a couple of iron-barred gates that owned locks so old they appeared rusted. The heat and humidity grew, and so did the darkness. When he turned the bend, there were no more red lights overhead.

Everything was pitch-black.

He stopped. Took one cautious step forward. And suddenly a series of red lasers shot all over the tunnel – red crimson beams slicing through the blackness. Striker's first thought was of the laser tripwires he'd triggered in the sewer systems behind the A&W parking lot.

They're just laser trips, he recalled the bomb expert saying.

But were they now? And were they designed to stop someone from entering the room – or to prevent them from leaving? At the very least they would slow down someone's escape.

He aimed his flashlight down the pathway, scanning the floor for tripwires or pressure pads. When he saw none, he slowly, cautiously, made his way down the corridor, stepping over and ducking under each crimson beam in his path.

Beside him, the sound of the steam-pressurized pipes grew louder, moaning like a trapped beast desperate to break free. The heat coming off them was immense.

Thoughts of Oliver setting off a bomb in the tunnels brought a sick feeling to Striker's stomach. With the combination of darkness, locked doors, laser tripwires, and the never-ending maze, escape from the steam tunnels would be impossible.

Striker cut a final corner and found himself facing a steel door. There, he paused, unsure of what to do. Opening it could not only warn Oliver that he was coming, but trigger a detonation.

Yet what choice did he have?

He reached out and placed his flashlight hand against the steel. Then he readied his pistol and gently pushed open the door. What he saw caused his heart to constrict.

He was standing at the entrance to a control room. Everything was tinted dark red from the overhead lights, and the air was so hot it was suffocating. To his far left, slumped with his back to the concrete wall, was Mike Rothschild. His hands were cuffed to a large steel pipe and blood trickled down the left side of his skull.

His head hung low, his eyes were dazed.

To Striker's far right was another closed door. Steel, with a deadbolt across the facing. It looked heavy. Across the front was one word:

Maintenance.

'Welcome to the command room,' a weary voice said.

Striker turned and looked directly across the room. There, half in the shadows, was Oliver Howell. The man sat on a long steel table, next to a static-filled television monitor and what looked like a green-lighted router. He was wearing a policeman's uniform, complete with a radio, gun and flashlight – but where his bulletproof vest should have been, Oliver had made some modifications. Strapped across his chest were not Kevlar and trauma plates, but long cylindrical columns.

Explosives.

Striker counted six on the front alone.

'Oliver—' Striker started.

'Finally, we're all here.' Oliver spoke the words softly, weakly. He looked over at Rothschild. 'The man who murdered my father' – he looked back at Striker – 'and the man who murdered my sister.'

'I murdered no one.'

Oliver made no reply. He just sat there, the slick flesh of his face looking like broken-in red leather in the strange tint of the safety lights. Striker deftly scanned the man up and down. Oliver's right fist was closed tight. In it was a small rectangular clip of some kind.

A detonator.

Oliver caught his stare.

'It's a pressure release,' he explained. 'Just like the ones I used to disarm in the Green Zone . . . though I gave this one a ten-second delay.' He smiled weakly. 'Just enough time to let you think about what you did before it goes off and we're all bathed in blistering hot steam.'

'Where are the children?' Striker asked.

But Oliver only smiled. He opened his arms wide, and the exertion made his arms and shoulders tremble. 'Go ahead, Detective. Take your shot. All it takes is one single trigger pull – and then we can end this. Redemption for all.'

One Hundred and Forty-Seven

Striker did not react.

Time . . .

He needed to give Felicia time . . .

He stood there in the entrance to the control room and took in all of his surroundings. In the far corner of the room sat an opened crate. Inside it were supplies, most of which appeared to be technological gear and ammunitions. Next to it sat a small red cooler that had a medical emblem on the front. At the right end of the room was the closed steel door:

Maintenance.

Striker studied it and thought of Cody and Shana.

He turned back to Howell and met the man's stare. 'Are the children in there?' When the bomber said nothing, Striker added, 'They're not a part of this, they've done nothing wrong.'

'Nothing wrong?' Oliver laughed oddly. 'What *wrong* did my father do?'

Striker looked back at the man. 'Your father did nothing wrong. We both know that. You, on the other hand, have committed murder.'

'Retribution—'

'*Murder*, Oliver. Because what you think happened is all wrong.' Striker took a small slow step into the room, and Oliver's fingers tightened on the release pad. 'I know it all,' Striker continued.

'You think the Emergency Response Team betrayed your father. That Koda was the lead, and Rothschild was the shooter. You think Archer was shot in the back and blown up in the process, and you also think that Osaka covered up the shooting.'

Oliver's eyes narrowed at the words, but he said nothing.

Striker continued:

'You think that Dr Owens falsified her reports to hide the murder and that her cousin, Keisha Williams, was money-laundering the funds. And you believe that *everyone* is culpable, no matter how small or indirect their role in this mess.'

Still, Oliver said nothing.

'I also know you derived this belief from inconsistencies in the police and medical reports, along with the audio tapes.' Striker edged his way a little closer to the maintenance door. 'That's why you kidnapped Dr Owens – not to torture her, but to interrogate her. To corroborate what you already believed. And you think you got that from her.'

Oliver's expression remained unreadable. After a short moment, he nodded slowly. 'You're good at your job, Detective.'

'Better than you. I found the *truth*.'

A quick burst of anger flashed through Oliver's eyes. 'I know the truth.'

'You know nothing.' Striker took another step closer to the maintenance door. 'The fact is, you're right *and* you're wrong.'

Oliver's expression communicated nothing.

'Koda did cover up the shooting,' Striker said. 'And Owens did falsify the report . . . but that's as far as it goes. When your father was shot, Oliver, it wasn't because everyone betrayed him. It was because the entire scene down there was chaos. Rothschild didn't purposely shoot Archer in the back, it was an *accident*.'

For the first time, Oliver smiled. And he did so darkly. 'Do you take me for a fool, Detective?'

Striker met the man's stare. 'I take you for nothing. I don't have to – the evidence speaks for itself.'

'What evidence?'

Striker edged a little closer to the maintenance door. 'During that call, Rothschild had to reposition. He moved from a south to north position. He had to – because of the downward slope of the river. Otherwise he'd be shooting from a level position, lighting up his men instead of covering them.'

The dark look on Oliver's face turned from one of anger to cold suspicion, but he remained silent.

'You're a military man,' Striker said. 'You have a hundred times more experience than I do. *Wartime* experience. So you tell me: does that make sense to you?'

Oliver let out a long breath, wiped away the sweat from his brow. 'I've seen the radio reports.'

'I know you have. You got printed-up copies of the entire CAD call. But you didn't actually pull the *tapes*, did you? I know you didn't. Know why? Because *I did.* And the tapes don't match the call – just like the medical tapes don't match the written report.'

'The CAD call—'

'CAD calls are typed out by Dispatchers on the fly, Oliver. People miss things, they make mistakes. If you had taken the time to listen to the actual tapes, you would have heard Rothschild repositioning.'

Oliver's face took on a blank look, then it tightened.

'Liar,' he said.

Striker shook his head. 'No. I'm not. It was a rookie squad, Oliver. A bunch of novices thrown together at a moment's notice. When Chipotle started shooting, the men just panicked – all of them except your father, which doesn't surprise me because he was the only one who had seen wartime action.

Archer only turned to run when he realized he'd lost the entire squad. And that's when Rothschild tried to take out Chipotle. The bullet went through the living room window, north side, and exited out the south side through the dining room. It struck your father as he ran for cover. That's how he got hit in the back, Oliver. That's how the breach went off.'

'*Liar*,' he said again.

'It was an accident.'

Oliver's face tightened. 'It's fucking *bollocks*.'

But Striker only shook his head solemnly. 'Same goes for Osaka. His investigation was dropped only because he didn't have enough evidence. Why? Because Koda wrote the police reports and Owens doctored the medical reports. There was no cover-up on his part. He was just overburdened with work and the shooting looked straightforward.' Striker reached the maintenance door. 'You murdered an innocent man.'

Oliver's entire body began to tremble. '*Lies*.'

'It's true. Your father's shooting and the subsequent explosion was nothing more than a horrible accident in a chaotic gun battle. Osaka, Koda, Owens, Williams, the cops back at my house, even your sister's death . . . it's all been for nothing. You were wrong.'

'*LIES!*' Oliver roared.

Striker stopped talking and took a long look at the man. The flesh of his face had turned a purplish-red colour now and spit bubbles formed on his lips. Beads of sweat covered his face and neck regions, and his eyes were large and wild and glaring.

'Where are the children, Oliver?'

His stare was faraway, his voice quiet. 'It's not true.'

'They have no mother. She died just months ago.'

'. . . not fucking true.'

'Their father is all they have left.'

'. . . not true . . .'

'Oliver,' Striker said. '*Oliver*.'

But the man was no longer listening. He was zoning out now. Fading. And his posture was sagging, his entire body leaning to the left. Striker focused on the man's hands. They were trembling, weakening, slowly loosening on the pressure-release plate of the detonator.

'Oliver,' Striker said again. 'OLIVER!'

But it was no use. He was losing him.

One Hundred and Forty-Eight

Oliver heard his name being called, but the words seemed small – so distant that they were not only miles away but in another plane of existence. He was fading, he knew. He could feel it. Slipping away to that faraway place where he and Molly were kids again, where Mother was baking scones and Father was healthy and strong and alive.

'Oliver! Focus on me, Oliver!'

So hot . . . he was so goddam hot.

And so cold too.

Light. Swelling. Floating.

Recollections hit him. Memories slowly untangling in time:

Father was spinning him round in the air, giving him an airplane ride.

Then Father was leaving. Standing at the car. And he was sobbing, peeking out between the drapes, saying, 'Don't go, Daddy, don't go.'

Then he was off to war.

And Mother was crying, not wanting him to go.

His men were dying all around him – chunks of flesh being punched from their bodies by the AK47 fire.

And the helicopter was dropping down – the loud whup-whup-whup of the blades sounding like angry thunder . . .

Oliver looked up. Blinked. Let out a small laugh.

The memories made sense, the timeline was in order. And for the first time in as long as he could remember, his head felt clear. Like the clouds of confusion had finally dissipated.

He looked up at Striker oddly. 'Do you believe, Detective?'

The question seemed to surprise the big cop. 'Believe? You mean, in *God*?'

'In God. In flesh and spirit.'

'I believe there's *something* there, yes.'

Oliver smiled sadly. 'How fortunate for you. The feeling must be nice.' When Striker offered no other words, Oliver continued. 'You know what I believe in, Detective? I believe in *Semtex*. I believe in fuse kits. And copper jacket rounds.'

'Oliver—'

'I believe in dust and bones.'

'There's still a way out of this, Oliver. A way to make things right.'

But Oliver shook his head. 'You're a good man, Detective. I can see that now. I'm glad I never killed you . . . But you're wrong about everything.'

'Oliver—'

'You're *wrong*.'

One Hundred and Forty-Nine

Striker studied the man sitting on the table across the room from him. Oliver was fading now. Spitting out gibberish. Swaying. Sagging. Ready to collapse.

Striker looked at the detonator in his hand.

Too far.

It was *too far.*

He tried to rouse the man: 'The children, Oliver – where are the children?'

But Oliver offered no answer.

To Striker's left, Rothschild let out a moan, and a grating sound filled the room as his handcuffs slid against the steel pipe. Striker turned his eyes from Rothschild to the steel maintenance door, then back to the pressure-release in Oliver's hand. If he could reach Oliver in time, he could grab the man's hands and maintain the pressure . . . but there was thirty feet of distance between the men.

A lot of ground to cover.

Striker watched Oliver swaying on the table. When the man closed his eyes, Striker edged closer.

'I got him!' a voice suddenly said.

Striker was startled by the sound; he looked back towards the entrance of the room and saw Harry. Even in the strange red hue of the command room, it was obvious that the man's face was tight. His gun was drawn – aimed at Oliver.

'*I got him*,' he said again.

'Harry, no, he's holding a detonator—'

But it was too late.

The gun fired. Two loud explosions thundered through the room and the left side of Oliver's chest burst open. He jerked, lilted, rolled off the steel table and landed on the ground. Even as he fell, Striker raced towards him. Reached out for the pressure-release pad. But there was too much distance to cover.

The detonator had been released.

One Hundred and Fifty

Ten seconds. It was all they had.

A dozen thoughts raced through Striker's mind: the amount of explosives strapped to Oliver's chest; the hot steam powering through the steel pipes around them; the tripwires set up in the tunnels beyond; Rothschild handcuffed to the pipes beside him; and the children – where were the children?

He grabbed the steel maintenance door. Slid open the latch.

Nine seconds.

Yanked open the door and felt his heart drop.

No children inside.

Just supply boxes. Stacks of pipes. Some chairs. A panel of levers at the end.

Eight seconds.

Striker spun around, raced back into the room.

Seven.

Rothschild was conscious now, screaming: 'My kids – find my kids, Striker! Get my kids out of here!'

Six.

Striker ran over to Oliver. Grabbed him roughly. And suddenly Harry was there beside him.

Five.

They dragged the dead bomber into the maintenance room.

Four.

Dumped him behind the column of supply boxes and steel pipes.

Three.

Leaped from the room. Slammed the door behind them. Slid the latch.

Two.

They grabbed the steel table. Flipped it over.

One.

Yanked the table in front of Rothschild. Started to drop down behind it.

Zero.

The bomb went off – a vicious explosion raged through the room, sounding like a locomotive powering through a mountain tunnel. One moment, Striker could see and hear and think; the next there was only darkness and deafness and the air around them was wet and humid and suffocatingly hot.

The pipes, he thought. *The steam . . .*

It was hissing all around them now.

They were going to cook to death.

One Hundred and Fifty-One

Hot. He was so unbelievably hot.

He was burning up. Couldn't breathe. And there was blood. He could taste blood. In his mouth, in his throat. And the ringing in his ears was painful – a strange high-pitched whine.

Striker opened his eyes. Saw nothing but darkness.

Closed them again.

When he re-opened them sometime later, white lights were flashing. Hazy beams pierced through the mixture of mist and dust like light-sabres through smoke. The illumination came from the far end of the room, along with voices so soft and distant he could barely hear them.

'*Jacob*,' they sang. '. . . *Jacob*.'

Angels, calling his name.

'. . . the children,' he tried to say. '. . . find the children . . .'

But nothing would come out.

He felt hands take hold of him. Many hands. And suddenly he was suspended in the air. Floating, flying, his entire body lifting from the ground. He thought of Felicia, thought of Courtney, and how he needed to stay with them. But when the darkness came, fighting it was as useless as trying to stop time. It swallowed him whole, a tidal wave of warmth and blackness. And Striker felt himself go. He was fading into the nothingness now.

Dying.
Becoming dust and bones.
Just like Oliver . . .
Just like Oliver.

EPILOGUE

One

It was almost a full week later when Striker walked down the back alley of Trafalgar Street with a box of doughnuts and muffins in one hand and balancing two large coffees in the other – Timmy's mediums, double-double.

Cops' blend.

The sweltering heat wave had slowly soothed out into a softer, gentler balminess, and the soft blue colour of the sky made the mid-morning air feel fresher and brisker than it had been in a long while.

Striker relished the moment – it felt so good to be outdoors. Ever since he had been trapped in the dark depths of the steam tunnels, confined areas bothered him. He'd even been avoiding elevator booths. And the thought of it made him chuckle with self-admonishing thoughts:

I'm turning into Felicia.

He spotted Rothschild's house. As he neared, he heard the kids playing in the yard, and it filled him with a thankfulness he couldn't explain. There was a certain grace about children's laughter. Especially now, after he had been so terribly close to losing them.

He listened to Cody yell out, 'Don't touch that, it's *mine*!' and smiled. He stood there, behind the fence, eavesdropping on their conversation, and he knew if he stayed much longer he'd choke up. So he got his feet moving again.

Up ahead the garage door was open. Inside, the hood of the Cougar was up and there were chrome car parts lined up all along the work bench. Rothschild was leaning over the engine, looking down and pretending he had even a modicum of mechanical skill. When Striker was close enough, Rothschild spotted him and nodded.

'Hey,' he said.

Striker stepped inside the garage. It smelled of oil and kitty litter and solvent. He looked out the window at the children playing, yelled out *'Doughnuts!'* and Cody and Shana came running from the yard.

'Hi, Uncle Jacob!' Shana said.

Cody was too fixated on the box of treats to speak.

Striker passed the coffees to Rothschild and opened the box. The children overlooked the muffins and went straight for the doughnuts – a Boston Cream for Cody and some god-awful sprinkle mess for Shana. Treats in hand, they bounded off for the backyard again, and Striker thought of how long it had been since Courtney was that age.

It seemed a lifetime ago, and he missed it.

'Thanks for the brew,' Rothschild said. He opened up the lid and sipped some.

Striker nodded. 'I needed it today.'

'No sleep?'

He nodded. 'Not a bit – you been getting any ringing in your ears? It's been coming and going for me ever since the explosion.'

Rothschild snorted. 'Naw. No ringing. Just a new-found sense of claustrophobia. I can't even work on the car with the garage door closed.'

Striker laughed because he fully understood the feeling. 'When you going back to work?'

Rothschild looked out the garage door at the clear blue skyline. 'I dunno. Maybe never.'

At first Striker thought the man was joking, but upon closer inspection he could see the seriousness on Rothschild's face. All that had happened the previous week had taken a toll on the man. That much was clear.

'You just need some time is all.'

Rothschild looked back at him. 'I don't think so. Not this time.' He crossed the garage and again approached the window where he stared at Cody and Shana in the backyard. 'When that nutcase kidnapped them, it took something outta me, Shipwreck. Something *deep* . . . And I don't know if I'll ever get it back again.'

'And yet they were fine,' Striker pointed out. 'Safe and sound – heck, they were eating sandwiches and doughnuts in the back of a police cruiser a half-mile away.' When Rothschild said nothing, Striker joined him at the window. 'They don't even know anything was wrong, Mike.'

He nodded absently. 'And God keep it that way.'

Striker nodded his agreement.

He sipped his coffee and turned away from the window. He studied Rothschild's prized Cougar, and for a while the two men talked about life's smaller issues – when Mike had bought the car, how the unpacking was going inside the house, and of the possible trip to Disneyland Mike was planning for the children. After a while, Rothschild grabbed one of the chrome engine parts and began polishing it. Then the conversation – like always – returned to work.

'So what's going on with Harry?' Rothschild asked. He stopped polishing the manifold and looked over. 'Lots of rumours going round – he gonna get off, or what?'

Striker just shrugged. 'Who knows for sure? I gave what I had to Internal. It's up to them now. But from what I hear, there's already talk of a forced early retirement.'

'Retirement?' Rothschild laughed with scorn.

'They may not have much of a choice. All the evidence is either old, linked directly to Koda, or circumstantial. We're talking about something that happened *ten years ago*, and most of the witnesses are dead. Laroche assigned the case to John Reyes. And you know what a pit-bull that guy is – the file will go on for *years*.'

Rothschild said nothing. He just stood there with a rag in one hand and a shiny chrome exhaust pipe in the other. The talk of Harry had rankled him. 'Goddam Harry – he could have killed us when he shot Oliver like that. I hope he gets whatever's coming to him.'

A troubled look spread across Striker's face.

Rothschild saw it.

'What?' he asked.

Striker shrugged. 'Just Harry. The man's confusing.'

'What do you mean?'

'When Oliver dropped the detonator, Harry had two options – he could have run away and saved his own ass, or he could have stayed behind and helped me try to save you and the kids . . . He *stayed*, Mike. Helped me drag and tip that steel table in front of us. It was what made the difference.'

Rothschild let out a humourless laugh. 'So what are you talking about here, Shipwreck – redemption?'

'I'm just saying it should count for something.'

'So you're glad he's getting off?'

'No. I think he should be charged to the full extent of the law . . . but I don't have to be happy about it.'

Rothschild snorted but said nothing.

Striker sighed. He'd had enough of the dark conversation. He gestured out the garage window to Cody and Shana, who were playing in the yard. Giggling. Frolicking in the sun. It was a wonderful sight.

'There are better things to focus on,' he said.

The dark look on Rothschild's face stubbornly remained for a moment, but then the lines there lessened, and he nodded. The two friends talked and drank their coffees and polished the chrome engine parts together until Cody sheepishly poked his head back into the garage and begged for another doughnut.

Striker gave the boy one, plus another for his sister. Then he threw the box on the work bench. Soon there would only be muffins left. *Bran.*

'You still going over there?' Rothschild suddenly asked.

'Ireland?' Striker nodded. 'Yeah. Courtney's going to be there three more weeks yet. I know she's safe with Tate and his parents, and they're probably having a wonderful time . . . but I kind of want to see her.'

Rothschild stopped polishing and looked at him. 'What about Felicia?'

'She's coming too.'

He grinned. 'Well, well. Fancy that. How'd you spin that one, Spiderman?'

Striker shrugged. 'Wasn't hard. Felicia's never been there either. It will be a nice break for both of us. And you know what? We need it after all that's gone on this last week.'

Rothschild finished the last of his coffee, then looked at the empty cup. 'Want me to put on a pot?'

Striker shook his head. 'I got to be going. Got a dozen things to do before we leave and I haven't even packed yet. Besides, you know what they say' – he gave Rothschild a wry grin – 'it's a long, long way to Tipperary.'

Rothschild laughed softly and kept on polishing the manifold.

'Keep your day job,' he said.

Two

Striker picked up Felicia at her home and they made the drive to White Rock in less than forty minutes. Not that they were rushing it. The drive out there was nice. Traffic was sparse, the sky was clear, and the weather was balmy. It gave both of them some time to relax a little as they passed by the ebbing tide of Crescent Beach and, kilometres later, the forested hills of South Surrey.

Their first stop was the Davies house.

Striker pulled up to the small rancher and stared at the place. Everything was falling to pieces, and it made him feel better about what he had accomplished. Felicia climbed out, and Striker joined her. As he fiddled with the paperwork, Felicia hiked up the stairs and knocked on the door.

No one answered.

'We should have called,' Felicia said.

Striker just smiled. 'Doesn't matter.'

He stuffed the thick, legal-size envelope into the mailbox and closed the lid. Inside it were two bundles of paperwork: some legal documents, and some forms. The legal documents were from the Royal Logistics Corps. With Archer having passed away, the family was qualified to obtain assistance from the regimental fund of the British Army.

Enough to pay a good-sized monthly mortgage.

As for the forms, they were from the Police Mutual Benevolent

Association. The cops-for-cops charity had put forward enough funds to cover one year of a sports programme for each child – hockey for Logan and figure-skating for Rachel. Striker even added a cheque of his own to cover the required equipment expenses.

When they got back into the car and started driving again, Felicia reached over and grabbed his hand. 'That was really nice of you,' she said.

'The kids are both in high school now. But better late than never.'

'They'll remember this.'

Striker shrugged. 'I was eighteen when my parents died. I had to take care of my siblings and it was all we could do to get by. It hurt to see other kids playing sports when Tommy wanted to and couldn't.' He let out a long breath and found it odd how the memory still upset him. 'You know, playing hockey was the only thing Tommy ever asked me for, and I couldn't give it to him.'

'You did more for them than any other brother would, Jacob – you *raised* them.'

He shrugged. 'Same thing when Courtney was little . . . I think of all the time and money we spent on Amanda's sickness, and all the things Courtney sacrificed. I can never get those times back for her again . . . but I can do something good for someone else. I can do this.'

'You're too hard on yourself.'

Striker said nothing back, and Felicia tightened her grip on his hand as they drove down 16th Avenue towards Highway 99 in the noon-day sun. They headed back for Vancouver. For the subsidized apartment complexes of Creekside Drive. Where the Williams children lived.

Striker had a little package for them too.

Three

It was three o'clock when Striker parked his vehicle in the long-term parking at Vancouver International Airport. He and Felicia removed their bags from the trunk and took the skywalk from the second level into the main terminal of international departures.

The moment they had checked in their luggage and were walking into the waiting area, Felicia asked Striker to get them a couple of coffees and then beelined towards the nearest book store. They met up ten minutes later, Striker with a couple of coffees – a standard Americano for him, a caramel latte for her – and Felicia with a handful of magazines and two novels.

She handed him the latest Brad Thor novel, and Striker smiled. They sat down in a booth, sipped their coffees, and read. It felt so good to relax. Striker had barely finished page two of *Black List* when his cell went off. He looked down at the display and saw the words BLOCKED NUMBER.

That meant work.

He let out an exasperated sound. 'You gotta be kidding me.' He jammed the phone to his ear. 'Striker.'

'It's Kami,' came the response. 'Corporal Summer. From the RCMP.'

He laughed. 'I know who you are.'

'Oh.' She sounded surprised. 'Well, I just wanted to let you know that I put in my last evidence page into your report. So if this whole thing with Harry Eckhart ever goes to trial, you have everything you need from me. I'll post you my notes through the internal mail. Shouldn't take but a few days.'

'Much appreciated.'

'Call me if you need anything else,' she added.

'I will.'

Corporal Kami Summer said goodbye, hung up, and the line went dead.

The end of the conversation brought Striker a sense of relief. Over the past few days, he'd had enough work-related calls to last him a lifetime. He powered off the iPhone and stuffed it into his jacket pocket. When he looked up again, Felicia was eyeing him curiously.

She licked away a milk-foam moustache.

'Kami – with a K?' she asked.

'That depends on whether it's going to get me into trouble – with a T.'

Felicia just gave him a deadpan stare, and Striker laughed. She raised her magazine once more and went back to her column. Striker let her read for a few minutes, then broke the silence.

'I have a surprise for you.'

She lowered her magazine, intrigued. 'Go on.'

'We never did get away for your birthday, so after we spend a couple of days with Courtney and Tate, I'm taking you away somewhere special. It's already planned. *Booked.*'

Her smile widened and she put the magazine flat down on the table.

'Where?' she asked.

'Just a little bed and breakfast I found overlooking the Cliffs of Moher. Five-star accommodation. A room with a fireplace. Our own personal hot tub overlooking the bay. And of course, almond bark and champagne when we arrive.'

She reached out and squeezed his hand. 'I can't wait.'

Striker was glad to see her smile.

'Me too,' he said. 'No computers, no phones, no friggin' sirens and alert tones. Just the two of us. Finally, some quality time together.' He smiled. 'Quality time – with a T . . . Or would that be a *QT*?'

Felicia grabbed his hand and squeezed it . 'It's with a U and I.'

Striker laughed softly. 'Corny. But I'll take it.'

Felicia leaned forward, touched his face with her fingers, and kissed him on the lips – one long, slow, tender kiss. When she sat back again, her eyes were warm and caring, and they made Striker smile. He felt good. He felt relaxed. He felt *free* again. There was no doubt about it.

It was going to be one hell of a holiday.

Acknowledgement Section

The Guilty would not have been possible without the specific help of the following people:

- Sergeant Phil Chambers whose knowledge of explosives and vast experience as a former Breacher of the Emergency Response Team were invaluable to my research
- Sergeant Steve Thacker (AKA *The Silver Fox*), whose experiences in numerous Investigations sections offered me not only direction but a unique insight.
- Constable Kirk Longstaffe (AKA *Stone Cold*) who made sure I didn't commit any policing faux pas
- Joe Cummings (better known as *Python Joe)*, who is one of the best brainstormers I have ever worked with
- And Ian Bailey (no nickname; just plain old Ian – all six foot four of him), who never lets me forget the media slant of the inciting events.

On a professional level, I have to thank the following people who helped turn a good manuscript into an excellent novel:

- My editor extraordinaire, Emma Lowth, whose thoughtful suggestions no doubt enriched the story

- My copyeditor, Ian Allen, whose attention to detail was downright life-saving at times
- Publishing Director Suzanne Baboneau, who had belief in this series from the get-go
- And the rest of the staff at Simon & Schuster. Whether they are marketing the new book or designing the next jacket, everything they do is always top notch and much appreciated.

Also on a professional level, I have to thank everyone at the Darley Anderson Agency. For those of you who don't know, they have the patent on making dreams come true.

- Clare Wallace
- Mary Darby
- Rosanna Bellingham
- Darley, himself
- And of course my awesome agent, Camilla Wray, who is my lifeline in the publishing world and always a joy to hear from.

Last of all, I have to thank my lovely wife, Lani, who takes on the bulk of the family duties (the not-so-fun ones) so that I may have the time required to research, outline and write these novels, each of which seems to take an inordinate amount of time.

I thank you all,

Sean

Sean Slater

SNAKES & LADDERS

When staying alive is the only game worth playing...

Detective Jacob Striker has had more than his fair share of brushes with death. But this one really shocks him. When he is called to attend a suicide at a decrepit apartment on the bad side of town, he expects to find one more life lost to mental illness and drug addiction. But this time the victim is not just another sad statistic, this time it's someone Striker knows.

And one thing is obvious to Striker: this wasn't suicide.

Striker's investigation quickly leads him to the Riverglen Mental Health Facility. The victim was a patient from the support group overseen by psychiatrist Dr Erich Ostermann. And when Striker discovers Larisa Logan - a dear friend of his, and also a patient of Dr Ostermann - has gone missing, his investigation goes into overdrive.

Racing against time and a chilling adversary, Striker searches desperately for Larisa. It is a dangerous game they play, where one throw of the dice can catapult you to a place of dominance - or send you sliding to your doom.

Paperback ISBN: 978-1-84983-215-1
Ebook ISBN: 978-0-85720-041-9